Tessa Barclay is a former publishing editor and journalist who has written many successful novels, among them the four-part Craigallan Saga – *A Sower Went Forth*, *Harvest of Thorns*, *The Stony Places* and *The Good Ground* – and the Wine Widow trilogy – *The Wine Widow*, *The Champagne Girls* and *The Last Heiress*. She lives in south west London.

The Final Pattern

Tessa Barclay

HEADLINE

Copyright © 1990 Tessa Barclay

The right of Tessa Barclay to be identified as the author of
the work has been asserted by her in accordance with the
Copyright, Designs and Patents Act 1988.

First published in 1990
by HEADLINE BOOK PUBLISHING PLC

First published in paperback in 1991
by HEADLINE BOOK PUBLISHING PLC

10 9 8 7 6 5 4 3 2

ISBN 0 7472 3542 2

Phototypeset by Input Typesetting Ltd, London SW19 8DR

Printed and bound by
Collins Manufacturing, Glasgow

HEADLINE BOOK PUBLISHING PLC
Headline House
79 Great Titchfield Street
London W1P 7FN

CHAPTER ONE

The Earl of Thornieburn was being entertained
to tea by Mrs Ronald Armstrong, of Gatesmuir
and the Waterside Mills. The whole of Galashiels was aware of this unusual event, and was
greatly intrigued.

It was known that the Countess had written
a few days ago to the Mistress, as Mrs Armstrong was generally known in the town. The
communication system which runs between
one servant hall and another, and to the
tradesmen who supply them, had spread the
word: Her Ladyship had suggested that the
Earl might drop in on such and such a day if it
was convenient to Mrs Armstrong. Mrs Armstrong had sent back an immediate reply with
the messenger to say his Lordship would be
offered afternoon tea.

The cook at Gatesmuir had baked her light-
est sponge cake, her crispest shortbread. Sandwiches of ethereal thinness had been cut. The
kitchenmaid had washed and re-washed the
Worcester tea set till it shone with a brightness
that hurt the eye. The housekeeper herself had
cleaned the silver. The best lace cloth had felt
the sprinkler and the gas-iron over its fragile
surface oftener than was good for it.

Jenny Armstrong had met his Lordship

socially at one or two of the occasions by means of which Borders society amused itself in the summer months. That's to say, she had bowed politely and murmured 'How do you do?' if they happened to be watching the same archery contest, and they had sat a few rows apart at an open air country dancing display.

The Countess was slightly better known to Jenny. This year of 1872 had been one of the worst for wet weather ever known in the Borders. So far it had rained on two hundred and thirty-two days, and since it was only September there might be more to come. The roads were a quagmire.

Ten days ago, Jenny's carriage had become hopelessly bogged down on the road between Clovenford and Caddenfoot while she was on a visit to a retired employee. There she might have remained for hours except that the Countess of Thornieburn happened by while out riding, sent a handy estate worker for plough horses, and had her dragged out of the mud.

During the dragging process, Her Ladyship had strolled by the roadside with Jenny on the only dry piece of ground, an outcrop of stone. They had chatted about the rainfall – over forty-six inches so far – the plough horses and their strength, the outbreak of croup in Selkirk, and whether this new fashion, the bustle, was really going to 'take'.

It was an entirely amiable encounter. Safely home again, Jenny had debated whether to send a length of fine tweed with her thank-you letter. 'Do you think it would be "pushy", Ronald?' she mused aloud as she sat with pen in hand at the secretaire.

Her husband had even less *savoir faire* about such nice points than Jenny. He had come up from the ranks of the work force, and somewhat disapproved of the aristocracy on principle.

'Well, it'd be a good advertisement for the mill if she were to have it made up into a gown,' he said in his dry way. 'Is that what you want?'

'Husband! I only thought . . . if I were a farmer, I might send a few fresh eggs or – '

'No you wouldn't. There's nothing anyone else can give to the Thornieburns, since they're the biggest landowners in the district – '

'Aye, that's so – but their land isn't all that productive.'

'Dinna be sae daft! They've nearly as many sheep as an Australian! Not to speak of the property they own in the towns – '

'All right, all right, I'll simply write a sweet letter expressing gratitude.'

She had certainly never expected the Countess to take the acquaintance further.

Speculation was high in Galashiels about the Earl's visit. 'He wants to buy into the weaving business,' suggested Mr Dugald of the Braidstow Mills with some envy.

'Na, na, he's a man for the agriculture,' Thomas Mitchell objected, 'he disna ken a warp frae a woof.'

The town's chief lawyer, successor to Mr Kennet, shook his head in disapproval. 'We shouldn't speculate – '

'That's a true word, but a man canna help it.'

Nor could a woman. Every female inhabitant wanted to know why His Lordship should want to call on the mistress of Waterside Mills.

'It canna be an affair o' the heart,' sighed the milliner, 'because Her Ladyship herself writ the letter asking if her man could visit – '

'Happen he's a wily one and he's playing her for a fool – '

'Lizzie, mind your tongue and your manners!' Miss Gordon said with great sharpness to her chief trimmer, the more sharp because she'd thought that very thing herself.

What could be the reason for the visit? What could they be talking about?

What they were talking about was that most engrossing subject to parents – their children.

'I have to confess my wife is over-protective of Allen,' sighed His Lordship. 'But it's not to be wondered at. You've heard, I suppose, that he's the last left to us out of four . . . ?'

Jenny hadn't in fact heard that piece of information, but she wasn't surprised. So many families lost children in infancy. It was the most vulnerable time for a child, those first few years, when mysterious fevers could strike, whooping cough might cause convulsions, or the onset of some strange wasting disease would manifest itself.

Inwardly she thanked heaven for the health of her own two sturdy children, for her daughter, now aged ten and physically strong though still shy and reticent, and for the baby son born since she and Ronald returned from Australia. Maxwell, known as Max, was the apple of his father's eye – lusty, noisy, growing almost visibly from day to day.

Quite different, it seemed, was young Viscount Cairness. 'Damned doctors – oh, excuse me, ma'am! I have to keep reminding myself to watch my language when I'm with ladies. My wife doesn't mind what I say, and besides, she agrees with me about doctors – God knows we've had enough of 'em to examine the boy, but there's not a thing they can do. I don't think they understand a word about what's wrong with him.'

'I imagine you've had the best advice?'

'I should say so! And they've been poking and prodding the poor lad ever since he was a tiny mite. Yet he keeps wheezing and sneezing – '

'He's of a bronchitic disposition?'

'Hanged if I know, or anybody, for that matter,' His Lordship said with a sigh, and crunched his shortbread in a disheartened manner.

'Heather is somewhat subject to a cough in very cold weather – '

'But that's just the point! Weather seems to have almost nothing to do with Allen's complaint! I could understand it if he got a cold after being out on a long ride in wet weather. But no – he can be as right as rain that day, and then perhaps two days later, when it's perfectly dry, he can have streaming eyes and a running nose – it's a perplexity, ma'am, truly it is. And these attacks come on as much in the summer as in the winter; more, perhaps. The doctors say he'll grow out of it, but I don't know, I don't know . . .'

'He's twelve years old, I believe?'

'Yes, and you see, he should have gone to public school by now. I had him down for Fettes, of course, but the headmaster says – quite understandably – that they can't take the responsibility in view of his state of health. And that's why I'm here, Mrs Armstrong!' The

5

Earl, pausing, looked at his hostess with a serious, pleading expression.

Jenny was at a loss. He seemed to expect a response from her, but what could she say? She had only the ordinary layman's understanding of health matters, if that was what he had come about. Nor did she know much more about education than any ordinary mother.

It was true that she had had problems over Heather's schooling. Her daughter suffered from a disability which made it very difficult for her to fit into a classroom full of children.

Heather could express herself perfectly well when she chose. But an episode in her early childhood had made her timid, even fearful, so that she hardly ever opened her mouth with strangers. If she was sent to school, she was overwhelmed with dumbness. And children being as they are, half-tamed savages, she suffered from the unkindness of her classmates.

Jenny had withdrawn her from an excellent small school for the education of the children of local gentlefolk. She had tried to hire a good governess. The first, who came with excellent references and undoubted qualifications, had been a martinet who reduced the little girl to tears six times a day. The second, a sweet and loving girl who had brought Heather on amazingly in four months, had naturally been courted in marriage and had left only six weeks ago.

At the moment Heather had no teacher except Jenny herself. It was an unsatisfactory situation, for Jenny was the child of working class parents and had none of the 'accomplishments' necessary for a young lady of fortune, therefore she could pass on nothing to Heather except a good grasp of reading and writing and some slight artistic training.

'If you are asking me to recommend a governess – '

'Eh?' The Earl looked startled. 'No, no, dear lady. No, no, the tutors and all that are laid on. I thought I'd explained that.'

'No,' said Jenny, floundering. 'You haven't mentioned tutors at all, so far.'

'I haven't? What have I been talking about, then?'

He really seemed to want to know. Looking at the plump, muddled, bewhiskered face, Jenny murmured, 'Well, the Viscount's state of health, and your anxieties on that score . . .'

'Dash it, I'm getting more and more absent-minded every day! What must you think of me, Mrs Armstrong? I really thought I'd explained why I'd come.'

Whatever he had come for, it was certainly not to conduct any kind of flirtation with the Mistress of the Waterside Mills. Jenny was very glad she hadn't given in to the hints of her maid, Baird, that this was a good opportunity to wear her new bustle gown of violet taffeta. His Lordship had scarcely noticed her appearance, although she was looking (she thought) rather well in a gown of what was known as nun's veiling, the skirts full but not crinolined, and with some very fine lace about the neck and shoulders. Her dark hair, over which Baird had taken a great deal of trouble, was held up by cut-steel combs, a present from Ronald on the birth of their son.

'Perhaps we had better go back to the beginning again,' she suggested. 'You were saying you were anxious about your boy.'

7

'Yes, but that's only background. I'd better tackle it from a different angle. You'll recall that you and my wife ran across each other a couple of weeks ago?'

'Of course. Lady Thornieburn was so kind as to –'

'Yes, yes,' His Lordship interrupted with unintentional bad manners. 'Your carriage and all that. Well, Jemima took to you considerably . . . I hope you don't mind my saying that, ma'am?'

Jenny blushed. 'No, of course not. I'm very pleased . . .'

'She doesn't take to everyone, Jemima. It's because she doesn't socialise as much as she ought to. She stays at home fussing over Allen. We think of his well-being all the time – our one ewe lamb, you know. Well, of course, he's not a *ewe* lamb but it's the same idea . . . Where was I?'

'The Countess and I had chanced to meet . . . ?'

'Ah yes. Well, afterwards, she chatted to one or two friends about you – not mere inquisitiveness, I assure you, ma'am.'

'Of course not,' said Jenny, as if inquisitiveness was a fault that could never be attributed to a countess.

'And of course I'd heard a bit about you, in the course of business and so forth. Am I right, ma'am, in supposing your daughter Heather has some sort of handicap? A stammer?'

'Not exactly.' What could all this be about? 'For reasons that go back into her childhood, she is extremely shy, extremely wary of strangers. She speaks very little. A specialist who examined her called it "voluntary mutism" – in

8

other words, she can speak if she wants to but chooses not to.'

'Hmm . . .' said the Earl. 'It's a case of nerves, then, is it?'

'In some ways, although the child is quite brave physically. She suffered an experience in her early childhood that made her retreat into silence. She's been emerging slowly in the last few years. I must add,' Jenny said, 'that my husband doesn't share my views: he doesn't see how any experience so long ago could continue to affect the child. But there it is – before that happened Heather was a blithe, bonny baby, just like my baby son. Afterwards she was a silent little shadow. And though she is better – much, much better! – it is difficult to find just the right teacher for her.'

His Lordship rose from his chair and wandered to the rug in front of the fire. He stood in thought a moment, pulling at his greying side-whiskers. then he took up the traditional stance of the male human animal: back to the fire, hands under his frock coat tails to raise them a little so that the warmth could reach the grey-trousered expanse below. Jenny knew the pose. It meant that an important announcement was coming.

'Mrs Armstrong, my wife and I have a proposal to make to you. You've heard that our child too has a difficulty about his schooling. We've solved that so far by simply having a governess, because we kept hoping he'd be going on to college, but the boy's twelve now and unless we send him to an "invalid school" he's got no hopes of proper companionship and so on. So we've decided to, as you might say, extend the schoolroom at Thornieburn.

9

We're parting with the governess he's had up to now – an old fashioned soul, she's got a post elsewhere. We've engaged a younger woman, excellent qualifications, all that.' He paused.

'Yes?' Jenny prompted, still bewildered.

'There'll be special tutors for music and art, and we've been lucky enough to find a young clergyman who is interested in the natural sciences to give lessons two or three times a week. I don't know about some of the other things – dancing lessons, for instance, we haven't sorted that out yet but I daresay we could arrange it. So what do you say?'

'What do I say to what, Your Lordship?'

'To having your little girl share lessons with my son. Don't you think it's a good idea.'

She stared at her visitor in amazement.

'No? You don't like it?'

'But, Lord Thornieburn – '

'Perhaps I didn't make it sound attractive enough. Allen's a pleasant lad: quite intelligent, mad about horses and country life and all that kind of thing. We think of inviting another boy to share the classroom, David Buchanan – I don't know if you've met his father, a widower with a little place outside Kelso but I don't think it brings in much by way of an income.'

'I don't believe I've met Mr Buchanan, but that's not – '

'The point is, your child needs schooling and companionship, and so does mine. It can't be good for them to have no one to work with, to compete against, to talk to about what interests them. I remember my own school days; they were hard, by heaven, the masters used to lay into us if we were lazy or inattentive. But I made friends there who gave me a way to measure myself. And sometimes they saw things in a different way, and that taught me something. Latin, for instance, I was never any good at it but I pegged away because I didn't want Edgar Anstruther to outstrip me. And I've never regretted it, you know, it's stood me in good stead – '

'But Lord Thornieburn,' Jenny broke in upon the flood of memory, 'I'm thinking about the physical difficulties. It's nine miles from here to Thornieburn as the crow flies and a lot longer by road, even when they're in a good state. Heather could never make the journey there and back every day – it would be impossible.'

'Of course! Didn't I explain that? I thought I had. No, no,' said the Earl, pacing to and fro on Jenny's hearthrug, 'we thought of asking her to stay with us during the week – '

'Never!' cried Jenny.

Startled by her vehemence, Thornieburn stared at her.

'I'm sorry,' she said, recovering, 'but my daughter and I have hardly been parted since the day I – since the day we – since she was returned to me after a long absence. Heather would never be happy away from me.'

'But Mrs Armstrong! It would only be for five days in the week. The Countess and I thought that if school were held from Monday to Friday, the other two could go home to their parents on the Saturday morning so that they could pursue their separate interests – Allen would like to go hunting, I'm sure, if there was a meet, and I daresay your daughter might have a dancing lesson, and all that kind of thing. And then of course the family should

11

go to church on Sunday together, that's only natural.'

'No,' Jenny said, shaking her head, 'you don't understand. Heather would never agree to it.'

'But it's for her own good, ma'am,' said the Earl. 'You said yourself that you were having difficulties over her education. And I can assure you that the tutors at Thornieburn would have the highest qualifications – '

'That I don't doubt. But as to Heather's own good . . . You must forgive me, my lord. I can only go on my instincts here. My little girl has had more than her share of unhappiness in her short life. I don't want to inflict any more on her "for her own good".'

Lord Thornieburn looked dashed. He brushed his whiskers aside from his lips two or three times to give himself time to think. 'I could ask someone else,' he mused, 'but Jemima thought it would be particularly good for Allen to have a girl among his classmates – he sees almost no females except his mother and his governess and the maids. Friends, of course, they come to call with their children, but they don't get to know Allen well and of course if he happens to get an attack of the wheezes they get scared and run away from him. The girls especially. The boys hang round and laugh at him. The local lads call him "Bubbly", you know. Bubbly – they mean someone who's always bubbling, that's to say weeping or crying.'

'Oh,' said Jenny. 'I'm sorry.' After a moment's hesitation she said, 'The local children used to call Heather "the dummy".'

'There you are. I thought you'd feel we had

something in common, something that could be helped by private education in a quiet, understanding atmosphere.'

'Oh, indeed! If it weren't for the distance – '

'You wouldn't consider our idea of having your daughter to stay?'

'Heather would never agree. And I wouldn't dream of forcing a separation upon her.'

His Lordship hesitated. 'Shouldn't you ask your husband about this?' he inquired. He took it for granted that Ronald Armstrong ruled his household like a benevolent tyrant, as most men did. She herself had said that her husband didn't precisely share her views on their daughter's upbringing.

Jenny understood what he was after. She had dealt with wilier men than Lord Thornieburn in the course of business. 'Of course I shall speak to him. He is naturally interested to know the reason for your visit, my lord. But I think he too would be unwilling to make Heather accept an unwelcome parting.'

'Think about it, at least, Mrs Armstrong. It seems to me our idea solves a lot of problems.' He moved awkwardly from one foot to the other. 'Thank you for a delightful tea. My compliments to your cook – that's the best shortbread I ever tasted.'

'I'll tell her,' Jenny said, moving to the fireplace to ring for the maid. The summons was answered with suspicious promptness by Thirley, who had been hovering in the hall in hope of overhearing some of the conversation.

'Fetch His Lordship's coat and hat, and call his coachman.'

'Yes, ma'am,' said the housemaid, looking from one to the other as she turned to obey and hoping to read something in their faces – some hint of passion foresworn, or guilt, or any emotion that she could speak of to her friends. All she saw, alas, was polite attention from the mistress and a little dejection from the Earl.

In the awkward pause that comes when the carriage is awaited, Thornieburn said with a faint return of hope, 'How would it be if you just brought the child to have a look at us? She might not be so much against the notion as you think, ma'am.'

'Well . . .'

'I know the roads are bad, but at present we're having a dry spell. If you took the long route by Torwood and Blackhaugh, I think you'd find the going pretty fair.'

'I'll mention the idea to my husband.'

'Just send word. Almost any day will do. Come to lunch – my cook knows how to roast a pheasant.'

'You're very kind, my lord.' And very eager. Jenny felt guilty at dashing his hopes so firmly. 'I'll see what can be arranged.'

When Ronald came home from the mills at his usual hour, his wife had his peg of whisky ready for him. He sank into a chair, accepted it, sipped with a sigh of pleasure, and then regarded her over the rim of the glass. 'Well, I see you didn't run off with the Earl,' he remarked.

'Nor did he ask me to design an estate tartan for his servants.'

'Well, then, the other rumour was that he was going to offer an investment of ten thousand pounds in the business.'

'Not that either.'

'Ach, I'm no caring what he came for,'

14

Ronald said, stretching his feet out towards the fire and groaning with pleasure. 'It's been a terrible day at work. Richie couldn't get that new set to work without a gnarl in the weft – we had to stop four times. Four times! And I'm sad to tell you that the marigold yellow you want for the spring ladies' suiting is unsafe. I've tested and re-tested till I'm as yellow as a Chinaman myself but it defeats me. Add to that the fact that Ainsley is talking about leaving for a job in Yorkshire – '

'Never! Ainsley would never leave us, Ronald!' She was on her feet, throwing out her hands in horror.

'No, I don't think he will. It's his wife, you know. She's poorly and he thinks the climate in the Borders is too damp for her. But he thinks it every autumn and gets over it by Hallowe'en.' He finished his drink and made signs of moving. 'I'll go up and get changed. What's for dinner, lassie?'

'Halibut and a game pie.' The thought brought Thornieburn's promise of roast pheasant to mind. 'His Lordship asked us to lunch, Ronald.'

'Did he now? What for?'

She told him about the Earl's proposal. 'I said of course I would speak to you about it, but my first instinct is against it.'

'What does Heather say?'

'I haven't told her yet. I didn't want her to get anxious about something that will probably never happen.'

'Aye, well, I'm against it on principle. I don't want any daughter of mine hobnobbing with a lord! She'd only get ideas above her station.'

'I don't know about that,' Jenny said at once,

put out that he should think anything was above Heather's station. 'She's a nice child, daughter of reasonably important people, well brought up as far as we could manage it in the circumstances. What's so far above us in the Earl's household?'

'You know what I mean, Jenny,' Ronald said, a faint frown of irritation between his sandy brows. 'We both come from working class backgrounds. We've done well, but we've no pretentions to the nobility. If we were ever to start getting on friendly terms with the Thornieburns I bet what you like it would end up damned expensive for us – we'd have to move in circles that would expect a lot more than we aspire to.'

'Nobody's asking us to move in their circles,' she replied. The more Ronald explained it was unwise because of the social barriers, the more she felt she was as good as the Thornieburns. And after all, the Earl had only suggested they go to lunch. Surely they could just go, and take a look?

'I'm away upstairs to get out of these clothes,' Ronald said, to show that as far as he was concerned the discussion was at an end. She watched his spare figure move rather wearily into the hall. She ought not to pursue the discussion – he'd had a bad day and anyway the idea of Heather sharing lessons with the viscount was absurd.

But it would be rather nice to see inside Thornieburn Hall. And it really would be an occasion on which she could wear her new bustle gown. And Heather would enjoy the outing – she loved going in the carriage.

So it came about that in the course of daily

chat and discussion it became accepted that the Armstrongs would at least go to Thornieburn Hall to see what they could see. Jenny wrote a note suggesting they should come on the following Monday, the 30th of September, and received a reply by her own messenger joyfully agreeing.

They set out early to cover the thirteen miles by the long route. Jenny was in her taffeta gown and furs, Ronald was in his new frock coat and plaid waistcoat with pepper and salt trousers. Heather, her light brown hair in ringlets, wore a new bonnet with forget-me-nots round the brim, with a little wool coat and dress of the same shade.

Why she was so eager to make a good impression on the Earl and Countess, Jenny couldn't quite explain. She wasn't going to agree to any of this nonsense about letting Heather stay for lessons all week.

There, as it turned out, she was quite wrong.

CHAPTER TWO

It had been quite clear to Heather for the past week that the visit to Thornieburn Hall was of particular importance. First of all Baird, her mother's personal maid and ruler of the nursery wing at Gatesmuir, had unearthed a piece of forget-me-not blue wool intended for a coat and dress next spring. The dressmaker had been sent for, the costume had been made up at breakneck speed. When she asked why, Baird replied, 'Ye wouldna want to go to Thornieburn looking like a spurdie, would ye?'

Then Cook, smacking her wrist when she tried to steal a newly baked scone from the cooling tray, had said crossly, 'Ye'll need to mind your manners when ye break bread wi' a Nurl.'

What was a Nurl? Or should it be Gnurl? A cross between a gnarled and a churl? It didn't sound very inviting.

Matters became clearer as she listened to conversations between Mama and Papa. It turned out that they were going to visit an Earl and Countess. The Countess was Mrs Earl, though why she wasn't an Earless when a Mrs Prince was a Princess was never made clear.

Heather was an intelligent child but at ten years old she was often baffled by grown-up behaviour. Papa kept muttering that he didn't want to go to this lunch, and Mama kept saying, 'Well, we can say no as we leave, but it can't do any harm to go.'

Say no to what? In the end Heather inquired about that point.

Mama answered with many hesitations. 'Well, you see, sweetheart, there's a possibility you might share lessons with Lord Thornieburn's son. Would you like that?'

Heather screwed up her face so that her brows came together. At that moment she looked extraordinarily like her father when he was trying to come to a difficult decision. She was darker than Ronald but fairer than Jenny, with grey eyes often lowered in timidity when she was in company.

'What's Lord Thornieburn's son like?'

'That's what we're going to find out, dear.'

'Is he older or younger than me?' This was of course always one of the most important points in any relationship between children.

'He's twelve, Heather, and he suffers from an ailment that makes his breathing difficult and his eyes run – at least, so His Lordship told me.'

'Is the son an earl too?'

'No, he's a viscount.'

This was enough to puzzle over. She submitted to Baird putting her hair into curl papers to form ringlets for the great day, but was glad she wasn't forced to wear new boots – new boots were always uncomfortable, and the forget-me-not coat and dress were trouble enough, because of course Baird warned her not to get them dirty, because they were going to be put away again the minute she got back from Thornieburn and not taken out until the time came for her to wear them at Easter. 'By which time,' Baird sighed, 'the hems'll hae to be let doon . . .'

The carriage ride was delightful. Heather loved the carriage. It smelt of well-polished leather, it creaked and swayed on its springs, and the two big horses, Clynie and Rust, looked so fine with their braided manes and their tail bows. Dunlop the coachman beamed at Heather as she clambered in. The weather was dry though dull. The trees they passed had lost most of their leaves because of the heavy rains day after day, but the fields were lush, the sheep in their winter wool moving like dream creatures under the misty sky.

The village of Gairford was the point where they had to turn on to the road for the Hall. A respectful villager was waiting at the bend of the road to say that the coachman should take care at the top of the slope because the road surface had slipped somewhat and the laird's men hadn't yet been able to mend it. 'But if you draw in close to the wa' and haud your horses going doon into the vale, ye'll be grand.'

'How long do you suppose that poor fellow's been standing there in the damp to tell us that?' Papa said indignantly as they drove on. 'It's not right, Jenny! It's positively feudal!'

'Now, now, husband, don't let's have any of your radical opinions until we get home to Gatesmuir,' said Mama, laying a gloved hand on his sleeve.

Thornieburn Hall was indeed feudal. The main part was fairly new – that's to say, built in the eighteenth century in the Scottish Baronial style, very handsome. The west wing dated back to the fifteenth century, its frowning tower standing up in the vale to watch the surrounding hills for reivers.

The effect might have been sombre except that the building was of the glowing dark red stone of the district, had many windows let into the original facade, and was flanked by smooth green lawns on which strolled ornamental pheasants from China and the Himalayas. Close to the hall a series of low terraces had been made on which chrysanthemums held up indomitable blossoms to the rain-threatening sky.

As they drew up on the flagstones in front of the entrance, the big double doors were thrown open by a footman in livery and white gloves. Out strode the Earl, surrounded by a bevy of dogs – two collies, a red setter, a Dandy Dinmont and a Pomeranian. These pranced about, barking, while Thornieburn roared at them to 'Shut up!' and the visitors alighted.

'Dowter! Dowter! Come and take these confounded dogs away!'

A man in a green jacket and a hard hat appeared from round a corner. At a word from him the dogs cantered off, to be shepherded to some home near the stables.

'Sorry about that,' said His Lordship. 'Always spend a while with 'em in the morning even if I don't take out a gun. Now, how do you do, Mrs Armstrong? Mr Armstrong, I don't believe we've met, though of course I know of your work.' The two men shook hands. 'And this is the girlie, eh?'

He stopped. His whiskers came close to

Heather's face. She shrank back. The Earl, who had an instinctive understanding of nerviness in animals, straightened with a smile. 'Well, I daresay you'd rather speak to Allen. Allen! Allen!'

No one came. He led the way indoors, where coats and hats were handed over. The Countess came out into the hall, which was vast and paved with black and white marble. Behind her hovered a gangling boy in a knickerbocker suit.

'Ah, there you are, Allen. Come and say how-de-do to Miss Armstrong.'

Miss Armstrong? Who was Miss Armstrong?

The boy approached. He bowed. 'Miss Armstrong,' he said to Heather.

Heather gave him a nervous curtsey. Miss Armstrong, that's me, she thought. The man is an earl, the lady is a countess, the boy is a viscount, and I'm Miss Armstrong. She felt disorientated, bewildered. 'There!' said the Countess, fixing a shrewd gaze upon her. 'We've scared her out of her wits. Let's all get round the fire and be comfortable – what a dreary day for your first sight of Thornieburn.' Cheerfully talking, she ushered them into the morningroom.

Although the house was enormous and full of fine things, it was clear that in this room the Thornieburns were at their most informal. It was scattered with the items which had held their attention before the visitors appeared. The Countess had been working on a piece of wool crochet, her husband had been musing over accounts, the boy had been looking through a book of coloured pictures of exotic birds. Strewn about were that morning's newspapers, a box containing the bleached bones of some small countryside animal, two or three shotgun cartridges, a map and a magnifying glass, a dish with dog biscuits, two pairs of spectacles, and a fashion magazine open at a picture of the latest Paris gowns.

'Please forgive the mess,' said Lady Thornieburn. 'Come to the fire – did you find the journey chilly? We'll have coffee to warm you up. Or would you prefer something stronger? Sherry? Madeira? Luncheon will be served in about an hour.'

The men opted for sherry, the ladies and the boy took coffee, and Heather was supplied with hot lemonade. She took it quietly to the table on which the bird book lay. It was open at a page showing a mynah bird on the branch of a rain tree.

On their voyage to and from Australia, the ship had stopped at ports on the Indian subcontinent. Heather had seen mynah birds of many kinds in the wild – the Asian starling, as she had been told by one of the ship's crew.

She turned the page: cockatoo, white and yellow, pecking at a mango fruit.

'Those are Asian birds,' said a slightly breathy voice at her side. 'I'm studying them for an essay Reverend McMurdo wants me to do.'

Heather nodded.

He turned the page with a bony hand. He pointed. 'That's a Cacatua, from Burma. Brighter colours, you see. This pink one' – he turned over – 'is from Australia.'

Heather remembered that Mama had wanted her to take part in the conversation today. 'I've seen them,' she murmured.

'In an aviary? Yes, so have I – and you may

23

have noticed we have some exotic pheasants in the grounds.'

'Yes.'

Allen went from one illustration to another, telling what he knew about each. He was showing off, she realised. She understood his motives. If they were to share lessons he wanted her to know that he was not only older but brainier.

But she found him rather pleasing. His voice was gentle, his Celtic blue eyes were kindly, he let her turn back to look again at the prettiest birds, he waited for her to answer and when she didn't he seemed unperturbed. There was none of that impatient bossiness she'd met with in many other children.

Their parents were deep in a conversation of their own around the fire. Leaning towards her, Allen said, 'Are you good at French verbs?'

She shook her head.

'I can do them if I take them as if they were on the page of the book. But putting them into a sentence is awful.'

She nodded.

'What about Latin?'

She shook her head.

'Not good at it?'

'Don't know any.'

'I'm reading Virgil. He's *awful*!'

She turned a page of the book with one finger, quietly and carefully.

'Father said you didn't talk much.'

'No.'

'That's all right. I don't either, mostly because it makes me breathless if I go on a lot. But I'm supposed to chat to you.'

'Me too.'

'Want to look at my weasel bones?'

She nodded.

'I found it among the brambles on Ligster Hill. If you like I'll show you the place.'

'Thank you.'

They knelt by the box. Allen spread a piece of paper on the carpet and began to lay the bones out in the skeletal order. 'Bits missing, of course,' he mourned. 'Some silly rook's taken some bones for his nest, I expect. There's a big rookery among the pines at the far side of Ligster. We'll ride there but you have to wear a hat.'

Heather brightened. 'Do you ride a lot?'

'Every day. How about you?'

'Me too.'

'What do you ride?'

'I've got a roan mare, thirteen hands. Her name's Lucky.'

This was the longest passage of conversation from her since they arrived. Her mother, watchful though politely chatting, turned her head a little. Heather glanced aside and caught her approving smile. She began to relax. The visit wasn't going to be such an ordeal as she'd imagined.

When lunch was announced she was buoyed up with the promise that afterwards Allen would take her out to the stables. The meal, as a result, seemed interminable. Her Ladyship remarked that it was only a light meal, but there were six courses, one of them the promised pheasant with all kinds of trimmings.

But at length the children, having been told they might get down, escaped from the lofty

25

dining room and its shining array of silver and glass. Allen paused to put on a topcoat and long muffler, which he wound about his throat until his head emerged like a turtle's. 'Mother always gets in a fantash if I don't wrap up,' he said in apology. 'You'd better put your coat on – no wait, that silly pale blue will get marked. Here, borrow this!'

He thrust a boy's mackintosh at her. It came down almost to her heels, for he was considerably taller than Heather. They stepped out of the little room – which he told her was called 'the mudroom' because it was here boots and coats were shed in bad weather – into a court-yard from which a stone archway led to the stables.

The parents had removed to the drawing room, a fine contrast to the ease of the morning room, for it was graced with Chippendale and Sheraton, ornate gilt mirrors on two walls, an Adam fireplace, and carpets which, though worn, glowed with the colours of the Orient.

They were sitting by yet another roaring fire, talking comfortably about their children. 'Young Buchanan comes to stay at the beginning of the month. You haven't met him yet, but he's an able child. Not so inquisitive as Allen and therefore not so wide-ranging, but he works harder.'

'Rather greedy for his food,' the Countess put in with a little shrug.

'My love, you don't take into account how badly he fares at home. I daresay when he was offered cakes and syllabubs here, it was a great treat to him. Besides,' Thornieburn added, grinning, 'I was a good trencherman myself at his age.'

'Which is what, exactly?' Ronald asked.

'He's eleven. That puts him neatly between your child and ours. Miss Darnley, whom you shall meet in a moment, says she can handle the age group nicely. Then we have the Reverend Herbert McMurdo, the local minister, for the natural sciences and Latin, and a young gentleman called – what's his name, my dear?'

'Forbes, Andrew Forbes – '

'Ah yes, for music; he can instruct in piano or violin. I don't know if Heather has any talent in that direction?'

'She plays a little on the piano – '

'The same with Allen. David hasn't a note of music in him but then, poor lad, his circumstances . . . His father is the most inept landowner I ever came across, let himself be defrauded by a crooked estate manager so now he's deep in dept. I came to know him through my lawyer – we use the same man. I can vouch for him in case you are worrying on that point, sir – he's poor and silly but honest, and his son is poor and earnest and honest.'

All this was to set their minds at rest about the third classmate, if they should agree to the scheme. Naturally, they wouldn't allow their daughter to share teachers with anyone who could not be vouched for. But the Earl and Countess could see that though they both talked hard and enthusiastically, the Armstrongs remained unresponsive.

'Come and see the schoolroom,' Lady Thornieburn suggested. 'It's the one Robert used when he was a boy.'

'Aye, you'll find my initials cut in the table,' His Lordship said as he led the way upstairs.

They traversed various passages, coming at

last into a light, airy room on the second floor of the east wing. A young woman rose to greet them – Miss Darnley, the viscount's governess. Previously briefed by her employers, she showed them all the new books she had bought for her prospective pupils, let them notice her educational certificates hanging framed on the walls, and mentioned two previous posts in excellent families.

Jenny was very impressed. If anyone could help Heather fill the gaps in her knowledge, it was this brisk, bright young lady. If only it didn't involve an absence from home . . . But that was an inevitable pre-condition, it seemed. Their journey today had taken them two hours, and it would be two hours again back to Galashiels. And today the weather was relatively good. In January, for instance, when the snow lay on the roads, who could tell how long it would take or whether it would even be possible to get the carriage up and down those dangerous slopes? If Heather were to enjoy the advantages of the Thornieburn schoolroom, she would have to do it as a weekly boarder.

At that moment the door burst open and the two children came rushing in. 'There you are! Bissett said you'd come up to see Miss Darnley. Father, what do you think? Heather learned to ride in *Australia!*'

'Did she indeed?' said the Earl, looking with a surprised smile at the little girl in a raincoat far too big for her.

'Mama, there's the prettiest little horse in the stables, his name's Oatcake,' Heather put in. Her voice was still husky and uncertain but the words tumbled over themselves to be said. 'Allen says he's a palfrey – '

28

'A what?'

'Like in "Jock o' Hazeldean": "palfrey fresh and fair" – '

'Oatcake's been specially trained for a lady to ride,' the Countess explained. 'A nice little thing. Do you like him, Heather?'

'Oh, he's beautiful. His coat is just the colour of his name. And Mama, Papa! Allen says if I come and stay here for weekdays we can go out riding first thing every morning before lessons, and I should have Oatcake all for myself! So may I, Mama? Papa, may I? Please?'

In the face of so much eagerness, there seemed nothing to say but 'yes'. The only objection had been borne away – Heather herself wanted the separation, seemed not even to have thought of it as a thing to be feared.

Although Jenny had left Heather with others during their stay in Australia, Baird had always been with her: Baird, the staunch and patient friend. This time Heather would have a strange maid to do her hair and look after her clothes. Yet she didn't seem to mind.

Among the families they knew in Galashiels there were daughters who went away to boarding school – an adventurous, sophisticated thing to do, so Heather gathered, but too frightening for her even to contemplate. This was different. She was going to a house where everybody seemed to like her. She would only have two classmates and one of them, Allen, was as mad about horses as she was herself. So it would be much less scary than going to a school full of girls who were older and cleverer and prettier than she.

She watched with equanimity while Baird got her clothes together for the first week's stay, which was to start the following Monday. Dark dresses, ten pinafores (two for each day), outdoor clothes, underwear, her riding habit, some well-loved story books, hairbrushes, house shoes . . . 'Is there anything we've forgotten?' sighed Baird as she packed the portmanteau.

'We've forgotten Momo,' Heather cried, holding out a decrepit old doll made of sheepskin.

'Ye're no takin' that to the laird's hoose!' declared Baird. 'I'd be ashamed to let them think ye played wi' sic a thing!'

Momo slept on Heather's pillow at night. He had been washed many a time but he had a rather grimy appearance and the expression had been kissed off his painted leather face.

'I've got to have Momo,' she said.

'He'll be waiting here for you when you come home at the weekend,' Baird coaxed. 'Look, I'll set him on your pillow and cover him up, and yourself can uncover him when you get back on Saturday.'

'No, I have to have him with me!' Suddenly it seemed a long way away, Thornieburn Hall, and too big compared with Gatesmuir, and empty without Mama and Baird.

Baird explained the problem to Jenny when she came home from a session with buyers at Waterside Mills. 'We canna let her take the thing, mistress. It's disreputable.'

Jenny thought it over. She recalled a time when her little girl had recognised the woolly Eskimo doll and found comfort in it after a long parting. 'She must take it,' she said. 'I don't care what the maids at Thornieburn think –

Heather is more important than their good opinion, Baird.'

It was a good decision. On her first night at Thornieburn, Heather wept bitterly in her strange bed, even though the prospect of riding on Oatcake next morning should have brightened her thoughts. Clutching Momo, she fell asleep at last.

Baird, in her familiar bed in Gatesmuir, wept too, into her pillow, stifling her sobs with a handkerchief. 'Ye daft puddock, the bairn's aw richt,' she told herself over and over again. 'What makes ye think she canna do without *you*?'

Heather's mother didn't weep. But in the middle of the night, when Ronald was sound asleep, she stole quietly to the nursery to sit over the cot of her baby boy, her throat clenched tight to prevent the sobs breaking out. She knew she was a fool. She would be seeing her 'lost' daughter again in five days' time. She was a lucky woman – her husband loved her, their little son lay among his lace pillows blissfully sucking his thumb, they all had their health and strength . . . And yet she felt vulnerable, lonely, afraid – because Heather, to whom she had devoted almost her whole life for the last nine years, was not here in the house with her as the moon sailed overhead.

She was so anxious that on Friday she herself went to fetch her daughter home, instead of merely sending the carriage.

'Mama! You're usually busy on Friday – '

'I thought you'd like to see me – '

Heather dragged forward the governess. 'Mama, Miss Darnley can say poetry *in French!*'

'My dear child,' said the governess, laughing

31

while she tried to disengage herself, 'what have I been trying to teach you about polite conversation?'

'Oh yes.' The little girl straightened her shoulders, assumed an elocutionary stance, and remarked, 'It is a great pleasure to see you again, Mama.'

The two boys applauded from under the porch. Jenny exchanged a smile with Miss Darnley. One of the Countess's terriers put its paws up on Heather's skirt front to lick her hand.

Once they were in the carriage, Heather settled herself on the seat, took her mother's arm, then inserted Momo comfortably into the niche between them. For the first fifteen minutes she talked almost non-stop. Then her usual reticence returned. There was a long pause.

Jenny spoke of the little treats she'd arranged at home: mincemeat tart for pudding, a visit to see the stable cat's four kittens.

'Lovely,' murmured Heather rather sleepily. Her first week at school had proved physically tiring. 'You know,' she went on, 'Momo and I like it at Thornieburn. So why is it so nice going home?'

But before Jenny could answer the question from that creaky little voice, its owner had fallen into a happy doze.

The inevitable consequence of Heather's connection with Thornieburn was that the two families saw more of each other. The Countess didn't stir much from home, but she often invited Jenny to luncheon on a Saturday when Heather was being collected. The Earl would ask Ronald for a day's shooting with a party of local dignitaries.

Ronald had to admit that the Earl wasn't such a bad fellow, even though he was an aristocrat. He approved somewhat of Mr Gladstone and, though he seldom took his seat in the House of Lords, seemed to vote Whig when he was there. Any man who voted liberal couldn't be all bad, in Ronald's view.

His tenants spoke well of the laird: he maintained the village day school his grandfather had built, paid the teacher's salary, and even saw to it that any boy of more than average ability should go on to college. The houses in the village all belonged to him, of course, and he kept them in good repair, as he did the farms on his estate. His sheep grew good wool, which was another point in his favour: as a leading member of the weaving trade, Ronald had no opinion at all of farmers whose wool was useless to the tweed industry.

Unknown to Ronald, the Earl was learning more about this new acquaintance. The man was bright and alert, that was clear from his conversation, but others spoke highly of him. It had been said at first that he'd married Miss Corvill of William Corvill & Son for her money, but events had proved otherwise. He had acquired a substantial sum of his own – some said by finding gold in Australia – which he had promptly invested in the Waterside Mills.

He was a good employer. His workforce wouldn't be tempted away to other mills by offers of more pay. He seemed to have a talent for mixing colours unmatched by anyone else in the woollen industry – not that His Lordship would have rated that highly except that it showed the fellow understood something about science, which to Lord Thornieburn was a great mystery.

Over a period of about six months the regard between the two men grew. And it had its results. The Earl bestirred himself to use his influence behind the scenes, and the influence of a Whig peer in the Border district was considerable.

The Member of Parliament for West Tweed was a sick old man. At Lord Thornieburn's quiet suggestion he decided to resign his seat in the House of Commons. A suitable candidate had to be found – someone young, enthusiastic, level-headed and representative of the main industry, the weaving of woollens.

Ronald came home from an evening at the local Gentleman's Club to find Jenny working on a plaid design at her desk in the old study. 'Jenny, what do you think?' he burst out. 'I've been asked to stand!'

Taken by surprise, she floundered. 'Stand where?'

'Here! For the seat old Hammond has left vacant!'

'In Parliament?' she gasped.

'Yes, in Parliament! The Whigs are looking for someone who'll speak up for the woollen mills. I said I'd think it over. What do you say, my lass – shall I take it on?'

She got up, ran to him, and threw her arms around him. She was speechless. What an honour! To be asked to stand for the district – her husband, Ronald, the man she'd first known and loved when he was master-dyer for her father's works, from a humble background, often derided behind his back because he was married to that formidable woman, the Mistress of Waterside Mills . . .

At last he was going to take the place that was rightly his; a place of respect and public authority. She said nothing, but the strength of her embrace told him she was filled with enthusiasm for this new adventure.

Ronald Armstrong, MP – she tried out the title in her mind. Yes, it sounded right. He would stand, and he would win.

CHAPTER THREE

The by-election for the constituency of West
Tweed resulted in an increased majority for the
Whigs. The campaign was fought angrily by
Ronald's Tory opponent, who lost no opportunity to call him 'Miss Corvill's husband'. But
though some of the voters sniggered, many of
them thought it was no bad thing to be married
to the former Miss Corvill, who had a shrewd
head on her shoulders and was involved in
every stage of the weaving industry, the life
force of the district.

Moreover, Mrs Armstrong was pretty, and
the voters of course were all men.

When the results were read out by the Provost, Jenny was on the edge of the platform
party, gloved hands clenched together to keep
them from trembling with anxiety. She had
travelled daily through the countryside speaking to the men, smiling at the women, kissing
the babies. 'My husband will concern himself
with the welfare of Scottish weaving,' she
promised. 'My husband will try to reduce
import taxes. My husband will go on striving
to make the woollen industry safer and more
healthy for its workers.'

Once the seat was won, apprehensions that
she had held at bay came crowding in. Would

his new career take him away from her? She knew from experience that he was a man who liked to go after new things and give them his entire attention. Would he find family matters a hindrance? Would he meet women in London who could further his career, political hostesses who knew how to scheme and intrigue, women far more sophisticated than a provincial like herself?

Playing his part in the House of Commons would take Ronald away from home for long periods. True, he could head for home on Friday when the House rose, but not every Friday, because there were functions he would be expected to attend, committees he would have to serve on, party caucuses at which he must put in an appearance.

Luckily the Armstrongs had a London house. Some years ago Jenny had been on the verge of giving up the lease, but it had always had its uses. Foreign buyers who didn't wish to make the long trip to Galashiels could be entertained there. Some important social obligations could be paid off by dinner parties and evening entertainments in the pretty surroundings of Eaton Square. It was useful to have a base in London if one was travelling to the Continent. And so on.

The fact was, the London house held memories for Jenny. It was to the London house that she had brought her daughter Heather when she was found at last after being missing almost a year. Here Jenny had tended her, coaxed her back into something like her old self. Here she and Baird and Heather had made up a close, loving family, needing no one else at the time, concerned only with helping the child to recover from the terrors of that bitter parting.

Now the house would be Ronald's London home while he attended the House of Commons. 'You won't expect me to come south and be a political hostess, Ronald?' she asked with some anxiety.

'What, in my first year in the House?' He gave a snort of laughter. 'Dinna get delusions of grandeur, lassie! I'm an MP but I'm a political nobody, and will remain so for months, probably years – '

'But Mr Gladstone wrote to you – '

'He sent me a list of instructions, you ought to say. Well and fine, I'll do exactly as I'm told, because if there's any man worth taking orders from it's himself. But in fact all I've got to do is vote as I'm told by the Whips over the Irish Universities Bill this month – '

'But your maiden speech, my love – '

'My maiden speech has got to be as pure as a milkmaid and as harmless as the milk. When there's something coming up about the weaving trade I'll get up on my pins and utter five minutes' worth of platitudes and sit down.'

'But you will let me know in advance, Ronald, man? I want to be there to hear it.'

He went off to be introduced to Parliament and take his seat. He wrote home by that same night's post: 'Thank the Lord that's over. My knees were like jelly but there was nothing to it. Nobody seemed to pay any attention except a fellow in the Tory benches who made whooping noises as I performed my bow, out of boredom, I suppose. The Whips have looked at the Parliamentary calendar and recommend I speak for the first time on Thursday of next week, when there's a debate about money available for agricultural improvement – I'm going to get up and talk about sheep and wool and Scottish Border conditions.

'If you want to be in the Visitors' Gallery, my love, you'd better come down the previous day. I want you here so I can rehearse my speech to you. It's lucky we agreed I should stay in London this weekend, because I'm summoned to a meeting to plan tactics for the Universities debate. I can't see that my presence at the meeting is necessary because I've already been ordered to go into the lobby and vote as I'm told, but the Prime Minister is worried. It seems anything to do with Ireland has its pitfalls.'

Heather had just come home from Thornieburn as the letter arrived by the second post on Saturday. Jenny read out parts of it to her daughter.

'You mean Papa was nervous about taking his seat?' Heather murmured. It had never occurred to her that Papa could be nervous.

'Yes, and is even more nervous about making his first speech, even though he makes a joke of it.'

'May I come too and hear him?'

Jenny pondered. 'I don't know if children are allowed in the Visitor's Gallery. In any case, my pet, you have only just gone back to school after the New Year break – I don't think Miss Darnley would approve of my taking you away for three days.'

Heather made a face and tried to put forward arguments, but didn't object too strongly when she lost. It was clear she enjoyed her schooling with Allen and David.

The improvement in her was perhaps only noticeable to Jenny and to Baird, the two who knew her intimately. She was still wary with strangers, she spoke little more than before, her voice was still low and creaky. But her smile came more readily. She was more confident with those she already knew, sometimes venturing on quite long conversations with the coachman or the head gardener.

Miss Darnley, the governess, had given it as her opinion that Heather would always be slow to put herself forward in company. 'Something has destroyed her confidence in herself,' she said to Jenny. 'It's a pity, for she's a pretty little girl, and will be prettier when she fills out. And she's by no means lacking in intelligence – not academic, of course, but bright and eager to learn.'

'She's certainly learnt a great deal already,' Jenny said with gratitude. 'She regaled me last weekend with a recitation of the names of the monarchs of Scotland, going back to Kenneth McAlpine – '

'How dull! But one must dun such things into their heads; history seems to be full of lists of kings and battles.'

'That's exactly what I mean,' Jenny broke in. 'There's a certain background of knowledge that every child seems to have, and because of Heather's speech problems she's missed out on all that. I couldn't remember much history so I couldn't teach her – '

'But you've done marvels, Mrs Armstrong. You mustn't reproach yourself. Heather has a better grasp of geography than any child I've ever taught, thanks to her travels to Australia and back. And her arithmetic is excellent.'

'My word, so it ought to be! I used to take her to the mill office with me, you know. She'd sit in a little chair near my desk, reading books and doing sums I set for her . . .' Jenny sighed. It had all been makeshift and not suitable for the daughter of a leading citizen, but there had been something unique in that relationship. Now it was gone. She had handed her daughter over to someone much better qualified, and she didn't regret it, no she truly did not – but she missed the old days sometimes.

Especially now that Ronald would be spending so much time in London. Sometimes in the evenings, when she came back from her day at the mills, the house seemed strangely empty. Servants in the kitchen, a housekeeper upstairs in her own little apartment, the coachman and two grooms over the stables, a gardener in a newly built house on the far side of the extended grounds and a bothy for the two gardening boys – and yet she felt lonely.

Only in the nursery wing, playing with little Max or watching with Baird while his nanny, Semple, bathed him ready for bed, only then did she feel the strong current of affection that she had grown so accustomed to.

When Heather was returned to school on the Monday, Jenny sent to let Lord Thornieburn know that Ronald was to speak on Thursday and that she herself was going to hear him. She knew that the Earl took an interest in her husband's parliamentary career; more, she in fact suspected he had had something to do with it.

To her surprise and delight, Lord Thornieburn sent back a note with the coachman. 'I too should like to hear your husband make his debut. I look forward to meeting you in the Gallery of the House of Commons on the great day.'

Ronald himself conducted Jenny to her place on the visitors' benches upstairs. 'I shan't be called for another half-hour or so. Sit there and say a prayer for me!'

Thornieburn arrived ten minutes later. 'Don't look so nervous, Mrs Armstrong,' he whispered. 'He's only got to speak for five minutes, you know.'

'I do indeed. We timed it six times last night by the drawing room clock!'

'Don't worry, he'll do splendidly.'

The benches were not well filled when Ronald was called. Few members were interested in the Bill, which was a minor matter about granting funds to landowners willing to carry out programmes of experimental breeding on farm animals. 'Mr Speaker,' he began in a voice firm but quite unlike his own, 'the money provided in this Bill is quite insufficient. While many landowners have great financial resources, there are others working in small farms whose knowledge of animals, particularly sheep – '

An extraordinary baa-ing sound broke out on the Opposition benches. Ronald broke off, startled. Some laughter ensued, and stern hissings for silence from both Whigs and Tories.

'Mr Speaker,' resumed Ronald, 'er . . . Mr Speaker, in this country sheep are raised not primarily for their wool, but it would be very advantageous to the woollen industry, particularly the woollen industry of the Scottish Borders – '

'– If you were to shut up and sit down!' interrupted a loud voice.

Once again Ronald fell silent. Once again there was laughter from the other members, but there was something surprised in the note of it.

'Order!' said the Speaker in a cross tone. 'Order! Honourable Members will remember that a maiden speech is always heard with consideration and attention. The Member for West Tweed has the floor.'

Ronald glanced about rather wildly. He had a few notes in his hand to help him remember the points to make, but the rudeness of the interruptions had made him lose the thread completely.

'Wool supplies,' he began, 'wool supplies – That is to say, fleeces from British flocks – If we improve our sheep – '

'If we count our sheep, we can all have a quiet sleep instead of listening to this rubbish!'

'Order!' shouted the Speaker, rising from his chair to look over the benches. 'I will not have bad manners during a maiden speech. The member responsible for these interruptions is under my notice. Continue, the Honourable Member for West Tweed.'

'The cost of importing wool from the Colonies is considerable,' Ronald said, having collected himself and taken a hold on his thoughts. He spoke too quickly, however, wanting to make his point before his persecutor could shout again. 'The freight charges are high, and delays caused by ocean travel – '

'I wish you'd take some ocean travel,' came the stentorian voice. 'Then we wouldn't be bored to death – '

'Order!' called the Speaker. 'The Member for Spedlow and Nestholm will be silent.'

'I have a right to voice an opinion, Mr Speaker!'

'No member has a right to make himself objectionable during a maiden speech. It is quite against tradition. I direct that the Member at fault should be silent.'

'The Member at fault is the Member for West Tweed,' replied the mystery voice.

'Who is that man?' Jenny whispered in consternation to the Earl.

'Heaven knows. He's drunk, I suppose.'

'He doesn't sound drunk.'

'Well, then, he's out of his mind. What a way to behave!'

Ronald meanwhile had resumed. He made a few quiet remarks about the Scottish woollen trade then resumed his seat without interruption. But his intended speech had been lost, and the impression he had wanted to make – that of a steady, intelligent man who knew what he was talking about – had been destroyed.

As he picked up his scattered notes he was perplexed and angry. A member behind him on the Government benches slid along the seat to murmur, 'Extraordinary carry-on! Sorry, old fellow.'

About ten minutes later a messenger came to him to say that the Chief Whip wished to speak to him in his office. Still uncertain of his way in this handsome new building, he followed the man to the panelled room where Mr Glyn sat behind his desk, frowning with undisguised annoyance.

'Now then,' he began at once, nodding

Ronald to a chair, 'What's this between you and Unsworth?'

'Unsworth? Is that the man who's just created all that hullabaloo?'

'Yes, of course, Thomas Unsworth. Now what have you done to set him against you?'

'Thomas Unsworth,' repeated Ronald. He sat stiffly on his leather chair, like a schoolboy in disgrace, his spare figure upright, his shoulders squared. 'I never heard of him.'

'Come, come, Armstrong. Whatever your quarrel is, you mustn't let it spill over into parliamentary work. Tell me about it and I'll have a word with the Tory Whips and we'll sort it out.'

'I tell you, Mr Glyn, I never heard of Thomas Unsworth. I've no idea why he broke out in that way.'

'Unsworth,' urged the Chief Whip, tugging at the lapels of his black frock coat, 'sits for Spedlow and Nestholm.'

'I don't even know where Spedlow and Nestholm are!'

'It's a Lincolnshire constituency – a wide area with two sizeable market towns. If you haven't met the man personally, I presume you've had dealings with him in business or something of that kind – '

'No, I assure you,' Ronald interrupted. 'Lincolnshire, that's arable farming, is it not? I've dealt with farmers, of course, but it's always been wool-producers; Scottish mainly, a few in Wiltshire, but mostly Colonial growers. I know nothing of Lincolnshire and even less about the member for Spedlow and Nestholm.'

Mr Glyn huffed and tugged the collar of his coat. 'Now see here, Armstrong, I had high

45

hopes of you. The Prime Minister himself said to keep an eye on you because we're to have dealings with these new Trade Unions soon, and you're said to have good knowledge of that kind of thing. But I can't help you on if you're not going to be frank with me.'

Ronald stood up and raised his right hand. 'As God is my witness, I never heard of Thomas Unsworth, I never heard of his constituency, I never had any dealings with landowners or farmers in Lincolnshire, and I have not the slightest idea why the man chose to wreck my maiden speech.'

A short silence followed. The Chief Whip eyed the tall wiry figure before him: long, narrow face with laughter wrinkles about the eyes and mouth. A determined chin. Grey eyes that looked straight at him from under sandy brows.

'Sit down, sit down,' he said irritably. But the tone masked a feeling of goodwill towards the new member. Long experience had taught Mr Glyn to know the honest from the deceitful. He was sure that Ronald Armstrong was telling the truth.

Ronald sat. After a moment he said, 'You know, when I was presented to the Speaker, somebody broke out into catcalls.'

'Really?'

'I was too nervous to take much heed. But Farquharson, who was "supporting" me, looked about and glared at somebody.'

'Hm, It would be interesting to know if Farquharson was glaring at Mr Unsworth . . .' He rang a silver bell on his desk. A minion appeared. 'Kindly go to the Chamber and if Mr

46

Farquharson is sitting, ask him to spare me a moment.'

As it happened Peter Farquharson, a fellow Scot, had come to witness Ronald's debut and was now sitting on one of the back benches discussing the fracas with a fellow-member. He hurried to obey the Chief Whip's summons.

'Yes, it was Unsworth who wailed and moaned when Armstrong took his seat,' he said in answer to the Whip's question. 'And I can tell you he's lolling in his place now, grinning like an ape and disregarding the disapproval of the few Tories who're in the Chamber at the moment.'

'Unsworth, Unsworth,' mused Mr Glyn. 'He's a nobody, I believe? I don't remember that he's ever spoken more than ten words in the House.'

'That's what I think too,' Farquharson agreed. 'He represents a broad farming constituency, turns up when there's a debate that's important to his constituents, votes to protect the interests of the farmers and landowners, and says hardly a word.'

'Have you heard anything among the members? Any gossip? Has he been acting strangely in other ways? Or is he reported as saying anything about Armstrong?'

'I haven't made any inquiries, sir. I remember his outburst when Armstrong was introduced but I thought perhaps he'd had a drop too much. It didn't seem important until today.'

Mr Glyn turned to Ronald. 'Can you explain it? Have you any suggestion, however bizarre?'

'None,' said Ronald, with a shrug of bewilderment. 'I don't know the man, never did him any harm that I know of, have given him no reason since I got to Parliament to take against me – I repeat, I don't even know him, wouldn't recognise him if I saw him in the lobby.'

Glyn nodded dismissal to Farquharson, who went off looking baffled. To Ronald he said, 'We must hope that whatever set him off today is a minor matter. I'm very sorry he has marred your maiden speech. I hoped to be able to report to Mr Gladstone that you had done well, because although you are very new and will need some time to find your feet, he had some slight plans for you.'

'Would it help if I sought the man out and asked him what he was up to?'

'I think not. We'll ignore it and hope it is all over. If you'll excuse me, Armstrong, I have other things to attend to.'

Ronald went to find his wife, who was waiting for him with great anxiety among the staring political statues in the hall.

'My dear,' she said, flying towards him with her hands held out, 'what a shame! You hardly got a word out before that man – '

The Earl of Thornieburn came up at her side. 'Bad business, Armstrong. I should think his Whips will have him over the coals for that. Who is he?'

'Mr Glyn tells me he's a member for a Lincolnshire constituency, famous for saying hardly a word hitherto.'

'Why has he behaved like this to you, Ronald?' Jenny demanded, her brown eyes sparkling with indignation.

'It's a mystery.'

'But there must be a reason – '

'Not that I know of, my lord.'

'But a man doesn't hack another man about in public like that for no reason.'

Ronald shook his head. 'If there's a reason, it's unknown to me and everyone else so far.'

'You'll take him up on it, I suppose?' said the Earl.

'No, the Chief Whip says it's better just to forget it.'

'Nonsense!' cried Jenny. She was furious with this man who had spoiled what should have been one of the best moments in Ronald's life. 'You must have it out with him.'

'No, I have to follow the wishes of the Chief Whip,' her husband said. 'And I must go back into the Chamber – they'll call the division soon on this Bill.'

They had planned a celebration dinner at the Chinon Restaurant, one of the best in London. It seemed pointless to go on with it now. 'I'll come back to Eaton Square after the vote. Nothing elaborate tonight, Jenny.'

'I'll tell Cook.'

But dinner had to be put back twice, he was so late coming home. When he arrived about ten he said, 'I was called for a post mortem on this afternoon's affair. The Whips of the two parties have been talking to each other. The Tories called Unsworth in and put him on the carpet but it seems he laughed and treated it all as a huge joke.'

'A joke!' Jenny cried.

'He's been told to behave himself but I gather he shrugged off the scolding. The Whigs want to see if he'll obey orders so they've had a word with the Speaker and I'm to take part in the debate tomorrow and again on Monday, to see if he keeps quiet.'

He went upstairs to wash. Jenny rang for the meal to be served, but it was so late that they had both gone beyond hunger and could eat little. They went to bed, subdued, perplexed.

Jenny was to travel back next day so as to be at home when Heather returned for the weekend. She was weary, yet she couldn't sleep, her mind full of plans for tomorrow and recollections of today.

By and by she became aware that Ronald was still awake.

'What's the matter, dearest?' she said, turning on her pillows, trying to descry his face in the starlight glinting through the windows.

'I just keep thinking about what happened,' Ronald said, 'I felt such a *fool!*'

'You weren't the one who looked foolish,' she said, finding his hand and holding it. 'It was that silly man.'

'No. He made me look helpless, childish . . .'

'Put it behind you, my darling. It won't happen again.'

'I hope not. Oh, God, I hope not! I was told this afternoon that the Prime Minister was prepared to take some interest in me, but after a start like that . . .'

'Mr Gladstone has had years of experience, Ronald. He'll understand that none of it was your fault.'

'But why should it have happened at all? I just don't *understand!*'

She put her arms around him and hugged him close. 'Never mind, my love, never mind. You'll soon show them what you're made of.

Forget this afternoon – when you speak tomorrow and on Monday, you'll retrieve all the ground you feel you've lost.'

He buried his head against her shoulder. She lay holding him close to her breast, comforting him almost as if he were a hurt child.

When she left him next day, he was full of optimism and resolution. 'Everything will be all right today,' he said, as they lingered on the station platform outside the train carriage door. 'It was just some peculiar silliness that came over him, I see that now.'

'You'll write and tell me all about today's and Monday's debates?'

'Of course.'

The guard came along urging passengers to get into their carriages. Jenny mounted the step and sat in her place, the porter putting a heated footstool under her feet against the chill of the February day.

As the train pulled out she watched her husband's figure diminish in the dark early morning light under the glass canopy. He waved. His stance was upright, his voice was cheerful as he called, 'Goodbye, love to Max and Heather, warn Gaines about that pressing machine.'

In Galashiels business needed her attention on the Friday evening – correspondence awaited her in the office at the mills, and she had a vexed debate with her assistant manager, Gaines, over the pressing machine that had developed a fault. Then on Saturday there was the usual routine of sending the carriage for Heather and with it must go a friendly note to Lady Thornieburn. Should she tell her anything about Ronald's troubles? No, for her

51

Ladyship wasn't interested in politics and the Earl, when he came home, would tell her about it if he thought fit.

By the afternoon post came a note on Parliamentary notepaper. 'Unsworth repeated his performance. I'm to go to a meeting at the Chief Whip's house tomorrow (Saturday), to discuss tactics for Monday if he does it again. Mr Glyn thinks it best not to talk about all this, my dear.' He signed off with affection and messages to his children.

On Monday the *Border Beacon* published a paragraph about Ronald's debut. 'Mr Armstrong spoke on the subject of grants towards the experiments in improved animal rearing, with special regard to the production of wool. His remarks were sometimes not easily heard because of the intervention of an inebriated Member but on the whole the Member for West Tweed made a satisfactory first speech.'

It was faint praise indeed. And worse was to follow because by midweek the national newspapers, *The Times* and the *Daily News*, had taken notice of the strange events. *The Times* merely reported that Mr Ronald Armstrong, the Member for West Tweed, seemed unable to utter a word in the House without eliciting a distorted echo which seemed to diminish his efforts. 'His words are set at naught, but then from the Whig benches one expects naught in the first place.'

The *Daily News*, the supporter of the Liberal Party, was indignant. 'For some reason there is a campaign to prevent Mr Ronald Armstrong, the recently elected Member for West Tweed, from expressing his opinions in the House. It is some measure of how much the Tories fear his views that they have set on one of their more foolish supporters to bray and bark when Mr Armstrong rises. We hope that even the Tory Party will not continue in this absurd and pointless display of bad manners.'

Jenny read it with concern. She could imagine how tongues were wagging in Westminster.

As for Ronald, he had already noticed other members eyeing him with curiosity. Among his own party he had been given friendly nods, assurances of support. Some Conservative members added their regrets, but he could tell that there were a few who thought yet another great joke had been added to the store of Parliamentary buffoonery.

'What you want is a speaking trumpet, old chap,' they suggested. 'Don't be bashful, get up and shout through it. Hunterton's stock them, I believe.'

Infuriated, Ronald pushed his way through the group and found his persecutor, Thomas Unsworth, grinning to himself behind them. He had had the opportunity to pick out the man among the Opposition benches that evening. A tallish, broad man with rusty side-whiskers and a very ornate pearl-and-diamanté tiepin in his cravat.

He grabbed the man by the silk cravat. 'You!' he growled.

'Here, I say! No fisticuffs in the Palace of Westminster, Armstrong.'

'Why are you doing this? What is it for?'

'It's to make you feel uncomfortable, my lad. And it's working, isn't it?'

'But why?' Ronald demanded, shaking him.

Well-intentioned hands intervened, detaching

his fingers from the folded silk. The handsome tie-pin fell on the paving stones.

'Now, now, what's this, robbery with violence?' Unsworth said, looking down at it.

Someone picked it up and handed it to him. He pinned it into his cravat. 'You'd better mind your temper, Armstrong,' he said with his chin tilted up to accommodate the resettling of his necktie.

'Is that what you've been after? To make me lose my temper?'

'No, my poor Scottish sheep-stealer, it's to make you lose your seat.'

'What?' Ronald said, startled.

'If you don't like it at Westminster, you ought to go back home to the mists of the Borders.'

'You're trying to get rid of me? But I don't understand . . . What have you got against me?'

Unsworth patted his tie and beckoned for his coat. 'I don't like you,' he said. 'That's my reason.'

'You don't like me? But you don't even know me!'

'Oh, I know you, my friend. I know you and I don't like you.'

'But we've never met until now!'

'You don't have to know a man personally to take against him. And I've taken against you, Armstrong. You might say, I've made it a kind of crusade to make your life a misery. So if you've any sense you'll throw in the towel now and go back to making horse blankets.'

With that, taking his overcoat over his arm, he strode away, leaving Ronald staring after him in disbelief.

The man must be mad.

Ronald had heard of people who, caught up in the web of their own delusions, imagined they had reason to hate or fear some particular person.

That must be the explanation. Though why Unsworth should have chosen to weave his fantasies around Ronald was a mystery.

Whatever the reasons, this much was clear.

Ronald had an enemy who was out to ruin him.

CHAPTER FOUR

Easter was not until mid-April that year. Ronald promised to be home before then but became immersed in the Parliamentary session.

Jenny for her part busied herself with running the mills and looking after her family. The little boy, Max, was teething. Semple, his nursemaid, reported broken nights, and the baby often wailed during the day with the sheer pain of his gums.

When she was home, Heather was a great help. The baby seemed to find her strange little voice very soothing. She would take him in her arms and walk about the house with him, crooning with a reedy little sound that always seemed to Jenny like a cross between a reed warbler and a lark.

The little girl seemed very happy with the arrangements for her education. Her talk was sprinkled with phrases like 'Allen said' or 'David thinks' or 'the others told me'.

'Don't you ever have any say in what goes on among you?' Jenny teased. 'It sounds as if they order you about all the time.'

Heather swayed the baby to and fro in her arms. 'I suppose they do,' she admitted, 'most of the time.'

There had been an occasion just a few days ago when they had not ordered her about, where she had taken the initiative. They had been out riding, as was their custom in the early morning. The two boys had gone off on a side trail among the pines on Ligster Hill, with Heather bringing up the rear on Oatcake. A branch, weakened by a recent gale, came down unexpectedly, startling David's mount which took off at an alarming rate on the wooded path and towards a pond where wildfowl abounded.

Allen set off at once in pursuit and, at a point where the path widened as it came out on the banks of the water, managed to catch David's bridle and pull the horse aside. For a moment it floundered in the mud at the verge, then slid to its knees and stopped, tipping David off into the swamp.

Wild duck took off in a flurry of whirling wings and alarmed cries. Heather came out from among the trees to find David staggering to his feet, the front of his clothes and his face covered in mud and weeds. Allen was leaning forward in his saddle, helpless with laughter.

She drew up, her fright giving way to amusement at the sight of the solemn, sedate David in such a state. He, in a huff, led his horse out on to the dry bank and was about to remount and ride away when something strange about Allen made him pause.

The viscount was leaning forward in the saddle, his shoulders heaving. But he wasn't laughing. He was coughing and gasping and making a strange keening noise.

'Allen! Allen!' David ran up to him and

57

tugged at him, trying to get him down. 'What's the matter, Allen?'

The other boy could make no reply. He was clutching at the mane of his horse, his face almost buried against its shoulder. Heather had ridden up close without dismounting. She leaned forward on Oatcake. She could see that Allen's face was covered with sweat. He had gone very pale.

'Allen,' she said in her low voice, close to his ear.

'Pocket,' he gasped. 'Pocket. Help, pocket!'

'He's having one of his attacks,' she said over the horse's head to David. 'Help me – '

'Oh – God – he's dying!' cried David. 'Look, he can't even hold on – he'll fall – '

'Help me, idiot!' cried Heather. 'Feel in his pockets.'

She put her hands into the left hand pocket to his tweed jacket. David pulled himself together and felt in the right hand. It was he who came up with the little bottle.

'Here,' he said in a panicky tone. 'Is this it? What do we do?'

Heather grabbed it from his wavering hand. She felt the little spring attachment at the neck. It's a spray, she thought, like Mama uses to put on her perfume. She took off the cap to reveal a tiny nozzle. Without ceremony she took hold of Allen's hair, hauled his head back, and pressed the spray under his nose.

A little cloud of vapour came out in the morning air. Allen was still gasping horribly, trying to breathe. Heather pressed and pressed the spray, until by and by she realised that the boy was holding up his head and no longer needed to have it pulled back. She let go of his hair, rather horrified to think how much it must have hurt to have it pulled so hard.

'Is that enough?' she asked, waving the spray bottle in front of his eyes.

He nodded. 'J-just a m-minute . . . I'll b-be b-better in a minute . . .'

He sat, bowed over but much more in control of himself. His horse, Perkin, moved uneasily, disliking Heather so close on Oatcake and the general air of alarm. David stood staring at them, his mouth a little agape, his square face lengthened in a droll look of dismay.

'Do you want to dismount? Rest a bit?'

Allen shook his head.

'Sure?'

'I'm all right.' He gave a shaky smile. 'It was just one of my wheezes.'

'Lord above us,' said David, almost in tears, 'I thought you were going to die!'

'So did I,' Allen said. 'But I rarely do.'

Heather heard the words, then understood the sense, and laughed. She was filled with admiration. Anyone who could go through that ordeal and still make jokes was a hero.

'You were a marvel,' David said to her in admiration. 'You knew what to do in a minute.'

'No,' she said. It had just seemed common sense to her.

'What on earth brought it on?'

'Dunno,' Allen replied with weary annoyance. 'I got over-anxious about you running away, I think. Almost anything seems to start me off.' He sighed. 'Damned nuisance.'

'Allen!' cried Heather, shocked at the swearword. But she knew it was bravado, a reaction against having been helpless in the grip of his ailment.

'Promise you won't tell Mother,' he said as they gathered themselves together and prepared to head for home.

'Oh. Oughtn't we to . . .'

'Promise, Heather!' He hated his illness and his mother's anxiety over it. 'Anyway,' he added, 'if you tell, we'll have to explain how it happened and David'll have to admit to being tipped off into a pond.'

David went red. Heather suppressed a smile.

'All right,' she agreed.

So she now said nothing to her mother about the episode.

It was strange to have secrets from her mother. After spending all her life sharing every single thing with her, now she had a life quite separate from her.

In some ways it was good, in some ways it was bad. She saw Jenny more dispassionately these days. She was able to think of her sometimes as others did – as Mrs Ronald Armstrong, 'the Mistress', the extraordinary woman who held her own in the world of textiles, who designed plaids and fine cloths that were exported to every fashion centre of the globe, who was held somewhat in awe by local worthies, often envied and gossiped about, sometimes courted.

One of those who came to pay court, Heather noticed, was the handsome Mr Brunton.

Mr Archibald Brunton was the owner of the largest estate in the neighbourhood of Galashiels. Everything he did or said was of interest to the local people.

Years ago, when Jenny Corvill first came to the town and built up Waterside Mills to pre-eminence, it had been widely expected that she and Archie Brunton would make a match of it.

However, much to the surprise of the townsfolk, Archie had at that time suddenly taken himself off overseas. More recently he had returned to the land of his birth, but by then the pretty, lively Miss Jenny Corvill had become the pretty, busy Mrs Ronald Armstrong.

And besides, said the gossips, Archie Brunton had such a roving eye . . . you couldn't expect him to be thinking of the Mistress nowadays.

In that they were wrong. Archie Brunton had learned a lot in the years that had gone by since first he had left Galashiels. He was now genuinely in love with the woman he had more or less jilted. There had been a time when he thought her marriage to Ronald was breaking up – Ronald had gone to the Antipodes on a so-called business trip and from what he could gather had got himself mixed up with some woman.

Seizing his chance, Archie had urged Jenny to divorce Ronald and marry him. Instead, to his chagrin, Jenny had packed up and set off to Australia to get back her erring husband.

Now that husband was away from home again, off politicking in Westminster. Jenny was lonely – he was sure she was lonely.

So, as a good friend should, he rallied around.

In the week leading up to Easter, the weather turned extremely mild and pleasant. Word went round among the gentry of the neighbourhood: Mr Brunton was sending out invitations to an *al fresco* afternoon on his estate, the idea being that the artistically inclined should be given the chance to sketch the spring scenery, especially the wild daffodils on the banks of a stream that ran through his grounds.

The fact was that Archie had heard on the servants' grapevine that Ronald Armstrong was not coming home for Easter. If Ronald had been in Galashiels, nothing would have tempted Jenny away from home. But what with the disappointment and the urgings of her friends, Jenny was just as interested to see the daffodils on the bank of the Bowden Burn as anyone else.

Carriages set off straight from church. A cold collation awaited them at Brunton's house, a plain, sturdy farmhouse much enlarged. Afterwards the artists wandered off with their easels and watercolours, the children were taken to be introduced to the sheepdogs, and the rest strolled about in the sunshine.

It was on occasions like this that Archie Brunton managed to get a few words of private conversation with the woman he couldn't cure himself of loving. They walked in the old-fashioned garden beloved by the late Mrs Brunton, Archie's mother. Not far off other idlers were noting the new shoots on the lavender bush or standing back to admire the ornamental cherry.

'You'll be disappointed Ronald couldn't come,' Archie suggested. He always found she spoke to him more readily if he mentioned that confounded husband of hers.

'He had to spend the weekend with one of

the political panjandrums at a country house.'
Jenny replied.

'He's been taken up by the bigwigs, then?'
Despite himself, Archie was impressed. He
had been intrigued when the Thornieburns
interested themselves in the Armstrongs, and
a little put out when, clearly at the instigation
of Lord Thornieburn, Ronald stood for the
local constituency. But he had never expected
Ronald to win.

In one way it was a good thing. It took the
man away to London. But on the other hand it
gave him importance. Archie could no longer
shrug him off as 'that nobody she married'.
Even the gold that Ronald was supposed to
have found on his trip to Australia could be
shrugged off as luck, or legend – but a man
helped into the role of MP for the district had
to be reckoned with.

And now, curse him, he was being singled
out for attention by the Whig party managers.

'How does Heather like her new school-
mates?' he inquired, since Jenny said neither
yea nor nay to his inquiry about the political
leaders.

'Oh, she's happier than she's ever been. She
gets quite conversational these days.'

'And the baby – how is he?' Archie said,
having already done his duty by her annoying
husband and her troublesome daughter.

'He's teething, alas.'

Jenny was inwardly amused. She knew
Archie didn't care a fig for her husband or
either of her children. But she was also sorry
for him.

He was, after all, forty years old, and the fate
foretold for him by his angry mother had come

about. He was still a bachelor, with no one close to him. Young ladies of the neighbourhood still hoped that they might have the luck to land Archie Brunton and his fine estates, but he was essentially lonely – and not quite so handsome or lively as he used to be. The once abundant brown hair was thinning a little, there was more flesh about his jaw-line than there used to be.

Nevertheless, he was still an attractive man, who helped his appearance by adopting the latest fashions the moment they appeared. For instance, he had grown Dundreary whiskers, luxuriant side-moustaches that left the chin free. Today he was wearing a short jacket of soft wool cloth over an informal striped shirt and beige flecked trousers. None of the other men had achieved such sartorial novelty – they were in frock coats, the nearest approach to informality being shepherd's plaid trousers or a round curly brimmed hat becoming known as a bowler.

'What did you think of the reshuffling of the government?' Jenny asked, feeling it was now her turn to make conversation. 'Did you expect Mr Gladstone to return to office?'

'I expect any manoeuvre from him that will keep him at the top,' Archie said tersely. He knew nothing about politics and cared less. Someone had mentioned to him that Mr Gladstone had resigned over the Irish Universities Bill in March, and come back into office again because Disraeli refused to form a government. Mr Gladstone seemed to be a fact of political life, always there. The only interesting thing he knew about him was that a fellow politician had nicknamed him 'Merrypebble' – which seemed to Archie the sort of name you gave to a race horse.

'Ronald was very worried about it,' Jenny said with a stifled sigh.

'Really? I should have thought he was too new to be involved.'

'Oh, of course – it had nothing to do with him personally. But it was felt as such a rebuff to the Prime Minister – and Ronald has so much respect for him.'

The more fool he, thought Archie. 'While he's away, I expect you often feel the need of an escort. I stand ready at any time, Jenny; a note will always fetch me.'

'You are very kind.'

They both knew she would never summon him. It would cause too much talk, and give Archie himself grounds for hope. If she needed an escort she would call upon some very elderly married man who could come to her aid but would bring his wife. But then, the Mistress of Waterside Mills was perfectly capable of going wherever she wanted to without a man to shepherd her.

'Are you well, Jenny? You seem to me rather paler than usual.'

'Not at all, I assure you – it's this dark dress, it makes me look pale.' She was wearing an apron-fronted gown of very rich brown, high at the neck and with no lace or trimming to lighten it there. Her Leghorn hat was dark brown trimmed with flowers made from sherry-coloured velvet.

But in fact, she was paler than usual and a little thinner. She missed her husband.

She missed him through most of the ensuing months. The Whig party was in a state of crisis, particularly in July. First of all there was the revelation that the funds in the Post Office Savings Bank had been put to improper use by the government. Then there seemed to have been irregularities in the awarding of the contract for the telegraph system to Southern Africa.

The Opposition enjoyed the scandals very much, the more so as William Ewart Gladstone took such a pious position in moral questions. Scenes in the House of Commons were often noted as 'ending in uproar'. Members met unofficially to discuss how to counteract the rot that seemed to be setting in.

'It will end with the Prime Minister resigning,' Ronald wrote. 'It has been rumoured for some time, but the party cannot spare him . . . The not-knowing when the blow will fall is very unsettling.'

Jenny went to London every time she could find an excuse. On these occasions she found her husband preoccupied, inattentive. New friends came to the house, men she didn't know and who paid scant heed to her even after they were introduced.

She told herself she must excuse them. They were worried, and worried men have no time to be gallant.

What made it worse for Ronald was that in the midst of the common troubles he still had his own: his *bête noire* continued to torment him every time he rose to speak. Jenny went to hear him, and discovered that he had found a quite effective way of dealing with Mr Unsworth and his heckling.

He was to take part in a run-of-the-mill

debate on foreign affairs. He got up and began, 'Mr Speaker – '

'Sit down, sit down!' shouted the member for Spedlow and Nestholm.

'I intend to, as soon as I have said what I have to say.' Ronald waited. No response. 'Since the Member for Spedlow and Nestholm is unaccountably struck dumb, I hasten to go on. The recent actions of the Russian Government in seizing Khiva and Bokhara are tantamount to – '

'Tantivy, tantivy!' carolled Mr Unsworth from his place on the back benches of the Opposition side.

'I am referring to the field of foreign affairs, not the hunting-field,' riposted Ronald. 'This is a serious matter and should not be treated as a joke.'

'You're a joke, my friend!'

'But not such a bad joke as someone who ignores parliamentary good manners. I repeat, Mr Speaker, the British Government must keep watch on the actions of the Russian Empire or else – '

'Why don't *you* go and perform at the Empire, you comedian – you belong on a music hall stage!'

'Order!' called the Speaker. 'The Honourable Member for West Tweed must be awarded the respect due to him. Pray go on.'

Ronald finished his remarks with only one more interruption, which he fielded neatly.

'I thought you were splendid!' Jenny told him at home in Eaton Square that night.

'Thank you, but I didn't go to Westminster to play the fool! He was right when he said we belonged in a music hall – it's not good sense to waste House of Commons' time like that.'

'Have you ever managed to discover what he holds against you?'

Ronald, putting parliamentary papers into his desk drawer, shook his head. 'We've come to the conclusion he must be a little unhinged.'

'Can't you have him dismissed? Is it in order for a Member of Parliament to be touched in the head?'

Ronald gave a wry smile. 'Some would say the House of Commons is the proper place for him. There are some very strange folk there, Jenny.'

She was in the doorway, about to go to the dining room where sandwiches and coffee awaited them. Ronald's hours were so unpredictable that meals were often delayed or cancelled, and a substantial snack even at this late hour was by no means unusual.

Something in his voice made her turn back. 'That sounds very disillusioned, lad.'

He closed the drawer with an angry shove. The key fell out on the carpet but he walked away disregarding it, to stalk past her into the passage.

He was normally so careful about his Parliamentary papers that she knew something was seriously wrong. She retrieved the key, locked the drawer, and followed to give the key to him.

The table had been set with two places, one at the head for Jenny to pour, and one at the side for Ronald. She filled two cups. He drank thirstily, despite the fact that the coffee was hot enough to scald.

'Tell me what's the matter.'

'Nothing.'

'Tell me, Ronald.'

He shook his head. 'It's hardly fit for your ears.'

'I'd rather know,' she said, frowning, 'since it's worrying you so much. Is it the money scandals?'

'It's something much worse, at least in my opinion.'

'What is it?'

He drew a deep breath. 'Very well. Mr Gladstone – our beloved leader – goes out at night to consort with prostitutes.' He coloured as he said it. One didn't use such a word in front of a woman one respected. Decency forbade it.

Despite what the menfolk might think, the word wasn't unknown to such as Jenny. In fact one of her charities in Scotland was in aid of women of ill repute.

Nevertheless, this was startling. 'I think it must be a mistake,' she said.

'No. It's well-known among the Members. They snigger and joke about it all the time.'

'Mr Gladstone?'

'He's always been interested in women of that kind. It seems when he was a young man he used to go to the Argyll Rooms after the debates ended – '

'The Argyll Rooms?'

'It's a well-known brothel.' Once again Ronald coloured. He had never in his life imagined himself having this kind of conversation with his wife, and it angered him all the more to have to do it. 'Some say he even kept a record of those he encountered and what they did – '

'Wait,' said Jenny. 'Didn't I hear that he used to work for some religious movement – '

'The Tractarian Society, yes, but that was thirty years ago. He *still* goes out at night in search of these creatures.'

'It's just evil gossip.'

'I tell you, sweetheart, men can put a name to some of them. There was a woman called Summerhayes, and the most recent is Mrs Thistlethwayte – Mrs T the Temptress, the jokesters call her.'

'But I've heard of her. She gives religious lectures – '

'There's some very strange religiousness mixed up in all this, but if you think he meets her in private to discuss religion, you're in the minority, Jenny. When I first took my seat she was in Egypt for her health, but she came back in April and since then the jeers and sneers have been unbearable. Disraeli calls her "The Returned Serpent of Old Nile".' Despite himself Ronald smiled at the phrase.

'Disraeli himself is considered to be something of a ladies' man – '

'But not like this! Dizzy has too much sense to get himself mixed up with "fallen women". People try to tell Gladstone he's being wildly indiscreet by seeing Mrs Thistlethwayte but he refuses to listen. And he seeks out others in the streets . . .'

'Is there any proof that he is . . . physically attracted to them? Perhaps he only wants to help them.'

'Oh, Jenny,' Ronald groaned. 'How can you be so naive? And even if he is doing it all from good motives, don't you think there's something *strange* in that? Here is the Prime

Minister and Chancellor of the Exchequer of Britain, choosing to spend his time and energy on prostitutes. If he wants to do it, why doesn't he resign his seat and enter the church? And if it's above board, why does he go out alone at night? Why does he have private meetings with Mrs T, whose history is well-known and who would be strongly disapproved of by his wife and family?'

Jenny got up, to put her arms about her husband's shoulders and give him a hug for comfort. He captured one of her hands and held it against his cheek.

After a moment she took the chair next to him on his side of the table, so that she could look forward and watch his face. He looked pale and exhausted.

'Eat something, husband,' she urged. 'Eat some food and get to bed.'

'I canna sleep with this on my mind, lassie! It's been haunting me for weeks! You can't know the *disappointment* of learning that a man you've respected all your life is a sham . . .'

She paused a moment to rally her argument. 'Think about it in practical terms, Ronald. Whatever Mr Gladstone may do in his private life makes no difference to the fact that he is an able politician, a superb orator – '

'And every time he gets on his feet in the House I find myself wondering, What did you get up to last night, old man?'

'But you're not alone in that – '

'That makes it the more distasteful! I don't think I'm cut out for a world where we have to accept such things. I think I ought to resign my seat, Jenny.'

'Never!'

'I didn't come to Westminster to listen to snickers and sneers about the Party leader. I thought I was going to be part of a team that would help the country – '

'But that's just it, Ronald! Your job is to carry out the business of running the country, and it's at Westminster that the work is done. You achieve nothing by walking away from it.'

'Peace of mind?'

She shook her head at him. 'Now who's being naive?' She thought it over. 'Listen, my lad, did you ever promise the electors you would look into the morals of the Prime Minister when you got to Westminster?'

'Of course not – because I never thought they needed looking into!'

'Very well. You were elected to help the weaving industry and the folk who make their living by it. Are you going to fail them by giving up?'

Ronald took a sandwich and bit into it in an absent-minded way. Hunger seized him. He finished it and began another. 'But it's all so depressing,' he objected. 'We have these meetings and weekend house-parties. They talk and talk about how to manage affairs, how to keep the cover on the Prime Minister's oddities, how to repair the damage after the Post Office Scandal. But really everyone is out for himself. Everyone is cynical and self-seeking.'

She understood his feelings only too well. Even dealing in the business world was no preparation for the scheming and plotting that went on in politics, because in politics the rewards were so much greater.

'Think of yourself when you were asked to stand for Parliament by the Whigs in Galashiels,' she urged. 'Had you ever given much thought to politics?'

'As much as most men. I thought I could suggest things to improve the world a wee bit.'

'So you came here full of idealism and good intentions. The awakening has been a bit hard, my dear. But it doesn't make your intentions less worthwhile. And those intentions can only be carried out under the leadership of Mr Gladstone.'

'Even that is by no means so certain,' he replied, his tone mournful. 'People say he's not so deft as he used to be, and even I can see he's losing his grip. He tells his friends he's tired, wants to stand down as leader.'

'Surely not!'

'It might be best. If he went now, it would be with his good name intact. As things stand, he can be disgraced at any moment and so can the Party. It only takes one enemy who decides to speak out about his foibles.'

'And I suppose he has many enemies.'

'We all have enemies,' Ronald murmured. 'Even a nobody like me has a lunatic called Thomas Unsworth for an enemy.'

'What a good thing,' murmured his wife, 'that there's nothing to your detriment that Thomas Unsworth can get hold of.'

The conversation languished. Ronald was really too weary to keep his anxiety and dismay at a high pitch. They finished the snack almost in silence and went to bed.

They slept rather late. After a meal that was half-breakfast and half-lunch, Ronald left for a committee meeting at the House. Jenny sat in the drawing room with the blinds lowered against the strong July sunshine, going through her business engagement diary, crossing out appointments already attended to, making notes for those still to come that afternoon.

The butler entered. 'A person wishes to see you, ma'am.'

'A person?'

'A young woman. She had no card to send in but she says her name is Mrs Eynsham.'

'Mrs Eynsham – I don't think I know her.'

'She said to tell you she has recently arrived from Australia.'

'Australia! It must be someone I met out there. Show her in, Graves.'

A few moments later he ushered in a tall figure in a worn jacket and skirt of thick grey cotton. Under the faded pink bonnet clusters of curls glowed with the lustre of well-polished mahogany. The face was not easy to distinguish in the diffused light of the room, but the voice was unmistakable.

'I hope this isn't too big a surprise for you, Mrs Armstrong.'

It was Dinah Bowerby, the woman from whose clutches Jenny had had to rescue Ronald in Australia four years ago.

CHAPTER FIVE

The last place Jenny had seen this girl was on the quay at Sydney, as the steam-clipper moved out of the harbour taking Jenny, her husband and her daughter home to Scotland.

The picture would never fade from Jenny's memory. In the grey, misty drizzle, Dinah had stood quite apart from the little crowd bidding farewell to the passengers aboard the *Cumberland*. She was on some bales of wool awaiting shipping. As the distance between ship and shore increased, Dinah had mounted to the top bale so as to get a better view.

Jenny knew the girl was looking at Ronald. But Ronald was calling last instructions to their shipping agent. His attention was totally on the group of business acquaintances on his right. Dinah, on her vantage point, was too far off to the left for him to notice her.

As the *Cumberland* manoeuvred out towards the open bay, the girl stared with a consuming gaze at Ronald, the man she loved but had given up. At last a faint breeze was rising, the curtains of drizzle were being blown a little.

That breeze took hold of the old oilcloth raincoat Dinah was wearing and blew the folds against her body. And in that moment Jenny realised the girl was heavily pregnant.

The baby was undoubtedly Ronald's. Whatever her passionate nature had led her into, Dinah was essentially what the farmers' wives called 'a good girl'. Ronald was her only love, on whom all her hopes had been pinned until she discovered that his wife – that unknown, uncaring, unkind woman – loved him enough to cross the world to get him back.

'A good girl'. Brought up in an orphanage where moral values were based on stern church teaching. 'Whom God hath joined together, let no man put asunder.' Dinah bowed to that law. Ronald was a married man, his wife had the rightful claim. With simple obedience Dinah had stepped aside.

Until that moment of departure, Jenny had never suspected there was a baby on the way. Her first instinct had been to tell Ronald, to make some move – but what? They were on their way home, to start their married life again on a new, hopeful footing. Everything concerning Dinah Bowerby was to recede into the background.

Besides, if Dinah had wanted Ronald to know about the baby, there had been plenty of opportunity to tell him. Everything that the Armstrongs did in Sydney was subject to public notice, especially after Ronald came back from the Lachlan River with gold nuggets in his saddlebag.

But Dinah had kept her secret. And after hours of anguished thought, Jenny had decided to do the same. Before leaving Sydney – before ever suspecting the pregnancy – she had made arrangements for money to be available to Dinah if ever she needed it. She felt no enmity towards her, only pity, and the more so when she thought about the coming child.

The disclosing of that secret she had left to Dinah. No letter had come, no word of any kind.

Until now.

The two women studied each other. Jenny saw that the years had not been too kind to Dinah. There were lines already on the creamy skin that goes with dark Titian hair. Her hands, always workworn from her life in farm kitchens, were softer now after the long voyage from Australia, but they were thinner, with a scar caused by some scald or burn on the back of the left one.

Her clothes were poor – creased from having lain for weeks in a trunk, badly cut in the first place. She stood in an attitude of anxious attention, as if waiting for an order from someone.

Dinah for her part saw a more elegant version of the woman who had taken Ronald away from her that dreadful day on Ma Fowler's sheep station. Even then, away out in the bush, Jenny had seemed a magazine illustration with her neat travelling suit and her kid gloves. Today, in a gown of high fashion – pale blue watered silk, the skirt very full at the back and looped at the front into ovals edged with lace – she stood with sparkling, alert brown eyes fixed on Dinah with an air of instinctive authority.

'Dinah! What are you doing – ? But no, come in, sit down.'

Braced for animosity, Dinah was taken aback. She moved forward into the elegant room, her gaze travelling over graceful small tables, lamps with sparkling hanging crystals on the shades, richly upholstered sofas.

'Here, sit here.' Jenny came to her, took her hands, and urged her to one of the sofas. They sat down together. 'Let me look at you. How are you?'

There was a tremor in Jenny's voice, audible to herself. She had had one of the greatest shocks of her life. But above all she must not let this meeting begin with any suspicion of illwill on her part. She had thought that Dinah Bowerby had vanished for ever from their lives but, now she was here, she would be treated well.

'I'm fair, I s'pose,' said Dinah. 'I didn't enjoy the trip. Weather was poor and I discovered I ain't a good sailor.'

'I know what you mean. When did the ship dock?'

'Day before yestiday. We had to spend a couple of days getting our land legs and resting up.'

'Would you like anything now? Coffee? A drink?'

'A drink? If you mean liquor, I'm a total abstainer, Mrs Armstrong. But I could go a strong cuppa.'

Jenny rose, pulled the bellrope by the fireplace, and came back towards Dinah. But she didn't sit down, she stood openly studying her. 'Things haven't been going well with you, Dinah.'

'You could say that. I just didn't seem to be able to make a good go of it. And when I saw that in the paper – '

Graves appeared.

'Tea, Graves – and please ask Cook to make

it stronger than usual. And something to eat?'
She glanced at Dinah. 'Scones? Biscuits?'

'Just the tea, ta.'

Graves raised his eyebrows, bowed slightly
at Jenny, and took his departure. Even his back
showed how offended he was at the idea of his
mistress entertaining such a low-life character.

'Who's *he*?' said Dinah. 'Is he what's called a
major-domo?'

'Oh, goodness, no, we don't run to quite
that state of things.'

'But you really are rich. Ron used to say you
were.'

'Rich enough, I suppose. Dinah, why are
you here?'

The girl's clear skin coloured up. 'Not for
anything bad,' she said quickly. 'I haven't
come to cause you any trouble, or that. But
when I saw that in the paper about Ron becoming an MP – it just didn't seem right,
somehow.'

'You saw it in the paper?'

'Yair, it was in the Sydney papers, look.' She
took from the pocket of her jacket a man's
wallet, very worn. From it she extracted a
newspaper cutting, much creased and going
yellow, which she handed to Jenny.

'News from London. Ronald Armstrong,
who will be remembered by Sydney residents
for his visit of four years ago, has been elected
Member of Parliament for the constituency of
West Tweed in Scotland. Sydney-dwellers will
recall the good fortune of Mr Armstrong
during his stay with us, when he was one of a
numerous party prospecting for gold on the
Lachlan River and was blessed with the reward
of several large alluvial nuggets.

'His wife, it will be remembered, inherited the famous woollen firm of William Corvill & Son which has its premises in the Scottish Borders. This interesting couple purchased Giddiring Sheep Station before they returned to their native shores so their link with New South Wales continues.

'We wish Mr Armstrong every success in his Parliamentary career and couple this with the hope that he will not forget his Australian friends if an opportunity occurs in the House of Commons to further their interests.'

This flowery tribute had clearly been read and reread during the voyage. 'What did you mean when you said it "didn't seem right"?' Jenny asked in some perplexity. 'In essence, this is quite true.'

'I meant it didn't seem right that the boy should have so little, such poor prospects, and him the son of a Member of Parliament.' Dinah's voice was full of respect, almost of awe, as she said the words.

Jenny nodded. 'So your baby was a boy.'

'Yair. Say, how did you know?' The words, after a moment, jerked out in surprise.

'I saw you on the dock as we left.'

'You saw me? Well, fancy. I saw you, of course, but I thought you were looking at all your posh friends that'd come to see you go.'

'No, I was looking at you, Dinah. I tried to attract Ronald's attention so as to point you out, but he was busy. And afterwards . . . Afterwards I decided to say nothing.'

'Glad you did, Mrs Armstrong. I never wanted to make any call on your charity, you know.'

The door opened, Graves came in with the

tea in its silver pot on a silver tray and with the pretty Chelsea cups. He set it down and at a nod from his mistress poured two cups. He handed Dinah her cup and a fine lace napkin which looked very out of place when she spread it on the creased cotton of her skirt.

When he had taken his disapproving departure Dinah drank thirstily then said, putting her cup down with a clash, 'I want you to understand that I haven't come here to get anything for myself. But Ron's boy deserves better than I can give him, especially now with his dad being in the Houses of Parliament – I mean, it's not right, him growing up to nothing better than sheep herding or driving a cart. I though it over after I saw that piece in the paper – '

'What's the boy's name?' Jenny put in gently.

'Clive. I called him Clive. It's a nice name, don't you think?'

'Very. Is it in your family?'

'Nah,' said Dinah with a shrug. 'You know I was an orphan, Mrs Armstrong, didn't have any family. No, Clive was the name of a nice old gent that used to come into the restaurant where I was working and so I picked that. I'd really ha' liked Ronald, but I thought that would put ideas in folks's heads.'

'Was this old gentleman the one whose name you took? Eynsham?'

Dinah sighed, looked down, and after a moment held out the cup to Jenny. 'Could I have another cup, missus? I got a lot to tell you and it's dry work, talking. I've never been much good at it, can't seem to get my thoughts organised.'

Jenny refilled the cup, then sat down alongside her again on the sofa. 'Take your time, Dinah. But try to tell me everything.'

'Yeh, well, when I knew I'd fallen for the baby, I was in a state, I can tell you. I anguished a lot over whether to get in touch with Ron, but you know, it's a rotten thing to drag at a man who's shown you he's got over what feelings he had for you.' She paused. 'Am I making myself clear?'

'You felt Ronald had no regard for you.'

'Reckon he wouldn't have cleared out so fast if he'd been as fond of me as I was of him. You know, lookin' back, I see I made all the running. But when you appeared on the scene and he went back to you, I knew it was absolutely all over for him and me.'

'But the baby . . . ?'

She moved restlessly, smoothing her creased skirt, returning the napkin to its original folds. 'I only come to realise about that later. And as by then I'd understood it was no go, I decided to deal with it my own way. I left Ma Fowler's – we had a big row, but I didn't want her looking at me as I got bigger and wagging her finger at me. And I went to Newcastle and got this pretty good job as waitress in a restaurant.'

'Where Mr Clive used to come in.'

'Yair. And so did Tim Eynsham, only he always had the cheapest dish on the menu. That was what made me think he'd be agreeable.'

Jenny was surprised at the word. 'Agreeable to what?'

'To marrying me and giving a name to the baby. See, Tim was in the coalmining but what he wanted, he said, was to have a little place of his own, above ground, something to do with livestock. And I had me savings – not a lot but he had this chum who had a little patch of land outside Newcastle, so I give him the money, he bought the smallholding, we got married, and I had my marriage lines to shake in the face of anybody who got funny with me. I was already Mrs Eynsham when I come down to Sydney to see your ship leave.'

It was the kind of solution many a woman had found to such a problem: a good-natured man willing to take on the responsibilities of another, for some slight monetary reward.

'Did he agree to your coming to England?'

'Oh, he cleared off,' Dinah said with an angry shrug. 'I was a real mug – I see that now. We started off on the little farm right enough, and it coulda been a winner, really it could. We were going to supply milk and butter and cheese to the shops and restaurants in the town. I'm good on the dairying side, the shop-keepers were keen to get my stuff. But Tim didn't like getting up at break of dawn to milk, and nor did he like having to be there again to milk at tea-time – he liked to be off with his mates. So I found it getting too much for me, for I was feeling pretty crook, see, after the baby come. And as I've got a bit of a temper, we had words.'

'What's he like?'

'Not much of a looker, but he's got winning ways.' Dinah looked back at the past. 'We could have made a go of it. I promised to be a good wife to him and I meant to keep my bargain, but you see, he wouldn't believe me when I said I felt rotten and if he tried to be lovey-dovey . . . you know . . .'

'Yes,' Jenny said, with unfeigned sympathy.

'So one morning I got up at me usual time, fed the baby, went out to the cowshed, and there was the poor beasts dancing about with discomfort 'cos they hadn't been milked. And after I done that I went round looking for him, and discovered he'd packed up his clobber and gone.'

'Poor Dinah.'

'Aw, I brought it on mself. I jump into things, you know – and then think about them after. I remember I once saw a report about me at the orphanage school. It said, "This child has an eager spirit but little judgement," and I reckon I haven't changed since then. Well, then, what happened, Mrs Armstrong, was that I found he's sold the smallholding from under me.'

'It wasn't in his name!' Jenny cried, aghast.

'Yeh, it was. A born mug, ain't I? So I had to either get out or stay on as an employee, and that's what I did, and I managed to get by fair enough, for the new owner and his missus was sorry for me, having been deserted, like.'

'Eynsham didn't come back?'

'Naw, he went off looking for gold, and there's never been a word of him since. It was what he'd always wanted to do. I hate to think it, but mebbe he always intended to from the outset.' For the first time there was the sparkle of tears in her dark blue eyes.

'Don't say that. He did actually marry you. He might just have run off after you gave him the money to buy the land.'

'That's true.' Dinah sniffed, fetched out a small handkerchief, and rubbed hard at her nose and mouth. 'I'd resigned myself to soldiering on for ever as a farm servant – it was what I was good at, you understand, and the boy was thriving, and anyhow I didn't seem to have any ambition any more . . . And then I saw that bit in the newspaper about Ron, and though at first I didn't give it anything more than a bit of admiration, it grew on me – I wasn't ever going to be able to do much for Clive, but a Member of Parliament . . .' She pronounced all the syllables – 'Parl-i-a-ment'.

'You never thought to get in touch with Samuel Chalmers?'

'Chalmers? Chalmers . . . I think Ron mentioned him a coupla times. Didn't he work for you in an office in Sydney?'

'He's our shipping agent. I left a sum of money in the bank, under his care. If ever you were in need he was to make you a payment from it, or agree an allowance for you.'

Dinah stared at Jenny. Colour mounted in her face. 'Gee!' she sighed. 'I wish I'da know that! I needn't ever have come here and caused a fuss.' She looked down. 'Tell the truth, Mrs Armstrong, I thought you'd have had your lawyers on to me by now – I never thought we'd be having a cup of tea and a chat.'

'Lawyers?' Jenny echoed. 'What do we want lawyers for?'

'Well, I reckoned you'd deny Clive is Ron's son and you'd hate me for breaking in on you –'

'I don't hate you, Dinah.'

'You don't?'

'Do you hate me?'

A pause. 'Well, I did,' the other woman confessed. 'After that time you came out and laid down the law at Ma Fowler's. But that all died away, 'specially after Clive was born. I mean, I realised then that you were just trying to keep your family together, and I'da done the same in your place – done it for Clive, just as you did it for your little girl.'

Jenny decided not to say that it wasn't only for Heather that she had travelled around the globe to find Ronald. She wanted him back for herself – but to speak about that kind of love seemed out of place now.

What they had to consider was what to do next.

'Where's the little boy now?'

'I left him with my landlady. She's a decent soul, it's a nice boardinghouse that the purser on the ship recommended.' Dinah braced herself for what she had to say next. 'But it's pricey, and I haven't much money, so I got to ask you, Mrs Armstrong, if you could lend me a little –'

'Lend you! Good God, Dinah, that's Ronald's son at the boardinghouse. We must do better than lend you something. As you rightly say, Ronald owes it to the boy to see he's looked after, to give him an education –'

'I don't want him took from me and sent to school!' Dinah cried. 'He's too little to be parted from me.'

'Of course he is. That wasn't in my mind at all, my dear! He's – how old?'

'Just turned four.'

'There's no question of separating you, then – and never will be, unless you wish it. Dinah, I want you to understand . . .' She leaned towards her, took her hands in hers. 'I want to see that you and your son are looked after. Ronald will feel the same, I know. You've nothing to fear from me, I promise you. But the next step is to let Ronald know you are here.'

'Will he be home for his dinner?' Dinah said, looking at the gilt clock on the mantelpiece. It was well past one o'clock.

'Not today. His comings and goings are quite unpredictable. He's at the House now, although they don't sit till mid-afternoon. Then, if I remember rightly, there's a vote expected about six-thirty or seven.'

Dinah sat looking lost at this information. 'Does that mean he'll be home this evening?'

'Not necessarily. Though you seem to have a high respect for MPs, Dinah, they have to do what they're told to a large extent. But even if the Whips want Members in the House later, he ought to be able to get away after the first vote. I'll send a message – though where it will catch up with him I don't know.'

'So what's the plan, then, missus?'

'I think it will be best if we come to the boardinghouse rather than have you bring Clive here.' Already Jenny's mind was full of the awful possibilities inherent in this situation. Supposing Dinah were to come back to Eaton Square bringing with her a boy who looked very like Ronald Armstrong. The servants, quick to notice everything, would immediately begin to talk. No, better by far to go to the boardinghouse to see the child.

She sat down at the bureau to write a note to her husband. When Graves appeared at her summons, she handed the envelope to him. 'Send Robert to the House with this. If Mr Armstrong is not there, Robert is to go on to wherever he is and hand the note to him. I don't want Robert to come back until he has delivered the note to Mr Armstrong – is that understood?'

'Yes, madam.'

'Please call a hackney.'

'Immediately, madam?'

'Yes, please, and tell Baird I shall want my hat and gloves in a moment.'

'Very good, madam.'

Dinah had witnessed all this with awe. 'What's the cab for, Mrs Armstrong?'

'I'll take you back to your lodgings.'

'Oh, that ain't necessary, I can walk.'

'You walked here?'

'Yeh, it's only quarter of an hour.'

'How did you find the address, Dinah?'

'Oh, that was easy. I asked the landlady how to find out the address of an MP and she said ask the cabbies on the rank at Westminster, 'cos they was used to taking the MPs home at all hours of the day and night. And she was quite right, the second one I asked told me.'

'I must just go up for my things,' Jenny said. 'Have more tea while I put on my bonnet –'

'There's no need to come with me, missus, I can –'

'I have to go out,' Jenny said. 'Most unfortunately, I have an appointment with a buyer from Switzerland who is leaving for home tomorrow morning. I *must* see him.'

'You do that sort of stuff – go in for business and all that?'

'Yes, I always have, and all the more so now that Ronald is taken up with Parliamentary matters.' She turned the silver teapot towards Dinah and hurried out. Upstairs, Baird had put the bonnet that matched her gown on the bed, together with her gloves and the calf document case she always carried on business outings.

Her maid was gazing at her with some anxiety. She had heard about the visitor and, knowing much more about Jenny's personal life than anyone else in the house, was worried.

'Who is she, mistress?'

'It's Dinah Bowerby – Dinah Eynsham, as she is now.'

The shock washed pallor into Baird's weathered face. 'Ach, what is she here for? Trouble?'

'No, no.' Jenny came close to say in a low voice, 'She's got a little boy, Baird.'

'Heaven preserve us!'

'I'll explain it all to you later. I've written a note to Ronald, asking him to come home by seven. If he arrives before then, Baird, keep him here, don't let him go back to the House.'

'Very well, mistress.'

The cab had arrived by the time she reached the hall. Dinah came to join her and, with obvious enjoyment, climbed in. 'I only ever rid in a cab once before in my life,' she confided. 'And it wasn't as posh as this one.'

She watched the traffic on the London streets in something like fear. 'Isn't it a foofaraw! Dunno how you put up with it.' In a few minutes they pulled up in front of the address she had given, a sedate house not far from Victoria Station. 'We'll be here about seven, Dinah,' Jenny said in farewell.

Dinah looked up at her. Colour came and went in her cheeks at the thought of meeting Ronald again. 'Do you think he's going to be very angry with me?'

'Oh, Dinah . . .' Jenny pressed her hand, sat back, and ordered the cabman to drive on.

Robert the footman had meanwhile set off on a search that ended at last in a gentlemen's club in Pall Mall, where Ronald had gone with a Parliamentary acquaintance for a drink, a snack and a chat before attending the evening's session. The club porter brought the note on a salver. 'The messenger is waiting, sir.'

Ronald tore open the envelope.

'Dinah Bowerby is here from Australia. Please return home by seven o'clock at latest. There is something I *must* explain to you before we go to see her this evening.'

He felt his hand jerk with startlement. He sat staring at the sheet of the paper.

'Anything wrong, old boy?'

'No, it's just . . . my wife wants to see me urgently.'

'Ah, that's the trouble with wives,' said his friend, who was a happy bachelor. 'Always wanting you at inconvenient moments.'

Ronald made no response. The club porter said, 'Any reply, sir?'

'Tell him I shall be home by seven.'

'Shall you, old boy? We'll probably be still walking through the lobbies then.'

'I'll speak to the Whip.'

The vote was in fact taken at six, and the count having been made without too much delay, Ronald got away by six-thirty. He drove home in a cab from the rank where Dinah had made her inquiries that morning.

Jenny had returned, and was waiting for him in the drawing room. He could see by the tension in her stance that she was extremely anxious.

'What is all this?' he demanded as soon as the door of the drawing room had closed on them. 'Dinah here?'

'She came about one o'clock.'

'She came here, to the house?'

'Yes. Mrs Eynsham, she was announced. I couldn't think who – '

'She's married, then?'

'We-ell . . .' She hesitated, then decided to get it over at once. 'Ronald, she married him to give a name to your baby.'

Her husband drew back. He frowned, the sandy brows coming together in an effort to comprehend what she was saying. He put up a hand as if to ward off the information. After a moment he said, 'No.'

'Yes, my dear. He's about four years old now.'

'But that means . . . she must have known when we parted from each other – '

'Not quite then. But she was expecting the baby when we sailed from Sydney.'

He felt for a chair, and like a man who has been taken suddenly ill he sank into it.

'You . . . you speak as if it's . . . as if it's no surprise to you.'

'Not as much as you might think. I saw her on the dockside when we sailed, Ronald. I could tell how things were with her.'

'You *knew*?'

'Yes.'

'You knew then, you've known all these years – and you never told me?' He sprang up. 'How dare you?'

They faced each other. He was angry – at himself, at her, at the whole world. Just for that moment, violence hovered in the room.

He could have struck her for having kept it from him, for telling him this awful news *now* when he was unprepared, at a loss.

'It wasn't my secret to tell, husband. If Dinah had wanted you to know, she would have sent word.'

'I don't understand! Why didn't she tell me?'

Jenny took his hand, led him to the sofa, and sat down with him. 'What good would that have done? She didn't want to make any claims on you – she thought she could manage on her own. But things have gone badly for her. Ronald, man, she's a simple woman. She saw some news about your having won the seat in Parliament and she felt it was wrong for your son to have to struggle in poor circumstances. She seems to think that being a Member of Parliament is something like being a prince of the realm. So she came to get justice for the boy.'

He sat as if in a dream. After a long moment he said, 'The boy . . . You've seen him?'

'No, not yet.'

'She must bring him to see me. I want to see him –'

'Not here, Ronald!'

'What?' he said, vaguely, catching the urgency of her tone but not quite understanding what lay behind it.

'Dinah mustn't bring Clive here. In fact, we've got to be discreet about the whole thing –'

'But she's come all this way, from the other side of the world –'

'I know, I know, but *think*, husband. I've had all afternoon to think. What will people say if they know a woman has arrived on our door-

92

step with a little boy, and then we begin taking an interest in them? Gossip has sprung up from less than that, and as an MP you're more vulnerable than if you were an ordinary citizen – '

'Damn the gossip.'

'No, listen, the last thing Dinah would want is to harm you. Listen to me, Ronald! You were saying only last night that Mr Gladstone himself could be destroyed if the rumours about his behaviour – '

'But this is different – '

'To us it is different, because the boy is your son. You want to see him and take care of him – that's what you want, isn't it, Ronald?'

'Of course!'

'It doesn't help him to be the centre of a scandal. Do you want that label put upon him – "bastard"?'

'Jenny!'

'Do you think it wouldn't be said?'

'I – I – '

'It's best if we don't give anyone the chance to say it. We'll see Dinah and the little boy, but we'll go to her lodgings.'

'Yes,' Ronald said, giving up the argument for the moment. 'Let's go now. I want to see him.'

To some extent, Jenny was comforted by that statement. He had said, 'I want to see him.' He hadn't said, 'I want to see Dinah.'

And truth to tell, among all the miseries and anxieties that had whirled in her head that afternoon, not the least had been that Ronald might still feel some attraction towards Dinah Bowerby. He had assured her that it was all over, when first she caught up with him in the Australian outback. And she had believed him.

Yet how could she be sure that some spark wouldn't flare up again into a fire when he knew Dinah was here in London?

A cab was waiting for them outside. They were driven in silence to the boardinghouse. The maid who let them in was clearly much impressed by the elegance of the lady and the fine tailoring of the gentleman. Her opinion of the careworn colonial went up: she must be *somebody* if people like this came calling on her.

There was a small writing room off the passage beyond the hall. Here the maid led them. She threw open the door. 'Mr and Mrs Armstrong,' she said.

Dinah rose from an armchair by the empty fireplace. The evening sun shone on her dark chestnut hair.

By her side, clutching her skirts, stood a small boy. He was rather tall for his four years, the flesh spread sparingly on his bony frame.

But other than that, he had no resemblance to Ronald Armstrong. He had his mother's colouring, his mother's blue eyes, her round chin and stubborn mouth. Even the way his hair grew down in a widow's peak upon his forehead was like Dinah.

Jenny studied him, her heart turning over at the thought that this was Ronald's son.

At that moment, all her hard-won tranquillity vanished. The hours she had passed today, being sensible, being brave after Dinah walked in – they counted for nothing.

Ronald's son. By another woman.

She was jealous. Her entire being seemed consumed in a fire of jealousy. Anger, resentment, a need for revenge – they sprang at her like tigers. How dare she! How dare she come here, in her ignorance and naivety, to make claims on her husband. My husband, she said to herself in her deepest heart, *my* husband – he belongs to me, he always has and always will. How dare she tempt him from me. I hate her, I hate her, I wish she were dead!

This boy . . . totally unlike Ronald but flesh of his flesh, conceived in passion under strange stars and a different sky . . . this boy was as much Ronald's as little Max at home in bed in workaday Galashiels.

He had no claim, none, none! Max was Ronald's son, this child was a nothing, a mistake, a reminder of past sins – sins, yes, the church in which she had grown up would say this was a child of sin.

Let him die, the cruel voice inside her raged on. Let him vanish, let him cease to be. He is proof that Ronald was unfaithful to me. I hate him, I hate his mother, I wish they were both dead! Let fire descend from the heavens, let the earth open and engulf them, let them *never have been*!

'Jenny?' her husband said in a questioning tone.

She came back to herself as if rising up out of the pit of hell. 'Yes?'

'Are you all right?'

She couldn't make her lips frame any words. No, she wasn't all right. She was stricken, she was destroyed. Not only at the sight of the child, but at her own reaction to him. Hate? Could she possibly have let herself even think the word, concerning a *child*?

All her life she had known she had strong

emotions. They had swept her in her youth into more than one love affair. From these she had learned the painful lesson that she must rule her heart with her head.

Yet here she was, wishing the death of a little boy, and of his simple, open-hearted mother. Was this Jenny Armstrong, the Mistress of the Waterside Mills, renowned throughout the Scottish Borders for her good sense and understanding?

'I'm all right,' she murmured through stiff lips. 'It was just . . . a bit of a shock . . . to see him.'

'I know,' Dinah said in her flat tone, yet with sympathy. 'Hits you, don't it? I went through that, when I found out about Ron being married.'

Ronald made a stifled sound. It was a mixture of guilt, remorse and sheer embarrassment. To stand here, between the two women who had borne him children, and hear them struggle with their emotions was a torture. Yet he wouldn't have given up this moment. The boy was a revelation. Handsome, sturdy, like the mother who had somehow ensnared him with her very innocence.

Jenny felt herself trembling in the reaction to the spasm of pain she had undergone. She made her way like an invalid to a chair, and sat down. She looked from her husband to the boy. She could see already in Ronald that pride which men must feel in their sons – the pride that goes back to Biblical times, to the very dawn of history.

She drew in a slow breath. Yes, Dinah had been right to come. The boy was innocent of any wrongdoing and needed his father. The

96

boy was a promise of Ronald's immortality, in the same way as any child of his legal marriage. He needed their help. And she, Jenny Armstrong, the level-headed, the patient and shrewd, must so arrange matters that he received that help, no matter what difficulties might lie in the path.

Already her mind was working, thinking ahead, planning. She was thinking, He doesn't look like Ronald. No one could ever guess he was the father. It lessens the danger.

For danger there was, no matter how Ronald might belittle it for the moment. Careers had been wrecked on rocks like this. An MP must be upright, honourable – or at least the public must believe him to be so, otherwise why should they let him vote on their behalf on matters that affected their very lives?

A mere breath of suspicion could mean the end of Ronald as a politician. And though last night he had talked about throwing it all up, she couldn't help seeing that today he had gone back to the House with renewed vigour. His career in Parliament meant a lot to him – and rightly so, for he intended to use this influence for the good of his compatriots.

His political leaders wouldn't want any gossip or tittle-tattle. They had problems enough to deal with this summer as the House prepared to rise. For that reason, it was important to be discreet.

But – even more important – what would that apparently implacable enemy Thomas Unsworth do if ever he knew Ronald had fathered a child outside the bonds of marriage?

CHAPTER SIX

Ronald Armstrong was a man who lived very much in the present. He seldom made plans for the future beyond the next few weeks or months. He almost never looked back.

Particularly, he had blotted from his mind the events of six years ago and their consequences. At that stage, he had felt his whole life had gone wrong.

His wife was devoting all her time and, it seemed, all her love, to their daughter Heather. The little girl herself seemed a stranger to him; she, who had been his little darling, his angel, was now a silent, wide-eyed waif whom he could scarcely recognise as his own and who would not even speak to him.

Behind all that was the continuing misery of having to manage the Waterside Mills. Ronald was not by nature a manager. He would rather have been on the floor of the carding-room with his workmates, or in the dye-room using his skills on the yarns that would make the famous cloth. But no, he had to deal with accountants, foreign buyers, other mill-owners who objected to the new Factory Regulations which Ronald thought thoroughly justified.

And when they disagreed, he had the feeling that there was always a hidden sneer in their manner. Who is he, anyway, they seemed to him to be saying. A nobody, a nothing, only of importance because he's Jenny Corvill's husband.

That had been a very bad time for Ronald Armstrong. When he considered it later, he knew that he handled everything badly. He had been self-centred, intolerant of Heather's needs and Jenny's reaction to them.

All he was aware of then was that he was somehow alienated from everything that made his life bearable. If he had been a little boy his cry might have been, Nobody loves me! But as a grown man he couldn't sob out his misery. He kept it hidden, and longed for things to be different.

His chance came when he and Jenny began talking about having an agent in Sydney, Australia, devoted to the business of getting good wool for William Corvill & Son. It had become almost a necessity to have their own representative there, for the London banking houses were backing the wool staplers so that they bought up the clip almost before it was off the back of the sheep, and then the prices went up to those who couldn't do the same.

Ronald and Jenny had discussed sending out a young man from Galashiels, someone who understood the Borders woollen industry and could act for them. They had looked at one or two possible applicants but there were reservations about almost every one.

And then Ronald had said, 'I think I'll go myself.'

Whether he had really intended to go, at that moment, he couldn't have said. Perhaps he merely wanted Jenny to cry, 'No, no, don't leave me!'

But she did not, because she thought he had grown restless within their marriage. He had always been a restless creature, moving from job to job, travelling abroad more than any other man in search of knowledge where dyes were concerned.

So Ronald had gone to Australia. And there – incredible as it seemed afterwards – he had got entangled with a young woman who insisted on seeing him as a sort of knight errant on a white charger.

Anyone less like a knight errant than Ronald Armstrong would have been hard to imagine. He was then past his mid-thirties, not unhandsome but unlikely to cause romantic dreams. He was nimble of intelligence, kindly by disposition, and had educated himself to a standard above many men who had been to expensive schools.

But to Dinah Bowerby he was like a creature from the kingdom of faerie. He rescued her from a situation of danger and violence – herders with too much pay to spend had got drunk and were quarrelling over cheating at cards. When he talked to her, he spoke of worlds she had never known: London, Berlin, Milan. He didn't order her about and look down on her because she'd been brought up in an orphanage. He was considerate, kind.

She fell head over heels in love with him. The force of her passion swept them both along, the more so on Ronald's part because his wife wrote coolly in response to his letters of admiration for this great, new, free country where a man could start afresh.

Shameful to say, Ronald grew tired of Dinah rather soon. She was beautiful – no one could deny that. But she was . . . not exactly silly, but simple, as if she lived her life in blinkers and could only see what she wanted to see.

She was also very stubborn and very apt to break out into bursts of anger or indignation or resentment. Perhaps it sprang from her upbringing – she'd had to fight for her place in the pecking order of the orphanage, and she did the same in the world at large.

But what was her place? With her splendid looks – regular features, creamy skin, dark fiery hair, a figure like a goddess – she could have made a living in the theatre. Except for the sad fact that she had an unpleasing voice, rather flat in intonation, with undernotes of harshness which hurt the ear especially when she was emotionally upset.

It was her voice particularly that began to grate on Ronald. He was ashamed that he found her boring and difficult, but when she began again on her demands for a place of their own where they could settle down, he found himself thinking, What a noise she makes . . .

On shoals like these even the most passionate affairs can be grounded. And this had not been a very passionate affair on his part. He had been lonely, in need of the mere physical warmth of a woman's body, adrift in a strange society. Once his physical hunger had been assuaged, once the male conceit of having such a beauty at his beck and call had worn off, he found himself tied to a girl he would rather not have bothered with.

It was disgraceful. He felt guilty. But when his pretty, intelligent and loving wife appeared

101

like an angel from the clouds to save him, he could scarcely prevent himself from bursting into a hymn of thanksgiving.

Jenny saw Dinah at the farm where she had found a job once it became clear Ronald didn't want to settle down on a homestead with her. Jenny convinced Dinah that it had all been a mistake. Jenny told Ronald he had nothing further to worry about.

He was very pleased to believe her.

So they had come back to Galashiels and resumed their normal life. Things were better. Jenny no longer concentrated all her energies on Heather. Heather had improved to the extent that she could be quite conversational with her father, though only in a muted way. Jenny bore him the son he longed for, to be called after Ronald's father, Maxwell. The Thornieburns befriended them, Ronald had become a Member of Parliament. Dinah Bowerby had faded entirely from his thoughts.

Until now.

She was as beautiful as ever, almost. The tall rounded figure was perhaps thinner, and the direct gaze of her dark blue eyes was more inclined to waver – and no wonder, when he thought of what Jenny had told him. Dinah had had a hard time. And all because of him, Ronald Armstrong, who had walked away from her and never given her another thought.

The little boy at her side was his son. His son Clive, from the other side of the world.

He stooped, held out his hand. 'Good evening, Clive,' he said.

The little boy hunched his shoulders and tried to disappear in the folds of his mother's skirt. Who were these splendidly dressed people? Why was he here in his sailor suit instead of in bed? His wide eyes peeped out to study them.

'He's shy,' Dinah said. 'He didn't see a lot of people on the farm. And everything's been strange for a while now.'

'Of course.' Jenny sat on a chair by the shelf of books that gave the reading room its name. She produced a package. 'This is for you, Clive.'

No response from the little boy.

She set the package on the floor by her skirt hem. To Dinah she said, 'Ronald and I have been talking about the situation.'

'Ye-es,' said Dinah, looking with anxiety at the man she used to know and love so well. To her he seemed a total stranger now. Gone were the loose shirts, the cotton duck trousers, the canvas boots and the wide-brimmed hat. In their place fine black serge, a formal frock coat with an upstanding collar, custom-made boots of well-polished leather.

And his manner . . . his whole aura . . . no longer easy-going and tolerant, but solemn, almost austere in this moment of meeting.

'Ain't you going to say welcome to England, Ron?' she asked with faint defiance.

It was then that she saw something of the old Ron in him. He smiled his wry, critical smile. 'Welcome to England, Dinah,' he said. 'But a letter would have been a good idea.'

'Ronald,' Jenny rebuked him.

'No, he's right, missus, I shouldn't have rushed into things the way I did. But you know I'm no hand at the letter-writing, and besides, I didn't know if you'd believe me, Ron.'

At that he was shocked and, coming to her, took her hand. 'You were never a liar, Dinah.'

Meanwhile the boy, seeing that the grown-ups were too busy with their own affairs to notice him, had stolen across the room and begun to open the package. He gave a little cry of delight. 'A sodger!'

He held the toy soldier to him. It was of tin, with a flat cap edged with much gold over a moustachioed face, and a rigidly military body. 'He winds up,' Jenny said. 'If you turn the key in his back, he raises his hand and salutes.'

'Naw!' breathed Clive.

'Yes. Try it.'

But the key was too tight for his hand. He held it up towards the grown-ups for help, and it was his father who took it.

Next moment the two of them were together in the centre of the worn carpet, Ronald turning the key, the boy holding on to his sleeve and waiting with bated breath for the toy to go through its marvellous performance.

Over their heads Jenny said, 'There's a lot to settle, Dinah, but we want you to know that we're going to do all we can for you and Clive. However, I must ask you to be very discreet.'

'Discreet?' She repeated the word as if she weren't quite sure what it meant.

'Ronald has a position to keep up – you understand that, I'm sure. It would be dangerous to refer to Ronald as the boy's father . . .'

'Oh, yeh – yeh, I wouldn't want to cause him any trouble. I thought I made that clear.'

'You did, of course you did. But any rumours would do great damage to his standing as an MP. He might be made to resign if anything came out.'

'Oh no, that mustn't be – I wouldn't want Clive's dad to lose out from anything I did.'

'Good,' Jenny said, 'but that's the kind of remark you have to avoid. "Clive's dad" – that's Tim Eynsham, legally.'

'Yair.' A pause. 'You needn't fret, Mrs Armstrong. I'm used to holding my tongue about it.'

'What does Clive know – about his father?'

Dinah shrugged. 'Seemed best to say he was dead. I mean, you can't go on for ever saying to people that your husband's off prospecting for gold. It'd be a joke. Anyhow, Clive doesn't ask about it. I think he only once said, "Have I got a dad?" and I just said, "No, he's died and gone to heaven" – which I doubt,' Dinah added in a grim tone.

'In the next few days we must talk over what we ought to do. Do you think of staying in England or going home?'

'Home? This is Home,' Dinah said, with utter simplicity.

It was so. To all the Australians Jenny had met during her visit there, Britain was 'Home'. Even those born and bred in Australia spoke of the old country as 'Home'.

'Of course, if you want to stay here, that's what we'll do – '

'I mean,' Dinah interrupted, 'there's nothing for us in Australia. It's not as if I had a lot of friends and relatives waiting there for me to go back. Tim's vanished and even if I knew where he was, I dunno that I'd want to have anything to do with him – he and I just didn't hit it off. So I don't have anybody, 'cept Clive. And you know, it's pretty much a man's world back there. A woman on her own ain't much, and a woman with a little boy . . . reckon he'd get more of what he deserves if we stayed here. I mean, education and manners and all that, a good start in life, more sort of gentlemanly ways . . .' She faltered into silence at the end of what was, for her, a long speech.

Jenny sighed. 'London isn't full of well-mannered gentlemen, my dear – but never mind, if you wish to stay here that's agreed. We must find you a place to live, and a school for Clive by and by, and of course you must have an income – '

'I didn't come here to grab your money!' Dinah said, colouring up.

'No, no.' Heavens, how easily she got hold of the wrong end of the stick! But of course, this was a very difficult position for her. She had come here out of the blue, demanding his rights for the boy, so she would be touchy about any imputation of greed.

'You must have an income,' Jenny said with careful calm. 'You'll need it to look after Clive. He must be properly fed and clothed, mustn't he?'

'Well, ye-es . . . So long as it's understood that I'm not pocketing anything for myself – '

'But Dinah dear, you must use some of it for yourself. You must buy some decent clothes – '

'What's wrong with my clothes?' exclaimed Dinah. 'This is my best dress!'

No doubt. It was a faded blue silk-poplin, wide-skirted and with a shirtwaist top that fitted snugly. There was nothing wrong with it except that for London eyes it was much too plain, lacking any lace, braid or fringe, and it had clearly seen its best days. One glance put her in the servant class. Nothing wrong with that, of course, except that if she were to appear to be on friendly terms with the Armstrongs, she couldn't be a servant. The inexorable laws of Victorian society forbade it.

Jenny decided to take a firm line. 'If you're going to go up in a thunderstorm at everything I say,' she remarked, 'it will make life very difficult! I'm saying that you need to have a suitable place to live and an income to go with it, and you need to have clothes that will pass muster in your new surroundings. No one asks you to dress like a London fashion plate or put Clive into velvet suits, but if you won't accept our advice as well as our support, it was pointless to come here in the first place.'

Ronald got up from his knees. The little boy confidingly took his hand, the other still clutching the mechanical tin soldier.

'Are you two having a row?' Ronald asked, with just enough of the patronising male in his tone to unite both women.

'Not at all,' Dinah said. 'We're just having a sort-out. I reckon you and your missus will want to have a real good talk-over about things, 'cos of course I sprung all this on you very sudden. I'll state my side. I come here to get his rights for Clive, but I don't want any more than that and I don't want to do any harm to anybody. I'll go along with anything you say so long as it's proper.'

Ronald sighed. 'Give us a day or two, Dinah. In the meantime, would you like to move into a more comfortable hotel? The Hyde Park, for instance – '

'Ronald,' Jenny said, touching his hand, 'her clothes aren't right for the Hyde Park.'

Jerked into awareness of mundane matters, he paused, looked at Dinah, and nodded. 'Jenny's right, Dinah. You'll need to buy some dresses.'

'I'll do as I am!'

'No, Dinah,' Jenny objected, 'you won't. Please believe me, it's going to make things much more difficult if you don't make some changes. I've brought a purse with me. If you'll just take it – '

'No!'

Jenny let some of her irritation show. 'Listen to me, Dinah. You want a place to stay for yourself and Clive, don't you?'

'Of course.'

'Well, if we took you to see rooms or a house in some good neighbourhood, the landlord probably wouldn't accept you as a tenant dressed as you are now.'

'You're joking!'

'Not at all,' Ronald put in. 'Appearances matter here in London, far more than they do in the outback. You've *got* to accept our advice, Dinah, otherwise we might as well throw in the towel at the outset.'

After some discussion Dinah unwillingly accepted the money. They arranged to call again next day at the same time. Parliament would rise tomorrow, and after that Ronald would be more at leisure. Jenny, who had expected to go home to Galashiels with him, would now have to send word that they would be delayed. It was important that when visits were paid to Dinah, Ronald should never go alone. It must be established from the outset that Mrs Eynsham was the friend of *Mrs* Armstrong, a friendship begun during Jenny's visit to Sydney.

It took them a week to find a home for Dinah and her son. They chose a little house in Chelsea because Dinah had asked for somewhere with 'a bit of green' – she found London with its mass of buildings and stone overwhelming after the spaciousness of the farm. Chelsea was something of a village, just beginning to be settled by the Bohemian fraternity. It was relatively quiet and rural, yet near enough for Jenny and Ronald to be able to visit with ease.

Dinah resisted the idea of having servants. She had looked after herself for twenty-seven years, and would do so until she went into her grave.

'But, Dinah, you can't do your own housework! It isn't – '

'Why on earth not? Six rooms, I can whisk through them and be finished by midday!'

'But it isn't *done*, Dinah!'

'Well, I've always done it.'

'Look here, you want Clive to fit in with the other boys he's going to meet once he goes to school, don't you? I can assure you he'll be the only one whose mother does the cleaning and the cooking!'

The reasoning prevailed. Dinah accepted a cook and a housemaid.

Next it was necessary to persuade her to have a companion.

'Clive's all the companionship I need, Mrs Armstrong.'

'Of course, I understand! But look at it this way. You've come into a different world now, and so has Clive. He needs to learn how to bow and open doors for ladies, and how to address his teachers once he starts school . . .'

And she needed someone to look after her while she learnt how to fit into this different world. Ronald would soon have to give his attention to politics, for storm clouds were gathering over the Whig Party. Jenny would have to return to Galashiels; the pattern book for next spring must soon be launched, and she must see to its final make-up. Besides, she had a baby boy and a daughter whom she hadn't seen in three weeks.

She left Dinah to think it over for twenty-four hours. The other woman, though she wasn't quick or clever, had some insight into her own ambitions. She had always wanted to 'be someone'. She wanted Clive to 'be someone' when he grew up. Clearly her own twenty-seven years in the outback had not prepared her for 'being someone' in London society even in a limited way.

'All right,' she agreed, 'but I don't want no disapproving spinster with prunes in her mouth.'

A spinster she got, but a kindhearted one, Miss Kinsman, elderly sister of a parson lately dead. Miss Kinsman was very pleased indeed to land this post, with only one widowed lady and a little boy to consider, they having some connection with the Armstrongs who, though in trade, were very well spoken of and who even had friends in the Marlborough House set.

To the companion, it seemed very kind-hearted indeed of Mrs Armstrong to take so much care of Mrs Eynsham, whom she must only have known briefly on her visit to the

Antipodes. The full extent of the 'kindness' was unknown to her; she had no idea that her salary and that of the servants, the money for the upkeep of the pretty little house, the wages of the dressmaker now busily engaged on making up suitable gowns for Dinah, and all the other living expenses came out of the Armstrong purse.

Under Miss Kinsman's gentle guidance Dinah soon stopped addressing her as 'missus' and even gave up such phrases as 'ain't never' or 'fair enough'. But nothing could change her voice, which was very far from the fashionable low and gentle cadences of admired young ladies. Nor could she always remember to move with small steps, to sit with her ankles crossed, and to drink her tea noiselessly.

Yet she was so lovely to look at that much would be forgiven her, thought Miss Kinsman. Moreover, people would be charitable towards her: she was, after all, a colonial.

For his part, young Clive was happy. There were far more people to talk to here than there had been on the farm in New South Wales, the house was more comfortable, water came not in a bucket but from a tap, and though outdoors was often very chilly and wet nevertheless there was always something to see in the streets.

Christmas in London was strange. Snow fell, and there were people going about in the evenings with lanterns, singing songs called carols. They went to a real church where there was a little crib with a baby and toy animals around it. Mr and Mrs Armstrong visited Ma soon after, coming in at the door with presents for what they called 'firstfooting'. Clive opened his present, hoping for another soldier, but got something even better: a wheeled truck with a handle which he could push or pull along and into which he could load his soldier, or a piece of cake, or building bricks, or any other thing that needed to be transported from one room to another.

Mrs Armstrong was very nice. She let him clamber up and sit on her lap. Mr Armstrong, who at first had seemed his special friend, seemed to be thinking about something else all the time.

This was no less than the truth, for all the warning signs of the summer had culminated in the promised storm. William Ewart Gladstone sent a sombre message to his friend and adviser, Lord Granville, saying that he felt the Party to be in a state of fundamental weakness for which the only remedy might be resignation and a rallying for a new election.

Granville resisted the idea. A week later Gladstone came back to London, although Parliament was in recess and it was his habit to spend the Christmas period in the country. Arguments were heated among Cabinet members because the Prime Minister was asking for reductions in expenditure which they had no intention of agreeing.

In mid-February Gladstone resigned. Although it had been foreshadowed, the blow was tremendous, the more so as he resigned during the Parliamentary Recess without allowing a chance for the Party in general to discuss it.

Ronald hurried north to fight for his seat, so recently acquired. His constituents were faithful: although the Whigs in general suffered a big defeat Ronald was returned for West Tweed with an increased majority. But now he was a member of a party in disarray and in opposition. The once-powerful leader had made it clear he no longer wanted to fill that role. Gloom and something like panic prevailed.

He was busy in London, busier than ever, it seemed – in the elections he had been shown to have popularity beyond that enjoyed by most of the Liberal candidates. So for the moment he was a favoured child of the Party Whips, even though still handicapped by the strange antagonist in the Tory Party. Ronald had looked at the election results with more than normal interest once he knew his own seat was safe. He hoped to see that the abominable Mr Unsworth might have been rejected. But no: the confounded lunatic had been returned, he too with an increased majority. But even so, the managers of the Liberal Party felt Mr Armstrong would be a useful tool in the House.

As spring approached again that optimist Archie Brunton saw a clear field before him. From all he heard, it seemed very unlikely Armstrong would have much time to be at home between now and the summer recess.

Moreover, some very strange stories had begun to reach Archie's ears. It seemed there was a goodlooking girl stowed away in a little house in Chelsea. Not an uncommon thing – after all, Parliamentary men were only human, in need of a little feminine company like everybody else. Even Archie, whose heart truly belonged to Jenny Armstrong, found himself in need of a comforting soft pair of arms from time to time.

He didn't think any the less of Ronald for having a *petite amie* to console him during his absences from home. In fact, it was all to the good.

Archie began to be more persistent in his efforts to be a particular friend to Jenny. His view was that if Ronald had a particular friend, Jenny was entitled to the same freedom.

Jenny knew Archie very well by now. She sensed the change in his attitude almost at once. There was something protective, almost possessive, in his manner.

Things came to a head at an evening occasion at the house of Mr Aitchison of Melrose. Jenny was suffering from a headache so withdrew somewhat from the main gathering, who were listening to a noisy rendering of a new piano work by Herr Brahms.

The younger son of the house, Harry, came to coax her back into the room. Archie intervened. 'Now kindly leave Mrs Armstrong alone, Harry. She doesn't like Brahms.'

'Oh, Mrs Armstrong, I'm sorry – '

'I do like Brahms,' Jenny began.

'Now, now, there's no need to be polite about it. You're entitled to dislike the man if you want to. Run along, Harry.'

Rebuffed, Harry withdrew. Archie sat down beside Jenny on the settle, by a French window giving a view of the grounds lit by a young moon.

'I'll fetch you a headache powder,' Archie began, disregarding the romantic possibilities of the situation.

'Thank you, Archie, I'm quite all right.'

'Fiddle-de-dee! Do you think I don't know when you have the headache? And all that jingle-jangle next door!'

'It so happens that I like German music, Archie. Unfortunately Mr McEwan plays with more gusto than taste.'

'Isn't that what I said? It's nothing but a jingle-jangle, and if you want to have a few minutes peace and quiet, I'll see that you get it.'

'Archie, please don't adopt the role of guardian – '

'Well, who else is there to do it? That husband of yours is never here!'

Jenny was vexed, her head hurt, and she had had enough for one night. 'What is it you want from me, Archie? You're always at my elbow these days!'

'You know what I want, my angel. I want to give you comfort and affection and all the things you're missing.'

'You can't seriously think I'd become your lover?'

Archie was shocked into silence. He hadn't intended to go that far, or to put it into so many words. He felt himself colour up, and was glad of the soft lighting in the room which helped to hide his discomfiture.

After a moment he said, 'You know I've never thought your marriage was worthy of you. Most people would say I was wrong, because Ronald has made his mark, but at what cost to you and your family! He neglects you – '

'He does not. He comes home when he can – '

'And stays a few days and then is off again, when his political masters whistle for him.'

'But I expect him to be busy, Archie! He didn't go into Parliament to twiddle his thumbs!'

'No, certainly not. He has plenty to keep him occupied. And you may as well know it, Jenny – one of the things that keeps him occupied is a certain young lady in a little nest in Chelsea!'

To his amazement she didn't exclaim in horror. Instead she rose up from her place, turned to look down at him, and he could just distinguish the cold smile on her lips.

'Archie,' she said, 'you're months out of date. I've known about it all the time.'

'Known about it?'

'Of course.'

'Jenny! You mean you condone – '

'Condone? Condone? Listen to me, my laddie! The next time you come to me with scandal about Ronald Armstrong, make sure it's based on solid fact. I know the lady at Number Fifteen Cheyne Terrace. Her name is Mrs Dinah Eynsham and she's a friend of mine from Sydney, Australia.'

Dumbfounded, Archie rose to his feet to look closely at her. But it seemed to be true. Her features were composed, with only a glint of anger in the eyes – anger against *him* for his unfounded suspicions.

'I . . . I'm sorry, Jenny.'

'I accept your apology. And I hope you haven't said this kind of thing to anyone else?'

'No . . . But I've had it said to me.'

'By whom?' she demanded.

'Well, I can hardly remember. It's being said, that's the only way I can put it.'

116

'Then I'll thank you to contradict it the next time it's said! Mrs Eynsham is a perfectly respectable widow woman living with her little boy and an elderly companion. Make sure your gossiping friends know that!'

The last thing he'd expected was that he should be charged with the duty of defending the good name of Ronald Armstrong. He muttered that he would do his best, glad to hear the piano in the drawing room coming to a thundering climax that ushered in silence and polite applause.

Jenny decided to relent far enough to let him escort her back into the drawing room. But the fact that he had broached the subject with her was enough to alarm her. It must be something that was widely gossiped about.

She had had a difficult time coming to terms with herself over Dinah Eynsham. On the one hand her intelligence told her that Dinah was only doing what she thought best for her child. Moreover, since the child was also Ronald's, it was an absolute duty to do everything she could for mother and son.

But on the other hand, she had resented her. Jealousy had gnawed at her as she saw the other girl's looks, damaged by the hardship of the sea voyage, come back to their former glory in the restful atmosphere of the Chelsea cottage. And she wore her new clothes so well, with so much unconscious dignity. Her speech had improved, and she had learned to hold her tongue when she had nothing important to say. A silent beauty is a very attractive being.

But even more than Dinah herself, Jenny had felt jealousy over the boy. It was clear that Ronald found him charming: open, uninhibited, odd. She wanted to say, Don't love him! You have a son at home!

But that was foolish. Ronald surely had enough love for two little boys and his daughter. And for his wife, even though she was older than this pretty creature of the wilderness – older, and somehow feeling insecure and troubled these days.

These emotions had battled in Jenny until the time of the disastrous election. Then she had set to work once again to help her husband hold his seat. She had seen Ronald worried, exhausted, baffled, disappointed – and she had been the one to whom he turned.

Her hidden fear and resentment towards Dinah waned and died away. Even the little boy was no longer to be thought of as a rival to Max. Ronald knew that Dinah and the boy were his responsibility and so he would always feel concern for them. But when he needed comfort, advice or encouragement, it was to the family at Gatesmuir he looked.

All the same, it was good to have an excuse to go to London and see him. There were designs for the next pattern book that she needed to discuss with Wilson, London agent for William Corvill & Son. Moreover it was always as well to check the housekeeping at Eaton Square – Ronald needed to be comfortable when he came home late from the Commons.

She was sitting over a cup of coffee at the breakfast table when Graves came in bearing a note on a salver. 'A messenger boy brought this, madam, and is waiting with a hackney outside to take back your reply.'

Jenny took it with a pang of anxiety. Some

crisis with Ronald? He had gone out early to meet some visiting Parliamentarians off the boat train from France.

The writing she recognised at once as Dinah's straggling hand. 'Dear Jenny, Please can you come, a strange man is hanging about outside and Miss Kinsman and me are scaired.'

'Graves, my cape!'

She snatched it from him and hurried out. The messenger boy was standing by the carriage. She gave him sixpence, nodded dismissal, and got in. Within a quarter of an hour she was set down at the corner of Cheyne Terrace.

It was a gusty April day. Lilac not quite ready to bloom lashed about like a wild green wave in front of Number Fifteen, spilling over the low fence that bounded the small garden.

Sure enough, as the note said, there was a man there. Hunched under the boughs of the tall lilac bushes – sheltering from the wind, or perhaps trying to stay out of sight?

When he saw Jenny he pulled down the brim of his hat as if to shield his face from view, and retreated. She called, 'Hi you!'

He hurried away without looking back.

CHAPTER SEVEN

Indoors Jenny found the household in a state bordering on panic. Dinah was pacing up and down the sitting room with her hands clasped in front of her, Miss Kinsman sat by the fire looking pale and drawn.

'Did you see him?' Dinah burst out as she was shown in.

'Yes. I spoke to him but he made off.'

'That's what always happens.'

'You've no idea who he is?'

Dinah shook her head. Miss Kinsman said: 'We were each under a misapprehension for some days – '

'Some days! You mean this isn't the first time he's been here?' Jenny exclaimed.

'No, Mrs Armstrong, he's been there for at least ten days and perhaps more. At first, when I noticed him I thought . . . ahem . . . that he was some poor fellow romantically attracted to Mrs Eynsham – '

'Utter rubbish!' Dinah interrupted with great vigour. 'You know I don't even *know* anybody yet, Miss Kinsman.'

'But I thought, you see, that perhaps he'd seen you when we go out for our walks, or something of that kind. However, yesterday Mrs Eynsham asked me whether it was acceptable to have the servants' men-friends hanging about like that and then I understood that – '

'You see,' Dinah took it up, 'I don't know what's allowed and what isn't hereabouts, so I took it for granted this fellow was a "follower" of Daisy's. But even so, I thought he'd have stood waiting around the back door. But the minute I said that to Miss Kinsman – '

'Yes, at once, I realised we had both been under a misapprehension, ma'am, and we were then both very alarmed. It was Mrs Eynsham's thought to send word to you first thing today.'

'I'm glad you did,' Jenny said, frowning and shaking her head. 'What happens? Does he just stay there?'

'I . . . I rather think he has followed us, but I cannot be certain, I fear.'

'Has he spoken to you? Either of you?'

'No, not a word. In fact, when one tries to address him, he moves off. It is rather unnerving.'

'I'm going out to speak to him.'

'It's a waste of time, Jenny.'

'We'll see.'

She went out at once, hoping that her sudden reappearance would take him by surprise. He was certainly there, lurking in the lee of the lilac bushes. As she came down the path to the gate she caught a glimpse of his tweed-clad shoulder. But by the time she opened the gate he was disappearing round the corner of the terrace.

She went back indoors slowly. It was, as Miss Kinsman had said, unnerving. Who on earth was he? What did he want?

'I think we must tell Mr Armstrong,' she said

when she re-entered the sitting room. 'I'll send for him.'

A note was dispatched. They waited an hour, during which Daisy brought in tea and Clive trundled his cart from room to room.

Jenny's note had merely asked Ronald to come at once, as a matter of urgency. He arrived thinking someone was ill. Jenny put his mind at rest as he came in, adding, 'Did you see a man lurking outside?'

'Well, yes, funnily enough. He was hidden from the house by the lilac bushes, though. How did you know he was there?'

'He's been there for a couple of weeks at least, Ronald.'

'What?'

'Watching the house.'

'But that's absurd. Watching the house?'

'It's a fact, Ron,' Dinah said. 'We're really scared about it, Miss Kinsman and me.'

'What does he want?'

'That's what we don't know.'

'But he can't be allowed to skulk about – '

'Did you speak to him?'

'No, he moved away when I got out of the cab.'

'I think he's planning to rob the house!' broke out Miss Kinsman in a quavering voice. Her face was wan, her mouth trembled. She was under great pressure from fear, and Jenny didn't blame her.

Ronald went to the window to look out. The lilacs blotted out part of the street outside. If the watcher was there, he wasn't to be seen.

'He can't be a cracksman,' he objected. 'If he's made no secret of the fact that he's spying on the house, he's spoiled his chance of getting in unnoticed, hasn't he?'

'Then what does he want?' cried Miss Kinsman, putting her thin hands up to her face and rocking back and forth in misery. 'What does he mean by it? Oh, Mr Armstrong, it's a dreadful feeling to know he's there all the time. Perhaps even at night . . .'

The three women drew in a breath. It was somehow a more frightening thought even than his constant daytime presence – that he should be out there in the dark.

'I'll go out and tell him to clear off.'

'Don't waste your time, Ronald. Dinah has tried that and so have I. He walks away.'

'But he must give a reason if he's challenged – '

'The difficulty is to challenge him. He's elusive.'

Ronald paced about the little room for a moment. Then he said, 'Very well, we'll have to trap him. When he walks off, where does he go?'

'He generally walks towards the nearest corner, off to the left as you leave the house.'

'Very well. The back door gives on a lane that runs parallel to the terrace, doesn't it? I'll go out the back door and wait for him at the corner. Jenny, you go out and drive him towards me.'

He went through the house, Cook in the kitchen looking up in surprise as he walked through her domain. In a few rapid strides he was out in the lane, and then at the corner. Almost immediately the man in the tweed jacket and hard hat walked into his arms.

'Good morning,' Ronald said, taking him by

the lapel. 'Would you mind telling me what the devil you're up to?'

'Up to?' said the man. He had been surprised at the encounter, but he recovered at once. His face was bland, his manner calm.

'Why are you watching that house?'

'What house?'

'Number Fifteen, in the terrace.'

'Am I watching Number Fifteen?'

'You've been hanging around there – '

'What makes you think so?'

'Do you deny you've been spying on the house?'

'I do, sir.'

'You deny it?' Ronald said, taken aback by the flatness of it.

'Of course I deny it.'

Ronald gave his arm a shake. The man detached himself from his grip.

'Sir,' he said, 'please don't resort to physical violence.'

'I'll break your neck for you if you don't clear off!'

'But what's your complaint?' was the quiet reply. 'I'm not doing any harm.'

'Not doing any harm? You're scaring Mrs Eynsham and Miss Kinsman out of their wits.'

'Mrs Eynsham? Miss Kinsman? I don't have the honour of the acquaintance of those ladies.' He spoke clearly, but not quite in the manner of a gentleman. He had confidence, but not enough to raise his voice in response to Ronald's anger.

'I know damn well you're a stranger to them! That's why they're frightened: they've no idea why you're subjecting them to this intrusion and – '

'I'm not intruding,' said the man. 'I haven't intruded. If you'd be so good as to step out of my way, sir, I should like to walk on.'

'Walk on?' cried Ronald. 'If I let you go you'll be back on watch outside the house – '

'If I choose to stand on the pavement and enjoy the air, what harm does it do to anyone?'

'But the ladies are frightened – '

'Oh, ladies, my good sir, they have such vivid imaginations. Please, if you'll allow me, I'd like to make my way along the street.'

There was nothing for it. Ronald turned aside, the man walked on, and while Ronald watched him he continued to walk away from Cheyne Terrace towards the King's Road.

Baffled and angry, Ronald went back into the house. 'He's gone,' he said. 'I don't know whether I've scared him off for good.'

'Who is he?'

'We never got to that! I challenged him to explain why he was hanging about outside and he said he had a perfect right to stand there if he wanted to.'

'That's ridiculous!' cried Dinah. 'He can't have no right – any right – to make a pest of himself like that!'

Ronald looked doubtful. '*Has* he made a pest of himself? Done anything, said anything?'

'Not a word, Mr Armstrong. In fact he's avoided actual contact. It's just that . . . one feels the pressure of his presence . . .'

'I understand you perfectly. The best thing is to inform the police, I think.'

The nearest police station was in Pimlico. He walked there at a brisk pace, forced along by irritation at his own lack of effectiveness.

The desk sergeant listened phlegmatically to the beginning of his story.

'Stands outside the house, you say?' he murmured. 'What else does he do?'

'Nothing.'

'Beg pardon, sir?'

'He doesn't do anything. Except that he scares the daylights out of Mrs Eynsham and her elderly companion.'

'No man in the house, sir?'

'No, only Mrs Eynsham, who is a widow, her companion, and two female servants.'

'Is he known to the servants, this feller?'

'No, not at all. And when I spoke to him he didn't claim to be known to them.'

'It's always the same man, is it?'

'So far as I know. I've only seen him a couple of times, this morning. The women speak as if it's always the same man. Why do you ask?'

'Well, if it was a criminal plan, there'd be a team, more likely. One man on and one man off, something like that. Did he cut up rough when you nabbed him?'

'Not at all. He was perfectly calm – calmer than I was, in fact.'

'Didn't swear at you? Behave tough?'

'No. In fact, all he said was that he wasn't doing any harm by standing there.'

'Well . . . As a matter of fact, he's in the right there, sir.'

'What?' roared Ronald. 'He can prowl about every day – and perhaps at night – outside the house of two helpless women and he isn't doing any harm?'

'I'm afraid that's the case in law, sir. He's a perfect right to stand about wherever he likes.

Unless he commits a breach of the peace, we've no reason to try to stop him.'

'Can't you arrest him on suspicion?'

'Suspicion of what, sir?'

'Well, he might be planning to break in – '

'What, and give a couple of weeks' notice by standing right outside?' said the sergeant with an affable smile. 'No, no, chummy isn't planning a robbery.'

'Then what is he planning?'

'Nothing, Mr Armstrong. We've no evidence that he's planning anything.'

'You mean you aren't going to do anything?'

The sergeant pulled at his luxuriant beard. 'Well, sir, what we could do, we could send our foot patrol round there more frequent. The constable usually goes along Cheyne Terrace twice in daylight hours and once at night. I'll tell him to double back on himself each time in the day, so he'll go past four times.'

'Has he reported seeing this man?'

'No, as a matter of fact, sir, no, he hasn't. But as you tell me, the feller makes himself scarce if anyone comes up to him. So I daresay he's picked up on the times Constable Medlar goes by and just moves off for a few minutes.'

'You don't find that strange?'

'Oh, yes, I do, sir – the whole thing's queer, no argument. But he's committing no crime. That's the long and short of it.'

Whether he might have bestirred himself more if Ronald had told him he was a Member of Parliament was open to question. As it happened, Ronald didn't think to mention that fact.

Late that night, when Miss Kinsman had gone to bed with a tisane to calm her, and little

Clive was in dreamland, Ronald, Jenny and Dinah sat down to talk over the problem. A problem it remained, for after Ronald had gone to speak to the police the watcher had returned to his post, had been there all afternoon, and for all they knew might be outside at this moment.

'It's an utter mystery,' he groaned. 'The police can suggest no explanation and declare there's no action they can take.'

'You mean we just have to put up with this?'

'I'm afraid so, Dinah, unless we can work out what it's about and make a move to stop it.'

'Ronald,' Jenny said, and stopped.

'What?'

'Someone in Galashiels told me there had been . . . some talk . . . about this house and Dinah.'

Her husband looked at her, and a mixture of emotions flickered in his eyes – anger, apprehension, dismay, defiance.

'Oh, lor . . .' muttered Dinah.

'What are you saying, Jenny?'

'I wondered if the man could be a reporter from one of the scandal sheets?'

There was a pause while they considered that. Then Ronald said, 'But surely he'd have put something into print by now? You say he's been here for at least two weeks, perhaps longer – standing out there, perhaps following you when you go on outings, Dinah. Surely by now he'd have got tired if there wasn't a story in it?'

'What do you suggest he's after, then?'

'I wondered if he was some friend of your husband's.'

'A friend of Tim's?' Dinah's voice climbed in incredulity.

'Well, you know, when I was off with the gold-prospecting crowd, that was one thing they all talked about. How if they made their pile, they were going to go Home and buy a mansion and live in style. It crossed my mind that perhaps Tim – '

'That man outside isn't Tim – '

'No, but if some friend had made a good strike and actually made the dream come true, travelled Home and settled in London – perhaps he'd come seeking you out, if Tim had talked about you.'

'But Tim doesn't know I've come Home!'

'He could have found out. And asked his friend to look you up.'

'But that man hasn't done anything but stand out there and frighten me. He hasn't brought any message, offered any word – '

'That's true, Ronald, he deliberately avoids being contacted. He can't be there bringing a message from Dinah's husband – '

'Well, then, *you* explain it, Jenny.'

'I wish I could. What I do know is, it can't go on like this.'

With that the conference broke up, Dinah barring and locking the door noisily behind the Armstrongs as they left. If the watcher was still there, they couldn't see him in the dim light of the few street lamps in the terrace.

They returned to Eaton Square arguing all the way in the cab. They went to bed still in perplexity but during the night Jenny's mind must have been at work because in the morning she had a plan.

She sent for Henry Baxter.

Mr Baxter was an ex-sergeant of detectives of the Metropolitan Police, who now ran a small detective inquiry agency in Marylebone. It was thanks to his indefatigable inquiries that Jenny had got back Heather when she went missing years ago. From time to time since then Jenny had used his services – in finding a debtor who had absconded, in recovering some cloth designs stolen by a rival manufacturer.

He heard her story with raised eyebrows. 'The police could move him along,' he began.

'Only if they see him there. I think you must accept the fact that this man is wily, Mr Baxter, he knows how to make himself scarce if a constable appears.'

'Wily. Or experienced. Or both.'

'The only explanations we've come up with are that he is a reporter or that he is some friend or associate of Mrs Eynsham's husband. Mrs Eynsham has let it be supposed she is a widow, but her husband vanished in the gold fields of Australia a few years ago. So that last idea is a possibility – but not very likely.'

'What do you want me to do?'

'Well, I think we should try to establish whether Mr Eynsham is alive or dead. Do you have associates in Sydney or Melbourne who could undertake the inquiry?'

Baxter brushed his iron-grey moustache one way and the other above his lip. 'Not personally, no, ma'am, but this sort of inquiry for a person missing in the colonies isn't unknown. I have contacts in London who have contacts in Sydney – but you must understand, ma'am, it will take time. The very least you can expect is six months' delay.'

130

Jenny frowned and sighed. 'I understand that, of course.'

'In the event that our associates find Mr Eynsham, what would you wish them to say or do?'

'Nothing, I suppose. We mustn't take it upon ourselves to give Eynsham any information about his wife without her permission. And to tell the truth, I think she would be very loth to be in touch with him again. But it would be a sensible thing to find out whether or not the man is in the land of the living and whether, if it can be done discreetly, he is in any way responsible for the spying being carried out upon her.'

'If I may say so, ma'am . . .'

'Yes?'

'Mr Armstrong's idea that this watcher is a friend or agent of Eynsham is a bit unlikely. I mean, the man's behaviour is inconsiderate, to say the least. If Eynsham were trying to find out whether his wife wished to have a reconciliation, this sort of thing is the least likely to bring it about.'

'That's very true, Mr Baxter, and to tell the truth I don't put much faith in the idea of it having anything to do with Eynsham. That simply arose because none of us could think of why anyone should be so persistent in spying on Mrs Eynsham.'

'You yourself thought it might be a reporter . . . ?'

'That idea crossed my mind.'

'Er . . . ahem . . . is there any reason why a reporter should be interested in Mrs Eynsham?'

Jenny pressed her lips together. She had no

intention of telling even the sensible and reserved Mr Baxter the relationship between the Armstrongs and Mrs Eynsham. 'Can you undertake to catch this man and tackle him in some way?'

'But you said Mr Armstrong had already done that, ma'am.'

'Yes, but he was so taken aback at the rogue's calm manner that he didn't use the opportunity to best effect. I thought . . . perhaps, if he's a criminal . . . you know more about handling such people than . . .'

'Quite so,' said Baxter with a smile that had some grimness in it.

'If you do manage to grab him – and he seems as slippery as an eel – you will be careful, won't you? It may be that he is a little, well, touched. Some people can be quite dangerous.'

'Ho, don't worry about that, ma'am. I daresay I can handle him if he cuts up rough.'

'No, I meant, dangerous as to the kind of thing he might say. He might claim he had been hurt, assaulted . . .'

'I get your drift. Leave it to me, Mrs Armstrong.'

The law firm with whom Baxter worked closely were able to provide an address in Melbourne where he could write, entrusting the task of looking for Tim Eynsham to their employees. After a day or so tidying up some other jobs he was engaged on, Mr Baxter looked into the matter of the constant watcher himself.

He had no intention of having a confrontation. Instead he spied on the spy, from a vantage point in a cabman's shelter at the far end of Cheyne Terrace. When the man left in the dusk of the early May evening, Baxter accompanied him home on the same horse omnibus.

Having found out his address, Baxter made inquiries. He was a respectable fellow, Charles Woodcott, working in his own employ as a sort of messenger, his neighbours thought.

Next morning Mr Baxter was waiting at the omnibus stop where the man had alighted. By and by Mr Woodcott appeared. As they waited for the omnibus it was quite reasonable to drop into conversation – about the weather, the latest concert at the still new Albert Hall, and whether the style of beard adopted recently by the Prince of Wales would become a general fashion.

When Mr Woodcott alighted, so did Mr Baxter. They walked together from King's Road towards Cheyne Terrace. As Mr Baxter showed no signs of parting company, Mr Woodcott ceased to chat, and began to look uneasy.

'Whereabouts are you headed?' he asked.

'Wherever you're going. I'm out for the fresh air, you know.'

'I, er . . . I go round this turning.'

'Well, so will I.'

'But . . . er . . . I'm not going any further.'

'No? Calling at a house here?'

'Yes. No, that is . . .'

'Listen, matey,' Baxter said, taking the man by the arm in a friendly way, 'you'll end up in big trouble if you go on bothering Mrs Eynsham like this.'

Woodcott gasped. 'Mrs Eynsham? I don't know any Mrs Eynsham – '

'Not to speak to, you mean? I know you don't. Now, see here, Woodcott – '

'How do you know my name?' squeaked Woodcott in alarm.

'Do you take me for a cuddy? I followed you home yesterday, no trouble, and I've got your name and address and quite a bit about you written down in my notebook.'

Woodcott had recovered himself. 'Copper, are you? Well, that doesn't scare me. There's no charge you can bring against me.'

'Oh, think you're a defty dodger, do you? I dessay I could think of something.'

'Go on then! See where it gets you!'

Baxter cocked his head on one side as he studied the other. 'You know what I'm talking about, eh? Understand the lingo – but you're not a hedge-bird. What are you up to?'

'I don't have to tell you, friend, and so I wish you a fare-thee-well.'

'But I told you, I've only myself to please, I ain't going anywhere. I think I'll stick along of you for the rest of the day.'

'Get out of it,' said Woodcott in exasperation. 'I don't want you here.'

'I quite understand you. If you hang about on the pavement and do no more, nobody can touch you. But if I stay here and start some fisticuffs with you, we'll both end up in the coalhole with a charge of disturbing the peace, at least. Right?'

'Clear off!' snarled Woodcott.

'Not a chance. Come on, let's cut this short. Who hired you to do this glims-on lark?'

'None of your business.'

'Righto, then I start pasting you round the head after a count of three, and you can be sure the local constable will be round the corner the minute he hears the row – '

Woodcott huffed out a breath. 'You mean you've tipped him the wink?'

'I said I thought there might be an outbreak of violence. Handy, ain't it, to be able to call on favours from old friends.'

'I got you,' Woodcott said. 'You're a private agent.'

'Right.'

'Well, well . . .' Woodcott grinned, quite at ease now. 'So am I.'

'You what?'

'Charles Woodcott, discretion guaranteed. Didn't you find that out when you were nosing around my neighbours? No, I s'pose not. I don't let it out that I'm in that game – discretion, you know.' He tapped the side of his nose in the ancient gesture for 'I won't let on'.

Baxter was surprised but not overwhelmed by the information. At least the man wasn't some lunatic who had an obsession with the beautiful Mrs Eynsham.

'So who hired you, then?'

'You know better than to ask that, matey. But seeing as you've been so clever in putting me off my stroke this morning, I'll tell you this much. I'm being paid by Drayward and Ford of Clerkenwell – look 'em up in the law books, they're as good as gold.'

Baxter had in fact heard of the firm of solicitors. He frowned at the other man. 'What's your brief, then?'

'Me, I'm just told to watch the lady. I asked, Keep it under the hat? And they said it didn't matter if she saw me, all they wanted was to have her under observation during normal working hours and a report turned in every day. So that's what I do – on duty at eight-thirty in the morning, sandwich in my pocket if I feel hungry, sign off at day's end. Easy work, the lady don't go anywhere much and sees hardly anybody at home. 'Cept the pretty lady with the dark eyes and the bright manner, and the tall fairish bloke I take to be married to the dark lady.'

'You haven't found out who they are?'

'That wasn't part of the instructions. I just report the comings and goings, and that's it.'

'I think I might knock you down a time or two and shout for help, just the same,' murmured Baxter.

'Please yourself. If I'm put in the nick they'll just hire somebody else.'

'That's true.' Baxter nodded, tipped his hat, and walked off.

He took a hackney to Clerkenwell. There he had to wait before anyone at Drayward and Ford would see him, but at length he was shown into a dim and dusty office with the name D B Ford on the door, where a youngish man sat behind a paper-strewn desk.

'Well, sir . . . What is your business, Mr, er, Baxter?'

'My business is to find out why you have hired a man called Charles Woodcott to keep observation on Mrs Eynsham of Cheyne Terrace, Chelsea.'

'Ug?' said the young man, gulping in horror.

'Why have you undertaken this work, Mr Ford?'

'Sir . . . I . . . How did you come to . . . One moment!' He leapt up, almost ran round Baxter, and rushed out of his office. Baxter could hear his feet on the linoleum of the passage outside. He took the opportunity to lean over the desk for a look at the papers lying about, but none of them had anything to do with the present case.

After a few minutes the young Mr Ford returned with an older man, clad in lawyer's black but with much gold in the way of watch chain and seals and fobs on the front of his expansive waistcoat.

'Mr Baxter?' he said, looking with cold pale eyes at the detective.

'Yes, sir. You are . . . ?'

'This is my father,' said the young Mr Ford.

'Mr Ford,' Baxter said, 'I repeat my question. Why are you persecuting Mrs Eynsham by keeping watch on her?'

'That is none of your business, sir.'

'I'm being paid to make it my business.'

'Then I am afraid that you are being paid to no purpose. I have nothing to say to you, sir.'

'There's no reason why you shouldn't tell me, Mr Ford, if you are not ashamed of it.'

'Don't be absurd. It is a confidential matter. I shouldn't dream of discussing it with you.'

'A confidential matter? You mean you are doing it on behalf of a client?'

'I should like to know how you became aware of my firm's part in this.'

'No doubt. That is a confidential matter. Who is your client?'

'You know I will not tell you that, sir.' The lawyer gave a cold, sour smile.

'Doesn't it trouble your conscience to make the lady, and her elderly companion, quite alarmed?'

'Alarmed? They have no reason to be so if their conscience is clear.'

'I don't understand you, sir. Do you mean you are having Mrs Eynsham kept under observation because you believe she's involved in some crime?'

'What I believe or don't believe is not to the point. I am carrying out instructions – '

'Instructions to harass a widow in her own home? I can't believe a man of your standing would accept instructions to that effect, Mr Ford.'

'I say, Father,' put in his son, 'what he says has a lot of sense in it. I never liked this from the outset – '

'David, hold your tongue! We have nothing further to say to you, Mr Baxter. Kindly leave.'

'I'm glad one of you has some kind of conscience,' Baxter said, moving slowly towards the door. 'I should think you'd be ashamed, taking money from some stranger to scare a decent woman – '

'But our instructions aren't from a stranger – '

'Will you be quiet, David! We have no obligation to justify our actions to this man. We're doing nothing illegal.'

'But we're doing something very ungentlemanly!'

'We may very well be justified by what eventuates – '

'Eventuates! And in the meantime we keep this poor lady in a state of distraction – '

'What d'you expect to learn,' Baxter put in, 'that could possibly justify your campaign?'

'Sir, I believe we have already said that this conversation is at an end.'

'Tell me at least this much. You say you've received instructions from a client – '

'I said no such thing!'

'Your son said the instructions come from someone "not a stranger". At least satisfy me to this extent: this someone – is he respectable? In full control of his faculties?'

Mr Ford composed his face so that it looked like a slab of stone. With a stiff arm he gestured to the door. Baxter saw nothing was to be gained from him by staying longer. He went out into the passage.

David Ford came to close the door behind him. Just as it began to swing to, he leaned out and said in a low, anxious voice, 'Our client is of excellent standing and has been with us for many years.'

A client of excellent standing? Interested enough in Dinah Eynsham to have her watched in this strict, almost cruel fashion?

Mr Baxter shivered a little as he put on his hat and walked out into the May sunshine.

CHAPTER EIGHT

Baxter's report of what he had so far discovered caused Jenny some consternation. She
took the news to the Chelsea house in hopes of
some enlightenment, but Dinah was baffled.

'Someone who's been a client of a posh
London lawyer for years?' she repeated in her
rather flat voice. 'I don't understand it at all!
I've only been in London a few months, and I
didn't know anybody here before I came –
'cept you, Jenny, and Ron.'

Try as they might, they could make nothing
of it. And to make it worse, the watcher was
still there – not Mr Woodcott, who was probably thought inefficient since Mr Baxter had
been able to trace the law firm through him –
but another man, more subtle though equally
assiduous.

'I tell you, it makes me feel like a stump-
tailed lizard trapped under a rock!' Dinah
cried. 'He's always there – I can feel him even
when I can't see him!'

Baxter had said he felt there was some
charge that could be laid against Drayward and
Ford, no matter how invulnerable they seemed
to think they were. 'There are other clever solicitors,' he'd said to Jenny. 'Somebody could
find a case against them.'

But the likely publicity made Jenny shy away from it. Once it got into the courts, newspapermen would take note. And once newspapermen became interested, who knew what they might learn or suspect about Dinah's status?

So there seemed no way of getting rid of the paid spy. However, there was an alternative. They could take evasive action.

'You must get away for a while, Dinah,' she suggested.

'Get away? Where to? Another London house?' Dinah looked mutinous. 'I hate London! It's so full of people and houses, and the air seems somehow so heavy . . .'

'You'd prefer the country?'

'Oh, anywhere; anywhere where there's more green grass than houses, and where you can see open sky when you look around . . .' She threw wide her arms and took a deep breath to illustrate her meaning. She looked magnificent – her darkly gleaming head thrown back, her rounded breasts thrusting against the discreet boning of her bodice.

'It's like that where I come from, my dear.'

'Where? You mean Scotland? Ron used to tell me about it. Rolling hills and valleys. And sheep . . . you got sheep there, haven't you?'

'Yes, the Borders are full of sheep. Would you like to come?'

'But where would we stay, me and Clive and Miss Kinsman?'

'With me. At Gatesmuir. There's plenty of room.'

'In *your* house?'

'Why not?'

'But, I mean . . . me being who I am, and

Clive being who he is . . . I mean, Jenny, do you really want us?'

It was a good question. Did she really want Ronald's former mistress and his bastard son coming to stay with her?

Yet, on the other hand, the relationship couldn't remain static. Ronald seriously wanted to look after Clive and his mother, oversee his education, help him eventually with a career. The two families couldn't be kept compartmentalised. They would have to meet eventually – and perhaps now was a good time for it to happen, before the children were old enough to wonder why Ronald should interest himself in the wellbeing of a boy from a different family.

Besides, against all the odds, Jenny was growing fond of Dinah. Particularly since the persecution by the spy. Something in Dinah's reaction to it had called out a protective affection for her in Jenny. Somehow the girl seemed to need looking after. She was so beautiful to look at but so simple, so artless.

'I think it would be a good idea if you came, Dinah. For one thing, Drayward and Ford will find it hard to hire anyone to watch you in Galashiels, and if they send a London man he'll stick out like a sore thumb. Besides, it would be a lot more uncomfortable standing outside the gates of Gatesmuir, in the wind off the hills!'

'But I mean . . . Jenny . . . who're you going to say I am?'

'I'll just say you're a friend from Australia, a widow lady with a little son. I'll say I owe you gratitude for being kind to me while I was out there. Border traditions of hospitality are strong – they won't question it.'

'Well, jeez . . . I'd love it, Jenny!'

'I must warn you,' Jenny said, 'it's more open and expansive than London – but it's also a lot colder.'

'But it's coming on summer.'

'Scottish summers are colder than Australian winters,' Jenny laughed. 'But never mind, we've plenty of woollen cloth in Galashiels to make you some new dresses!'

Miss Kinsman elected not to come. She felt the cool damp atmosphere of the Cheviots would be bad for her chest. Since she had accomplished a great deal already in polishing Dinah for presentation to society, Jenny gave the elderly gentlewoman a handsome money present and an excellent reference, and dispensed with her services.

Packing was done quietly. The cook and the maid were not told the house was being closed up, so that the news couldn't leak out to the man watching out in Cheyne Terrace. One day three or four boxes were taken away by a carter – these were the belongings Dinah and Clive had accumulated since arriving in London. Next day Dinah took Clive out for a walk in the grounds of the Chelsea Hospital.

Mr Baxter arranged matters so that an associate innocently bumped into the lawyer's spy near the gates in Royal Hospital Road, detaining him for five vital minutes. Dinah thereupon walked rapidly through to the Embankment of the Thames, where Jenny was waiting for her in a carriage to whisk her off to Euston and the train for Carlisle.

News that Mistress Armstrong was bringing

home a foreigner to stay had already leaked out to the ladies of Galashiels. Quite a few of them had found reasons to be in and around the main street on the day she was known to be arriving. Thus when Dinah stepped into the Armstrongs' carriage, holding Clive in her arms, she was closely observed.

'Yon's a pretty lass,' remarked Mrs Hamilton to Mrs Kerr. 'She'll not be to her thirties yet, by the looks of her – puir soul, she's young to be widowed.'

'Aye, and a fine wee laddie with that rich dark hair. He'll be a playmate for the Mistress's wain.'

'Na, na, he's ower auld – Max is only a bairn by comparison.'

'You're forgetting, Maisie, Max is over two years old the now.'

'My, how time flies . . !'

Cards were quickly left at Gatesmuir, signalling a desire to be introduced to the newcomer. Archie Brunton and one of his friends were among the earliest of the gentlemen to call.

'Australia?' he murmured to Jenny as they strolled in her garden a little apart from an afternoon tea party on the terrace. 'What's she doing in Scotland, then?'

'I brought her here – you know that, Archie.'

'No, what I meant was, why did she come to Britain in the first place?'

'Because it's Home, and she had no relatives in New South Wales.'

'It's the devil of a long way to come just to look up a friend you knew for a few months some years ago!'

Jenny said nothing. They were joined by Mrs Kennet, and the conversation changed its course to discussion of the new roses being imported from France.

But Jenny saw Archie's eye upon Dinah, and more importantly upon Clive.

She felt sure there was nothing to suggest that Clive was Ronald's son. The child took after his mother in every way except that it was clear Nature intended him to be tall and angular in frame, whereas Dinah's body wasn't longlimbed.

She noticed that Archie tended to avoid Dinah. This was remarked upon by the local worthies. 'Fancy Archie not making a set at the handsome widow! He's never been so slow in going after a pretty woman in all the years I've known him!'

'Aye, but,' said Mr McMahon, the town's hatter, 'she's a particular friend of Mistress Armstrong's. He would be carefu' about offending the Mistress by acting free wi' her'. And she's no exactly a sparkler, is she? Archie likes young leddies wi' bright smiles and empty heads.'

Through the weeks of summer, when Border folk liked to mount events like the Braw Lads Gathering so as to be out enjoying the sunshine together, Dinah was taken hither and yon by Jenny and Ronald. The general verdict was that she was an agreeable lady, interesting enough when you got her talking about life on a farm in Australia but with little to say otherwise. Goodlooking, of course – oh yes, many a young man cast languishing glances at her. The oddity was, she didn't seem to know what to do with them. There seemed to be nothing of the coquette in her at all.

The maids at Gatesmuir had their reservations

about her. With that instinctive wish to have everything in its place, they had decided that Mrs Eynsham was 'not quite a lady'. Thirley, the head housemaid, was quite put out about her. 'I canna see why the Mistress bothers wi' her. She doesna even ken what knife and fork to pick up at mealtimes! And I can tell you, from snatches I've overheard, her conversation's nothing to glory in.'

'Well, she was welcoming to Mistress Armstrong when she was ower in them foreign parts wi' the kangaroos,' said Cook. 'She feels an obligation to her.'

'Humph,' Thirley grunted. 'A few weeks' hospitality on a farm at the back of nowhere doesna deserve months of bed and board in one of the best houses in the Borders – '

'Months?' queried the kitchenmaid.

'Well, she's having winter clothes made. Mistress Carstairs is coming the morn to take the measurements.'

'Staying on into the winter, is she?' Cook mused. 'I wonder if she's ever had black-bun or the Captain's punch?'

'She's used to plain fare, you can tell that. When I told her the other night that the entrée was a ragoût, she was at a loss.'

'Ah well,' said Baird, 'she's a colonial, poor soul. She canna help it.'

Baird was the only person other than Mrs Armstrong who knew anything about Mrs Eynsham in her Australian setting. Baird had gone with the Mistress on the long, dangerous voyage to the Antipodes. But Baird was uninformative. When cross-questioned, she would say that she had stayed at a sheep station – a sheep station! Who ever heard of keeping sheep on a station? – had stayed with Heather, while Mistress Armstrong travelled elsewhere. So, she averred, she knew nothing much about Mrs Eynsham.

Dinah was scarcely aware that her status was a subject of interest to the servants. In the first place she was unused to servants and in the second, she didn't know her status or what to expect from her new surroundings.

She loved the Scottish Borders. True, the climate was cooler than she was used to, but the wide horizons, the hillsides with sheep moving across the pasture, the workaday life of the town, all these things pleased her.

London had frightened her very much. The pressure of so many people living close to her had been strange, almost unnatural. And then the intricate elegance of society – the society for which Miss Kinsman had tried to groom her – had filled her with dread.

Here people had their finery, and were justifiably proud of it. They enjoyed wearing good clothes, riding in their own carriages. But they seemed to attach less importance to these matters. They had an easy, comfortable style. She could often feel quite at ease with them.

Each time Ronald came home, however, she was jarred into embarrassment. To see him at Gatesmuir, knowing that he belonged here, that the carriage he ordered out so easily was *his*, that the woollen mills he had shown her on the banks of the Gala Water were under his control, to note the respect which greeted him both as employer and Member of Parliament for the district – all these things made her feel she had been a fool.

A fool ever to think he wanted to marry

her, to try to force him to stay with her . . .
Sometimes when she remembered how she
had railed at him she would colour up with
shame. She, a nobody, an uneducated girl
from an orphan school – to think she could be a
match for Ronald Armstrong of Gatesmuir and
the Waterside Mills . . .

When Ronald came home on brief visits she
was always subdued. When the Parliamentary
Recess began, she was very apprehensive,
because she would see him daily for weeks.
She felt that he must feel irritated with her
every time she crossed his path – a silly,
stupid, demanding woman who should have
stayed in her own place on the other side of the
world.

She was quite wrong. Ronald had not been
in favour of having Dinah to stay at Gatesmuir
when Jenny first proposed it, but she seemed
little trouble. She occupied herself mostly in
helping to look after the two boys, her own
and little Max.

Although Ronald was proud of them he held
the current view that children should be seen
and not heard. He only saw them at set times:
in the morning before he left for the mills, in
the evening at nursery tea if he was home in
time for that.

So he and Dinah were mainly required to be
sociable at dinner if he were not called out to
some political event, and on Sundays. Ronald
was relieved. Sometimes, even, he was wryly
amused.

For a positive friendship seemed to be grow-
ing up between his wife and his ex-mistress.
Jenny was the one who knew how to handle
Dinah during one of her outbursts of touchi-

ness. Jenny it was who coaxed her into accepting the dull Scottish Sunday without loud complaints of boredom. From Jenny she would take hints and even criticism she would never have tolerated from anyone else.

Jenny helped choose her clothes, steered her away from bright unsuitable colours and shoe styles that included too many cut-steel buttons. In the matter of white kid gloves, however, Jenny was tolerant. During her stay in New South Wales she had observed that 'ladies' wore new white kid gloves whenever possible, and that those who were not 'ladies' longed to do the same. So when Dinah asked to have a dozen pairs of white kid gloves, she not only agreed, she increased the order to two dozen.

Sometimes, seeing the two women with their heads together over a fashion magazine, Ronald would wonder if this was what it was like to be a member of that American sect, the Mormons, and have two legal wives . . . But irony apart, he was grateful for the way things had turned out so far. He could do his duty in looking after mother and child, without wrecking his marriage. His admiration and affection for Jenny on that score were boundless.

The trouble was, he had few chances to express them. His duties as an MP he took seriously: he had tasks to fulfil in the area, he was called upon to open fairs and address meetings. He met the Secretary for Scottish affairs on several occasions to ask for more funds for technical schools in the Borders. Those were run-of-the-mill. More demanding were the anxieties of the Liberal Party at this time.

There was still uncertainty about the leadership. Mr Gladstone insisted he no longer held that title but no one else seemed to have it. In the House the last session had been marred by some unseemly rows, especially in May when Trevelyan's Bill for the extension of household suffrage had been heavily defeated. Called upon to speak in the debate, Ronald had had a severe mauling from the unrelenting Thomas Unsworth, but had acquitted himself well enough to be asked now for his views on reforming the Party.

As the year rolled round to the opening of the next session, Ronald was invited to gatherings of the Party planners, so that he could give what was called 'the Scottish view'. From all he could learn, it seemed there were as many opinions as there were members. But worse than that, there was an active minority who seemed determined to disagree no matter what was proposed by the Party leaders. It was almost as if they had decided to make a career out of being in disagreement, when what was needed if the Whigs were to win the next election was unanimity on a common cause.

He went back to London for the opening, very preoccupied and worried. Once he was gone, Mr Brunton considered whether to try once more for a close relationship with Jenny. He felt sure he was useful to her during these absences – a woman alone, he told himself, needs a man to advise her. This quite disregarded the fact that Jenny was running her household and the Waterside Mills with perfect efficiency and great success.

Archie managed to 'run across' Jenny at a gathering in Lauder arranged to discuss what, if anything, to do with the ancient Tolbooth, until recently used as the town jail but now falling into disrepair. Subscriptions from the local gentry would be needed if the old building were to be preserved.

Tea was served afterwards in the Manse, and thither Archie escorted Jenny. 'You didn't bring your friend Mrs Eynsham with you,' he remarked with a little smile that expressed some complicity.

'No,' said Jenny, 'this isn't the kind of thing that would interest her.'

'I wonder what *would* interest Mrs Eynsham? She seems totally out of place in her present surroundings.'

Jenny chose to ignore this question. The servant brought tea freshly poured by the minister's wife together with a scone oozing butter, and a napkin. The difficulties of handling all these items with gloved hands and hampered by a capacious document case took up her attention.

Archie proved his worth as an escort by relieving her of the document case and summoning up from nowhere a small table. Upon this they set down their afternoon tea. It had the added advantage for Archie of forming a slight barrier to anyone else who thought of strolling across the room to join them.

Determined to make some way past Jenny's defences he asked point blank: 'How long is that woman going to stay in your house?'

Jenny spread the napkin over her fine worsted skirts. 'That isn't a very polite term. To whom are you referring?'

'Mrs Eynsham, of course. How long are you going to put up with her?'

'Mrs Eynsham will stay until she feels like leaving.'

'Huh!' grunted Archie. 'She's not likely to leave while she has such a downy nest to snuggle into. You should send her packing!'

'Archie, I think you're under a misapprehension. Mrs Eynsham is a friend of mine – '

'Havers! She's the woman you rushed off to rescue Ronald from – don't deny it.'

'You're quite mistaken.'

'I am, am I? When she strolls around the grounds at Gatesmuir with a little boy who's the image of his father?'

'He is not!' cried Jenny, startled into indiscretion. 'He doesn't look a bit like Ronald – '

'Aha . . .' Archie sipped tea and looked pleased. He had got what he wanted, confirmation that the boy was Ronald Armstrong's son.

Jenny was vexed with herself. She kept silent.

'You have the goodness of an angel,' Archie took it up, 'to put up with having your husband's fancy woman living in your own house.'

'Archie, why are you talking like this?'

'I'm trying to show you how thoughtless and selfish your man is – '

'Ronald isn't selfish.'

'What kind of man would bring a doxy into his home?'

'You had better choose your words more carefully, Mr Brunton.'

'Oh, it's quarrel with me, is it? When an old friend tells you you're being insulted by the presence of that loose woman – '

Jenny set her cup and saucer down so hard

that they rattled. 'Listen to me, Archie Brunton! Who are you to preach about loose morals? Have you forgotten I know the kind of life you've led, and that you still seek out a little pleasure in out of the way places?'

'That is not what we are talking about,' Archie said stiffly. 'We're discussing – '

'*You* are discussing. The subject is no choice of mine. But since you insisted on bringing it up, let's see what right you have to be superior about Dinah. You've made love to every girl that caught your eye and been to bed with a good many of them, those that were silly enough to listen to you. You've sought out some who took money for what you got free from the others. Do you deny – '

'That's entirely different. A man – '

'Entirely different! You dare to tell me it's entirely different? If Ronald had a love affair, that was bad and wrong. If you had a score of love affairs, that's entirely different?'

'But I would never have the bad taste to drag my mistress into my home life – '

'Listen to me, Archie. It was I who brought Dinah here. It was I who invited her to stay as long as she wishes. So you see – '

'Oh, you're just saying that to make it look better.'

'Nothing of the kind. There's a little old lady in London who was acting as companion to Dinah – I'll give you her name and address and you can write inquiring who gave Dinah the invitation to Gatesmuir – '

'Don't be daft, Jenny, you know I'd never write to some old woman – '

'No, but you think it's your right to interfere – '

'It's only because I think so highly of you, my dearest. You know I'm yours to command. You've given me your friendship and in the past you confided in me – '

'Yes, and bitterly I regret it!' she cried.

'What? Jenny!'

'Just because in a moment of weakness I told you years ago that Ronald was involved with another woman! I wish I'd cut my tongue out first! What can I expect next – that you'll gossip with everyone and tell them you've more or less forced me to admit the truth? Is that it?'

She was very angry, and looked to him all the more beautiful – the great dark eyes flashed fire, the warm skin was flushed, her lips were parted in a smile of defiance.

'Jenny . . . People will be staring . . .'

She bent forward to pick up the plate with the scone, pushed the scone about with her finger for a moment, and replaced the plate on the table. It gave her a few moments to compose herself.

'Archie,' she said in a calm tone, 'I admit to you that Dinah is the woman Ronald fell in love with for a while. Clive is his son. But I beg you, if you have any real friendship for me, to keep the secret.'

'As if I would tell anyone!'

'Then why did you start out this conversation with so much force and lack of tact – '

'Because I feel it's undignified for you to have to put up with – '

'But I like her, Archie.'

'You *like* her?'

'Yes, I have a fondness for her.'

'Impossible!'

'What makes you say that?'

'Well, every time you look at her you must remember – '

'Oh, blethers! That's all in the past. And let me tell you, it seems as strange and unlikely to Ronald now as it does to me.'

'So he says – '

'He doesn't say it, he doesn't need to. I can see it in him. It all happened to another Ronald Armstrong, who sailed off to the other side of the world to try to get a new grip on life. I can even see it in Dinah. She can't understand how it came to be – but it happened and she has a little boy and we must all do what is best for him. You do see that, Archie?'

Archie picked up his teaspoon and stirred his cold tea. After a long moment he said, 'Aye, I suppose I can see it. I did things in the past myself that seem mighty odd to me now . . .'

'Yes,' Jenny agreed.

They were both thinking of that time years ago when Archie had had an affair with Lucy, the wife of Jenny's brother. How strange, how long ago . . . Lucy Corvill, miles away now in Richmond, Virginia, never mentioned by anyone because of past wickedness. It seem incredible now to Archie that he had once wanted Lucy Corvill so passionately, and she him.

The maid came up to ask if they wished for more tea. Archie was called away by a friend. The episode was over.

Jenny was relieved. She had known for a long time that Archie had guessed the secret. It was as well to have his promise to let it remain so. The little boy needed a good start in life, and Ronald's good name needed to be protected.

In London, Ronald was unaware of the pact over his reputation entered into by his wife and his rival. He was concerned over other matters.

Mr Baxter the detective had called at the House to give him another report on the inquiries he had undertaken. The two men were in a quiet corner of the Members' Bar, Ronald with a reasonable whisky and Baxter with a fine brandy.

'I never went to Cootamundra,' Ronald said. 'When I was there I don't believe there was any gold reported in the area.'

'There was a lot of prospecting, it says in the report, but no mention whether much was found, Mr Armstrong.'

'And he's definitely dead?'

'Yes, sir, a knife fight. It's all in the report.' Baxter took a document out of his inner jacket pocket to offer to Ronald. 'Seems he was going under the nickname of Timmo, but Mr Logan has gone into it thoroughly and there's no doubt he was Timothy Eynsham.'

'When was this?'

'It'd be the February of 1872, I think. Nobody remembers the date exactly and such belongings as he had are separated up – I daresay you know how it is in a place like that, anything useful would be carried off, sir. But the man who took his tools remembers the name scratched into the handle of the pick – Tim Eynsham.'

'Well,' said Ronald, rubbing his forehead, 'so she really is a widow, it seems.'

'Yes, sir, that's the fact.'

'I don't expect she'll shed any tears over him.'

'No, sir, he wasn't much cop as a husband, I imagine. The knife fight that killed him was over a woman.'

He finished the brandy in his glass. 'Another?' Ronald inquired, and signalled the waiter, but Baxter shook his head.

'No, thanks, I'll just report on that other matter and then I must be getting along.'

'What other matter?' Ronald asked, surprised.

'Why, Mr Armstrong – about who hired the man who was spying on Mrs Eynsham's house.'

'Oh. But I thought you'd done all you could in that respect.'

'Not at all, sir, not at all,' Baxter said, tolerance in his tone. These innocent clients – they'd no idea what you could ferret out if you really put your mind to it. 'And it turns out very important – shall I give you the gist?'

At the nod of acquiescence, he cleared his throat, took out his notebook, and began his report. 'You'll recall we'd got as far as Drayward and Ford, Solicitors and Commissioners for Oaths. Old Mr Ford was frosty-faced about it and young Mr Ford was too scared of his old man to say more. But you know sir, even the most confidential business leaks out, and all you've got to do is find out where the leak can be started.'

'And you did that, did you, Baxter? What did you do, break into the office?'

'Goodness, that would have been against the law, besides being wellnigh impossible. No, sir, I just hung about until I found out where the staff went to take their midday meal, and I discovered they mostly went to the Eagle in Clerkenwell Passage which does a very decent ordinary from twelve till two-thirty. So I began to take my grub there too, and after four days I was passably chatty with a young feller they hired recent at the law firm.'

'And you bribed him?'

Baxter looked shocked. He brushed his moustache with dignity. 'Nothing of the kind, sir. The poor lad was having a terrible time making ends meet on the wages they was paying him, what with two kiddies and another on the way, and as it happened I knew of a position going where he could get another two shilling a week.'

'How did you manage that?'

'Oh, it was quite genuine, sir, a cigar importer I know of was looking for a ledger clerk. So he went and they took him on. Out of sheer gratitude he asked if he could do anything for me and I said, "Well, while you're working out your week's notice at Drayward and Ford it would be a nice thing if you happened to look at the file on Mrs Eynsham."'

'I wonder if that cigar importer knows this man's so easy to trick?'

Mr Baxter looked bland. 'He told me next day there was no file on Mrs Eynsham but he would make inquiries quiet-like.' He paused and drew a deep breath, watching Ronald rather anxiously. 'So he did, the following day, in a chat with the chief clerk, and the chief clerk let on the file was in the name of Massiter.'

'Massiter!'

'Yes, sir. You recall the name?'

'Massiter! Shall I ever forget it. I never thought to hear of the man again.'

'It's not the man, sir, it's the lady, Mrs Harvil Massiter, sir, of Greybridge, in Lincolnshire.'

'Lincolnshire?'

'Yes, sir. Greybridge is a village, sir, I looked it up in the gazetteer. There's a manorhouse too, of the same name. The nearest town is Spedlow.'

'Spedlow!' Ronald gasped.

Mr Baxter eyed him. The conversation seemed to have become a series of echoes – he would give out a piece of information and Mr Armstrong would repeat it in a tone of dismay.

'The town means something to you, sir?'

'It's the constituency of a man who has been harassing me in Parliament from the moment I took my seat. I couldn't account for his animosity. But now . . . now I begin to understand.'

'How's that, sir?'

'You say Mrs Massiter has an estate in Lincolnshire?'

'Yes, sir.'

'Large?'

'I made a few inquiries – she's got a lot of first-rate property, owns most of Spedlow.'

'Yes. So she would have influence on the nomination of the local candidate.'

'Well, yes, if she were to bother to exert it, Mr Armstrong.'

'Oh, she bothered, all right,' Ronald groaned. 'And she hired a man to spy on Mrs Eynsham when the Member for Spedlow and Nestholm reported a rumour that Mrs Eynsham was in some way connected with me. I

159

would never have believed she would go on hating us so much for all these years . . .'

Baxter had been involved in the case, years ago. 'If you remember, sir, I called on Mrs Massiter at her London home after your daughter disappeared, to see if she could put me on the track of the husband and . . . er . . . the lady with him. She refused any help of any kind in tracing him, and I got the impression then that she was a good hater.'

'Ten years ago,' Ronald said, looking back into the past, 'her husband was fool enough to get entangled with a very pretty, silly woman who wanted to run off to the romantic land of Italy. So they went. Harvil Massiter took all his wife's jewellery and anything else he could lay his hands on, to say nothing of leaving a pile of debts for her to pay.'

'And made her look a fool.'

'Yes, Baxter. He made her look a fool.'

They sat in a cocoon of quietness in the hubbub of the Members' Bar. They were both remembering the terrible events of years ago.

Harvil Massiter had agreed with that very silly, pretty woman to elope to Italy. To his horror, she arrived at the rendezvous, an inn in Holborn, with a baby – her little niece, whom at the last moment she had impulsively picked up and carried off.

The little niece was Heather Armstrong, then aged about eighteen months. The pretty woman was Lucy Corvill, sister-in-law to Jenny Armstrong, whose baby she had stolen.

If anyone in the world had reason to hate, Jenny Armstrong had reason to hate Lucy Corvill: for nearly a year and a half of anguished separation from her little daughter, for years of anxiety after the child was found and brought home and patiently coaxed back to something like normality.

Yet Ronald felt that, as far as she could, Jenny had put all that behind her.

Maud Massiter, however, had not ceased to hate the woman who had taken her husband from her. Maud Massiter was still trying to get revenge.

Since Lucy Corvill was far off in the safety of Virginia with her still-adoring husband Ned, out of reach of Maud Massiter, Maud Massiter would wreak vengeance on anyone connected with her. That meant Ned's sister Jenny Armstrong, who had had the impertinence to send a detective agent to question her about her missing brat.

It meant also that upstart husband of hers, Ronald Armstrong, who had the impertinence to stand for Parliament and actually win.

Ronald could imagine how she must have smiled at the news. A Member of Parliament is very vulnerable, especially if you have a toadying dependent in the House ready to jeer at him, spy on him, and harm him in any way possible.

Yes, Mrs Massiter was an enemy to fear, all the more so because it seemed as if she were no longer entirely rational.

CHAPTER NINE

Over the next few weeks Jenny and Ronald had discussions about what Baxter had discovered.

Should they confront Mrs Massiter? Could they bring any kind of suit against her?

'Baxter says we could. He says we could bring a suit for damages – but then, you see Jenny, it means the thing becomes public.'

'Yes. And once it's known that Mrs Massiter has been having Dinah watched, people are going to ask what reason she has for bothering Dinah. And though nothing definite might emerge, it could do harm.'

'What do you think, then?'

In the end, much though it went against the grain, they decided not to take legal action. This was partly because, at the moment, Mrs Massiter was doing nothing. There was of course no watch on the empty house in Chelsea, where only the housemaid remained as caretaker.

But Ronald could not resist a swipe at Thomas Unsworth. He sought him out at the exit from the Aye lobby where he was emerging after a vote on a first reading. Ronald took care there were plenty of witnesses.

'Mr Unsworth.'

'Yes? Oh, it's the woolly moth from the weaving district. What do you want, Armstrong?'

'Just a word, Unsworth. You have a patron who's made it easy for you to win and hold a Parliamentary seat – '

'What?' Unsworth said, startled. The face between the mutton-chop whiskers went red.

'I want you to pass on a message to the lady when you see her over the holiday. Tell her she can spend money on putting a man in the House of Commons, and hiring spies, and any other silly thing she likes. She'll be wasting her time.'

'I don't know what you mean,' spluttered Unsworth.

Other members, mostly Tories, had gathered to see what the fuss was about. Ronald turned to them.

'I want you fellows to know,' he said, 'that the Honourable Member for Spedlow and Nestholm is financed by a lady – a *married* lady, mind you, and not married to Unsworth.'

'What?' cried the listeners, greatly amused. 'Unsworth, you rogue!'

'What's more, the lady thinks so highly of him that she helped him get into Parliament – '

'Hi, hi, Unsworth! A political mistress?'

'It's a lie! It's slander! I'll – '

'You'll tell your lady friend she's making a fool of herself, and getting nothing for her pains. Tell her that she'll get nothing by it, because there's nothing to be gained from spying and harassing the Armstrongs and their friends.'

'Up the Borderers!' cried a wag. 'Is this going

to end up in sword play – claymores and all that?'

'I don't need a claymore to cut him down to size,' Ronald said with scorn. 'I'll admit for a long time he had me mystified. I couldn't understand why he seemed to hate me so much. But now I know he doesn't hate me. He's just doing what he's told – like a puppet on strings. Gentlemen, I introduce you to Thomas the Teetotum – give him a spin and round he goes, whatever direction you please.'

'Thomas the Teetotum,' chorused the group. 'I say, jolly good. Thomas the Teetotum!'

Ronald knew enough of the customs of the House to feel sure the nickname would stick. He had disarmed Unsworth. From now on, though he might continue his campaign of disruption and cause laughter, the laughter would be against him, even on the Tory benches.

Now that December had come with pleasant mild weather, Dinah decided she would like to accompany Jenny on one of her trips to London. 'I'd like to buy some Christmas presents,' she said. 'Now I've got more confidence, I'd like to have a go at the London shops.'

'I'm pleased to have your company,' Jenny said. 'But I'm only staying two days – will that be long enough for you?'

'Well, I'd like to stay longer. Clive wants to see the ships at the Pool of London and I hear there's a play for children on at Astley's, *Jack and the Beanstalk*. I'd like him to see that, he's never been to a theatre.' Nor have I, she might have added. In conversations with the ladies of Galashiels Dinah had acquired a great longing to see a play.

At first Jenny took it for granted that Dinah and Clive would stay at Eaton Square. But then there came consideration of the fact that Ronald was there, and would still be there when Jenny went home to the Borders. It would hardly be seemly for Dinah and Ronald to be alone in the same house (alone, it ought to be remarked, with six servants, but alone in terms of convention).

'I'll be right,' insisted Dinah. 'I'll put up at my own house in Chelsea.'

'Just you and Clive?' Jenny was thinking of the apprehension Dinah had felt there.

'Oh, I've grown out of all that,' Dinah said. 'Got more sense now, and know my way around better.'

This was a welcome step. Jenny was fond of Dinah, but she wasn't an ideal companion. If she could be encouraged to live a life of her own, so much the better.

The housemaid-caretaker at the Chelsea house was instructed to hire a cook and a boy to do the rough work. The house was made ready. Dinah had some slight feeling of 'coming home' when the door was opened to her with a flourish to reveal a Christmas tree decked with tinsel and the servants smiling a welcome.

For perhaps the very first time in her life, Dinah Eynsham was able to please herself. She had money in her pocket, a little boy to entertain, and the whole of London before her. There was no sly watcher outside the house to frighten her.

Unfortunately the weather turned very cold. Dinah slipped on the icy pavement on leaving Astley's with Clive at her side. Kind onlookers helped her into a hackney for home, where she was put to bed with hot water bottles and brandy. In the morning the doctor pronounced no bones broken but a severe bruising of hip and shoulder.

'A day in bed and then a day sitting up with cushions at your back,' he recommended. 'Then you can go out the following day if the weather turns milder.'

'But, doctor, I'm travelling home to Scotland tomorrow – '

'Dear lady, that would be very foolish. You would be very uncomfortable indeed, and hardly able to give attention to your little boy.'

For Dinah, that settled it. Her first thought was always for Clive. She bowed to the doctor's orders, even though it meant spending Christmas here in London.

That wasn't so very bad. The people of the Borders celebrated Christmas, but it was New Year that claimed their true allegiance. It wasn't so bad to miss Christmas, but they must be back for New Year.

Dinah and Clive quite enjoyed themselves, once Dinah could hobble out to a carriage to take him to see the sights. There were magic lantern shows, street performers with their clever dogs and monkeys, Punch and Judy at street corners.

Jenny had been worried when the letter came saying that Dinah wouldn't return on the expected date. When she wrote two days later that she would come home for New Year, Jenny felt she ought not to travel unescorted, especially if she were still suffering from the after-effects of the fall.

Archie Brunton was in London. He had travelled south by the same train as Jenny, 'accidentally' meeting her at Carlisle Station. For him this was an ideal chance to spend some hours in the company of the woman he loved without causing her too much embarrassment. For the look of the thing, he had stayed on in the capital after Jenny went home: to travel north with her again would have been a little too much of a coincidence. She was quite capable of having the compartment door locked against him if he tried that trick.

Besides, London was agreeable, even without Jenny. Archie looked up a few friends, spent late hours at his club, found himself a pretty lady companion for a couple of nights, and was on the whole pleased with the world.

His complacency was jolted when he received a telegram from Jenny: 'Mrs Eynsham not quite fit, please accompany her and Clive home to Galashiels, address as follows.'

'Damnation!' said Archie.

He couldn't refuse. It was the first time Jenny had ever asked anything of him, and if he failed her she would never ask again. He wanted her good opinion more than almost anything else in the world.

So, with a head that ached from too much champagne at the Royal Opera Hotel the night before, he went to Cheyne Terrace to call upon Mrs Eynsham.

Dinah was in the sitting room fondly watching Clive play one of his endless games with toy soldiers. When the maid came to say there was a gentleman caller, she could hardly believe it – her only visitors had been Jenny before she left, Miss Kinsman, who now had a post in Harrow, and sundry neighbours. When she looked at the card and saw 'Archibald Brunton Esquire' she was amazed.

'Good afternoon, Mrs Eynsham, Mrs Armstrong sends word that you're under the weather?'

'No – yes – well, I slipped and fell on my – ' She closed her lips on the uncouth word she had been about to utter. Miss Kinsman had warned her early in their acquaintance that it was unladylike to mention such portions of the anatomy under any name.

'Good heavens,' said Archie, genuinely concerned. 'What happened?'

She gave him a quick summary of the little accident and the five days of recovery.

'You're feeling well enough to travel?'

'Yair, I reckon. Still ache a bit, though.'

'Mrs Armstrong asked me to act as escort. What train are you taking?'

'Tomorrow's early train, the one from King's Cross. I want to get to Gatesmuir for New Year.'

'Of course, quite understandable. Have you reserved a compartment?'

'Not yet, I was going to send the kitchen boy – '

'I'll see to all that, if I may.'

'That's very kind of you,' Dinah said, at a loss. This gentleman had scarcely said two words to her hitherto.

'Have you a maid travelling with you?'

'Just me and my boy.'

Archie looked round. Near the window Clive crawled about, urging a miniature guncarriage and horses forward, uttering sounds appropriate to warfare.

'I see he's acquired a few toys in London.'

168

'Oh, yair, he's loved it. We saw the Changing of the Guard – he liked that. I've promised to take him to see Edinburgh Castle once we're home – he's mad about soldiers.'

For a moment Archie felt an impulse to join the boy on the floor and set up a mock battle. He had a sudden nostalgia for his own childhood, with its plaster fortress under the schoolroom table. But he checked himself. He was here to be polite, and to oblige Jenny, nothing more.

'Leave it to me, Mrs Eynsham, I'll see to the arrangements. I'll call for you tomorrow morning at seven. Will you have the lad bring down your trunks, ready to be put in the carriage?'

'But it's putting you to a lot of trouble, Mr Brunton.'

'Not at all. Anything to please Mrs Armstrong. Until tomorrow, then.'

The day was as dark as any December morning, and even darker because of the heavy clouds lowering overhead. The air was icy cold. Carefully Archie escorted Dinah down the path, across the pavement, and into the carriage. Clive skipped behind, hugging a wooden toy.

At the station Archie summoned up luncheon baskets, footwarmers, and travel rugs. The luggage was stowed in the van. Telegrams were sent on ahead to intermediate stations where hot tea or coffee would be ready for them to take aboard.

Having done his duty, so far, Archie helped Dinah and Clive into the compartment and prepared to suffer heroically the three hundred and fifty miles to Galashiels. As it turned out, he was pleasantly surprised. For once Mrs Eynsham had some sparkle about her. The stay in London had enlivened her, she talked with animation about the sights she had seen.

This was very much Archie's world. He too loved a play, loved German bands and performing poodles. He chatted comfortably about performances he had seen not only in London, Edinburgh and Glasgow, but in Paris and in New York.

Probably nothing in the world is so pleasing as being listened to with appreciation. Archie found he was enjoying himself. As for Dinah, this was just the kind of conversation she liked – one in which she could ask naïve questions and be answered without feeling patronised.

It was Clive who noticed the snow. 'Mama, look, that stuff's falling again!' He recalled it from the strange experience of last Christmas in Chelsea. 'They have it here too!'

'Good heavens,' Archie exclaimed. 'It's coming down quite fast. And what is it called, my little man?'

'It's snow,' Clive replied with some indignation. He'd seen it in book illustrations. But witnessing it coming down outside the train window was different from the pretty white flakes in the pictures. It was whirling aslant, driven by a northeast wind.

When the waiter brought their hot coffee at Newark, he was muffled up in an overcoat and woollen mittens. Questioned, he reported that the snow had been falling all day in Nottinghamshire and, as he had heard from travellers from the north, for a day and a half in Yorkshire and Northumberland.

As they drank their hot drinks the station-master came to apologise because the train was running behind time. 'It's the weather, I'm afraid. We're having some difficulty with the signals – the snow further north has settled on the arms so that they're too heavy to raise and lower. The telegraph advises of some frozen points too.'

'Oh dear,' said Dinah, at a loss in face of an element she had never encountered in her homeland. 'What time will we get into Newcastle, then?'

'Might be a matter of a couple of hours late. I'm very sorry, madam.'

She looked at Archie, who didn't seem too perturbed. Snow storms were something he was used to. She sat back. 'Drink your hot milk, Clive,' she admonished.

They handed back the tray, the doors were shut on the passengers, the guard whistled and waved his flag, the train grunted and puffed in the way Clive found so admirable, and they were off.

By and by it became clear to Archie, who knew the line, that they were taking a detour. After Selby should have come York, but they appeared to be making a wide loop to the east. Eventually they reached Pickering, where passengers alighted to try to make their way west towards York and perhaps the train connections they had now missed. Hot punch and newly-filled footwarmers were supplied.

Off they went again, Clive in high spirits at this adventure. The compartment was very cold, but they had plenty of travel rugs and comforters, besides a hot meal provided by the catering staff at Pickering. In fact, they felt so

171

snug that the grown-ups settled down for a nap after the hot pies and punch.

The dark winter day had faded into night when at last the train, after many stoppings, startings, and detours, edged into Newcastle. 'We had better stay over,' said Archie.

'But we won't be in Galashiels for New Year!'

'I doubt if we could get there before midnight, judging by the speed the train kept up on the main line. We had better put up at a hotel.'

He was unwilling, because it meant finding a hotel for Dinah and Clive and another for himself. Gossip being what it was, it would never do for the two adults to stay under the same roof.

Wisdom prevailed, they stayed over in Newcastle. Next morning they came out of their respective hotels to find the snow had stopped and the streets were being cleared.

The train for the Borders line was waiting at the platform. Their luggage was put on board, off they went once more. By now Dinah was heartily tired of trains. The cold ate into her bones despite the thick woollen cape and the fur tippet. The motion was monotonous when it occurred, though this journey had been more famous for its periods of waiting than its movement.

It was New Year's Day 1875, the day of one of the worst blizzards in living memory in the Scottish Borders. By midday, when they should have been at Galashiels, they were in the midst of a thick snow storm somewhere in the Cheviots.

The train chuntered and came to a stop. Half

an hour went by, during which the snow slackened and at last ceased. Archie wound his muffler round his neck, let down the window on the strap, and looked out. Ahead of them, right across the line, was a great bank of snow.

'We're stuck,' he said, bringing his head back in.

'Stuck?' Dinah echoed, aghast.

'Oh, goody!' shouted Clive. 'Can I get out and make a snowman?' Those too had featured in his picture books.

'Certainly not! Sit still, Clive – here, let me button up your coat.'

A five-year-old boy seeing for the first time a vast expanse of virgin snow was unlikely to sit still. 'Can't I get out, Mama? The train's standing still. Can I get out?'

'Of course not – it's cold and nasty out there.'

But a moment later there were sounds of voices approaching, and footsteps muffled by snow. Archie looked out again, to find the guard and the engine driver walking towards each other for a conference from the opposite ends of the train.

Carriage doors opened. Men jumped down to ask what was happening. 'I'll just get out and have a word,' said Archie.

'Me too – can I come?'

'Sit still, Clive – '

Too late. Clive had jumped down after Mr Brunton, who now approached the two train-men with an air of expecting to be taken into their confidence. The child clung to the tails of Mr Brunton's thick overcoat, loving the feel of the cold, soft snow crunching at each step. 'In his master's steps he trod . . .' The words drifted into his memory from hearing them sung at London street corners. So this was what it meant!

The news was that a snowdrift ten feet high blocked their way. What lay beyond was as yet unknown – perhaps other drifts over the line. The first thing was to go forward on foot to see how the land lay. The second was to go across the fields to a farm, in the hope of borrowing tools to dig them out, since the train was only furnished with six shovels.

The guard volunteered to go, and other passengers offered to accompany him in case he got into difficulties. The driver remarked that the firebox would provide the means to light fires along the embankment if they could find dry wood. 'It'll help keep the leddies warm if they'll step doon, but michty me, their lang skirts are likely to get draggled.'

Archie and Clive set off into the woods at the top of the embankment. Under the boughs, sheltered from the snow, there were twigs and pieces of wood. Arms full, they returned. Then the difficulty of descending the embankment with a burden became clear. Clive solved it by sitting down in the snow and tobogganing down. He arrived at the foot of the slope encased in snow to his waist, spluttering, red-cheeked, and laughing.

When the fires were lit, the womenfolk were helped down from the high carriages. Food was brought out and shared round. A picnic atmosphere developed. The driver, fireman and some of the passengers attacked the snow drift with the available shovels. Hot tea was made over the fire and carried to them by willing hands.

Dinah proved adept at making twig tripods to hang tin mugs or other containers over the fire. 'Where did you learn that?' someone asked.

'Oh, I've lived in the open back home,' she said with a shrug. 'Mind you, never in snow – that's real new.'

In fact, Dinah had been in outdoor camps and lived harder than perhaps any of the other people on the train. She had had 'adventures' before: once a bush fire had almost engulfed the shearing camp, once she'd been trapped with another woman in the midst of a stampede of wild horses, and once she'd been on a station where the men fought over cards so wildly that she had had to be rescued by none other than Ronald Armstrong.

That didn't mean she was enjoying herself particularly now. She didn't share her son's enthusiasm for snow. She thought it cold, wet, nasty stuff. Her clothes weren't designed for moving about in it – the hem of her skirts became sodden, and brushed against her ankles continually, making her suede ankle boots feel icy. Her hands became so frozen she could hardly feel them.

When the early winter night was falling, the party who had set out to find a farm came back. With them came a team of plough horses and four farm hands with rakes, pitch forks, dung shovels, buckets, and all the lamps the farm could spare.

'Mr Ramage's eldest boy's gone to get help, but the road's in sair condeetion so the guid Lord kens when he'll fetch any. In the nonst, gentlemen, the best thing is to keep digging through the nicht by the light o' the fires and the lamps.'

At this suggestion from the guard, teams were formed. As the first group was about to move away, the guard said, 'Oh, by the bye, Mr Ramage wishes us a' a Happy New Year and sent us this.'

'This' was a large drum which proved to contain spirits. A thimbleful was served out to every man, and the old wishes for health and prosperity were exchanged over the cup of kindness.

Clive begged for a sip. 'No, of course not,' scolded Dinah. But Archie had already stooped and let the little boy take the tiny dregs in the bottom of his cup.

'Ooh,' he said, 'it burns your tongue, Mr Brunton.'

'Yes, it's genevers. Do you like it?'

'Oh, yes, it's lovely,' said Clive manfully, trying not to screw up his face. Anything that Mr Brunton liked, he was determined to like.

He ran about with the other children, playing snowballs in the firelight until they were checked as too much of a hazard. Then they all began on a snowman. This character arose on the slope of the embankment, tilting a little but reaching fair proportions before sleep began to claim the little boy.

Dinah peeled off his snow-sodden clothes, put him into his flannel nightshirt, wrapped him in a travel rug, and tucked him into a corner of the compartment. He was in dreamland in a moment.

Later, when Archie had finished his stint at snow-digging, he too came into the compartment. The fires outside were dying down.

Only two were to be kept going overnight, as a means of warmth when the diggers rested, as a source of torches and light.

There was almost nothing left to eat in the picnic basket which they had replenished in Newcastle. Dinah offered Archie a roll and some German preserves. To drink he had weak tea made over the fire in an empty humbug tin.

'It isn't much after such a hard day,' she apologised.

'It's fine, thank you, Mrs Eynsham.'

'Listen, I know you're soaked to the skin so when you've eaten I'll get down to the track and you can change into dry clothes.'

'Thank you.' He felt an unexpected respect for her. Few ladies of his acquaintance would have thought of anything so practical.

As she clambered down to the ground she looked up at him. The firelight picked out the planes of her lovely face, put a glow into her dark blue eyes. 'Give me a call when you're ready,' she said – alas, in the flat nasal tones that were the flaw in her beauty.

When she got back into the compartment, Archie was sitting on the seat alongside Clive, clad in fresh trousers and two pairs of socks, a clean shirt, a woollen cardigan, and his jacket.

'Now how about you, ma'am – your skirts are very wet – '

'I'm just going to turn 'em up,' she said. 'If you'd be so good as to look the other way until I do that and wrap a rug around me . . .'

He stared out of the window while she took hold of her skirt hems, turned them outwards to the depth of about a foot, and sat down on the seat. Next she unbuttoned her soaked boots, peeled off her stockings, and folded a travel rug around herself. She swung her legs up, lay back along the seat, and surveyed herself in the dimness. Perfectly decent: she was cocooned so that her feet and ankles were invisible.

'Righto,' she said.

Archie made no reply. When she leaned over to look at him, she found he had gone to sleep with his forehead against the windowglass.

The night was icily cold. They slept fitfully, wrapping their rugs around themselves in attempts to keep warm. More snow fell. When in the dark morning Dinah was awakened by sounds of activity outside, she found the fires had been replenished. In their light she discovered that Clive had crept close to Archie for warmth. He was asleep with his head across Archie's knees.

The overnight snow had stopped, to be replaced by a glittering sky of stars. A vast pot of porridge had been brought from the farm. Smells of bacon sizzling over the flames reached her. Quickly she sat up, brushed back her rumpled hair, unfolded her skirts, found dry stockings in her overnight bag, and unwillingly forced her feet into her damp shoes.

She helped serve the morning meal. It was so like old times on the sheep station she felt estranged, displaced. Slowly the daylight strengthened. The teams of men went on with their work.

Clive appeared, badly packed into his outdoor clothes. 'Mr Brunton helped me,' he explained. 'Can I have some hot water, in this, please? He'd like to shave.'

Importantly he held out one of the horn cups

that was part of the picnic set. Dinah poured hot water into it, and watched him carry it with infinite care back down the line.

By mid-morning sounds could be heard from the other side of the snowdrift. A team of workers from the village of Hobkirk had reached them.

Six hours later the train steamed hesitantly into Galashiels. There was a reception committee awaiting them. Shouts of relief, greetings and questions filled the air as families and friends found each other. Jenny and Ronald were there with the Gatesmuir carriage. Dinah and Clive were wrapped in shawls and quilts, then gently put inside as if they were precious porcelain.

Archie Brunton found himself being ushered into the carriage. 'No, no, I'm for home – '

'Archie, man, the road's impassable. Come along, now, we'll put you up at Gatesmuir for the night.'

There was no help for it but to accept Ronald's invitation. At Gatesmuir, after a hot bath and a change of clothing from his luggage, Archie came downstairs to be put through an eager interrogation. How had they managed? Had they been frightened? How did Archie come to have bad blisters on the palms of his hands?

The travellers for their part leaned that the New Year celebrations at Gatesmuir had been very muted because of anxieties about their wellbeing. Word came through that travelling was very bad because of the weather. Delays of up to ten hours were being experienced. The roads around Galashiels were almost impassable because of snow but the streets of the town itself had been cleared after each snow-fall. Partygoers could not be deterred from going out for the usual New Year firstfooting.

Then came the news that the main Borders railway line was blocked. The party going on at Gatesmuir gave up music and dancing. Instead they sat around discussing the situation. At about one in the morning a new fall of snow had begun, and most people went home for fear of not being able to get through if they left it later.

Friends trudged on foot now to inquire about the travellers' welfare. 'Archie, you dog,' the men said to him with a nudge of conspiracy, 'trust you to be trapped on a snow-bound train with the handsomest woman in the Borders!'

'Dinna be sae daft!' he growled, seriously annoyed for once. 'I spent most of my time digging with a confounded dung shovel!'

Jenny sought him out on the morning of the next day to say she was sorry for having involved him in such an episode.

'Not your fault, Jenny. You couldn't have foreseen the weather.'

'I'm afraid you'll have to put up with a lot of knowing glances and silly jokes . . .'

'They'll get tired of it when they see I really have no interest in Mrs Eynsham.' His tone was tart.

'You found her a trial?'

'Well, she's got more to her than I used to think. But that harsh voice of hers . . .' He broke off. It wasn't gentlemanly to criticise a lady openly. He reviewed the hours he had spent with Clive, in search of something favourable to say. And to his surprise he found it. 'The boy,' he said, 'the boy is a charmer.'

The words surprised Jenny. 'A charmer? Even despite the ideas you have about him?'

'That he's Ronald's boy?' He shrugged. 'If he is – and I'm sure he is – he's inherited something extra from some other forebear. I can't tell you exactly what it is about him but he's a very nice little boy.'

Jenny could have told him what it was: admiration. Clive admired Mr Brunton. He talked about him as if he were a model of fortitude, kindness, bravery, and every other male virtue. 'Mr Brunton digged very hard to get us out of the snow.' 'Mr Brunton never got cross like some of the other gent-a-men.' 'The train-man asked Mr Brunton to see the food was shared out proper.'

As a rule Archie avoided children. But during the two days he was trapped by the weather at Gatesmuir Jenny saw that he watched Clive and Heather and little Max rushing about in the snow. She even saw him laughing to himself when Clive began ordering the others about in the building of a snowman.

'Mr Brunton says you have to pack the snow *hard*,' Clive explained. 'But you mustn't tread on it with your boots 'cos then it gets grey and nasty and the snowman won't look so good. The one we left on the 'bankment was lovely, with eyes and a nose and everything, and Mr Brunton give us a real cigar to put in his mouth.'

When Archie's carriage at last made its way along the snowy roads to fetch him home, it almost seemed he was loth to go. For the first time in his life, the Home Farm at Bowden seemed dull and shabby. It still contained the furnishing his mother had chosen forty-five years ago. She had said to him, 'When you bring your bride home then she can choose new carpets and curtains.'

That bride should have been Jenny – if Archie hadn't thoughtlessly thrown away the chance of marrying her. Now there was no one for whom to improve the house. Hitherto he had enjoyed its bachelor cosiness but now he though it merely out of date.

Jenny sensed something of this through the following months. Archie was changing. From being a self-satisfied 'gay dog' of a bachelor he was becoming a lonely middle-aged man. She noticed he continued to like little Clive, but alas that didn't seem to mean he was also attracted to Clive's mother. To Dinah he was polite always, and sometimes more friendly than in the past. But that was all.

When other men teased him about having shared a compartment with her overnight, he would smile and make the same reply: 'I shared the compartment with Mrs Eynsham *and* her alert little boy.'

'But that doesn't make any difference to the fact you've got first claim on a beauty that Mr Rossetti would love to paint!'

'Mr Rossetti is welcome to her. But if his ear is as sensitive as his eye, he might not want her.'

'Ach, she canna help the way she speaks! She's a colonial, poor soul.'

He would shrug and turn away from the wits of the Gentlemen's Club. Although the timbre of Dinah's voice worried him less than at first, his heart still belonged to Jenny.

There were other matters to take the attention of the Gentlemen's Club, which interested itself somewhat in politics. Mr Gladstone had at last, definitely and publicly, resigned the leadership of the Liberal Party in the House of Commons. In February, somewhat to the dismay of Ronald and Lord Thornieburn, the Marquess of Hartington had been elected to succeed Gladstone.

'I think he's too emotional,' His Lordship sighed to Ronald. 'I was told that he was practically in tears of rage with the Old Man about the Irish Universities Bill – that's not the kind of man we need as leader.

'But he kept to his principles, I hear. We need someone with a bit of determination, my lord. That Prussian fellow Bismarck is getting to be a real danger to us.'

'War? You don't really believe he meant to threaten a war with that stupid piece in the *Berlin Post*?'

'Not against us – not yet. But the French government is very worried about him, I hear.'

'Don't let us get embroiled, Armstrong,' begged the Earl. 'War's bad for trade – and you're doing so well for us with your Scottish Trade Group at the moment, it'd be a pity if exports were curtailed.'

Certainly the export business was booming as far as the tweed industry was concerned. Ronald had persuaded mill-owners to invest in the founding of technical schools, helped by a grant from the Scottish Office. Young technicians were coming into the work force who could deal with the ever-more complicated machines. Weaves and textures were being refined. Patterns Jenny would once have put at the back of her folder as being beyond the reach of her mills were now in production.

She had to spend more time at the mills with visiting foreign buyers. Luckily her household was running smoothly so that her attention could be given to business without feelings of guilt. Little Max continued to thrive, Heather still enjoyed her lessons at Thornieburn Hall, and Dinah had now so much confidence in herself that she travelled back and forth with Clive to the Chelsea house whenever she felt like it.

She had gone south at the beginning of August, to take Clive and herself to the untried pleasures of a South Coast seaside resort. Ronald had just returned to Gatesmuir for the Summer Recess. The countryside was green, the Braw Lads Gathering had been a more than usual success in the glorious sunshine of a fine summer. Jenny was feeling very pleased with life.

She should have known it was tempting fate to be so smug. And fate dealt her a blow that swept away every vestige of contentment.

The blow came in the form of a weighty envelope at the side of her breakfast plate. She took it up, drawing in an anxious breath at sight of the black border around it.

'What's the matter?' said her husband, looking up from the pages of *The Scotsman*. 'Oh . . .' He had seen the black edging.

'It's . . . it's from America, Ronald.'

He got up, came to her side. From America? It must be something about her brother Ned. She never mentioned him these days, but he knew she still loved him somewhere in the recesses of her heart. The brother she had looked up to all through her childhood, whose career she had furthered with all her might – and who had married a girl from whom she had received nothing but envy and enmity.

Jenny slit open the envelope. Within was a letter and some documents. The letter was on paper headed with the name of a law firm and written in characters produced by a strange new machine designed by a Mr Scholes for an American company owned by a Mr Remington. The hard, unfriendly characters leapt up to meet her eye.

Dear Madam, I write at the instigation of Mrs Edward Corvill to inform you with the deepest regret of the death of her husband, your brother Mr Edward Joseph Corvill, of The Hayes House, Richmond.

Mr Corvill passed on eight days ago after an illness of some duration. I enclose a medical certificate which you will see denotes the cause of death as scarlet fever inducing nervous excitation and toxaemia. There is no doubt that Mr Corvill contracted the infection during his solicitous visiting of the Negro areas of our fair city. An epidemic of scarlet fever had been in progress among the freed slaves for some weeks, but despite warnings of the inadvisability of visits, Mr Corvill took his duties too seriously to discontinue them.

My fellow citizens and I appreciated the work of Mr Corvill on behalf of the former slaves and attended his funeral with all reverence. In due time we shall erect a monument in honour of the assiduity he showed in the cause of educating and raising the Negro population.

His widow nursed him with great devotion during his illness, to such an extent that she is now prostrate from exhaustion and grief. She asks me to impart her sorrow to you, his loving sister. She also instructs me to say that she will arrive by the steamer *Parvilla* at Liverpool on or about the 15th August, from which port she will travel to Galashiels as soon as possible.

Mrs Corvill longs to see her homeland again; the climate of Virginia has unfortunately never suited her. She tells me that there are moreover legal matters to be settled which require her presence in Scotland even if her health had not made it seem advisable.

Enclosed is a copy of Mr Corvill's will together with copies of other documents, notably of a power of attorney granted by Mr Corvill to you in the year 1864. By the death of Mr Corvill this now becomes invalid and all powers return to Mrs Corvill, his legatee. However, at her request I hasten to add that she is content to have you continue to act in her behalf until she arrives in person in Galashiels.

Once more expressing my sincere regrets at your loss, I remain, dear madam,

Your humble and obedient servant,
Ludvic Guildstrant,
Attorney at law.

The letter fell from Jenny's shaking hands. Tears welled up to blind her.

'My dear lassie,' said Ronald, taking her up into his arms, 'dinna greet, it's a long, long time since ever you saw him.'

For a moment sobs stifled her. Then she exclaimed, 'To die . . . so far away, so far from home . . . Oh, poor, poor Ned!'

He held her close. 'It was his own choice, my jewel. He went of his own free will.'

'Never!' She wrenched herself free, almost glaring up at him through her tears. 'He went because he knew if he didn't take that woman away, we would have had her put in prison for what she did to our baby!'

'Hush, now, hush . . . That's all in the past, all over and forgotten.'

'No!' She shook her head from side to side. 'She's coming back! She's coming here! That woman!'

'Jenny – '

'I've spent eleven years trying to forget what she did, eleven years holding my tongue so that Heather should never be troubled by the memory of it! And now it's all going to be raked up again!'

'No, Jenny, we can deal with it calmly – '

'Calmly? When the mere mention of her name makes me want to scream and shout? I don't want to deal with it – I want never to think of her, ever, ever!'

Her husband held her in his arms and stroked her dark hair. He was thinking thoughts that he dared not yet express.

They had to 'deal with it'. For Mrs Edward Corvill was coming to claim her inheritance. And the truth was, the Waterside Mills on which their wealth and status were based belonged, not to the Armstrongs, but to the widow who was now crossing the Atlantic to claim them.

CHAPTER TEN

Twenty years ago, Jenny Corvill had been the unknown daughter of unknown but hard-working parents, websters in the Huguenot enclave of Edinburgh. Her brother Ned was destined also to be a weaver, but longed to go to university, to study philosophy, to be a gentleman.

For his sake, but also to make known her own talents as a designer, Jenny had presented a length of tartan to the Prince Consort for use in the recently rebuilt castle of Balmoral.

Money flowed in after that. Ned had fulfilled his ambition, gone to Edinburgh University. Jenny had wrested her father from his safe, snug world to set up by the Gala Water in the Borders, where the best woollen cloth in Scotland was being made.

A couple of years later Ned returned to them in triumph with a philosophy degree – and a young bride. A Dresden shepherdess girl, with pale gold hair, milk-and-roses complexion, a shy, pleasing manner.

Sitting now at her breakfast table, the memory flooded into Jenny's mind, as fresh now as when the scene had presented itself before her eyes: Lucy stepping down from the carriage in her delicate finery, looking up to seek their approval. A faery-like creature, and clearly adored by her young husband.

The family, startled at first, had been prepared to take Lucy to their bosom. Yet by and by it became clear Lucy was not pleased with her lot. She found old Mr Corvill's strict religious beliefs hampering, the simplicity of the household disappointed her. She had evidently thought she was marrying into the Borders aristocracy, with liveried footmen and a French chef at her command.

Perhaps out of boredom, Lucy set her cap at the man everyone said was going to marry her sister-in-law Jenny. Archie Brunton was quite amenable – he never said no if a pretty woman seemed to want his attentions. But Lucy took it too seriously. She had a tendency to do so; she wanted her life to be a fairytale come true, with herself as the princess and an endless succession of gallant knights coming to kneel before her.

It was because of Lucy that Archie had to leave Galashiels suddenly. His imperious mother ordered him away when she learned about the affair. Jenny remembered how disappointed old Mrs Brunton had been, and how everyone thought he had jilted Jenny. The fact was she had turned her back on him when she discovered the liaison between her almost-fiancé and her sister-in-law.

It seemed to her, when she looked back, that disaster was inherent in the marriage between her brother and Lucy. They were both weak people. Ned needed always to be buoyed up by grandiose schemes, idealistic ambitions. Lucy needed to be loved and admired. Certainly Lucy resented the fact that she wasn't mistress at Gatesmuir, that she wasn't even second to her mother-in-law but must take third place, a long way behind Jenny Corvill, 'the Mistress'.

When at length Jenny married Ronald Armstrong, Lucy was scornful – a mere workman, how embarrassing! Yet she couldn't hide her envy for their marriage with its open affection, its comradeship, and later its first child – a pretty, glowing little daughter they called Heather.

Boredom was always a problem with Lucy. Left at home while husband Ned was off on the latest of his grand undertakings – the raising of funds to help the Union Army in the American Civil War – she found solace in playing with Jenny's baby. Heather in return adored her. Here was an angelic adult who indulged her in every way, spent time with her, gave her sweet things and toys, never scolded or rebuked her.

The nursemaid said to Jenny, 'I canna do a thing with the baby, mistress. She's getting as spoiled as a rug!'

So Jenny, to give Lucy some occupation, had suggested her sister-in-law should find and furnish a London house for William Corvill & Son. It was a justifiable outlay; they needed a place where they could pay off social debts, entertain foreign buyers, and be available when the Royal Family wished them to come to the Palace on business.

This was where Lucy Corvill met Harvil Massiter. She fell wildly, blindly in love. In haste Jenny got her home again to Galashiels, out of harm's way. She knew later she had underestimated the strength of Lucy's obsession with the rash, handsome gambler. An elopement was arranged, Lucy stole out of Gatesmuir at dead of night to a waiting postchaise.

But, against commonsense and to the horror of her lover, she took to the rendezvous in London the baby she had come to love as a sweet, animated doll – she took Jenny's little girl, Heather.

Heather was then about a year and a half old. She disappeared off the face of the earth at that point. Massiter, faced with a mistress who expected to take someone else's baby with them to Rome, got rid of the child by handing her to a stranger at the Holborn inn. He got rid of Lucy too who, in tears of guilt over Heather, was by no means the pleasant companion he had hoped for. He abandoned her in Dover, taking with him all her money and jewellery.

Jenny saw again in her mind's eye the scene when at last the police tracked down the run-away wife. Lost and betrayed, Lucy was hysterical. To get any sense out of her Jenny had had to stifle her own grief, cosset and pet her, buy her new clothes and fresh linen, assure her she should have a maid to do her hair.

But nothing could be learnt about Heather's fate. All Lucy knew was that Massiter had been angry with her for bringing the baby, had taken Heather from her, and had given her to a woman to take home. 'A respectable woman . . . he assured me she was a respectable woman . . .'

A year of anguish had followed for Jenny. She refused to believe what the police hinted – that her little girl was already dead. Why should anyone bother to convey her the long way home to Galashiels? Much more likely the 'respectable woman' pocketed the guinea and threw the baby over the parapet into the Thames.

'No,' Jenny insisted stubbornly. 'I should know if she were dead. She's alive, I feel it.'

So much the worse, seemed to be the general view. A pretty girl baby, lost in the stews of London . . .

Ronald Armstrong had believed it certain his daughter was dead. His one thought was revenge. He would have Lucy Corvill punished by the extreme rigour of the law. The penalty for abduction was death by hanging.

Jenny had never cared whether Lucy lived or died. Her one obsession was to find her baby. It was Ronald who consulted lawyers, listened to counsel's opinion, wrote and rewrote the case as he knew it against his sister-in-law.

All in vain. As luck would have it, no one but Massiter had actually seen Lucy with the baby – and Massiter was off on the Continent somewhere, unlikely ever to give evidence for or against her. Coached by solicitors hired by her adoring husband, Lucy now said that she knew nothing about what had happened. Her mind was a blank. She was ill, unfit to give evidence. She remembered nothing about a baby, or travelling to London by stealth, or taking jewellery belonging to Ned.

Challenged, Ned had protested that his wife wasn't to blame. Harvil Massiter was the villain of the piece, in some way he had mesmerised poor, innocent, trusting Lucy. Poor Lucy was innocent of anything except falling temporarily under the spell of his evil fascination.

Yet Ned had sense enough to be aware his

wife could not be accepted back into society. Willingly he entered into an arrangement whereby Jenny should continue to manage the Waterside Mills, from the profits of which she would send him an income. He for his part would take his wife abroad, where her history would be unknown and where time could heal her wounds.

For some years now he had been living in Richmond, Virginia, working to set up schools for the slaves freed by Abraham Lincoln, finding paid employment for them when they could read and write. He had written once to Jenny, when the news filtered through that Heather had been recovered at last from a foundlings' home. He had taken it for granted that the little girl was unharmed, unchanged. He hadn't enough imagination to think what a year's separation in hostile surroundings could do to a child so young. He had expected and asked for Jenny's forgiveness – not for himself but for Lucy.

Jenny didn't even bother to reply to the letter. For eleven years the only communication had been through their men of business. Each quarter a handsome sum of money was made available to a bank in Richmond, and each quarter the arrival of the certified cheque was acknowledged.

But now everything was changed. Ned . . . poor Ned . . . had died. Jenny tried to picture him, but she couldn't imagine what he had looked like after eleven years' parting. All his life wanting to achieve something fine, needing to lose himself in great dreams and sometimes almost coming close to his goal . . . but marred by self-doubt, lacking in willpower, and besotted by the lovely innocent-looking girl he had married.

She was coming here – Lucy Corvill, his widow, the woman responsible for some of the worst things that had happened in Jenny's life. Jenny's mother had died as a result of the shock of Lucy's flight. Heather had been lost for a year: a year of agony for Jenny but how much worse for the little girl, abandoned and terrified among cruel strangers? Once she was unearthed by Mr Baxter in the foundling asylum, there had followed three years of almost complete silence on her part – the power of utterance seemed to have been torn from her. Only Jenny had known she really could speak, a few whispered words hardly audible except to the listening ear of a mother.

Those long, anxious years: coaxing the child back to confidence in her own safety, building around her a shield of love and care and kindness . . . Almost to the exclusion of anything else, Jenny had worked to bring her daughter back to something like her old self.

In so doing, she had almost lost her husband. Indirectly, Lucy's actions had been the cause of an estrangement between Jenny and Ronald. He had grown weary of her obsession with the wellbeing of Heather. He had chosen to go to Australia when an excuse offered. And there he had become involved with Dinah.

Lucy Corvill. The name sounded almost like a curse in Jenny's ears. Everything bad in her life had been associated with Lucy Corvill.

Her head whirling, Jenny sank down at the table, pushing aside the crockery, resting her forehead on her folded arms to hide her horror and dismay at the thought of seeing Lucy again.

Ronald knelt at her side. 'Come, love,' he coaxed, 'it's got to be faced.'

'No!' It was a muffled sob.

The door of the dining room opened. Thirley came in, alarmed by the sound of the Mistress's raised voice – an unheard of thing at Gatesmuir.

'Is anything wrong, sir?'

He frowned at her. 'Fetch your mistress a glass of brandy.'

She hurried to the sideboard, poured the brandy, brought it back. Taking it, Ronald said, 'Send a message to the mill office – the mistress won't be coming this morning.'

'Yes, sir. And yourself?'

'I'm not expected there, I have another appointment.'

She waited for instructions concerning that. He nodded dismissal. She hurried down to the kitchen. To the scullery-maid she said, 'Run out and tell Murdoch to go to the mills. The mistress wilna be there the morn.'

Off scuttled the maid. Cook said, 'Is she ill?'

'Awfu' upset. You remember I said there was a black-bordert letter in the post? It's that.'

Cook stirred thoughtfully at the sauce on the gas range. 'Ye should tell Baird.'

'Aye.' To the under-housemaid she said, 'Up to the first floor – Mistress Baird's either in the day nursery or the main bedroom. Tell her the mistress is taken badly.'

Baird came downstairs at a run. She found the scene in the dining room almost unchanged. Ronald was trying to persuade Jenny to take another sip of the brandy, Jenny was half-lying on the table with her face hidden.

The papers were lying on the floor. One glance at the black edging was enough to tell Baird what she needed to know. She elbowed Ronald out of the way, knelt beside Jenny with her arm over her trembling shoulders.

'There, there, my wee dove. There now, come on, look at me, look at old Baird. Come now, lift your head, my lassie, let me see your face. Och, you're blae as a slate. Now, now, then, come on, let's you and me help each other up the stairs. Up you come now, dearie, lean on me.'

Her voice was like the cooing of pigeons. She raised Jenny to her feet, letting her lean almost all her weight against her. They began to move towards the door. 'We'll go up to the wee boodwar and we'll hae a wee rest and a cup o' tea and a crack and you'll tell Baird a' aboot it. Come now, this is the way.'

In helping Jenny up she had scooped the papers and stuffed them in her apron pocket. She said over her shoulder to Ronald, 'Let you go oot for a stroll in the grounds. In a wee while she'll be better.'

'I've got to be in Kelso by lunchtime. It's an appointment I must keep.'

'Aye, aye, jist like a man – the roof o' the house comes doon on his wife's heid and he wants the world to wag on just the same.' With this tart remark she went out, leaving Ronald Armstrong feeling, as he often did, that she was closer to Jenny than any mother could have been.

In the boudoir Baird settled Jenny on the chaise longue. She brought a glass of water with a drop of hartshorn added. As Jenny was about to take a sip, she suddenly thrust it aside. 'I'm . . . I'm going to be sick!'

She rushed out to the bathroom. While she was gone Baird took the papers from her pocket, glanced through the letter, and with a tightening of the lips put it on the table.

Jenny came in, shivering, wiping her lips on her handkerchief. She sank down on the chaise longue.

'I dinna wonder you lost your breakfast,' Baird said in a grim voice. 'So she's coming back, yon vixen.'

'Why is she coming?' Jenny cried. 'She could have all the legal affairs handled by an agent.'

'Dinna fash yourself aboot her. Let her come. If she so much as sets foot inside the gates, I'll throw her out bodily my own self.'

'She won't come here. But she'll be in the town. I might see her – meet her – I can't bear to think – '

'Ach!' Baird said in disgust. 'How she'd triumph, to think she'd reduced you to a frichted, shivering jelly! She always wanted that – to have the high hand over you.'

If it was calculated to bring Jenny out of her trembling, it worked like magic. She sat up, straightened her shoulders, then looked about as if slowly becoming aware of her surroundings again. 'It's cold.'

'Not at all, not at all – but it's the shock of it. Bide a wee.' Baird brought a Shetland lace shawl from the bedroom to put around her shoulders. That done, she rang the bell. Thirley appeared like an elderly elf from a flower bud. She had been hovering out on the landing.

'Fresh hot tea,' Baird ordered, 'and tell Cook in a minute I'll want toast wi' honey spread thick. Oh, and tell the maister – in half an hour he can come up for a wee converse.'

Thirley beckoned Baird to the door with a jerk of her head. 'Wha's deid?' she whispered.

'It's Mr Ned in Americky. Now off wi' ye.'

Jenny drank the tea gratefully, and though at first when the sweet toast came she was sure she couldn't swallow it, she obeyed Baird's orders. She felt better after a few minutes – the icy grip of shock relaxed about her heart, she could breathe more deeply, her hands began to feel steadier, her shivering ceased.

When Ronald came upstairs he found her lying back on the chaise longue with the shawl loose on her shoulders, a tartan rug thrown across her feet. Baird let him in, saying as she took her leave, 'Easy does it. She's as hurt as if she'd been stabbed, mind.'

He drew a low buttoned chair to the side of the chaise longue and sat down. He took her hand. 'My treasure, you gave me a fright.'

'I'm sorry. I wouldn't have believed I could be . . . could be so silly.'

'We have to talk about the situation. Do you feel well enough?'

'You mean, to talk about it without going into hysterics?' A smile curved her lips, still pale from stress and horror. 'I'll try.'

'She's coming here, that's definite. On the *Parvilla*, arriving on or about the fifteenth. I looked up the shipping list – the *Parvilla* is due to dock on tomorrow's tide.'

'Tomorrow!'

'Good weather in the Atlantic, favourable conditions; all sailings are ahead of time at the moment. I presume she'll stay over the Sunday and perhaps the Monday to get her land legs. That means we can expect her here on the Tuesday.'

'By here you mean in Galashiels – '

'No, wife, I mean *here* – at Gatesmuir.'

'She's not to come here!'

'Now, now – calmly, Jenny. Without hysterics. Your brother's widow is coming back to her homeland after eleven years' absence. She *must* come to Gatesmuir.'

'I forbid it!'

Ronald pressed her hand and was silent.

After a moment she said, 'I don't care what it looks like. I'm not having that woman in my house.'

'You have to give her hospitality. You *have* to. If you don't, all the gossips in Galashiels will start up – '

'I tell you, I don't care what people say – '

'Perhaps not, but think of the reverberations. I'm the kind of person who ought to avoid being gossiped about. How will it sound – the Member for West Tweed is such an eccentric he won't give bed and board to his sister-in-law?'

'Ronald, I'd do anything in the world to preserve your good name – but not this!'

'The story will infallibly get to the ears of Mrs Massiter. She's got her listening ear in Parliament who will pick it up and pass it on. Don't forget – Mrs Massiter is just longing to know that Lucy Corvill is back in the country again.'

Jenny made a fierce, dismissive gesture. 'Let Lucy take her chances with Mrs Massiter. I don't care a jot if Mrs Massiter has her tarred and feathered!' She glared defiance at Ronald.

He nodded and drew a slow breath. 'And how,' he said, in clear and careful tones, 'are you going to explain all that to Heather?'

Silence fell in the pretty room. The August sunshine, muted by the yellow blinds, touched the gilding on the book bindings, the picture frames, the screen that stood in front of the empty fireplace.

Jenny had always taken care never to say anything that would cause Heather to remember the awful period of her life when she was lost in the slums of the Rookery and afterwards in the foundlings' home. Once, during a period when she was attending day school in Galashiels, she had asked, 'Haven't I got any uncles and aunts? All the other girls at school seem to have them. And cousins.'

'No cousins,' Jenny said. 'You have an aunt and uncle, in America.'

'America? What are they doing there?'

'Your Uncle Ned works to help educate the freed slaves. There was a war in America a few years ago, and after that the slaves on the plantations in the south were set free, and Uncle Ned helps raise money for schools, things like that.'

'What is he like? Have you got a picture?'

Jenny took out the old album from the cupboard of her boudoir, and found an early photograph of her brother – faded now, taken when he first put on his graduate's cap and gown.

'He's handsome,' Heather said in her creaky little voice. 'Like you, a bit – so he's your brother.' She was working out relationships. 'What is the aunt like?'

'Very pretty.'

'What's she called?'

'Lucy. Aunt Lucy.'

'Do they write often? May I see the letters?'

'They don't write.'

'Not at all?'

'No.'

'Not even at New Year?'

'No.'

'Do you write to them?'

'No.'

'Why not?'

'We've drifted out of touch.' She didn't want to dignify the situation by making it seem dramatic – no family quarrel, no tragic estrangement, but instead a simple drifting apart.

'May I write to them, Mama?'

That had given Jenny a fright. For a moment she thought of saying yes, and then when Heather gave her the letter for the post, merely destroying it. When she received no reply, the idea of rediscovering lost aunts and uncles would lose its attraction.

But deceit was never a good idea. 'My pet,' she said, 'they have no children of their own so we must suppose children don't interest them. I hardly think they would want to start a correspondence with you, but if you wish, you can write.'

'No,' said the little girl, colouring. 'I just wondered if I had aunts and uncles, like other girls.' It was something that always troubled her – being like other girls. She knew she was different – less inclined to join in games, to chatter over dolls. Where the difference came from, she could never tell. She'd thought it might have to do with the lack of relatives. *Something* must account for the barrier that seemed at that time to lie between her and the rest of the world.

From then on she sometimes mentioned the aunt and uncle in America – if some item of news brought up the subject of slavery, or voluntary work in education. When Jenny said the distant but kindly pair were still serving humanity, she seemed content.

But now . . . Now Aunt Lucy was coming to Galashiels. If Jenny refused to have her in their house, Heather would be aghast. Moreover, she would demand explanations. Heather had just had her thirteenth birthday and was proving an intelligent, thoughtful, sensitive young lady. She couldn't be fobbed off with polite lies. She would know that all the conventions of family warmth, social expectation, and simple humanity demanded that the widow of her mother's brother must be given bed and board at Gatesmuir.

'We'll say the house is being decorated. I'll send for Macdivitt today – '

'Jenny, don't be absurd! What are you going to do – move us all out and have the painters in? At a moment's notice?'

'No, but we can say the guest rooms are being redecorated.'

'And when Heather comes home this weekend she finds you've made this sudden decision, all at once, without having even mentioned it last weekend? And almost simultaneously with the news that Mrs Corvill was coming?'

It was a mad idea, and she gave it up with a hopeless gesture of dismissal.

'I don't want her in my house, Ronald,' she said, tears welling up in her dark eyes. 'I can't bear the thought.'

'But she lived here before, dearest – '

'And tarnished it, tainted it! Nothing was ever right again after she came in at our door!'

'It'll be different this time, Jenny. You won't have to think about sparing the feelings of your family, your brother. They're all gone now, past caring what Lucy says or does. You can handle her if you have only yourself to think of. And perhaps after all, it need only be for a few days, a week, perhaps. We can say we want to take the children to the seaside – join Dinah in Brighton, maybe. We can leave her to the servants.'

'Oh, God,' groaned Jenny, 'everyone would blame us for not taking her with us!'

Her husband frowned and looked away. It was time now to say the most difficult thing. 'We have to take this one step at a time, Jenny lass. And here is the next step. We can't afford to be in open opposition to Lucy Corvill because we have to have friendly discussions with her lawyers.'

He felt her gaze upon him and looking up, met her eye. They said nothing for a moment.

'Oh.'

'You've just realised the position?'

'It had been swept out of my head by my . . . my revulsion at the idea of seeing her.'

'But you do see, Jenny . . . Hate her though we may, we can't afford to despise her. She's our employer now.'

Jenny clenched her fists, hit the curved

wooden edge of the chaise longue with them. 'Damn her!' she gasped. 'Damn her! Of all the people in the world to be given control of my mills – *my* mills, *my* work, the things I've built up through a whole lifetime!'

The original mill had been bought in the name of William Corvill; it still bore his name. When he died, William, like the good Huguenot he was, had left everything to his son, giving only the house of Gatesmuir to his wife and daughter 'so that they might always have a roof over their heads'. He took it for granted that his son, like a good Huguenot, would never see them in want.

Jenny, though she was the moving spirit in the business, had only ever been an unpaid manager and designer. She had never had a salary for the work she did, although, when she married Ronald and he took over the management, Ronald had been given a contract and appropriate remuneration.

Nevertheless, under the power of attorney Ned had signed when he left the country, Jenny had had the power to handle everything. She had used the profits wisely, reinvesting, expanding. She had raised Ronald's salary, though it had not seemed right or proper to pay herself one. She was herself a Huguenot, bound by their Protestant traditions – only the men of the family could earn money through the family business.

If it was a paradox, it was one which had worked well and with which she had lived unquestioningly. But now came the moment of truth.

Their livelihood depended on the mills. And

the mills were now the property of the hated Lucy Corvill.

'She won't want to change anything,' Ronald said quickly. 'She'd be mad if she did. Money has been rolling in to the Corvills all the time they've been in Richmond. She'll want that to go on – why not? And you know what she's like – she's coming back to Galashiels because it's probably part of the "devoted widow" character she's playing now. Remember what the lawyer said? "Prostrate with grief and exhaustion" or some such havers. Once she's got all the sympathy and admiration she thinks she deserves, she'll get bored and want to go to Glasgow or Edinburgh or somewhere.'

'Yes.'

'I know I'm right,' he insisted. 'All we have to do is be objective about this. Just let her come, be polite, and get rid of her with as little disturbance to our affairs as possible.'

'Yes.'

'You agree?'

'Yes.' Once again that small, muffled voice. He knew that her intelligence was agreeing with all he said, but her heart was at war with it.

There was nothing more to be done for the moment. He must let her have time for the situation to sink in. 'I must go,' he said. 'I'm due in Kelso by one o'clock – they're holding a lunch in my honour at the Manufacturers' Society, in aid of funds for the new school. I *have* to be there.'

She nodded, her head bent and her face turned away from him.

'Jenny . . . Are you going to be all right?'

'Yes.'

He bent over her, kissed her cheek, hugged her shoulders, and left her.

As soon as he had closed the doors, the tears she'd been holding in flooded from her eyes. She laid her head against the wooden edging of the chaise longue and wept. She hated herself for the weakness, but she couldn't help it. Pain at the wounds of the past, revulsion at the thought of the future, dismay at her own feeling of defencelessness, and something like fear . . . all of these clawed at her, and she could only find refuge in tears.

Baird returned. 'Weel, whit's next, mistress?'

Jenny sat up, mopping her eyes with a sodden handkerchief.

'Tell Thirley to prepare the guest room, Baird.'

'Eh?' exclaimed her maid, her lined face suddenly reddening with anger. 'You're no having her *here*?'

'It seems we have no alternative.'

'Dinna do it! You'll regret it!'

Jenny met the angry eyes. 'I know it,' she said. 'No one knows it better than I do.'

CHAPTER ELEVEN

The return of Mrs Edward Corvill to Galashiels was a subject of the greatest interest to the townsfolk. Her absence had lasted nearly twelve years. It was known that her husband had taken her to 'foreign parts' – Ned Corvill, off on one of his great schemes to improve the world.

Now, they learned, Ned Corvill was dead. Mrs Corvill was remembered as a very beautiful lady, always finely dressed in the latest fashions. Women looked forward to her arrival – new styles from abroad, something to discuss and compare.

Some murmured that there had been a great mystery about Mrs Corvill's departure. The police had been involved. But wait, the police had been involved because the baby went missing at about the same time. True, there had been a great upheaval in the family, but what else could you expect? The Mistress had been beside herself with grief over the child.

It was difficult now to recall the course of events. Heather had come home again after a year's absence. Poor wee soul . . . Never quite right, afterwards. Everybody had taken to calling her 'the dummy' because she seemed unable to speak. But that was wrong, she could speak now, though seldom did. Howsomes-ever, that had naught to do with Mrs Corvill, for was it no the case that she had been in the Western Indies or some siccun a place?

Now here she was coming home. A poor lorn widow. Young, too – she could only be in her thirties still.

All agog, the town awaited her appearance.

She stepped off the train on a fine August day, with the sunshine coming through the glazed roof to catch the soft gold of her hair. She was wearing a plain travelling suit of silky black batiste trimmed with fine black lace, and her straw bonnet was covered with soft black gauze so that it looked as if a silky haze sur-rounded her. The bonnet strings, of broad stiff ribbon, were tied in a bow against a milky white cheek. Through the bonnet veiling, her eyes gleamed like forget-me-nots seen in the mist.

The elegance, the richness of her dress would have been enough to make the women-folk stare. But . . . at her heels walked a small boy, with a face as black as pitch under a little pillbox hat of pale blue. The rest of him was attired in a suit of sky-blue sateen, bum-freezer jacket trimmed with two rows of silver but-tons, trousers with silver braid down the side seams. His hands were in small white cotton gloves, his feet in shiny black shoes with silver buckles.

'Guid God, what's yon?' cried the station-master's wife, who had come out of their house to witness the arrival.

'Ssh, Marion it's her page boy.'

'Page boy? Whit'n the world does she need a page boy for?'

The answer was clear from the evidence before them. The page boy was needed to carry her parasol and a little travel basket containing smelling salts, fan, leather-bound novel, and a purse of money. He also opened the carriage door for her when she was conducted to the Armstrongs' brougham. The little crowd waited with interest to see what the page boy would then do – did he sit with the lady on the carriage seat? No, he climbed swiftly on to the box with the coachman and there sat, looking straight ahead, the travel basket on his knees.

The townsfolk were divided about the reception offered to the widow. Should the Mistress and her husband not have come to the station in person to greet their relative? But then, on the other hand, word had come from the servants that Mistress Armstrong was quite overset by the unexpected news of her brother's death. She'd aye been fond of that strange brother of hers. And true it was that she hadn't been to the mill office since the letter came from overseas.

While the luggage was loaded on the brougham the gardener's boy, who had sneaked out to watch the fun, ran home to Gatesmuir. 'Miss Thirley, Miss Thirley, d'ye ken what the lady's brocht? A wee blackamoor.'

'What?' cried Thirley.

'Aye, a wee black laddie aboot ten years auld, in a wee fancy suit – he holds her belongings and sits wi' the coachman.'

'Do ye say so?' gasped the housemaid. She ran upstairs to convey this astonishing news to the Mistress, who was sitting in icy calm in the drawing room.

'You mean a page boy?' Jenny said, surprised but too numb to sound so. 'You'd best make a room ready for him on the top floor, through it seems odd to make a little boy of ten sleep on his own in a strange house . . .'

Ronald was shaking his head in disbelief. 'What can she want with a page boy, Jenny? It seems . . . pretentious.'

'She always wanted liveried footmen,' Jenny remarked. 'Perhaps this is the nearest she could get. And besides, it may be the custom in Virginia.'

'She was always a little . . . odd. D'you think she's a wee bit peculiar? Gone astray a little in her wits because of losing Ned?'

Jenny gave her husband a glance of cool anger. 'She's not grief-stricken, Ronald. Don't begin by falling into any traps. She never cared a fig for Ned and she doesn't care now he's dead – of that you can be sure.'

'But a page boy, in a pale blue uniform . . .'

'I really don't care about her page boy, Ronald. She can bring a whole plantation of servants with her. I only want to see the back of her and everything to do with her as soon as possible.'

'Of course.'

The brougham rolled up the steep drive. They heard Thirley open the door, heard the footsteps across the hall. The drawing room door opened.

'Mrs Corvill, mistress.'

Jenny rose.

Her enemy walked in.

The gauzy veil was thrown back from the lovely features. Tears stood in the blue eyes like dew-drops on harebell petals.

'Jenny!' cried Lucy, moving forward with her black-gloved hands clasped. 'Oh, Jenny, how I've longed to be with you! You are the only one who can understand my loss!'

Despite all she could do, Jenny found herself being embraced. The natural reaction was to take hold of Lucy so that they shouldn't stagger and fall. She felt the shaking shoulders within her grasp. She thought, Perhaps she's really grieving. After all, twelve years . . . Perhaps she's changed.

Thus Thirley was able to report to the servants' quarters with absolute truth that the two women were weeping in each other's arms as she closed the door on them.

When she pictured this meeting, Jenny had wondered how she would survive it without shrinking from her sister-in-law. But now it was over, and Ronald was conducting the weeping woman to a chair, asking if there was anything he could do.

'My vinaigrette . . . in my travel basket . . . my page has it.'

Ronald put his head out the door. A small figure in sky-blue was sitting on the hall settle with the basket gripped between gloved hands. Uncertain whether this little creature spoke English, Ronald jerked his head. The boy leapt up, hurried into the room.

He knelt at Lucy's side, offering the basket as if to a goddess. Lucy's face was hidden by her lace handkerchief. Jenny found the restorative, took out the stopper, brought it close to Lucy's face. Lucy leaned away from it, sobbed two or three times, then sat up, dropping her hands.

'Oh, what a fool you must think me!' she

said in a broken voice. 'But this has been such a dreadful time. Jubal, a handkerchief.'

The little gloved hands delved in the basket. Another lace handkerchief was offered. She took it without glancing at him, patted her eyes and lips, straightened the black lace widow's cap which lay so beautifully among her soft hair. In her slight movements, she discovered Jubal was kneeling on her skirt hem. 'Jubal!' she said.

The boy squirmed aside, looking scared.

'So your name's Jubal,' Jenny said, stooping down to him.

'Yes'm,' he murmured, hunching his shoulders.

'And you've come all this way with Mrs Corvill.'

'Yes'm.'

'He's the son of my maid, the one I had to leave behind in Richmond. Poor Selina, she was too scared to make the journey overseas, devoted though she was. So instead she insisted – absolutely insisted – that I take Jubal to look after me. And he does, don't you, Jubal?'

'Yes'm.'

By previous arrangement, Thirley now appeared with a tray bearing decanters and ratafia biscuits. This was placed on a side table. 'What about the wee boy?' Ronald said, as he prepared to pour. 'He'll not be taking port wine or Marsala, I take it?'

'Good heavens, what an idea. Er . . . Thirley, isn't it?'

'Yes, madam.'

'Thirley, you can take him to the servants'

hall now, I don't need him for the moment. Go along, Jubal.'

'Yes'm.'

'Oh, goodness, don't be so silly, boy. Leave the basket here – what good would it be in the servants' hall?'

'Yes'm.'

The page followed Thirley. As he closed the door after the two of them he cast a glance back at his mistress. It was frightened yet it held appeal – she was, after all his only link with home in a strange place.

Jenny caught the glance. She smiled in encouragement. As the door slipped shut she saw the glint of his eye, rimmed with tears.

'Lucy, don't you think that little lad needs a –'

'He's all right,' Lucy said, 'although we had a very uncomfortable rail journey. Something went wrong with the arrangements for our refreshments. I must say, however, that I was agreeably surprised at the comfort of the voyage across the Atlantic. The most favourable time of year, of course, balmy winds and calm seas. But the smoke from the funnel is such a nuisance – it makes black smuts on white clothing.' She glanced down at the black folds of her skirts. 'Not that that perturbs me for the present.'

Ronald was lifting decanters. 'What will you take, Lucy? I think I said, there's port and Marsala, and a dry sherry.'

'A little sherry, I think. You cannot imagine how agreeable it is to be offered wine! In Virginia, the refreshments are mostly based on spirits, which you know are very bad for the skin, besides being inelegant for a lady.'

'I suppose so.' He brought the sherry, offered the biscuits. For Jenny he poured mineral water imported from Baden. He himself took a hearty swallow of Marsala.

He felt in need of something stronger. The sight of Lucy falling on Jenny's neck had unnerved him, and the sight of Jenny putting her arms around the sobbing figure had staggered him. Then, almost immediately, the old Lucy had shown through in her manner to the page boy. Poor little creature, he had a hard life ahead of him if he remained in Lucy's service.

There was little need to make conversation. Lucy had news to impart about her travels, about how desolate her Richmond friends had been at her decision to leave, about the anxiety on her behalf of the lawyer who had written to them.

'Of course we don't need to speak of that yet – anything to do with lawyers, I mean.' She glanced about the room. 'I see you've changed the furnishings, Jenny. And it seemed to me that the house looked bigger as we came up the drive?'

'Yes, we built on a wing to give us more room for a nursery. That was about four years ago.'

'A nursery?' She closed her lips on the question, because to speak of Jenny's children must bring back memories of Heather.

Jenny supplied the information. 'We have a little boy, Maxwell. He's three. You'll see them by and by, Max and Heather. They're in the playroom at present.'

The name had been uttered. Heather . . . Lucy stooped to take from the travel basket a pretty fan of black lace. When she sat erect again, fanning her face, there was a little extra colour in her cheeks – but that could have been caused by the exertion of stooping, or by the heat of the August day.

'It was always a grief to Ned and I that we had no children. But heaven never sent us that blessing.'

'We were very sorry to hear of Ned's passing,' Ronald said, in honour bound to offer condolences to the widow, although he had experienced no grief at the news – no grief, only apprehension.

'Poor darling Ned . . . He was so zealous in helping the slaves, you know. He never spared himself. Many a time I said to him, "My dearest," I said, "think of yourself a little, you have a right to a life of your own." But he said, "Darling," he said, "on this one point we must disagree. God has called me to help these poor people and I must do so." '

'You surprise me a little. I thought Ned had lost his faith in God.'

Lucy cast a look of hurt and surprise at Ronald. 'Oh, but that . . . you know, that was only a temporary mistake . . . All due to that dreadful Mr Darwin. When we were living in Kingston, Jamaica, amongst all the exotic flowers and trees and the strange creatures, Ned said to me, "My dearest," he said, "when I look around and see the variety of creation I know that it could never have come about by random changes." '

'My mother held that view,' Jenny remarked. She recalled how impatient Ned had been at her words. 'So he came round to agreeing with her . . .'

'Of course, he was helped in rediscovering

his faith by the fervour of the natives there. They are very strong in their faith. He was very involved with them.' She wrinkled her nose and waved her fan a little faster. 'I couldn't quite approve of their religious service, but then you see . . . it was more suitable for a gentleman to attend than a lady. They sacrificed small animals. The only time I went, it was a cockerel.'

'You mean Ned was interested in Obeah?' Ronald put in, startled.

'Oh, you've heard of it? I . . . er . . . it was new to me. I couldn't approve of it. But then Ned told me it was brought with them from their home in Africa and was merely another way of communicating with the Creator. ''All ways are good,'' he said to me. He intended to write a book about it.'

'Oh yes. That sounds like Ned,' said Ronald. 'Did he write the book?'

'Well, you see . . . my health was not suited to the climate there. I found the heat very enervating. And so much sunshine . . . it's so bad for the complexion. So in the end we removed to the United States, and there this cult is not so strong, although I must say, the manner in which they conduct themselves in church is very odd. They sing with so much enthusiasm, and shout out remarks. I thought it very strange. But Ned said, ''My dearest,'' he said, ''they are simple people using voice and heart to praise the Lord and so,'' he said, ''we must not criticise.'' He himself found it very affecting. He used to go to their chapel rather than the Presbyterian church. I had to go to church alone, you know, which was not really very correct, socially, but then . . . people understood that Ned was different, had these eccentricities. They made allowances . . .'

Her voice trailed off into silence. Jenny sat trying to picture Ned in these surroundings, carried away as always by whatever captured his enthusiasm for the moment.

She had been surprised to learn from the lawyer's letter that he had remained faithful to the cause of helping and educating the emancipated slaves for twelve years. Most of his other pursuits had faded within a year or eighteen months. But now, having heard Lucy, she understood. He had found something there to study, something as a basis for the book that was going to make him famous.

His life had been a series of attempts to be someone of consequence, of importance. First he'd thought the path led through university and the mere appearance of gentility. Next he'd wanted to make his name by writing a learned work about the influence of Greek philosophy on Scottish thought. When this proved too difficult he'd lost heart and turned to drink. Rescued from that by a doctor of strong Christian faith, he'd turned to the temperance movement and had lectured in favour of total abstinence from alcohol.

How that had embarrassed and distressed Lucy! How she'd hated being dragged round dingy lecture halls, to sit on platforms while her husband beat his breast in repentance for past faults. God, he assured his audience, had shown him the true path.

But then came Charles Darwin and *The Origin of Species*. Overnight Ned lost his faith and plunged back into drink. Luckily he had found a new cause when the American Civil

War broke out. Ned was strongly on the side of the North, in favour of emancipation. It was because he'd been so immersed in working to raise funds for the Union Army that he'd forgotten to pay attention to his wife, and Lucy had turned to Harvil Massiter for consolation.

These memories were like a shadow hovering above the sunshine that streamed into the drawing room. All three occupants were aware of them. Lucy feared them most, and it was she who rescued herself from them by turning to mundane matters.

'I hope the servants will have unpacked for me by now,' she remarked, rising. 'At what time is luncheon?'

'In about forty minutes, if all is well in the kitchen.'

'In that case I'll go up and get out of this travelling costume. I presume there's a maid to help me?'

'Er . . . If you ring the bell, Baird will come – '

'Baird? Don't tell me she is still with you?'

'Of course,' Jenny said in surprise.

'But she must be sixty years old by now!'

'Oh, she has still some way to go to reach three score years. In any case, what has that to do with it?'

Lucy shrugged. 'I always thought her rather disagreeable. And rather inclined to give opinions that it was not her place to entertain in any case.' She moved gracefully towards the door. 'One thing that could be said in favour of the black people, they knew their place . . . And of course, they were easily satisfied, so one needed to offer only low wages, and replaced them without effort if they were troublesome. You know, in Richmond, we had eight indoor servants. Eight! We could have had more but Ned thought it might look ostentatious. So of course I've grown accustomed to excellent service.'

She had reached the door, and now stood looking at it as if she expected it to be opened for her by some magic. Ronald, with a faint frown, hurried to do so. She smiled with a faintly patronising air. 'You see?' she said. 'In Virginia there would have been a servant waiting to do that the moment I moved towards it.'

'Aye, well,' Ronald replied, 'you'll find we still open doors for ourselves in Galashiels. I wouldna spend too long waiting the wrong side of one for invisible slaves to do it for you.'

Jenny shook her head at him. Lucy had walked on into the hall. 'Lunch at one o'clock, Lucy.'

'Very well.'

When she had gone husband and wife looked at each other.

'She's changed,' Ronald said.

'Perhaps suffering has changed her. Because she *has* suffered, Ronald. You can see it in her face.'

'And yet the extraordinary thing is she seems more beautiful than ever. Dammit, how can that be?'

'Before, she was artless and very pretty – kittenish, in some ways. Now she's "interesting". Her face has lost its childishness, there's a coolness about her that she never had before.'

Ronald picked up Lucy's glass to return it to the tray. 'I can tell you, when you enfolded her in your arms, I was astounded. If she managed that on purpose, she's a clever wee besom.'

'She was always clever,' Jenny sighed. 'It used to be an instinctive kind of cleverness. Now, somehow, I feel she's learned to plan things beforehand. And I must say that, for one moment when she was sobbing on my shoulder, I thought it was completely genuine.'

'Well, the first hurdle is behind us. We've actually managed to give her a kind of welcome. Let's hope she settles everything with Jamieson in a day or two and takes her leave for a place with a flock of servants.'

The solicitors for William Corvill & Son had always been Mr Kennet. But Mr Kennet had had to give up the practice after a stroke, so that now his nephew Harold Jamieson was in charge of their affairs. Ned's will, made at the time of his marriage, had reposed first in Mr Kennet's safe and then in Mr Jamieson's.

Advised of the imminent arrival of the widow, Jamieson had got out the document. Except for a codicil putting a small percentage of the profits into trust for Heather and any succeeding children of Genevieve Armstrong née Corvill, the will remained unaltered.

'This is not a generous document as far as you are concerned, Mrs Armstrong,' said Mr Jamieson when he had refreshed his memory by reading it through. 'Everything goes to Mrs Corvill.'

'I know that. It's always been so.'

'But, dear lady, this gives the widow the power to do anything she wishes.'

'I know that,' Jenny repeated. 'But she's unlikely to wish to change anything. She receives a very handsome income from the mills of William Corvill & Son under the present system.'

'Humph,' said Jamieson, who despite his services to the Armstrongs had a poor opinion of the business sense of women.

He told Jenny he would be ready to see the widow at a moment's notice. A message need only be sent and he would set aside whatever was under his attention. Jenny expected Lucy to pay him a visit the following day or the one after.

But first there was lunch to be got through. And after lunch, an ordeal for which she had been steeling herself ever since the letter came and she accepted the fact that Lucy would be staying in her house.

Lucy would have to be introduced to the children.

For Max, Jenny had no tremors. But Heather . . . Could Heather by any chance retain any vestige of memory concerning the journey she had made with Lucy, the journey by post chaise and train to London in the dead of night, the day at the inn in Holborn when her crying had annoyed Massiter and Lucy's placatory tears had had no effect? Would some instinct tell the child that this was the woman who had stolen her from her mother, whose vanity and selfishness had condemned her to a year of terror among strangers?

Heather was unaware of her mother's fears. For her, at home on school holidays for the month of August, the coming of this exotic American aunt was a great event. She had been told that Aunt Lucy was pretty, that she worked with Uncle Ned to help the poor slaves, that she was now a widow. A widow was someone to whom one must give kindness and consideration – like an orphan or an invalid. Heather was eager to show her goodwill towards this newcomer.

She and Max shared lunch in the schoolroom at Gatesmuir. Max, a boisterous three-year-old, was apt to throw his food around if he disapproved of it. 'Do be good,' Heather coaxed. 'I don't want spinach purée on my new dress. What will Aunt Lucy think?'

'Don't care,' said Max.

'Sit ye down and eat your food,' Baird said, rapping him on the knuckles with a spoon. 'Ach, ye're a wee limb of Satan. Sit still!' She turned a wrathful glance on Heather. 'And as for you, young lady, dinna put yourself oot too much to impress Mrs Corvill, for she's no great she-saint, and dinna think it!'

'Oh, Baird, you're always so hard on everybody – '

'Hard, aye, hard I am in head and heart! I know who our enemies are, if ithers havena the sense to remember it!'

'What are you *talking* about, Baird!'

'Niver you mind, niver you mind. Eat your mutton and spinach.'

At two-thirty, hands rewashed, hair brushed hard, faces shining from the soap and flannel, they were ushered into the drawing room where the grown-ups were being served coffee by Thirley in her best apron and cap.

'Children, I want to introduce you to your Aunt Lucy,' Jenny said in a firm voice.

Heather curtseyed. Max put his hand across his middle and bowed as instructed.

'How do you do?' Lucy said, turning in her chair to honour them with her attention.

Jenny's eyes were upon her daughter. She held her breath. Would any hint of the past flit through Heather's mind?

She need not have worried – on that score, at least.

Heather beheld a slender, golden-haired angel clad in soft black silk which threw into relief her milk-and-roses colouring. At the delicate ears, black pearls gleamed. A mourning brooch held folds of black lace against the long, fragile throat. The blue eyes had something in them – uncertainty? Apprehension?

Oh, thought Heather, there was no reason for her to feel apprehension! Surely she must know she was loved and admired wherever she went. So beautiful, so ethereal . . . Heather's heart was caught in that first glance. Beautiful, good, kind, a widow, a stranger in their midst . . . They must do all they could to make her happy as she deserved to be.

So what Jenny Corvill saw when she looked at her daughter was not some ghost from the past touching her with a cold finger. Instead she saw the girl fall headlong into passionate admiration of the woman who had harmed and abandoned her.

CHAPTER TWELVE

The citizens of Galashiels were eager to pay
their respects and offer their condolences to
Mrs Corvill. However, decency must allow a
few days' interval so that she could recover
from her journey. It was agreed that Sunday
after church would be a good day to call.

Meanwhile Mrs Corvill behaved in every
way as a widow should. She took breakfast in
bed, rose rather late, then went for a walk in
the grounds attended by her page. The
grounds were much more extensive than she
remembered but she became bored with them
after two days and went for a carriage airing.

Glimpsed by passers-by, she received many
bows from ladies. Gentlemen raised their hats
to her. She was pleased, reassured. That awful
period in her past, which now seemed misty
and dreamlike, was either unknown to the
residents or else was forgotten.

Next day her carriage outing took her to the
door of the solicitor's office. She remained with
Mr Jamieson for half an hour, then was driven
out to Abbotsford where she admired the view
and sent Jubal to pick some tansy from the
banks of the Tweed.

The fact that she had been to the solicitor
spread from the coachman to Baird to Jenny.

Jenny smiled to herself. She had estimated that her sister-in-law would lose very little time in paying that visit.

Ronald received a note next day at the office of Waterside Mills, inviting him to call on Mr Jamieson at his convenience. Since at that moment he was at leisure, he strolled along Overhaugh to High Street, and had himself announced to the lawyer.

Jamieson rose to greet him. 'Good afternoon, Armstrong. Thank you for coming to see me so promptly.'

'I was expecting you to contact me.'

'Indeed? You . . . er . . . knew Mrs Corvill had been here? She told you?'

'My dear man, a carriage can hardly stand outside your office with a little black boy sitting high on the box without attracting some attention. Of course I knew.'

'Of course. You must forgive me. I'm a little . . . flustered.'

Ronald studied the lawyer. He did indeed seem flustered. Youngish, florid, conventional, Harold Jamieson was less adept at keeping his countenance than old Mr Kennet.

'You have something to say to me?' he prompted.

'Yes, er, yes. I have to tell you that I fear I must cease representing you as your solicitor.'

'Eh?' Ronald said, truly thinking he had misheard.

'I must ask you to find someone else to act in your behalf, Mr Armstrong.'

'What the devil for?' cried Ronald.

'I, er, I feel certain that there will be a conflict of interests. As I am taking charge of Mrs Corvill's affairs, I cannot in all conscience continued to handle yours.'

Ronald stared at Jamieson. He was blushing with embarrassment above his grey silk cravat.

'What in God's name are you talking about, Jamieson?' he demanded. 'Mrs Corvill came to see you yesterday. All of a sudden you decline to handle my affairs. The one apparently follows from the other. Will you explain how?'

'Mrs Corvill . . . You know of course Mrs Corvill is the sole legatee of her late husband.'

'Yes, certainly. You and my wife looked through the will when she brought that letter to you from the American attorney.'

'Yes, Mr Armstrong. I understand then that Mrs Armstrong completely accepted the will.'

'You understand correctly. Apparently it is Huguenot tradition that the man has complete authority over the family property. Jenny accepts that.' He frowned at Jamieson. 'And so what follows from it?'

'Mrs Corvill is now the owner of William Corvill & Son.'

'Yes, man, yes. Get on with it!'

'She has decided to sell the firm.'

As soon as he had said the words Jamieson began examining the inkwell very intently. A silence followed. When he dared at last to look up, Ronald Armstrong was shaking his head to himself in silence.

'No doubt it comes as a surprise to you, sir.'

'A surprise? It's a thunderbolt! *Sell*? To whom?'

'Oh, that isn't settled as yet. But there will be no shortage of buyers when the news gets out.'

'Sell? Out of the blue like that? Damn it, man, she can't do that!'

'I . . . er, I think we just agreed that she could in fact do that.'

'Well yes, she can, of course – she has a right to. But why the hell should she?'

'She wishes to sell and invest the money in property.'

'In property? In *property*? But nothing she could invest in would bring her such good returns as Waterside Mills! Business is booming!'

'Mrs Corvill is aware that if she sells and re-invests in houses and land she will take a slight loss in revenue. But she has assured me it isn't important.'

'Not important? To lose a few thousand a year? You didn't explain things to her – '

'I did, I assure you, Armstrong. But you know, ladies have very scant understanding of business matters and Mrs Corvill was ada-mant. She wants to sell the mills and re-invest.'

'She must be mad! Look here, Jamieson, if you're representing her, it's your duty as a lawyer not to let her do something to her own disadvantage – '

'Mr Armstrong, a solicitor takes instructions. He cannot give orders.'

Ronald leapt to his feet and strode about the fusty room. 'It's absurd! What possible reason can she have for doing such a thing? Did you ask her, Jamieson?'

'I did indeed.'

'And what was the answer, for heaven's sake?'

'Mrs Corvill feels that it is not genteel to be connected with commerce. That is why she wishes to sell up and take her money to some-thing more in keeping with her status.'

228

'Her status? What in God's good name is her status? She's the widow of a weaver – '

'We had a long conversation. She explained her views to me with great openness, I assure you. She is the daughter of parents from very good backgrounds, her father having been a younger son of a landed family who had to make his career as an officer of the Royal Navy. Her mother was a Miss Douglas of the Ayrshire Douglases – their seat was at Rankinston. Mrs Corvill has always felt it rather unsuitable to be connected with the weaving industry although, as she sweetly put it to me, love blinded her to the – '

'I never heard such rubbish in all my life!'

'Mr Armstrong!'

'Love never blinded Lucy Corvill to anything, I can assure you of that!'

'Mr Armstrong, I must ask you to lower your voice and speak of Mrs Corvill in a correct manner. She is, after all, your sister-in-law and a recently widowed lady.'

Ronald Armstrong sat down and gazed at the lawyer. And what he saw was a man who had fallen under Lucy's spell.

He had seen it before in the old days, when she lived at Gatesmuir and had wanted to make herself the leader of the local society. Men had been brought to her feet quite easily. It was always the women who resisted her charms, or who recovered very quickly if at first they gave in to the fascination.

He knew it was useless to say anything detrimental about her to this new devotee. He took a deep breath, controlled his temper, and went back to purely business matters.

'When does Mrs Corvill intend to offer the mills for sale?'

'Well, at once. I waited overnight to collect my thoughts on the matter then felt it only right to have this interview with you. You do see my difficulty, Armstrong? Mrs Corvill has asked me to handle her affairs. I feel that it would be impossible to represent you as I have done in the past, because now, naturally, your interests are not the same as Mrs Corvill's.'

'You never spoke a truer word. Did Mrs Corvill happen to mention what her plans were for myself and Jenny?'

'Her plans?'

'Well, she's selling the business out from under us. What does she intend that we should do?'

Jamieson opened and closed the lid of his inkwell. 'If I may say so without offending you, Mr Armstrong, it is not Mrs Corvill's concern to make any plans for you. When one comes to look at it in the strictly legal sense, you are her employee. You manage the mills on her behalf. Mrs Armstrong is not employed – receives no salary. That is the case, is it not?'

Ronald felt as if cold water had been thrown over him. 'Yes,' he said, on a gasp of shock.

'When the business is sold, I have no doubt your services will be retained by the purchaser. You are so highly thought of that your position is assured. As for Mrs Armstrong, hers is a strange case. Her abilities are well-known. And yet, you know, this might be an opportunity for her to step aside. I have always thought it odd to have a woman taking so active a part in the running of affairs. Circumstances no doubt forced her into it. But circumstances are changing. And perhaps for the best.'

'Listen to me,' Ronald said, holding his anger in check with an effort that almost strangled him, 'Waterside Mills belongs to Jenny. They only exist because she brought them into being. Their success depended on her skill as a designer, her business acumen. If control is taken away from her, the driving force is gone. Any man who buys Waterside Mills and expects them to go on leading the industry *without* Jenny is living in Cloud Cuckoo Land. And if Jenny is shut out from control of her own mills, I will never work for anyone who buys them.'

Jamieson seemed almost to shrink away from so much emotion. 'I . . . I cannot entirely share your view, sir. I can tell that you hold it very strongly but, seen in a purely business sense . . . You must see, sir, that anyone buying a property so large would be astonished at the idea of having a woman in charge – '

'Anyone buying Waterside Mills would know that Jenny *is* Waterside Mills!'

'Perhaps so, perhaps so. You know more about the weaving trade than I do, Armstrong. We must wait and see what ensues. For the present, my task is to advertise the property for sale – '

'Damn it, you'll do no such thing! I forbid it!'

'Excuse me, sir, you can have no say in the matter – '

'Twenty years of Jenny's life are invested in that business! You can't advertise it for sale without – '

'My instructions are to sell the property, Mr Armstrong.'

'And you can actually do it? You can accept instructions like that? Good God, man, you've dealt with Jenny, you've discussed business with her – she probably imagines you're her friend – '

'My first loyalty must be to Mrs Corvill, as you should easily understand. Mrs Corvill has no one else to turn to. I must do what is best for her.'

Ronald got to his feet again. 'Jamieson, if you advertise Waterside Mills for sale in the newspapers I will never forgive you. The hurt and humiliation to my wife would be beyond bearing.'

Perhaps having this tall angry man looming over him intimidated the solicitor. Perhaps he did feel some touch of pity for Jenny Armstrong who for so many years had taken pride and joy in the weaving mills she ran so successfully.

'Let me say this, then. I will put out private feelers for a buyer. There are one or two people I can write to who are looking for property for clients. And the mills are so well known that there may well be inquiries merely on hearsay.'

It was a concession, and Ronald should have said thank you for it. But the words would have choked him. He picked up his hat from the side table and stalked out.

Out in the High Street he tossed a penny to a passing lad, calling to him to run to Waterside Mills with the word that he wouldn't be returning there that afternoon. He himself set off for home at a fast pace, despite the fact that it was three o'clock on one of the hottest days of the year.

By the time he reached Gatesmuir he was so covered in sweat that he had to go into the downstairs cloakroom to put his face in a basin of cold water. Then, smoothing his wiry hair down and taking a deep breath, he went up to the old reading room, once the domain of Jenny's father and now the room in which she carried out business to do with the mills.

She was looking through the pattern books of previous years. As he came in she said, 'I think I might try a variation of the Ben Nevis plaid for the spring book. Do you think you could find a tint just this side of sage green for the sixth line?'

She held up the book. Her hair was a little out of place, she had dust on her nose from the binding of the heavy old volume.

'Where's Lucy?' he inquired.

'She's taking a nap. This heat tires her, she says – no wonder she hated the West Indies.'

'Jenny, I have something to tell you.'

'Yes? You look put out. Have you had tea? Ring the bell, it's time for it.'

'Jenny, never heed tea, never heed pattern books. I have something truly terrible to tell you. I've been to see Jamieson.'

Slowly she closed the book, letting it fall on the desk with a heavy thump. She drew a shivering breath. 'What has she done?' she asked in a whisper.

'She's selling the mills.'

'Selling?'

He nodded. 'I thought you'd guessed, some-how. When you asked what she'd done . . .'

'I just suddenly knew – when you said

Jamieson's name – that it was about her visit to him. Selling the mills?' Her voice was dull, toneless.

'We won't let her, of course. It's against natural justice to let her – '

'It's not a question of letting her. The mills belong to her.'

'Not if we contest the will. We can – '

'Contest the will? Ronald, if you think a Scottish judge would uphold the claims of a woman to set aside her brother's will – '

'But you can plead that the mills have reached their success only because of *your* work – '

She spoke in a voice that quavered with the effort to be calm. 'If I wanted to make any claim, I should have done it when Ned inherited, or when we made him sign the power of attorney leaving me in charge. Lucy's lawyer will point to those occasions and say, quite rightly, that I've been content with the way things were.'

'But that was when you expected the mills to stay in the family – '

'And I blame myself for that!' she broke out, throwing her hands up to her head in dismay at her own folly. 'I thought they were both so . . . silly and uninterested in business affairs that things would never change. Until in the end, in the natural course of events, the mills would pass to our children. Because you see, I always remembered what Lucy told me just after Heather was born, when she was so angry and envious. She said she could never have a baby. So I thought . . . I simply took it for granted . . . It never occurred to me that either of them would want to sell!'

'Wife, we must talk her out of it. Her reasons are so idiotic.'

Quickly he went through his conversation with Jamieson. To his surprise Jenny began to shake her head before he had ended. 'Oh, Ronald. I'm afraid she . . . she won't be dissuaded.'

'But it's such nonsense! "Weaving isn't genteel enough for one of her good breeding" – '

'You don't know how nonsensical it is! There's not a word of truth in that story about her parents. I know who they really were – an actor and actress from a travelling theatre company. But that's not what matters. It's what she *believes*, what she's talked herself into over the years. She probably played the lady in Richmond – '

'On the income we provided! All her luxuries, all her comforts – and this is how she repays us!'

'Ronald, it's no use being angry with her about it. She's the way she is, and if for the past twelve years she's been embroidering her tale about being wellborn, she thinks of it now as being almost the truth. And from her point of view, quite rightly, she wants to rid herself of her commercial connections. I don't think she can be talked out of it.'

'I'm not letting her sell William Corvill & Son out of our care!'

Jenny put her hands with love and respect on the old pattern book on the desk. 'All our work,' she said sadly. 'All we've built up . . .'

'We're going to keep it. Hell's fire, Jenny – I won't let that silly snip take our whole life away from us!'

But in the midst of the shock and distress

they were feeling, they couldn't begin to plan a defence.

A housemaid came to say that Cook had the tray ready if they wished to take tea, and if so, should she bring it to the reading room?

'We'll have it in my boudoir.' Pulling herself to her feet, Jenny led the way to that refuge. The shades were drawn here against the sunlight, the room was cool and calm. Ronald threw himself into a chair, the tea was brought and poured.

'What are we going to do?' he muttered.

'I can't seem to think. My mind's in a whirl.'

'We'll have to find someone to take care of the legal side for us – '

'We're not bringing a suit, Ronald!'

'No, all right, I agree it would cause a scandal and might drag on for years. *And* we might very well lose. But we've got *some* rights, for God's sake! And if Jamieson's deserting us – deserting us, in favour of our enemy – !'

'He doesn't see her as an enemy. He sees her as a poor lady who needs someone to handle her business affairs.'

'Oh, aye, he's fair beglamoured by her – '

There was a tiny tap on the door, and Lucy herself walked in. 'Oh, Ronald – I didn't expect to find you here too. The maid said tea was being taken in the Mistress's boudoir.'

With her face bathed to refresh her after her nap, her hair newly brushed and tied into her widow's cap, she looked the very picture of fragile womanhood. She moved to a chair by the fireplace, filled now with ferns and palms for the summer. She touched one of the leaves with her white hand, then looked expectantly at Jenny. 'I hope it's China tea,' she said. 'I told

Thirley yesterday that I only like Indian tea for breakfast.'

The utter silence her entry had caused seemed at last to sink in. She looked from one to the other.

'What's the matter?' she said.

'I've been to see Jamieson, that's what's the matter,' Ronald replied.

'Oh? Yes, he said he would probably speak to you today. What kind of a price do you think I shall get for the mills?'

'What kind of price . . . ?'

'Of course Mr Jamieson will look at the ledgers and things like that, and let me know whether I'm being made a fair offer. He told me I could rely on him for all that kind of thing.'

'Lucy, you can't really intend to sell Corvills!'

'Of course I do. I've always thought, if you'll forgive me for saying so because of course you're married to a woman who does undertake business matters, that it's quite unsuitable – really unwomanly and certainly unladylike. I hope you're not offended at my opinion,' she added, pretending a little wince at protestations they might be about to make.

'But you don't have to play any part in business, Lucy!' Jenny cried. 'You can go on as we've always done – you can leave the management to us and simply take the income.'

'But if anyone asks me where my money comes from, I should have to say it came from trade.'

'But in God's name, who is going to ask you such a personal question?' Ronald demanded in loud perplexity.

'Well . . . it could come up . . . there could be an occasion when such things would be discussed – '

'I can't think of a single one!'

Lucy smiled. 'Oh, that's so like a man! You never think of the finer things, the things of the heart – '

Jenny had been studying her sister-in-law. Now she began to sense what lay behind the words. 'Lucy, this occasion when your source of income might be discussed . . . are you talking about a courtship?'

'What?' Ronald said in astonishment.

'That's it, isn't it? You're thinking of marriage – '

'Good heavens, Jenny, how can you be so crass! My dear husband has only been in his grave six weeks – '

'What else does it mean, then? Who else but a suitor would expect to know about your income?'

'You're rushing ahead too fast! That's all in the future. But . . . if I must speak the truth . . .'

'Oh, do,' said Ronald in a tone of irony. 'Do tell us your plans.'

'Well, I know very well that I'm not suited to living alone. Even six weeks of widowhood have shown me I'm not able to cope with the harder side of life. Just making the journey home, with only Jubal as a companion – it was most disagreeable in that respect. If it hadn't been that the purser on the ship was extremely considerate towards me, I could have been quite at a loss from time to time. No, no, I don't enjoy the single life. And so, although I adored my dear husband and shall never cease to

238

grieve for him, I think that in time I shall probably remarry. I know Ned would have wanted me to.'

The Armstrongs stared at her, and then looked at each other. Ronald was thunderstruck. Jenny, who had seen some little smiles of false modesty in Lucy's manner to prepare her for the announcement, took it better.

'I see,' she managed to say. 'I understand . . . at least, I can understand in part. But I must admit I'm a little taken aback that you . . . you have this plan already in mind.'

'Oh, it's not a plan. Not really a plan. You could call it a hope.' Lucy straightened her back and squared her shoulders, as one who is facing the future with courage. 'One must go on,' she said, 'even after such a loss as I have endured.'

'Oh, quite.'

'I wonder if you would be so good as to pour my tea now? Otherwise it will be quite cold, Jenny.'

'Yes.' Mechanically Jenny picked up the teapot and poured. She put in milk and sugar, handed the cup to Ronald, who carried it across the room to his sister-in-law as if in a daze.

Lucy sipped. 'It really is rather tepid, Jenny. Perhaps you would ring for fresh?'

'Very well.' At her nod, Ronald pulled the bell pull. 'Lucy . . . as to your hopes . . . After all, you would wish me to put all the practical points before you.'

'Why, that's very kind of you, Jenny. You always have had such a practical mind.'

'In some ways, yes. Lucy, it occurs to me that by selling the mills and re-investing you will take a loss in income. It would really be more sensible, from the financial viewpoint, to let things stay as they are. Even supposing that in the end you decided to remarry, no man with any sense could object to the weaving industry as a source of revenue.'

'It's not a matter of mere sense, it's a matter of refinement,' Lucy said in a tone of mild reproof. 'There are people, you know, who think trade is very low.'

Ronald stalked unexpectedly to the door, went out, and closed it sharply behind him.

Left to deal with this lopsided view of the world, Jenny put out feelers. 'Who, exactly, would think such a thing? What I mean is, Lucy, if a man really cared for you, he would surely not be put off by – '

'Oh, in certain circles, my dear sister-in-law, it's very important to be careful about breeding and background. Those who move in the upper spheres of society would certainly never wish to be romantically linked with a member of the weaving trade.'

Jenny's mind was in a haze, but instinct was coming to her aid. The upper spheres of society? Breeding and background?

In came the housemaid. 'We'll have fresh tea, Betty.'

'Yes, mistress. Mistress Baird reminds you that the children want to show you their garden before dinner, mistress.'

'Oh yes. Tell Baird I shall be there in about half an hour.'

'Their garden?' Lucy said. 'Is that what they were doing? I saw them digging and delving down by the burn when I took my walk this morning.'

'It's Max's idea. He imagines by taking flowers from the flower-beds and setting them in a plot of his own, he's making a garden. Heather knows better, of course.' While she spoke, her intuition was at work. Upper spheres of society who might be repelled by a woman with an income from trade?

It came to her as if in a flash of lightning. Lucy was going husband-hunting, and what she wanted was a husband with a title.

The clarity of the vision was utterly convincing. Now she understood why Lucy had come back to Scotland, why she wanted to rid herself of her workaday connections. She had always longed for a fairytale marriage, with acres of land, a huge and handsome house, liveried footmen and carriages with crests on the doors.

Now was her chance to have all that. She was a widow, she was beautiful, and soon if she had her way she would be a rich and elegant prize with a fortune invested in highly respectable property.

It would have been no use looking for a duke or a baron in Richmond, Virginia. Titled men were only to be found under a monarchy. Jenny knew of – could have named – three or four members of the British aristocracy who wouldn't say no to a rich and beautiful wife.

She became aware that Lucy was speaking – complaining, rather.

'– when I asked her what they were doing. In fact, she never says a word to me. I find it very impolite.'

'I beg your pardon? What were you saying?'

'I was saying that Heather never replies when I speak to her.' Lucy's chin came up, she

241

looked faintly belligerent. 'I suppose you've told her all kinds of bad things about me!'

'What!'

'About what happened, that time. It's most unfair! You must know I was ill at the time, didn't know what I was doing – '

'I have never said a word to Heather about you, Lucy.'

'Not in all these years? You expect me to believe that?'

All at once Jenny lost her temper. 'You are so vain and self-centred!' she cried, jumping up from her chair. 'You're one of those people that imagine, after you've left a room, that everyone sits there talking about you – as if you were the most important thing on God's earth! I never spoke of you to Heather! I tried never to think of you! To me you were and are wicked and callous and self-obsessed!'

'Well, really – '

'Yes, really! Heather doesn't reply when you speak to her because she's shy and frightened with people she doesn't know. *You* did that to her! You're to blame for almost every hurt my family has suffered since first you came to this house!'

'I will ask you to modify your remarks, Jenny. I am not accustomed to being spoken to in – '

'No, Ned sheltered you and indulged you because he was as silly as you are! He had to believe you were sweet and good otherwise his whole marriage was a farce. And now look at you – you could hardly wait for the earth to be shovelled over him before you came hurrying here to find yourself some blue-blooded idiot to give you a title. That's it, isn't it? That's what

242

it's all about! Selling up and getting yourself into high society on the prowl for a nobleman – '

Lucy's pale clear complexion went fiery red. 'How dare you,' she gasped.

'I should never have let you in at the door. I wanted to tell you to stay away, but Ronald said . . . Never mind, everything's changed, it wouldn't matter what we'd said or done because you always intended to take the mills away from us – '

'Take them from you? They never belonged to you in the first place – '

'And the more fool I, to think that you and Ned understood or valued what I had done! All these years – my whole life – and you want to grab it back from me to pander to your vanity – '

The maid came in with the teapot, looking hesitant and scared. Jenny waved her away. She went out in a flurry of alarm. Something very bad was happening. She had never seen the mistress look so angry.

'You can pack up,' Jenny said. 'You can put all your hypocritical widow's weeds back into your trunks and take yourself off. If the world thinks it's hard and unfeeling to turn you away, I don't care! I'll tell them the truth – that you're a selfish, grasping little toad who's already planning how to trap her next husband!'

Lucy gave a gasp. 'That's no way to talk! I – '

'Ah! Frightens you, does it? Queers your pitch in the matrimonial game? Go on, explain to everyone how innocent and honest your intentions are – I'm sure you have some tale to tell that will make you seem in the right. But once it's known you're selling Corvill's you won't find any friends in this town. I'd like to see you trying to convince them it's all my fault that you have to sell up my life's work.'

'I shan't stay another minute in this house,' Lucy said in a high, thin voice. 'I won't stay here and be insulted. You've never liked me, never – you've always been ready to think the worst of me. Well, I shall go, and I shall sell Corvill's, and if you want to know, I think it serves you right because it made you think far too much of yourself, Jenny Armstrong!'

Jenny laughed. 'You won't take it away from me. You've caused nothing but trouble in my life, my dear little widow, and somehow you've always come out the winner. Not this time, Lucy. Not this time.'

Lucy Corvill had never been exactly clever, yet until now she'd almost always been able to turn away harsh words. But now she looked at her antagonist, and could find nothing to say. She rose and hurried out.

When the door had closed on her, Jenny put her hands to her mouth to check a cry of something like despair. 'You won't take it away from me!' A vain boast – how could she prevent it?

There must be a way.

Almost her entire life had been spent on building up an industrial undertaking that had brought reputation, respect, fulfilment and, yes, money. She herself had taken nothing from the profits except to further the advancement of William Corvill & Son, but it had to be admitted it had given Ronald a good salary. It had also provided the handsome house in

London, and a style of living she would be sorry to lose.

Perhaps it could also be said to be the basis of Ronald's Parliamentary career, for Lord Thornieburn would scarcely have troubled himself for a man from nowhere. The fact that Ronald was manager of Corvill's, pre-eminent in the weaving industry, had been an important factor in his selection.

Yet more than that – it was her girlhood's dream, brought to actuality by her own efforts. She had never wanted to be the owner, she had wanted to be the *maker*, the maker of the finest cloth in Scotland.

If she let Lucy take it all away, twenty years of her life would go for nothing.

CHAPTER THIRTEEN

Lucy removed herself that evening to Carlisle, where she took up elegant lodgings not far from the cathedral. Her going was a shock to Heather.

'I thought she was going to stay a long time.'

'No, pet, it was only a short stay, to see her solicitor.'

'I wish I'd known. I'd have tried harder to speak to her.'

Jenny decided not to explain the situation to her daughter. Heather had had enough insecurity in her short life – she didn't need the knowledge that her admired aunt was about to sell the family business and put them out of work.

The news of the departure was a surprise to the townsfolk, particularly when it leaked out that there had been a resounding quarrel betwixt the Mistress and Mrs Corvill. But that became thoroughly understandable when the next nugget of information was mined out.

Corvill's was being sold up!

Tam Hay, foreman of the pressing room, came as spokesman for the workers to Ronald's office. 'Is't true, what they're saying, that you're selling the works?'

'I'm not selling. Mrs Corvill is.'

'What share does Mrs Corvill have in the works then, maister?'

'She owns them.'

Hay put his hands in his apron pocket, took them out again, and regarded them with bewilderment. 'Excuse me, sir – ye're saying Mrs Corvill owns the mills?'

'Yes.'

'Owns this?' He swept out an arm that took in the humming industry of the rooms behind and above them.

'Yes.'

'But I thocht . . . we a' thocht that the Mistress owned Corvill's.'

'No. Her brother Ned was the owner and he left it at his death to his widow.'

Hay shifted about in embarrassment and anxiety. 'What happens, then, to the jobs if we're sold?'

'I can't say. I imagine the buyer would keep on the workforce.'

'Mr Armstrong . . .'

'Yes?'

'Can ye no stop her? From selling up?'

'I'm afraid not, Tam.'

The facts spread consternation among the workforce. And it had a similar effect among the manufacturers.

The response to Mr Jamieson's 'feelers' was incredulity at first. When a buyer inquired, he had first to be convinced that Mrs Edward Corvill had the right to sell. One buyer, John McFee of Hawick, refused to believe it until he actually saw the title deeds to the mills. There it was – the original registration to William Corvill, the transfer at his death to his heir Edward Corvill, and now the lawyer's stamp saying 're-registration pending' and Mrs Corvill's name pencilled in.

'Well, I wouldna have believed it if I hadna seen it with my own eyes. And even now I dinna quite believe it, Jamieson.'

'I assure you, Mr McFee, those are the facts. Mrs Corvill is the owner of Waterside Mills.'

'Where does the Mistress come into all this?'

'She doesn't come into it at all,' Jamieson said, suppressing his irritation at hearing the question for the fiftieth time. 'She has no standing in the matter.'

'What's her view aboot this sale?

'She perfectly concurs.'

'She thinks the mills should be sold?'

'She assents to the sale.'

'Aye, aye . . . Where will she be when the sale is over?'

'Where? Why . . . at Gatesmuir, I suppose.'

'And Mr Armstrong? Will he continue as manager?'

'Mr Armstrong has indicated that he would not.'

'Not continue with a new owner?'

'No, he has said that he will not.'

'Man, Jamieson! That's the MP for the constituency you're talking about! He's not in favour of the sale, that's clear!'

'I have never said that Mr or Mrs Armstrong are in favour,' Jamieson said, forced to be utterly truthful as his profession demanded. 'What I have said is that they both agree Mrs Corvill has the right to sell.'

'Jings, Mr Jamieson, I'd never feel easy aboot a transaction that left the Mistress with nothing after twenty years in the industry! I'm no just easy aboot it.'

And so it went. Nobody would believe Mrs Corvill had the right to sell, and once he had been convinced of that fact nobody felt he had the right to buy.

The Armstrongs had meantime found themselves another lawyer to replace Jamieson. Mr Loomis heard them out with consternation.

'Are you telling me, dear madam, that you have worked nearly twenty years for this firm and never had a penny in pay?'

Jenny sighed. 'We were a weaving family. A woman who works for her family doesn't expect to be paid.'

'But in this case – !'

'It's no use regretting the past, Mr Loomis. What we want to know now is, what should we do?'

'You don't wish to take the case into court?'

A pause. Then Ronald said, 'My wife shrinks from the publicity and scandal that might ensue. And if you look at the legal facts, it's by no means sure we could win an action to have the will set aside.'

'That is alas only too true. By your own silence you have given consent to the situation finally brought about in the will. What is it you want, then?'

'We want to prevent the sale.'

'Dear Mrs Armstrong, you cannot prevent your sister-in-law from selling what is hers.'

'That seems to be the fact, on first considering the case. But perhaps there's some loophole . . .'

'If I might peruse the documents concerning William Corvill & Son?'

'Well, you see . . . Most of them are with Mr Jamieson. He was solicitor for Corvill's until this blew up. Still is, in a way, because he now represents Mrs Corvill and Mrs Corvill owns the firm.'

'I don't see what I could exactly do,' Loomis said. He grasped the lapels of his coat as if he were grappling with an opponent. 'If I ask for a Restraining Order, I must have grounds. Have you anything to suggest?'

'We . . . we've hardly got ourselves back into being able to think at all,' Jenny confessed. 'It was such a terrible blow that for days we simply couldn't take it in. All we know – what we feel – is that we have more right to Waterside Mills than anyone else.'

'If only it were possible to prove that,' groaned Mr Loomis through clenched teeth.

By year end, Mr Jamieson had not found a buyer among the weaving community of Scotland. He sent out a dove in the direction of the weavers of Yorkshire.

The cloth manufacturers of Yorkshire had heard the rumours, but had decided it was some manoeuvre on the part of those canny Scots. When Mr Jamieson's colleague in Leeds assured the board of Kirkstall Weavers that the rumours were true, that the redoubtable Mistress Armstrong was giving up, they began to express interest. A representative of the board, Henry Longshaw, was sent to Galashiels to inspect the premises.

He was shown round by Gaines, the assistant manager, stony-faced and icily polite. To be selling to a Yorkshireman, a 'suddron', one of those who copied the Mistress's beautiful designs the moment they appeared and tried to tempt workers away to the opposition by promises of more pay! It was unbelievable.

Mr Longshaw reported favourably to his board of directors. A fine set of premises, modern machinery in the carding rooms, beautiful designs in the pattern books, orders waiting execution – what could be better?

Having said a short prayer of gratitude, Mr Jamieson went to see Lucy in Carlisle to report that he had found a buyer. Kirkstall Weavers were offering one hundred thousand pounds for the factory and goodwill.

'That is a good price?'

'Excellent. I assure you, Mrs Corvill, this is a fine offer. It somewhat reflects the fact that they are removing a strong competitor.'

'But why has it taken you so long?' she inquired with a downward, half-petulant glance under her lashes.

He gave her a long apology to which she scarcely listened. One hundred thousand pounds . . . Invested in even the three-per-cents, it would bring her in a more than adequate income. But Mr Jamieson had looked about and found some property which would bring in six per cent per annum, in building and land in the Midlands.

With her smile of gratitude lighting his way, Mr Jamieson returned to his wife and family in Galashiels. Next day he wrote to Longshaw to say that the sale had been agreed by the owner. He would have the documents ready for signature in about two weeks.

Meanwhile, he felt it only fair and decent to tell Ronald Armstrong. As Mr McFee had remarked, the man was MP for the district. And he fortunately happened to be at home that weekend, although Parliament had not yet risen for the Christmas Recess.

He felt it would be more polite to call at Gatesmuir rather than invite Armstrong to his office. He sent word of his visit, and arrived at about four o'clock on Saturday afternoon.

Mrs Armstrong was also in the drawing room when he was shown in. He was rather put out. He'd never been entirely at ease when dealing with Mrs Armstrong.

'This is a business call, you implied,' Ronald said, offering him a chair.

'Yes, although in fact there was no necessity on my part to make it. But I felt, sir, that it would only be good form to tell you that Kirkstall Weavers are buying Waterside Mills.'

'I saw Mr Longshaw being shown round,' Ronald said with politeness. 'He approved of the premises?'

'Certainly. In fact, he said to me that the place was a credit to the management.'

'I'm overwhelmed. So. What is Kirkstall Weavers buying?'

'I beg your pardon?'

'What is included in their price?'

'I don't understand you, sir. Kirkstall Weavers are buying Waterside Mills lock stock and barrel.'

Ronald looked at Jenny. Jenny looked at Ronald.

'You have of course read through all the documents concerning Waterside Mills?'

'Certainly, Mr Armstrong, it would have been remiss of me to do otherwise.'

'You noticed, I daresay, that the carding sets are actually owned by me?'

'Yes, yes, I noticed that. Bought when you returned from your trip to Australia.'

'Just so. I had the good luck there to find

gold – actually to find gold lying in the roots of a tree. So when I came home I decided to invest in William Corvill & Son, and the investment I decided to make was in machinery. Improved carding sets had just been produced by a Sheffield firm and we re-equipped the carding room. Didn't we, my love?' he said to Jenny.

'We did indeed. And excellent machines they have proved.'

'I know all that, Armstrong,' Jamieson said with suppressed annoyance. The man was treating him as if he were a child needing a lesson in business. 'The machines are leased to William Corvill & Son. There's no mystery about it.'

'On a renewable lease.'

'Yes, of course.'

'Well, I have decided not to renew my lease.'

Mr Jamieson felt as if he had received a kick in the stomach by a mule. 'What?' he gasped.

'I told you that I didn't wish to work for a new owner. I feel my machines should not work for them either. So I shall take my carding sets out of Waterside Mills if you sell to Kirkstall Weavers.'

'You can't do that!'

'I certainly can.'

'Take out the machinery? But then . . . but then . . .'

'Then Kirkstall Weavers would be buying a set of empty buildings. Exactly.'

'You can't *do* that!' shouted Jamieson, going a dark red.

Jenny rose, rang the bell, and when Thirley came asked for the brandy decanter. She poured Mr Jamieson a glass, which he took in a shaking hand.

When he had drunk enough to give him some strength she said gently, 'We quite agree that we don't own Waterside Mills. But we were forced to look with great attention through every agreement and contract that we had ever made, and I found that, acting by power of attorney for my brother, I had leased twenty carding sets from my husband. I have paid him a yearly fee for the use of that machinery for the last four years. At the end of five years the fee would have been reduced, and again at the end of the next five years, by which time I would probably have replaced with new. But if the works are no longer under our control we don't have to consider such matters. We simply remove the carding sets – '

'But . . . but . . . where would you remove them *to*?' groaned Jamieson.

'To other premises. I've no doubt we could find a factory where we could set up – '

'Set up?'

'In opposition to the new owners of William Corvill & Son. We think of calling the firm Mistress Armstrong Tweeds.'

'No,' said Jamieson.

'Yes,' said Jenny.

Mr Jamieson protested, they responded. They went over the same ground three or four times. But it became apparent to him in the end that there was no way he could sell Waterside Mills complete with its machinery to Kirkstall Weavers.

'What is your intention?' he said at last, feeling as weak as a kitten from frustration, misery and defeat.

'Our intention is that the mills should not be sold to a buyer of whom we cannot approve.'

'Approve? You want to have a say in who buys?'

'In a nutshell.'

'You don't approve of Kirkstall Weavers?'

'Not at all.'

'Then who? Have you someone in mind?'

'Oh yes.'

'Who? Is it one of the Hawick firms?'

'No. We want to buy Corvill's.'

'You? But the price is in the neighbourhood of one hundred thousand pounds!'

'Only if the machinery goes with the buildings. The buildings alone, with such equipment as the dying vats and pressing rollers, would go for somewhat less.'

'Yes,' Mr Jamieson said in a faint voice.

'Nevertheless, it's still a great deal of money. And we need time to raise it.'

'Time,' echoed Jamieson. 'How much time?'

'As long as it takes to raise the money.'

'But my client – her hopes have been raised –'

'Your client is living quite pleasantly on a very large income which is supplied by the mills she is trying to sell. She has nothing to complain of at present. What she'll say when you tell her you overlooked the matter of the machinery –'

'I didn't overlook it!' cried the lawyer. 'I took it for granted that you would renew the lease –'

'We took it for granted that the mills would be left in our hands to manage,' Jenny said with a tinge of cruel satisfaction. 'You see what a mistake it is to take anything for granted.'

After Mr Jamieson had been shown out, an observer could have seen Jenny and Ronald Armstrong hugging each other and laughing with relief and delight.

Harold Jamieson had no such feelings. He went home to change for an evening party, which he attended with very little taste for the seasonal merriment. Next day, ashamed to go in person with his news to Mrs Corvill, he wrote a long apologetic letter, setting out clearly the manner in which Ronald Armstrong had got the upper hand in the negotiations for selling Waterside Mills.

'You will observe, dear madam, that up until yesterday I had no reason to suppose Mr Armstrong would change the conditions under which he leases the carding sets and looms. I know you will understand that I was not to blame, and I assure you of my continued endeavours to get the best price possible for the mills, according to your original instructions.' He begged to remain her humble and devoted servant, and sat back to await her letter of reply.

There was no letter. Mrs Corvill came in person, two days later. She walked past his confidential clerk and into his private office, waving the letter in her hand.

'What is the meaning of this?' she cried.

'Mrs Corvill – madam – I didn't expect – '

'You told me yourself everything was settled!'

'No, no, I told you the papers would be drawn up within two weeks – '

'There would be no reason for drawing up the papers if everything had not been settled! Mr Jamieson, you have failed me!'

'No, no, I assure you – it will still be possible to get a good price – '

'I don't want you to get a good price. I want you to go through with the sale to Kirkstall Weavers for the best price!'

'No, madam, I assure you, that's no longer possible.'

'Don't be absurd, Kirkstall Weavers wouldn't be put off by a silly thing like this! They can easily replace – '

'No, Mrs Corvill, alas, Kirkstall Weavers have withdrawn.'

'Withdrawn?'

'Yes, by this morning's post – but I expected that.'

'Withdrawn? How could you let them? Write to them at once and tell them I expect them to go on with the sale – '

Jamieson urged her into a chair and sat down himself, to explain to her why Kirkstall Weavers no longer wanted to buy the Waterside Mills. He thought he'd explained it already in his letter, which had cost him many pains. But no, it seemed she didn't understand.

For the next half an hour he went over the case again and again. It began to dawn on him that Mrs Corvill was not perhaps the very brightest of business brains. Moreover, she insisted on blaming him for not being able to make Kirkstall Weavers buy. He had the feeling that perhaps Mrs Corvill was not such an angel of sweetness as he had at first believed. In fact, he would have been very glad if he had never met Mrs Corvill.

She sat on his hard office chair, the slender figure upright in its gown of fine black cloth, the cheeks glowing pink with indignation under a black bonnet trimmed with sable. Her clenched fists rested on a muff of the same fur. She said for the twentieth time, 'But they cannot back out! They agreed to buy!'

'They agreed to buy on the understanding they were to get the premises and contents, not to mention the goodwill. Now they find that all they are getting is the buildings. The main machinery belongs to Ronald Armstrong and as to the goodwill – who is going to continue to buy from William Corvill & Son when their chief designer and their dye-master are setting up in opposition a few miles away under the name Mistress Armstrong Tweeds?'

'But the designs,' Lucy said with surprising shrewdness, 'the designs Jenny made for the mills – they could still be made and sold – '

'I don't know whether even that is the fact,' Jamieson said miserably. 'I believe she could bring a suit to say that those designs are her personal property – '

'Nonsense! She made the designs for the firm – '

'But she has never been paid by the firm. Nor has she ever signed any paper making a deed of gift of the designs. In fact, Mrs Corvill, they belong to Mistress Armstrong alone, if she wishes to claim them.'

'How can you argue on *her* side?' Lucy cried. 'How can you think of her when you should be thinking of me?'

'I am thinking of you,' groaned Jamieson. 'I'm trying to make you see that the sale of Waterside Mills depends on the approval of Mr and Mrs Armstrong. Without their approval the property cannot be sold as a going concern

'– and nobody wants an empty factory, at least not at the sort of money we at first presumed.'

'To think that you let me fall into this trap!'

'Madam! Dear madam! Trap? This is a purely business matter! Mr and Mrs Armstrong are defending their position –'

'But you told me they *had* no position! You told me the factory was legally mine!'

'So it is. Waterside Mills – extensive premises on the Mill Lead at the Gala Water – is yours, every square yard of ground and every stick and stone. But not the machinery. And not the designs, which the Mistress may claim as her personal property. All you can sell is the land and buildings – unless you make an agreement with the Armstrongs.'

'Make an agreement?'

'I explained it in my letter. An agreement. Ronald Armstrong will buy –'

'Ronald Armstrong has no money,' Lucy said with scorn. 'He's a paid employee, always has been – nothing but what he earns from day to day and a few pounds in savings put by for a rainy day!'

'He can get money. I set all this out in my letter. Madam, did you *read* my letter?'

'Of course I did! And I was very hurt and disappointed –'

'I understand. I do understand. But we must face facts. You cannot sell Waterside Mills without the concurrence of the Armstrongs. And in fact that boils down to this: you can only sell to the Armstrongs.'

'You mean, let them have my property?' To his surprise, he discovered it was possible for those soft blue eyes to flash.

'Dear lady, they would give you a fair price – '

'Fair? When has Jenny Armstrong ever been fair to me? She hates me!'

'Mrs Corvill!'

'She has persecuted me all my life!'

'My *dear* Mrs Corvill, you are over-wrought – you don't know what you are saying . . .' Beside himself with embarrassment and dismay, Jamieson leapt to his feet, opened a cupboard in a cabinet, and brought out a bottle of brandy and a glass. He poured some, stooped over Lucy, and made sure she sipped some. When he had persuaded her to take the glass into her own hand he went behind his desk again, poured himself a stiff peg, and downed it.

This was one of the worst interviews ever to take place in his office. He heartily wished his visitor would take her business elsewhere. It was no intention of his to get embroiled in family feuds.

The interruption had allowed Lucy time to gain control of herself. The fire left her glance, she drooped a little, pathos seemed to make a soft halo around her. 'I . . . I am so confused,' she murmured. 'I haven't really recovered from the death of my dear husband. You can't know what a grief it was to me, Mr Jamieson.'

'Of course, of course.'

'As a result, it's my earnest desire to break all ties with the past and start anew, with nothing to remind me of the dear dead days of happiness in Galashiels. That is why I want to sell out – to sell out and go away, perhaps to London where the bustle and activity will occupy my mind and keep me from sad thoughts.'

'I quite understand.'

A pause. 'How much do you think the Armstrongs will pay?'

Thank God, thought Alexander Jamieson. 'That remains to be negotiated. But I believe we can come to a good arrangement.'

'But how will they get the money? I don't wish to be paid . . . what is the term . . . ? in instalments.'

'I believe Mr Armstrong will have no great problem in raising a loan. His credit and that of his wife, although it is unusual to take the wife into account . . . However, I believe it will be accomplished before too long.'

'Perhaps.' Lucy sipped her brandy.

'Mrs Corvill, if I may offer a word of warning . . .'

'Yes?'

'I should be careful in what you say. Your best chance of doing well out of this transaction is to be on good terms with your in-laws.'

'Good terms? Of course we are on good terms! Mrs Armstrong is my darling Ned's sister – we are united by ties of the deepest affection.'

Mr Jamieson made a great effort and held his tongue. Perhaps she had forgotten the awful words she had just spoken a few minutes ago. Perhaps she merely wished them to be forgotten. Whichever it was, he was perfectly ready to go along with it.

The rumour that the Armstrongs were going to buy Corvill's and keep it in action lightened for the workforce the gloom that had been hanging over the season of Christmas and Hogmanay. The money hadn't yet been raised, but everyone from the carding room to the packing shed took it for granted that the Maister would get it easily enough.

It would in fact have been surprisingly easy to get the money. There were many men and business firms only too eager to have Ronald Armstrong, Member of Parliament for West Tweed, under an obligation. Through this quagmire Ronald trod delicately, declining most of the approaches. By Hogmanay he had offers which would have brought him to within twenty thousand of the price now agreed between himself and Mr Jamieson, but that last sum could not be found without compromising himself.

He rode to Thornieburn Hall to talk it over with the Laird. 'I'm sorry to talk business on such a day, sir – '

'Not at all, not at all. We have guests in the house but Jemima's taken them out shooting. Fine shot, my wife. In fact, perhaps you'd take a brace of pheasants home with you, Armstrong – the house is glutted with pheasants!'

They sat in what the Earl called 'my snuggery': a smallish room with dark panelling hung with sporting prints, maps, and old dirks and targes. Ronald had declined whisky and was drinking hot chocolate, a rich and comforting drink after the raw wind on the hill.

'Well now, I can guess what brings you here,' said His Lordship. 'It's the money, eh?'

'Thank you for broaching the subject, my lord. Yes, it's the money. I've got promises for most of the sum I need but the last stretch may have to come from Harrington. You know Harrington?'

'Of Harrington & Cryer, Exporters. Yes, I've met him.'

'I'm very unwilling, sir. He's made it fairly clear he expects favours in return. He's trying to influence the Tax Rebate Bill. He says – for the record – that he expects nothing from me by way of influence on the Bill, but even if he really means it, it would look so bad.'

'I see,' said the Earl. He went to the window, to stare out at the dreary winter garden. 'We'll have a frost tonight,' he observed. 'Put paid to the blossom on the viburnum, I shouldn't wonder.'

'What do you think I should do, my lord?'

'I think you should speak to a banking friend of mine. In fact, I wish you'd done so in the first place, Armstrong. It would have spared you a lot of anxiety, I believe.'

Ronald said nothing. It had never occurred to him to talk to the Earl about business – he was so vague and absentminded. He had only come today to ask advice about Parliamentary and Party loyalty.

'I'll give you a letter of introduction. You'll have to go to Edinburgh to see him. Can't do it now until we recover from our sore heads at New Year, eh? Never mind. New Year, new start. You'll like Lockhart – he was at Fettes with me, clever laddie, always won all the prizes for algebra and geometry and such, but not vain of his cleverness.'

'Lockhart?'

'Of the London-Scottish Commercial Bank. I expect he knows all about you, really. Makes it his business, keeps his finger on the pulse, see what I mean?'

'But, I was intending to keep the matter among Border firms, sir – to keep investment local – '

'Admirable, of course. But you needn't perturb yourself on that account. LSC have money invested in factories throughout the Borders, and elsewhere, I believe – Paisley, places like that. Yes, yes, Armstrong, I think you'll find this is the best way. Any road, talk about it to Lockhart. He won't expect you to go into the wrong voting lobby as a return for money – he's a banker, he only wants the interest due, that's all.'

When Ronald reached Gatesmuir in time for a very late lunch, he was able to add to the cheer of Hogmanay by telling Jenny that the money for the purchase of Corvill's was as good as in their pockets.

Jenny, clad in a working smock, was supervising the decorations for the Hogmanay party. Heather and Max were 'helping' – Heather was making festoons of red and green crepe paper, on which Max was sticking drunken stars with great blobs of paste. The gardener's boy was on a ladder pinning these to the cornice. In a safe spot on the floor and covered with tissue stood the bowl of carefully sheltered Christmas roses, among which white tapers had been interspersed so as to shine from the hall table as guests began to arrive.

Flowers stood in massy arrangements at every point on which the light would fall. The fireplaces were decked with festoons of greenery. From the gasoliers hung pieces of mirror glass on wire, to lend sparkle to the scene. The

Yule log lay in the hall fireplace, waiting to be set alight – an apple log, which would smell sweet and send its light smoke all through the house.

The house itself had been washed and swept, cleaned and polished, so as to start the New Year in the way the housekeeper intended to go on. The 'housekeeper' at the moment was Jenny, but if all went well with their purchase of the mills, she would be spending most of her time at Waterside. They had decided that she should be given the title 'Directress' and take full control of the running of the business – subject, for legal reasons, to Ronald's approval.

Ronald was unlikely to argue with any of the directress's decisions. He would be busy in Westminster, during a year in which Parliament was expecting an important report on the finances of Egypt and the prospects for Egypt's cotton crop – a serious matter for the Lancashire spinners.

Jenny went with her husband into the morning room to sit with him while he ate lunch. The dining room was out of bounds at present, because the caterers were setting out the buffet on the long table. Ronald ate his hot mutton pie and winter greens with appetite. 'The Earl seemed sorry I'd not gone to him at first,' he said between mouthfuls. 'To speak the truth, I never thought on it.'

'No, he's not the first man one would turn to over business,' Jenny agreed. 'Still, I'm glad to have his help over Corvill's. He's been a good friend to us, husband.'

'You may say so,' Ronald nodded.

The housemaid brought in his pudding – hot

brandy snaps with cream. 'I'm surprised Cook has time to make things like this for me,' he remarked. 'She's overwhelmed, surely, with preparations for tonight.'

'But most of the work's being done for her. Listen, Ronald, about tonight . . . Can I ask your opinion?'

'Of course.'

'And you'll be honest?'

He waited, eyebrows raised.

'Do you think . . . you see, it's almost exactly six months since Ned died . . . Do you think I could go out of mourning tonight?'

Ronald, who had expected something enormously serious from her tone, had to suppress a grin. 'Och, please yourself.'

'No, tell me – do you think it would cause comment?'

'Listen to me, wife. Yon brother of yours was gone from the family for twelve years and when he left us it was with no good feelings – so to go on in mourning a minute longer than you need to is mere pretence.'

'It's not pretence!' Jenny said with surprising emphasis. 'I do mourn for Ned. I mourn the little boy I used to love as a clever, lively elder brother. Today especially I'm thinking of him. He once led me into a scrape on Hogmanay – we got into the parlour before the guests arrived and drank ourselves dizzy on forbidden port wine . . .'

Her husband got up, gave her a hug, and made for the door. 'I'm sorry I spoke harshly of him. But I think you should follow your inclination and wear something coloured – in fact if you want to wear scarlet I wouldn't object.'

266

'Ronald! You know I don't own a scarlet dress! No, I thought . . . my pearl grey dinner gown . . . and the coral necklace you gave me for my birthday . . . Is that too bright?'

Ronald waved a hand in agreement, then hurried out. He had to get to the mills before they closed, to wish the workforce a Happy New Year as they left and present each with the florin bonus which had become a tradition at Corvill's.

It was almost four o'clock and growing dark. Jenny followed him into the hall, clapping her hands. 'Now, children, come along. You've been indoors all day making decorations. It's time to go out for some fresh air before it's black outside.'

'Oh, Mama!' wailed Max. 'I've got lots of silver paper still to cut!'

'We've got enough stars for one firmament,' Jenny said, scooping him up and thereby getting paste from his sticky hands all over her shoulders where he hung on. 'Come along, my treasure – up you go to the nursery for your coats and scarves. Heather, my love, tell Baird you're to go round the shrubbery and the kitchen garden twice, and then when you come in you are to go to bed for an hour.'

'Oh, Mama!' wailed Heather, sounding exactly like Max for all the ten years' difference in their ages. 'I shan't sleep if I go to bed!'

'That doesn't matter, you'll be resting. You know if you don't have a nap, you'll never stay awake to see the New Year in.'

'Yes I will – '

'I'd stay awake if I could stay up,' shouted Max, squirming to be put down. 'Let me stay up, Mama.'

'When you're ten years old, darling. Heather didn't stay up until she was ten years old.'

'But she's only a girl! Boys can stay awake –'

'Boys and girls must go to bed at their usual time until they're ten years old,' Jenny proclaimed, shaking a finger at him. 'And girls who are allowed to stay up must take a nap beforehand, otherwise when the New Year comes in at the door, they'll be off in dreamland, like a certain party last year.'

'I wasn't asleep!' cried Heather.

'No? Then why were you snoring in a corner of the sofa?' Jenny laughed and put an arm around her daughter's waist. 'Now, my joy, go upstairs and get your coat and scarf – and take this sticky boy with you and make sure he washes his hands before he touches anything. Off with you.'

Grumbling, the two children went upstairs. Jenny stood in the hall watching them go, and was suffused with happiness.

Everything was turning out well after all. They would raise the money to buy William Corvill & Son and though it would probably take them ten years to pay off the loan, that didn't matter, because now they'd be working for themselves. Better to pay out money every quarter to a bank or a finance house than to send it to Lucy Corvill – better to break off every connection with her at last.

Moreover they would have preserved one of the greatest names in Scottish weaving. William Corvill & Son would go on as it had before: pre-eminent in design, famous for the fineness of its cloth, leaders in new techniques.

Today was a day for looking back and giving thanks. She had so much, so very much, to be thankful for. Two fine healthy children, a husband who loved her, friends and neighbours who would come tonight to share the celebrations.

As for herself . . . She looked in the mirror as Baird did her hair in preparation for the party. She was thirty-nine years old. Her hair was still as dark and thick as ever, her eyes still shone with the old eagerness for life. True, there were faint lines around them, but they had to be expected – she didn't imagine she could look young for ever.

She said to Baird, 'Do you think it's all right to wear the pearl grey?'

'Ach, I wish you'd wear the blue. You always look your best in blue. But the grey's bonny. And I'll tell you what, Sangster's got some coral-coloured carnations in the greenhouse, I'll make you up a wee spray wi' some maidenhair, for your corsage – who'd criticise a lady for wearing a wee flower on New Year's Eve?'

Later Baird went to put Heather into her party frock. The girl was in a tither with excitement. Always shy, she was screwing up her courage to wish the guests a Happy New Year as they arrived. But she was looking forward to the dancing, the games, the sight of the women in their ball dresses, the jokes and laughter. She might even be allowed a sip of the Captain's Cup, a notorious rum punch made after the recipe of a long-dead sea captain and only prepared on very special occasions.

'Haud still now, will ye!' scolded Baird, dragging back Heather's pale tawny hair into a bow of white ribbon. 'Look now, you've made me tangle the brush! I wisht your hair would keep a curl for ten minutes thegither.'

Heather sighed. 'It's no use, I'm never going to be a fashion plate, Baird.'

Baird brushed harder. She would have liked to say, Yes you are. But though Heather was a pleasant-looking girl, something was lacking. She held herself badly despite weekly lessons in deportment by the governess at Thornieburn. Her pale skin seldom seemed to sparkle with vitality. Her hair, though the colour of the Venus painted by Botticelli rising from the shell, would not be dressed fashionably into curl clusters.

Clothes never seemed to help much. The plain dresses and pinafores of everyday were not calculated to make her look particularly feminine, but even party dresses of muslin and gauze looked uninteresting when she wore them.

Only on horseback did Heather come into her own. There, in a habit of dark green worsted, her hat tied on with green ribbons, she looked fully alive as she made her mount canter and curvet, sidestep and trot. When she helped unsaddle her horse, when she stroked him and talked to him softly, her eyes would glow with warmth and friendship.

But a young girl couldn't live her life among horses. Baird was waiting and hoping for the day when Heather would look as vivid in the drawing room as she did in the stables.

When she took her charge downstairs, Jenny and Ronald were already greeting the first guests. Heather made her curtsey, busied herself with fetching punch and shortbread. The band began to tune up – two fiddlers, a flute, and a drummer.

By eleven the house seemed to be bursting at the seams.

For younger guests a magic lantern show was going on in the morning room. Grown-ups were dancing the Dashing White Sergeant. Elders were sitting at innocent card games – no gambling allowed on Hogmanay.

Heather looked at the clock. She had promised Max she'd tiptoe up and wake him at five minutes to twelve so that he could creep down and see the New Year in. Every child in Scotland somehow expects to see a physical presence enter the house as the clock strikes twelve on Hogmanay – a personification of hope and happiness, glowing and gleaming under the light that streams from the open door. Max was determined to see it tonight even if cruel adults sent him to bed as usual at six.

Unaware of this plot, Jenny was dancing her way down the line with Peter Laidlaw. Her husband was off in a corner of the drawing room, chatting with old Mr Kennet who had been their solicitor until he retired.

'So,' said Kennet, 'I gather my poor nephew has made a complete fool of himself.'

'He hasna covered himself with glory, certainly,' Ronald agreed.

'I only became aware of it after he'd made the decision to act for My Lady Nibs. If he'd spoken to me first, I'd have warned him off.'

'I doubt if he'd have listened. He was fair carried away.'

Kennet sipped his punch. 'He's mebbe recovered. He gave his wife an unco splendid present for New Year – a wrap of French velvet. Poor Elsie hardly knows what to make of it, but I think it's guilty conscience – '

'You mean, he's seen the error of his ways and he's trying to make up for it?'

'Aye, just about. As to that, Armstrong . . . is there anything he could do to make up for his clumsiness towards you and the Mistress?'

'No,' Ronald said with great terseness.

'Ach, man, Harold's no the first that's lost his head over yon lady, and he winna be the last. Be merciful to him, Armstrong.'

Ronald took a deep breath and smiled. This was Hogmanay, no time to be speaking harsh words. 'You know, Kennet, I would have left the business of William Corvill & Son with your old firm for as long as I lived. It was your nephew who broke the connection, and I have to tell you I've little confidence in him now. So when Corvill's really is ours, I think we'll stay with Loomis.'

'Damnation,' sighed Kennet. 'Wherever she goes, Lucy Corvill spreads trouble.'

Kennet was drawn away by his wife, who insisted he should sit down and rest his stroke-weakened leg. Ronald asked Miss Pollock to dance, but his mind was elsewhere. Poor Harold Jamieson! But Kennet had summed it up – Lucy Corvill spread trouble.

The night wore on towards the great moment. Thirley, a little giddy from secret sips of tawny port, set open the front door. Somewhere out on the drive, visitors waited to come in with the chimes, bearing first-footing presents. Out in the frosty air the jingling of bits and the stamping of impatient horses could be heard.

The fiddlers retuned their strings to be ready for the New Year rendering of 'Auld Lang Syne'. Jenny cast an eye about to make sure there was plenty to eat and drink for the first-footers.

There was a shriek of delight from Heather. Jenny heard her footsteps speeding to the door. She spun round.

'Aunt Lucy!' cried her daughter, and threw herself in an embrace of welcome upon Mrs Lucy Corvill.

CHAPTER FOURTEEN

Lucy had gone back to Carlisle from her interview with Jamieson in a state of alarm and dejection. At a certain point in the discussion, she'd seen the lawyer's expression change from anxious devotion to something like irritation. Something she'd said or done had caused it. But she couldn't remember what.

This had happened now and again over the past few years. She would have a little *crise des nerfs* and when she recovered from it, she had an imperfect recollection of what had happened.

Ned had always insisted it was nothing to worry about, a quite natural consequence of the dreadful time she'd had with . . . with . . . that man, that man who had gone away and left her, all alone, with no money and no one to turn to, in Dover, where she was a stranger, where people looked at her with questioning eyes because the man who was supposed to be her husband had simply gone, leaving her, he had gone though he'd vowed he loved her, and she had loved him, yes, she had, but that was over, Ned said it was over . . .

She drew herself back from the giddiness that sometimes seemed to threaten her when she let her mind stray towards that bad time.

Ned said it was in the past. But Ned was gone too. Well, she could manage on her own, she wasn't the fool she used to be, no, no, she'd learned something in the school of hard knocks.

Jamieson had grown cool towards her. All in a moment. But it didn't matter, Jamieson was only a provincial attorney, a nobody, a booby.

Still, it seemed to be true, what he said, that she was going to get a lot less for Corvill's than she'd expected. Just like that low, common Ronald Armstrong to have some devious plan to cheat her out of her inheritance!

Not all of it. She still had something to sell. And she would sell it, because she knew what a hindrance it was to be connected with trade, if you were seeking a good match. Look at Jenny! Nobody would take her because she insisted on working every day in that awful noisy, dusty factory. She'd been almost an old maid – in her mid-twenties – when at last she was forced to take Ronald Armstrong.

Lucy was determined nothing like that would happen to her. She wanted a husband, she needed a husband. The world was too frightening to deal with for long on her own. And it must be a husband worth having, the kind she'd thought she'd landed when she married Ned. She'd had no idea then, silly innocent that she was, that when he spoke of getting his income from industry, he actually meant his family owned spinning and weaving mills. And that all the family friends were connected with the cloth trade. He had deceived her, with his fine clothes and his gentleman's manners!

But that was in the past. All in the past. She

would sell up and she would find someone really suitable, take her proper place in society at last.

Mr Jamieson had said the sale of her property could go on, but under different circumstances. A letter next day, by special delivery, stated the case again, in short sentences and with no legal terminology, so that she would be sure to understand it.

The mills could not be sold as a going concern. Nevertheless, the buildings and certain fixed machinery – the boilers, for instance, which were of the latest design, and the loading bays with rail tracks for freight wagons direct to the rail system – these had high value.

An unbiased assessor had said he thought Ronald Armstrong's offer for these assets was more than fair. Mr Jamieson advised Lucy to take the offer. If she refused, and looked for another buyer, she might get less. A new buyer would have to bring new machinery and fix it in place, and this would be an expense. Therefore a new buyer would want to pay less for the premises. He hoped she followed all this?

He awaited her instructions, wrote Mr Jamieson anxiously, but in the meantime he wished to mention a matter which had caused him some concern. He begged her not to speak in a slighting fashion of Mr Armstrong or his wife.

From her words he gathered she felt some resentment for a wrong of the past, but he hoped she would set that aside, for Mr Armstrong's reputation was of the best. As Member of Parliament for West Tweed, he had many influential friends, among whom could be named most of the manufacturers of the Scottish Borders and the Earl of Thornieburn, the chief titled landowner of the district.

In view of the above, Mr Jamieson hoped he could rely on discretion and a practical acceptance of the actual business position. He remained her humble servant, Harold Jamieson.

Lucy had to read the letter twice. The first time, the passage at the end blotted out all that had gone before. A Member of Parliament? It was the first she'd heard of it.

Lucy had stayed only three days at Gatesmuir. Ronald had been at home and had gone each day to the mill office. Nothing had been said about Parliamentary duties. He had kept that from her! Sly and deceitful . . .

But wait, it had been August. Perhaps Parliament had holidays, like everyone else? So he had been at home on holiday, and had not thought perhaps to mention it. Or there had not been an occasion to do so, because of course she had been aloof and tending to seek solitude, as was only fitting for a widow.

For the same reason, she'd met none of the citizens of Galashiels. People had left cards, but no one had actually called by the time she went away. So no one had had the chance to speak of Ronald's career in the course of polite conversation.

She had come immediately to Carlisle, where her new acquaintances had mainly been the gentlefolk who had lodgings in the same handsome house, and ladies she'd met at Mudie's Library.

She'd mentioned to no one that she was connected with the Armstrongs – it was something she preferred to forget. Beyond saying that she was in the process of selling up property in the Scottish Borders, she'd mentioned nothing about her dead husband's relatives.

And of course she never read anything in newspapers except the advertisements and the society column. All the rest was so dreary. That was where she might have seen Ronald Armstrong mentioned. In the Parliamentary report. But who read the Parliamentary report? Only prosy old men or people such as clerks and cashiers . . .

A Member of Parliament . . . It meant he could put the letters MP after his name. And, as Jamieson reported, he knew important people.

He knew the Earl of Thornieburn. He was friends with an Earl!

The title echoed in her mind. She'd heard the place mentioned at Gatesmuir. Something about Heather. Jenny had said to Heather, 'When you go back to Thornieburn.' Lucy had paid no heed, she'd thought it was the name of a school, because surely the context had been something about lessons . . . Something about taking a new box of water-colours for lessons with the art master . . . Was that it?

Heather took lessons with a tutor at the home of Lord Thornieburn? She cudgelled her brains to remember more, but nothing came to her.

After a long interval she reread the letter. The first part now made complete sense to her. She could sell at a good price, it seemed. But . . . if the Armstrongs were now so well-placed in society, perhaps it would be better to keep the connection with them? If they already had the entrée to titled society, perhaps it would make more sense to be part of their world?

She was in such a state of fright and dismay that she had to send Jubal running for the sal volatile and afterwards lie down for an hour. When she got up to change for the evening meal, the parlourmaid who acted as personal maid noticed that Mrs Corvill seemed abstracted. But her mind had cleared.

The first thing was to find out more about Lord Thornieburn.

It was quite easy. Over the long and substantial dinner served by the landlady, she brought in the Earl's name.

It appeared he was quite well known in the Borders. Yes, he owned a lot of land, was very rich, but very stick-in-the-mud. Never bestirred himself, almost never went to town, had a wife who thought only of horses and hunting and dogs, and a son who was a complete weakling, so much so he couldn't be sent to school but had to be educated at home. She inquired the age of the son. About fifteen, said her dinner companions. Any other children? No, all the rest had died in infancy.

She thought it all over in bed that night. There was nothing there for her. A provincial laird who didn't like town life, a son nowhere near marriageable age – no, no, she could do better by sticking to her original plan.

She would sell up, take her funds, invest them according to Mr Jamieson's advice, and on the proceeds she would move between London and the spa towns. Somewhere in that circle she would find a match that would give her the life she deserved – a house in town for the season, a hall in the country in a land-scaped park, status and respect.

All the same, she'd be a fool not to take advantage of the springboard provided by the Armstrongs and their unexpected eminence. 'My brother-in-law is Member for West Tweed . . .' 'Lord Thornieburn – perhaps you know him? – my little niece visits at their country house . . .'

She had fences to mend. When she thought how she'd thrown away this advantage by let-ting a foolish quarrel develop, she was vexed with herself.

But never mind. Tomorrow was Hogmanay. She would go to Gatesmuir. The door would be standing open. Who could stop her from walking in?

The time wasn't yet midnight. She rose, called Jubal from his pallet on the landing out-side her door, and sent him to the kitchens with word that she would require breakfast next morning at seven.

When it was brought, she was already up and half-dressed. By eight she had given instructions to the parlourmaid to pack certain clothes in a portmanteau and have them taken to the station. Next she went out looking for a gift to take to Gatesmuir, with Jubal trotting at her side to carry the package.

By nine she was in the train for Selkirk. Arriving there, she took a postchaise to the Halfway House, a well-known coaching inn halfway between Selkirk and Galashiels. She took a room for that night and the next, then had her portmanteau unpacked.

From four until eight she slept. She ordered a meal to be sent up. Afterwards she dressed with the help of the landlord's wife, who was very admiring of the gown she had brought with her from New York and never yet worn.

At eleven she called for a chaise, wrapped herself in her sable-trimmed cape, gave Jubal the present to carry, and set off for Galashiels. The night was starlit and frosty, the road was good. They turned into the steep drive at Gatesmuir as midnight was approaching.

Alighting, she told the driver to draw up round by the stables. 'It may be a long wait,' she said.

'Och, aye, mistress, what else wad I expect on Hogmanay?' he said with equanimity, aware he had a bottle in his coat pocket for company.

Lucy walked up to the open doorway from which the light streamed. It was one of the most frightening things she had ever done – more frightening than anything since that night when she had run away from this very house to meet Harvil Massiter in London.

She stepped across the threshold. And everything was all at once made easy, for her niece Heather flew across the hall to fall upon her neck in welcome.

By the time it was necessary to look up, others had gathered around – some in greeting, some in mere curiosity. Since Heather was still hanging on her right arm, Lucy made a little gesture with her left. Jubal stepped from behind her, a little blue-clad figure bearing a sky-blue velvet cushion on which reposed a little packet wrapped in silver tissue. The group gathered around her stood back in admiration. What a way to go first-footing – attended by a little page to carry the gift!

Lucy had intended it for the mistress of the house. But one glance at Jenny told her the package might well be thrown back in her teeth.

Jenny had been taken totally by surprise at the appearance of her sister-in-law. Flashes of anger and alarm went through her mind.

I'll have her thrown out! But Heather's kissing her on the cheek. And it's Hogmanay – I can't turn anyone away on Hogmanay. And everybody's staring. God, what am I to do? And what is the little witch up to now?

While she was still trying to make up her mind what to do, Lucy spoke in her soft, clear voice. 'I wish you the Auld Wish – strength to the roof of this house, health and happiness to all within. A Guid New Year!'

A little movement of her gloved hand directed Jubal to give the first-footing gift to Heather.

Heather uttered a cry of delight. She took the package, untied the ribbon to reveal a small silver box. Inside were cachous of coloured sugar bearing suitable words such as Happiness or Success.

Alight with pleasure, Heather began offering them around. Onlookers replied heartily to Lucy's greeting: 'And a Guid New Year to you, Mistress Corvill.'

It was a fait accompli. She had made her entrance and nothing could alter the fact that she was once more inside Gatesmuir.

Afterwards some of the women guests were heard to say that the gown revealed when Thirley took her cape had somewhat too much sparkle and glitter of black bugle beads for a family Hogmanay party in the country. The younger ladies protested that she had looked marvellous, like a mourning Princess in a stage play.

'Indeed,' agreed their elders drily.

Heather had elected herself guardian of this Princess. She led her into the dining room for refreshments.

Jubal followed at their heels. 'Little boy,' said Jenny in concern as he passed her, 'have you no greatcoat for this weather?'

He paused, looked up at her. His black face was purple-blue with cold.

'Good heavens, you're shivering. Here, come to the fire! Betty, fetch some hot coffee.' She put a hand on the blue-clad shoulder, urged him to the hearth where the flinders smelt so sweetly of burning applewood. 'What's your name again?'

'Jubal, mam.'

'Are you hungry, Jubal? Did you have supper?'

'Yes, mam, at eight o'clock.'

'But that seems a long time ago, I expect. What would you like? Cold ham? Salmon? Hot soup?'

'Thank you, mam. But Miz Corvill will want me – '

'Oh, fiddlesticks,' said Jenny, looking at the small burdens he bore, 'Mrs Corvill won't need her fan or her reticule for the next few minutes.'

Betty appeared with the hot coffee, to which she had liberally added cream and sugar. The black face was buried in the large cup. When he emerged, Jubal looked a little less likely to die of cold.

'Where have you just come from, Jubal?'

'We in the Halfway House, mam, t'ree mile down de road.'

'Since when?'

'Since dis afternoon, Miz Armstrong.'

'I see. Well, Jubal, sit you there and in a minute Betty shall bring you a tray with some food, and mind, I want you to eat it all up, every scrap.'

'Yes, mam.'

He sat down cross-legged on the rug in front of the hall fire. A draught inevitably reached him from the open front door. Jenny could see the sateen-clad shoulders hunching themselves against it. She twitched an ornamental shawl from a chairback to drape around him. 'There, that's better, isn't it?'

He smiled, a sudden flash of white teeth in a black face. Jenny was startled. She realised it was the first time she'd seen the child smile.

She hurried now in search of Ronald to tell him about their visitor. He was in the morning room with some of the men who wanted a quiet smoke. The heavy fragrance of cigars wafted out as she opened the door and beckoned.

'What's up?' he asked at the sight of her face.

'Lucy's here.'

'Here?'

'She just walked in as a first-footer.'

'I hope you told her to walk straight out again.'

'I couldn't, Ronald, Heather was hanging on her arm.'

'Oh, Heaven and Hell!' He closed the door of the morning room, drew her aside. 'What do you suppose she's after?'

'Who knows?'

'We'll go and ask her.'

'Ronald . . . Don't let's have a scene in front of Heather. It would be bad for her.'

'I'm not going to make a scene. I just want to know what that little cat is up to.'

They went into the dining room, which had a fair gathering of guests sitting at small tables. These had been eating and talking, but were now principally engaged in watching Mrs Corvill. They knew there had been a family quarrel over the selling of Corvill's. They wanted to see what was going to happen. As Jenny and Ronald came in, their attention noticeably increased.

Heather was filling a plate for Lucy, who stood smiling and protesting at the bounty. As she saw her host and hostess approach, her smile grew warmer.

'Ah, Ronald, so there you are – Ronald, here's wishing you a happy and prosperous New Year!' She lifted a filled glass from the buffet, raised it in toast.

'Lucy . . .'

'I wanted to come on this night of all nights,' Lucy said quickly, giving the little speech she'd been rehearsing all day, 'because there should be no coolness between members of a family.' She turned to Jenny. 'You and I, sister-in-law, said some things to each other in the heat of the moment. But I know you didn't mean them any more than I did. So here's to you and here's to us, and a new beginning in a new year!'

'Hear, hear,' murmured those who were near enough to catch her words. 'A new beginning!'

'Of course, of course,' Ronald said, nodding

here and there in assent. To Lucy he said, 'But I'd like a private word – '

The clock in the hall began to speak with a silvery chime. The band at the end of the hall played a loud chord. 'Happy New Year!' the shout went up.

Everyone hurried to the hall. The fiddlers led the way out into the sharp night air. The revellers spilled out after them. The song began: 'Should auld acquaintance be forgot . . .'

Ronald caught Jenny and Heather round the waist to urge them out under the night sky. For the moment everything else must take second place. Midnight had struck, the old year was behind them, it was 1876!

Later, when the first excess of hugs and handshakes had subsided, the gathering began an open-air eightsome reel. Lucy was swept away in the arms of some merry gentleman, and Ronald lost the opportunity of speaking to her in private.

Jenny exchanged a glance with her husband. They knew they had been outmanoeuvred. No use now to try to tell Lucy she was unwelcome at Gatesmuir. She was once more within their family circle, all they could do was accept her and keep their guard up.

Later, when some of the gentlemen teased her about her decision to sell Corvill's, Lucy passed it off with a little laugh. 'Oh, I've no head for business, never had, you know. I'm selling out, but only to my brother-in-law. It will stay in the family. Family ties are so important, don't you agree?'

Who could argue with that?

The words were repeated to Ronald. 'So she

knows she's got to sell to us, does she?' he muttered to Jenny. 'It's what you might call making the best of a bad job on her part, but she's managed to get an advantage out of it.'

Heather recalled, to her shame, that she had forgotten to rouse Max to see the New Year in. She comforted herself with the thought that he still hadn't learnt to read the time on the clock face. So she woke him, told him it was midnight, and let him have a view of the festivities though the banisters. By bribing him with a piece of shortbread and a chocolate mousse, she had him tucked up again by one o'clock.

As she was coming quietly back downstairs, she witnessed a curious episode. Archie Brunton had just arrived to first-foot the household, carrying a great sheaf of hothouse flowers. He walked in through the open front door, saw the black page boy squatting by the fire, stopped, and looked around in what seemed like dismay. For a moment Heather thought he was about to walk out again.

'Mr Brunton!' Heather cried, and ran to greet him. 'Happy New Year!'

'Er . . . Hello, Heather . . . Happy New Year . . . The little black page . . . what's he doing here?'

'Aunt Lucy brought him, isn't it wonderful? She's come back for New Year!'

'Come back?' Once more Mr Brunton looked about him, as if he were longing to escape. Heather couldn't imagine what was wrong with him. Generally Mr Brunton was so full of fun and so interested in everything at Gatesmuir.

'You didn't meet her when she was here

before, did you, Mr Brunton? It was only a very short stay.'

'No . . . I was busy with estate business. But I knew her years ago, you know . . .'

Still he looked as if he might depart at any moment but for Heather's hand on his arm.

Her mother came up to take the flowers and exchange New Year's greetings. 'Now, Heather dear, it's long past midnight and time you went to bed. Off you go.'

'Oh, Mama!'

'Look at you, you're like a ghost from weariness. Up to bed with you.'

'May I go and say goodnight to Aunt Lucy first?'

Jenny sighed. 'Of course, dear.'

'She'll be taking breakfast with us? I'll see her then?'

'I think not, dear. She'll take the dawn snack and leave, I imagine.'

'But Mama! Surely you're asking her to stay?'

'She has a room at the Halfway House and a hired chaise waiting to take her there – '

'But we could send the chaise back – '

'Heather, your aunt has her own plans. You can't expect her to change everything.'

'No,' Heather said, looking penitent. 'No, I see that. Very well, Mama. But may we have her here again soon? And may we go and visit her in Carlisle?'

'We'll see, my love, we'll see. This is a busy time for us – '

'Surely we're not too busy to visit Aunt Lucy!'

'Heather, we have the buying of the mills to see to. And you'll be going back to your lessons at Thornieburn. Later in the year, we'll see . . . we'll see.'

Heather held up her cheek to be kissed, then went off somewhat droopingly to say good-night to her aunt. Archie jerked his head towards the page boy. 'When I walked in and saw him . . . I'd heard she'd brought a little negro when she came in August.'

'She arrived just before midnight.'

'But I thought she went away in a huff?'

'So she did. But she's back again.'

'Lord, Jenny, this is embarrassing! I don't want to meet her!'

'Then say a few words to a few people and take yourself off again.'

Too late. Lucy was brought by Heather, all aglow at the thought of re-introducing old friends to one another on this auspicious night. 'You told me you used to know Aunt Lucy,' she said. 'Aunt Lucy, do you remember Mr Brunton?'

Lucy stopped in her tracks. For a moment she faltered. Heather, a little ahead of her, turned back to see why she hesitated.

Lucy made a sharp gesture to Jubal, who leapt up to bring her her fan. Taking it, she spread the black ostrich feathers before her face, fluttered them a few times as if she were too warm.

'Mrs Corvill,' said Archie, bowing. 'It's many years since we met.'

'Mr Brunton,' she replied, with a faint incli-nation of her fair head.

'May I wish you the season's greetings?'

'I wish you the same.' She smiled and walked away.

'Oh,' said Heather, disappointed. 'I thought she'd be pleased . . .'

'Darling, go to bed,' commanded Jenny.

Yawning, Heather obeyed. She was unaware of any real awkwardness, and the rest of the people at the party were in the same case. No one in Galashiels knew that Archie Brunton and Lucy Corvill had once been lovers, except themselves and Jenny Armstrong.

'Jenny, don't ask her to stay here,' Archie begged.

'Certainly not,' Jenny agreed. 'She'd never have got in here at all if she hadn't used Hogmanay as an excuse.'

'*Why* is she here?'

'I don't know, Archie, but I'm sure she hopes to gain something by it. It's gey awkward – my poor little girl has taken a juvenile passion for her.'

Lucy had wanted to achieve the appearance of a good relationship with Ned's family. So far she had succeeded. The arrival of Archie Brunton had shaken her, however. She had almost forgotten about Archie Brunton – so much else had happened in her life since that distant affair. And yet to see him again, still handsome, still rich, and apparently a close friend of Jenny's . . . It was upsetting.

All at once she felt she had had enough. It was time to go. She called Jubal, told him to order up her coach and fetch her cape. Then she went to say her goodbyes to Ronald, who was exchanging toasts with newcomers.

'Brother-in-law, it has been wonderful to see you again. Thank you for a happy party.'

'You're leaving?' said Ronald with ill-disguised relief.

'I find I'm tired. Talking so much to so many old acquaintances . . . dancing Scottish dances . . . one never had such things in Richmond. Dear Ronald, goodnight – or rather, good morning. I wish you every success with the mills once you become full owner.'

'Thank you.'

'Mr Jamieson explained everything to me,' she said with a departing smile. 'I've no business sense, you know. I didn't quite understand things until he explained. But he assures me – and I accept his assurance – that a fair price will be arranged.'

So that's it, thought Ronald. She wants to make sure we're not gypping her. 'You can rest easy on that score, sister-in-law,' he said.

'I think I explained that I wanted to re-invest. I shall do so, and when I have settled in my new home, perhaps you and Jenny will come to visit me.'

'Where do you think of settling, Mrs Corvill?' asked John Dyers, who was standing shamelessly eavesdropping.

'Oh, London, I think. I've always loved London. And after travelling so much, you know, I'm accustomed to lively surroundings. Yes, a small house in London, I think. That's one of the projects for the New Year. Good morning to you, sir. Good morning, Ronald. Give my love to Jenny.'

'I'll fetch her – '

'No need, no need, she has her duties as hostess – and here is my chaise, I believe. Goodbye, everyone.'

'Goodbye, goodbye!'

They stood in admiration as she was helped into her chaise by the page boy, who leapt up to the box as the carriage moved off.

'A fine-looking leddy,' said Dyers, 'verra sweet to speak to . . . I hope the New Year has good things in store for her.'

Archie Brunton stayed on as he usually did, to share the meal that was served at 'dawn', the hour of five o'clock, at which Hogmanay was considered to be over and New Year's Day began. There were still eighteen merrymakers at Gatesmuir at that hour, but they straggled off by five-thirty.

Jenny signalled to Thirley to close the door. Even now it would not be locked and bolted but could be opened by merely turning the latch for the rest of the day.

But no one else would come for the next few hours. Everyone, even the most stalwart reveller, had gone to seek some rest. Jenny watched the servants make a hasty clearance of the remains of the party food, saw the chairs and tables set straight, and decreed that everyone should go to bed.

She and Ronald went upstairs arm in arm. 'It was a strange party,' said Ronald, 'not at all the one I was looking forward to.'

'She spoiled it.' Jenny shook her head sadly. 'She spoiled what I thought was going to be one of the happiest nights of my life. We had almost settled the problem of the money to buy Corvill's – everything was turning out well. Our friends were all around us, they were pleased for our sake. I felt the world was turning on its axis as if to a waltz tune. And then she walked in.'

'I think she wanted to make some sort of

appeal to us, not to be hard on her when it comes to settling the price.'

'Oh,' cried Jenny, 'if I weren't so tired I'd be angry!'

'Don't let her upset you. She's not worth it.'

'But Ronald, it makes me a little anxious that Heather seems to think so much of her.'

He opened the door of their bedroom. 'Don't worry about it,' he said. 'She's going to settle in London. She told me so herself as she was leaving. With a little good footwork we can avoid ever seeing her there.'

Jenny went in and let herself fall on the bed. 'If I never see her again until I die,' she said, 'that will be too soon.'

As she made preparations for bed in a daze of weariness she was vowing that she would take care never to meet Lucy in London.

She was quite unaware that her sister-in-law had different intentions. Lucy, awake and restless in her bed at the inn, could see how the Armstrongs might be very useful to her in the new life she was planning. She had learned a lot from conversations at the Gatesmuir party.

Oh yes. 'My brother-in-law, the Member for West Tweed . . . highly thought-of by Lord Thornieburn . . . his little girl shares lessons with Allen . . . that's the Viscount, you know, Viscount Cairness . . .' How well it sounded!

Far too useful to let slip, the Armstrongs. What a good thing Mr Jamieson had alerted her in time.

CHAPTER FIFTEEN

When Jenny said to Heather that they would be busy in the New Year, it was no idle excuse.

Mr Lockhart of the London-Scottish Commercial Bank was perfectly willing to advance money to the Armstrongs. However, he suggested it would make more sense if they took the whole sum from his bank rather than from a series of smaller banks and merchants. It would be easier, he remarked, to send out one cheque for repayment each quarter than to send out half a dozen.

The formalities were soon settled. Jamieson received the selling price on behalf of Lucy Corvill, and at her request re-invested it. He reported that she had gone to London. Soon it was noted in the society columns that Mrs Corvill was now residing at 14 Chelmer Street in Mayfair, and that the elegance of her new furnishings and decorations was beyond praise.

In March Jenny Armstrong had to go to London on business. The new pattern book was out, so William Corvill & Son were giving a series of small parties at hotels and at the house in Eaton Square.

Jenny was inquisitive enough to have her hackney driver take her past the house in

Mayfair where her sister-in-law was now abiding. True enough – elegant, small, delicate, the place was the perfect setting for its new owner.

Jenny also visited Dinah Eynsham, who was now settled in her Chelsea house on a more or less permanent basis. Her little boy Clive, now eight, was attending a local private school and doing well. Dinah had friends now among her neighbours, some of them a little bohemian, since Chelsea was the home of many artists, but their easygoing ways suited Dinah even if she couldn't always understand what they were talking about.

'Is that right, that lady they mention in the newspapers, that Mrs Corvill, she's a relation of yours?' Dinah asked as she served tea to Jenny one afternoon. 'It's the same name as your firm and everything, and once it mentioned she was connected to the MP for West Tweed.'

'That's right. She's the widow of my brother Ned.'

'Fancy that! I read in the *Chronicle* where it said she'd given a party last week and some lady from Covent Garden sung some songs and everything. How did the *Chronicle* know about that?'

'I imagine she must have told them,' Jenny said, suppressing a smile.

'Honest? I wondered. Because, you know, I can have Mr Burne-Jones sitting right there talking to me and nobody ever hears about it.'

'Do you want them to?'

'Well, no . . . I don't think so.'

'There you are, then.'

'You mean, this Mrs Corvill wants people to know?'

Jenny sipped tea and considered Lucy's 'wants'. 'I think my sister-in-law wants to be noticed, but only by the right people and for the right things. Little parties where people chat and half-listen to music – that's proper and allowable. But sitting chatting to a painter with daubs of red and blue on his clothes – that's not quite respectable.'

'Well, supposing she wants to be noticed by the right people and for the right things – what does it get her?' Dinah asked with interest.

Jenny decided not to say what she really thought: that what Lucy wanted to get was a husband. 'I really don't know,' she said. 'Lucy and I don't have a lot in common, and she lived abroad a long time.'

'It's funny, wanting to be mentioned in the newspapers like that. It says she's very beautiful. "The beautiful Mrs Edward Corvill", they call her. Is she really? Beautiful, I mean?'

Clive burst in, home from school. 'Hello, Mrs Armstrong, Ma said you'd be dropping by. Can I have some real tea, Ma? You promised I could.'

'All right, all right, don't raise the roof.' Dinah poured tea into a thick china mug, adding very generous allowances of milk and sugar. 'There you are. And you can have a piece of sponge cake too – '

'Lovely!' cried Clive. 'Can I take it upstairs while I play with my soldiers?'

Dinah waved him away. When the door closed on him she said, 'He's all for "real tea" since he discovered Mr Brunton likes it.'

'Archie?'

'Yair, Mr Brunton dropped by just before Christmas, took us out to a place or two. We had a slap-up tea in a very nice restaurant and Mr Brunton happened to mention he liked his tea good and strong. Ever since, Clive's trying to get me to let him off milk-and-hot-water tea.' She laughed. 'Mr Brunton and Clive get on a treat.'

'I'm pleased to hear it,' said Jenny, intrigued. 'Shall they be seeing each other again soon?'

'It ain't . . . isn't likely. Mr Brunton mentioned he was trying to take more part in the running of his estate nowadays. I always thought it a bit rum, him having someone else to manage it for him when, after all, it's quite small.'

'It's very big, by Scottish standards, Dinah. Don't forget, we don't measure farms by square miles here.'

Dinah laughed. 'I'm beginning to forget what it was like back there, really. I've even got quite accustomed to having houses all around. Funny, isn't it? Mr Brunton says it's "acclimatisation" – is that the word?'

Jenny took her leave with the thought that a lot seemed to follow from what Mr Brunton said. It was an interesting notion.

On Saturday, her business allowing her a lull, she took Dinah on a shopping expedition. Easter was three weeks away. She wanted some Swiss piqué and batiste for dresses for herself and Heather, and it would be pleasant to buy something for Dinah and Clive – material for a gown for Dinah, for a sailor suit for her son.

In the Haymarket there was a shop which specialised in imported fabrics. They strolled to it through the busy London streets in the

297

March sunshine. The cottons department was to one side, but through an arch the silk department could be glimpsed.

'Dinah,' whispered Jenny.

'What?'

'You know you were wondering about my sister-in-law?'

'Eh?'

'You wondered what my sister-in-law Lucy was like.'

'Oh, yes.'

'If you look through the arch, you'll see her.' As Dinah strode towards the arch, Jenny grabbed her skirt and pulled her back. 'Ssh . . . Don't march in like that! I don't want her to see us.'

'You don't?'

'No. I told you, we don't have much in common.'

Dinah subsided into her place by Jenny's side. She studied Lucy, who was worth studying – out of mourning now, in a walking dress of velvet the colour of a dark ruby, a faery-like creature, slender and fragile.

'She's real pretty.'

The shopman, Arnolds, was a bachelor of fifty who had given his entire life to two things: fine imported fabrics and gossip. 'You're admiring the elegant customer?' he murmured. 'We had the honour to show Mrs Corvill our new spring silks last week. I imagine she's here to tell us which she has chosen for her season's ball gowns. You may have seen mention of her in the newspapers?'

'Yes, in the *Chronicle*,' Dinah said.

'She's quite a leader in her set – '

'Which set is that?'

'Oh, well, madam, perhaps it's too early to say,' Arnolds replied archly, 'but I do hear that one or two of the Marlborough House set are showing an interest in her.'

'The Marlborough House set?'

'That's the Prince of Wales and his friends. Rather fast, some people say,' he said with a little suppressed giggle. 'All to the good, perhaps, because I *have* heard there's some kind of scandal in Mrs Corvill's past.'

'Really?' said Dinah, round-eyed. 'You never told me that, Jenny.'

Jenny refused to take part. 'I think we'll have the narrow stripe piqué – eight yards should be enough. And do you have cotton gabardine in navy blue?'

'Ah, sailor suits, ma'am; I understand. Behind me on the shelf – there are two, one is a French navy, the other is an Italian cloth.'

They made their choice, Arnolds took away the fabrics to cut the lengths and make out the bill. The parcels would of course be delivered. Lucy meanwhile had moved further into the recesses of the silk department. Dinah took a peep through the arch, coming back to say in a startled voice, 'There's a little blackfeller sitting on the floor in there!'

'Ah, that is Mrs Corvill's page boy,' said Arnolds, showing the bill to Jenny. 'That comes to four pounds eleven shillings, ma'am.'

'Oh, they mentioned him in the papers. You mean she takes him shopping, and all?'

'Oh yes. Very chic, you know. I hear quite a few ladies are looking for small black boys to hire as pages.'

'Chic, is it? Can't say I'd care for it. Where I come from, the Abo boys are apt to take their clothes off and go walkabout as the mood takes them.'

Arnolds looked shocked. Jenny smothered a laugh. He went to fetch change from the five pound note she had given him.

At the shop entrance the door opened on a peremptory voice already saying, 'Lukas! Lukas! Where is the grosgrain you promised? My dressmaker says she hasn't received it!'

Jenny gave a start. The voice was unmistakable. 'Oh, lord!' she gasped.

'What's the matter, Jenny?'

'Stay here, then go outside as soon as you get my change, Dinah.'

'What? Where are you going?'

'Never mind,' Jenny whispered. 'Do as I say.'

She herself went through the arch holding a pattern book at face level as a disguise. She threaded her way past a display table, to where her sister-in-law was standing in thought before a fall of fine grenadine silk. She put her hand under her elbow and said in her ear, 'Lucy, quick, come with me, Mrs Massiter has just come in at the shop door.'

Lucy gave a cry of alarm.

'Ssh . . .' said Jenny. 'If you go through into the cottons department you can avoid her.'

'But – '

'Can't you hear her?' Jenny insisted.

And from the front of the shop the irritated voice went on, 'She should have been cutting out the gown today. I want the cloth delivered *at once!*'

'But madam,' stammered the hapless Lukas, who managed the shop, 'the parcel was sent out yesterday afternoon . . .'

'Then it's been delivered to the wrong address, nincompoop!'

'Quick, Lucy.'

There was no further argument. Lucy turned away from the silk she had been examining to follow Jenny through the arch. By going round one or two displays it would be possible to bypass Mrs Massiter and reach the door.

Unfortunately in their anxiety both women had forgotten Jubal. The page boy awoke from his drowsy waiting state to see his mistress opening the shop door. He saw himself left abandoned in a shop full of strangers.

'Miz Corvill!' he called, leaping up.

He collided with the edge of a display stand. Bolts of silk fell about him. Tangled, he flailed about, still calling, 'Wait foh me, Miz Corvill!'

Maud Massiter heard the name. She whirled, discovered the source of the cry in a little figure on its knees among folds of brilliant silk. She seized Jubal by the shoulder, dragged him up.

'You!' she shouted, shaking him. 'Where's your mistress?'

'Let me go!' wept Jubal, aware only that he was being held fast while, as he supposed, Mrs Corvill was hurrying away.

Jenny had turned back.

'Don't, Mrs Massiter,' she said, 'you're hurting him!'

Lucy had fled out of the shop door. But Mrs Massiter had glimpsed her. She gave Jubal a push that sent him staggering into Jenny's arms, and rushed after Lucy.

In the Haymarket on a busy afternoon the chances of hailing an empty cab were not good. Lucy was still on the pavement looking anxiously at the traffic.

Maud Massiter caught up with her in a flurry of nodding feathers and bonnet ribbons. 'Wait, Mrs Corvill!' she cried, seizing her by the arm with a plump but strong hand. 'I want a word with you!'

Lucy shrank back. 'Leave me alone!'

'By no means, my fine friend! I've waited a long time for this! So – you dare to flaunt yourself in London, do you? Advertising yourself in the newspapers like a fairground show – you and your soirées and your musical recitals!'

People had stopped to stare. Lucy gave a cry of dismay and buried her face in her hands. Jenny, elbowing her way through to reach her, said, 'Please, Mrs Massiter, this can do no good – '

'Nothing can do any good!' cried the other woman, her voice full of grief and unshed tears. 'But why should she crow from the top of the tree while my poor husband has to skulk abroad, for fear of being put in handcuffs if he comes home? *She* is the one to blame, not my poor Harvil!'

Dinah appeared on the fringe of the gathering crowd. She caught Jenny's eye, and nodded towards a hansom which had slowed a few yards further on. The driver was craning his neck to see what was happening on the pavement.

'It cannot improve matters to discuss it in the middle of Haymarket,' Jenny said, edging round so that Mrs Massiter turned towards her and away from Lucy. 'Come now, be sensible, let us go back into the shop.' She held out a hand as if to take Mrs Massiter's. The other woman half accepted, then snatched hers back.

'I have nothing to say to *you!*' she exclaimed. 'And why should you defend her? She brought disgrace on your family – '

Dinah had signalled to the hansom, the driver had opened the flap doors, and next moment she had pushed Lucy in and followed her. The hansom took off.

'Miz Corvill!' cried Jubal in despair.

Jenny caught him as he launched himself in the wake of the vehicle. The crowd broke into laughter at the expression on Mrs Massiter's face as she saw her quarry vanish. She struck out at nothing with her parasol, then staggered. 'Help her!' cried Jenny. 'It's no laughing matter – she's going to faint!'

Half the shop staff had come out to see what was going on. Mr Lukas sent for a chair, smelling salts were produced. Jenny quietly faded into the background, taking Jubal with her.

'Miz Corvill gwan be mad at me,' he said through his tears. 'She allus say I should stay handy, not get lost.'

'You aren't lost, Jubal. You're with me.'

'But Miz Corvill say I should be with her.'

'So you will be. I'll take you there.'

'You know where Miz Corvill lives?'

'Yes, it's not far.'

He sniffed two or three times. His tears seemed to pass. Then he said, 'We didn't get no silk. Miz Corvill gwan be mad we didn't get no silk.'

'Mrs Corvill isn't going to be worrying about silk, Jubal.'

They crossed Haymarket, heading for St

James's Square. 'This the way to Miz Corvill's house?' he asked anxiously.

'Yes, another five minutes' walk.'

'Shouldn't we take a cab? Miz Corvill allus say, it ain't ladylike to walk in de street.'

'I don't mind, if you don't,' Jenny said with amusement.

'Oh, I don't mind, lady. I like being wid you.'

He trotted at her side, occasionally glancing up at her. After a pause he said, 'That big lady – she shore was mad at me.'

'Not at you, Jubal. Don't worry about her.'

'Oh, I ain't worried about her now I'm wid you.' After that, conversation languished until they reached Chelmer Street. As they approached the door he said in a shaky voice, 'Will you wait while I ring de bell, lady? And explain to Miz Corvill I didn't mean to get lost?'

'Of course.'

The door was opened by a smart parlour-maid, who frowned at Jubal. 'Where've *you* been?'

'Be so good,' Jenny said sharply, 'as to tell Mrs Corvill her sister-in-law is here.'

'Oh, yes, madam . . . Mrs Corvill just came home a moment ago, madam . . . She's indisposed.'

Dinah came out of a door further up the elegant little hall. 'Is that you, Jenny? Everything's fine here. Mrs Corvill's a bit quavery but she's all right really. Can we scoot now? I promised Clive I'd be back by five.'

'We'll go directly.' She turned to stoop over Jubal. 'It's all right, little lad. Don't worry about anything.' To the maid she said, 'Please tell Mrs Corvill that I brought her page boy

304

home after she hurried away without him. Jubal is afraid she'll think he was remiss but he isn't in any way to blame. Is that understood?'

'Yes, ma'am.'

When they were out in the street, Dinah grinned at Jenny.

'I got some news for the social column,' she said. 'If Mrs Corvill had a little get-together promised for this evening, she's gonna cancel it.'

'I thought you said she was all right?'

'But not up to facing her fancy friends, I'd imagine.' They walked through the square into Pall Mall. 'Who was the fat old duck making all the ruckus?'

'Let's just forget it, Dinah.'

'Oh, go on, tell me – the traffic was making too much noise for me to catch what she said, but whatever it was it reduced Mrs Corvill to a jelly.'

'You remember what the shop assistant was saying, about a scandal in Mrs Corvill's past? Well, it was something to do with that.'

'A scandal! And she looks so milk-and-roses! Well, I'm the last person to hold it against her, I reckon.' They looked about for a cab. 'Don't let's take a hansom,' Dinah said, laughing. 'There isn't room in a hansom for two sets of skirts – I just found that out.'

When Jenny got home, Ronald was already indoors. They were entertaining a mixed group that evening, some Parliamentary colleagues and their wives together with two foreign buyers based in London. As they changed for dinner, Jenny recounted the afternoon's events.

'Sounds like quite a drama,' Ronald observed.

'I only made matters worse by trying to get Lucy away. Poor little Jubal, he set up such a wail. You know, Ronald, that little boy is frightened of Lucy.'

'I don't blame him. She's never been very considerate towards servants.'

'He worries me. He's so far away from home, and among strangers . . .'

'That's true, but his mother sent him with Lucy, didn't she? She must have thought it would be all right.'

'Yes.' Jenny sighed, and rang for Baird to help her with her dress.

Later, when they were alone again, she said, 'Mrs Massiter is really very strange.'

'Well, we knew that. She set that idiot Unsworth on to make life difficult for me in the House.'

'You haven't mentioned him recently.'

'No, he's been quiet for months now – hardly a peep out of him. I think after I faced him down he felt he'd better behave.'

'I wonder if anything may start up again. After all, I stepped in between Mrs Massiter and Lucy – it may set her off on some new tack.'

'Do you think so?' Ronald paused with his hairbrushes in his hands. 'I hope not. After all, she must have known Lucy was in London – there've been quite a few notices in the newspapers about her. Yet she never made any move towards her, until bad luck brought them together today.'

'You know, when Massiter ran off with Lucy, his wife was filled with rage. Baxter told me he approached her, trying to find out where Massiter had gone to, and she could hardly speak for the fury that was burning her up. Yet today – today she wasn't just angry. When she spoke of Massiter it was in such a piteous tone . . .'

'Oh, good lord, lassie, don't start feeling sorry for Maud Massiter!'

'No . . . But she said something very odd. She said her husband didn't dare come home for fear of being clapped in jail, or something like that. But surely she must know he's safe enough now. We couldn't bring a case against *him* if we couldn't bring one against Lucy.'

Ronald shrugged. 'I don't give a damn about Harvil Massiter or his wife.'

'Oh, neither do I,' Jenny hastened to say. 'But all the same . . . I wonder why he's never come home?'

Although Ronald told himself he didn't care one way or the other, enough curiosity remained to make him think of it next time he was at his club. He had actually heard Massiter's name mentioned in smoking room gossip. Over a cigar one evening, he let the name trickle through the talk again.

'Oh, Lord, yes, Harvil Massiter! What a card! He's living like a pasha out in Egypt now, I hear. Haven't seen him myself, but Somers – you know Somers? No, perhaps you don't, he's off in Asia Minor on some Foreign Office station, poor soul. Well, anyhow, he was saying – last summer, was it? – he ran across Massiter in Alexandria.'

'In Alexandria – he has a business there?'

'Massiter? You're joking! Massiter never raised a finger to earn money in his life. No, no, he's got this silly rich wife who sends him money.'

Ronald was astounded. 'Mrs Massiter sends him money? But . . . didn't I hear that he had left her?'

His informant grinned roguishly. 'Massiter spun her some yarn – I forget the details, old fellow, but he's somehow persuaded her it isn't safe for him to come back to England. Could be true, of course – he was up to his ears in debt when he skedaddled and who knows what he'd done besides! Somers said Massiter had just arrived from Cairo, where Mrs Massiter came out on a ship to find him. I seem to remember he practically got out the back door of his hotel while she was coming in the front. Haw, haw – damn fast on his feet, what?'

'I don't think I follow,' said Ronald. 'You're saying he avoids her and yet she keeps him in funds and so on?'

'Oh yes, he knows how to handle her. He don't want to go back to being a good little husband, and who can blame him. Ever met Mrs Massiter?'

'I've seen her, yes.'

'Well, I mean to say, old fellow – she's ten years older than Massiter and she never was a beauty. Why should he go back to the marital nest when he can finagle money out of her and live abroad to please himself?'

One of the group of men snorted. 'You can snigger about it, Loftus, but it's not gentlemanly, to treat a woman like that.'

'Never said Massiter was a gentleman,' Loftus replied through his cigar smoke. 'All I said was, he's a card. He's managed his affairs so that he gets enough to live on very comfortably. And Alexandria's full of those lovely dark-eyed girls – what?'

'You mean he keeps a mistress on his wife's money?'

'I'd imagine he would never live like a monk, my dear old chap. That's why he had to do a bunk when Mrs Massiter turned up. By and by he sends her some guff about how he had to move because the police were on his trail, and she seems to believe it all – she's not a clever woman, you know, though she's got bags of money.'

'She'd cut off his finances if she knew how he was using her,' someone remarked.

'Oh, I think she prefers not to know. She's built up this fairy story about her husband in exile – it's a sort of compensation to her for being left in the lurch.'

'But then how does she account for the fact that she doesn't go out to join him? There's really nothing to stop her, is there? Except for the fact that he doesn't want her!'

'As far as I recall, she always says he won't let her live in circumstances of hardship. And it's true enough, she wouldn't enjoy Alexandria – it's a man's town, from all I gather. Why doesn't she insist he lives somewhere civilised, I hear you ask, like Baden-Baden or Florence? Because, he says, his enemies could get at him in Europe.'

'And she believes him?' the cry went up.

'I told you he was a card! Could make a woman believe the English Channel is full of green pea soup, if he wanted to.'

It was a worrying conversation, as far as Ronald was concerned. It told of a woman being fed on fantasy, led to believe that the husband whom she still loved was being separated from her by the machinations of 'enemies' – those enemies being, supposedly, the Armstrongs.

As to Lucy, there was no knowing how she figured in Mrs Massiter's thoughts. She was the prime cause of all her misery – the femme fatale who had tempted her husband away in the first place. Yet there was very little Maud Massiter could actually do to Lucy. She couldn't prevent her from re-entering society, because Mrs Massiter had no influence in the kind of society Lucy was seeking. Mrs Massiter had never been one of the Marlborough House set.

Should he do anything? If so, what? Warn Lucy? But surely Lucy must realise, after that embarrassing confrontation in the Haymarket, that Mrs Massiter had not ceased to hate her.

He decided to let well enough alone, the more so as events were turning out so that he was able to keep an eye on Lucy.

Grateful to the kindly stranger who like an angel had borne her away from her accuser, Lucy called at Eaton Square to ask for her name and address so that she could write her thanks.

'Oh, she doesn't expect any thanks, Lucy – '

'I insist, Jenny. She was so sweet and kind to me.'

There was nothing for it, short of a direct refusal. And there seemed no reason to think any more would come of it than a polite note.

But Dinah, thinking no harm because after all the lady was Jenny's sister-in-law even if she said they had little in common, replied to the note. The two women met, an acquaintance was begun, with more warmth on Lucy's side than on Dinah's. Lucy had decided to 'take up' Dinah – so beautiful in the strong, russet-hued Rosetti manner, so naive and innocent in worldly affairs.

'You should wear more green, Dinah,' she explained to her. 'That is a very pre-Raphaelite colour, and excellent for your complexion. But do take care to keep out of the sun. Dear, dear . . . a skin like yours could be so charming if only it wouldn't freckle.'

'Oh, a few freckles across my nose don't signify – '

'Indeed they do! Look at the paintings! Do you see any freckles on those marvellous faces?'

Dinah, who had looked not only at the paintings but also at the models who sat for them, shrugged and let it pass. She had quickly become aware that Lucy attached importance to things that didn't really matter.

In the late summer the Armstrongs were in London. Jenny asked Dinah to dinner at Eaton Square, in a party to which Archie Brunton had also been invited. It wouldn't be quite true to say Jenny was matchmaking, but she felt it could do no harm to bring them together now and then.

Archie had offered to escort Dinah there and see her home afterwards to Chelsea. These two therefore stayed a little after the other guests had left. They sat by the open windows of the drawing room, looking out on to the lamplit square, chatting amiably.

Dinah began to describe an At Home she had attended with Lucy. Archie said, on a note of something like protest, 'You're not seeing Lucy Corvill?'

'Course I am. She and I are good friends.'

Jenny heard Archie take an indrawn breath. 'She . . . er . . . she's not quite the sort of lady I'd have thought you'd like, Mrs Eynsham.'

'You mean because of this supposed scandal in her past? Aw, we've all got things we'd rather forget, Mr Brunton. Tell the truth, I'm kind of sorry for her.'

'*Sorry* for her?'

'You can tell by the way she talks, she's really lost without her husband. They were bound up in each other. I wish I'd known your brother, Jenny,' said Dinah artlessly. 'He sounds a wonderful man.'

No one took this up with any enthusiasm. Ronald cleared his throat, Archie shrugged his shoulders in his evening jacket.

'Ah,' said Dinah, 'I can tell – there was some sort of family disagreement. But don't you think it's time you kissed and made up?'

'Dinah, I told you before, we don't have anything in common.'

'But that's no reason for giving her the cold shoulder! Gracious me, I bet lots of in-laws could say the same. You don't seem to appreciate how lucky you are, Jenny, to have family – I know from my own experience how lonely you feel without it.'

'Here endeth the First Lesson,' murmured Ronald.

'Sorry, I didn't mean to preach. And I s'pose it's true, she does go in for a rum crowd, not the kind of people you'd like, Jenny.' Dinah sighed. 'I wish she'd drop 'em. They only hang on to her for the free food and drink! But there you are – I saw a lot of that back home in

Australia – money thrown away on social-climbing.'

After a pause Ronald inquired, 'Does she ever refer to that incident in the Haymarket?'

'No, I think it embarrassed her to pieces. Poor little thing – she was so scared!'

'And the lady who scared her – does she pop up anywhere in this social whirl of Lucy's?'

'No, Lucy would run a mile if she did!'

That was satisfactory to hear. The less one heard of Mrs Massiter, the better.

'She's taking me to Cowes next month,' Dinah went on.

'Who? Oh, you mean Lucy!'

'Of course Lucy, who else? She tells me it's the "in" thing, but when I asked about the yachts she seemed a bit at a loss. I gather we're going to show off our dresses, stare at the latest debs, and stay away from the sea because it's bad for the complexion.'

'If you can speak of it with so much irony, Dinah, why are you going?' Jenny asked in perplexity.

'Because if I don't go with her, she'll be on her own, poor thing. Anyhow, Clive'll adore it. I hear they start the races with a little cannon, and there's fireworks at the end of the Week.'

'And have you also heard that Prince Teddy has a little love-nest there? Really, Mrs Eynsham, I wonder if you know the kind of people you're likely to be mixing with!'

Dinah laughed her flat, slightly discordant laugh. 'I'll be on the beach most of the time, watching Clive build sandcastles,' she said. 'Don't worry about me.'

'I wish you wouldn't go, Dinah.'

'I've given my promise, Jenny.'

Archie's carriage was announced, Dinah went to put on her wrap. Jenny shook her head in exasperation. 'Lucy is just using her as someone to lean on when nobody better is available.'

'She certainly seems determined to heal the breach in the family,' Ronald grumbled. 'I believe there's a quotation about "Where angels fear to tread"?'

'I suppose there's no need to worry about Cowes, really. It's only a week, after all.'

Archie could see Jenny was really worried. He felt an impulse of knight-errantry. 'I'll tell you what,' he said. 'I was planning a trip to Paris but it's not important, I can do it some other time. I'll go to Cowes to keep an eye on Mrs Eynsham and little Clive.'

'Oh . . . but . . .'

They were both thinking of his reluctance to meet Lucy. He said, quoting Dinah, 'We've all got things we'd rather forget . . .'

Ronald was not aware of the undercurrent. Jenny had never told him of the love affair between Archie and Lucy in those long-ago days. He said heartily, 'If you could really bring yourself to do it, Archie, it would be a great kindness. Not that I think Mrs Eynsham really needs a guard dog, but all the same, it would be better if the two ladies had an escort.'

It was settled. When they joined Dinah in the hall and told her of the new plan, she was naively delighted. 'Clive will be *thrilled*. He absolutely loves it when you can spare time to be with him, Mr Brunton.'

In a glow of pleasure she was spirited away in the carriage. Jenny went indoors a prey to mixed feelings. She was glad Dinah wouldn't be entirely in Lucy's hands for seven whole days, obliged out of politeness to fall in with her whims.

But she couldn't help wondering what Lucy would say when she discovered Archie was to be at Cowes.

CHAPTER SIXTEEN

Long years ago, Ronald Armstrong had been a humble employee at Waterside Mills who suffered considerable distress and unacknowledged jealousy when he heard the gossips say Jenny Corvill was sure to marry Archie Brunton. Ronald thought Archie unworthy of Jenny in every way.

Now that Ronald and Jenny were safely married he could be more tolerant of Archie, but he still thought him a lightweight kind of a man – rather shallow and trivial.

Whatever qualities Archie might lack, he had the social graces. Although Lucy Corvill looked taken aback when he first presented himself at their lodgings in Cowes, she came to appreciate him during the week that followed.

Because, alas, she received less attention from the gentlemen than she had expected. In London, menfolk were pleased to drop in at her luncheons or soirées – it made a pleasant stop, perhaps, on the way to Tattersall's or the Piccadilly Arcade. Her house in Mayfair was a place where you could take a lady-friend without having to give chapter and verse.

In Cowes it was different. One went with one's family to Cowes – one's mama or perhaps an aunt or two, and if one was married,

one had perforce to take one's wife. *And* the
children. And there was serious business
going on – there were races to take part in for
the yachtsmen, and to bet on for the landsmen.

Lucy found she was glad of Archie's companionship after the first embarrassment. She
wished he would spend less time with that
noisy little boy of Dinah's, but there . . . Somehow men did seem to enjoy playing beach
cricket or fishing among the pools for crabs.

She saw that Archie could be another lever
in her attempts to gain a footing in the Armstrongs' circle. Archie seemed to be an
acknowledged 'family friend' these days. So
clearly it was an advantage to be on good terms
with him.

She was surprised he was still a bachelor. He
was still goodlooking in his bluff, fresh-faced
way, he still dressed very à la mode, and he
was still very rich – even richer, perhaps, than
before. If only he had a title, she thought to
herself, he would suit me very well.

But she might have trouble landing him.
Although he was polite and attentive, she
often thought he didn't like her very much.
That was strange, because once he had pursued her and been very eager to take her to
bed. Perhaps he had a guilty conscience about
it? Conscience, she knew, could be a problem.
Ned often used to talk about conscience as if it
troubled him very much.

The dispersal from Cowes was a leisurely
business. Archie left them in Portsmouth,
having a cross-Channel trip awaiting him.
Lucy took Dinah and Clive back to their house
in Chelsea before heading for her own home.

As she walked in her own door, she felt a

dejection of the spirits. There was no sense of welcome here. The parlourmaid curtseyed, inquiring if she had had a pleasant time, but with no real interest. The cards on the salver on the hall table were fewer than she would have liked to see, and from no one who could be useful to her.

She spent a disagreeable evening alone at home, slept badly, and was really very pleased indeed when Dinah called next day to say her thank-you for the Cowes trip.

'London will be practically empty now,' Lucy remarked as they sat eating strawberry ice in the cool of her tiny shaded garden. 'I think I'll close up the house and go away.'

'But you just got back, Lucy!'

'Yes, but almost everyone I know is away.'

'Where would you go?'

'Oh, I don't know. Brighton, perhaps? But I don't really like the seaside, the breeze is so boisterous there, one can hardly keep one's bonnet on. Perhaps I'll go to Bath. Or Leamington – I haven't been to Leamington yet, I hear it's very agreeable.'

Dinah heard her with a pity she took care to conceal. Poor little lonesome creature. No one really cared what she did or where she went.

'Why don't you come to the Borders with me, Lucy?'

'The Borders?'

'Yes, Ronald and Jenny usually invite me to spend the late summer with them. Clive and I generally stay through until the beginning of October. Ronald likes to see – ' She broke off. She'd been about to say, Ronald likes to see Clive. But she was always very careful never to link the two together so that anyone could ever have the slightest hint of the truth. 'Ronald likes to see his little boy Max have other children to play with,' she went on, 'and Clive loves it there. The two of them play with toy soldiers all round the nursery.'

'I'm not very good at playing toy soldiers,' Lucy said, half annoyed and yet half wistful. At least Dinah had an invitation to go to stay with friends. No one had invited Lucy anywhere.

'Oh, come on, dear, don't brush it off. I know it isn't as fashionable as Brighton, but there's that thing they all turn out for – the Braw Lads Gathering. Then the men will be going shooting – I hear Lord Thornieburn's having a lot of guests at the end of the month. And there's a regatta at Ayr this year, they tell me; not on the scale of Cowes, but Jenny was saying we might make an expedition to watch some of it, and she says Ayr is a very pleasant town. And there'll be a Summer Ball in Peebles. Doesn't all that sound good?'

The thing that sounded best to Lucy was the mention of Lord Thornieburn. Dinah had said it as if she expected somehow to be included in the events at his shooting party. A man of so much standing in Borders society . . . There was no knowing who else might be there, eligible men perhaps.

But there was a problem. 'I don't think Jenny would want me as a house guest, Dinah.'

'Oh, gracious, you're not still worrying about that coolness. It's time it was all forgotten, whatever it was – '

'No, Dinah, it's not as easy as that. I'm not on terms with Jenny where I can just invite myself to stay at Gatesmuir.'

'But if I write a note and ask her – '

'No, it would be embarrassing if she said no.'

'I bet she'd say yes if I told her I specially wanted you to come.'

'It's sweet of you, Dinah. But Jenny's never forgiven me . . .'

'What's it all about?' Dinah burst out, despite a good resolution never to pry.

'Oh . . . well . . . I don't know if she talks about business to you, but when my dear husband died he left the mills to me.'

'Jenny's mills?' Dinah said, amazed.

'They didn't belong to her, they belonged to darling Ned. But you see, he wasn't a businessman. He was so good and kind, he never could be hard – and you have to be hard in business . . .'

'I suppose you do.'

'Well, we went abroad – Ned had a call to work among the black people, you see, so we went to the West Indies. And because Ned was so unworldly he left Jenny in complete charge and really, though I don't wish to say anything against her, I think she began to believe Corvill's really belonged to her.'

'Well, I always thought it did, and that's a fact.'

'I suppose I handled things badly,' Lucy said in a tone of deep regret. 'I wanted to sell out because, goodness me, anyone can tell I have even less talent for business than my sweet darling Ned. And somehow other people began to offer for the mills and Jenny . . . well, really, she got very angry with me about it though she must have *known* that I would far rather sell to her and Ronald than to anyone else.' A tear glinted on her lashes. 'She said some very unkind things to me, Dinah. And though I went there last New Year on purpose to smooth it all over, it didn't really work quite as well as I hoped.'

Dinah was really perplexed. She had good reason to know that Jenny had a forgiving nature. Yet family relationships were so strange, from all she could learn – and if business problems were involved too, that probably made it more complicated.

'I'll tell you what!' Lucy's mind had been at work. 'I don't need to ask Jenny to invite me, do I? I took lodgings in Cowes; I could do the same in Galashiels.'

'Lodgings? I don't know if there's accommodation on the same scale – '

'No, perhaps not . . . Not in that sense . . . But there are houses, near the Parish Church, along the edge of Gala House grounds. I drove past them in the carriage last year when I was there on business. You can't tell me the builder who put those up has found buyers or tenants for all of them.'

'But . . . they'd be empty – what about furniture?'

'That can all be arranged. I assure you, Dinah,' Lucy said, sparkling with animation now that she had something to do, 'if you had moved house as often as I have, following in the train of my dear husband's work . . . What I shall do is this: I shall send a telegram to Jamieson asking him to find a few properties to rent, and then, don't you see, I shall stay in Peebles for a week or so while the staff get the house ready . . . And even if it isn't a complete home at the outset, what a pleasure it will be to choose furnishings for it. You shall help me! It will be such fun!'

Dinah had arranged to travel north on the 15th. Jenny had her met at the station by Baird, who took Max and Heather along as a welcoming committee. There was a boisterous reunion. It wasn't until the evening when the children were in bed that she had a chance to mention the coming of Lucy. It wasn't well received. 'You mean you actually invited her?'

'Well, she was sweet about taking me with her to Cowes – '

'I thought you told me you only went because you thought she was lonely.'

'Well, true enough. But I had a great time, and so did Clive! And it seemed so rotten to leave her there in London, not knowing what to do with herself. You don't really mind, do you, Jenny? She isn't actually coming to stay here. She's making arrangements to rent a place.'

There was no denying the relief that showed momentarily on Jenny's face. Dinah felt guilty. She'd been so sure it was a good idea, bringing the family together again – but if Jenny really didn't want to have her sister-in-law in the house, perhaps she'd made a big mistake.

'She put her lawyer on to finding a house,' she went on hastily, 'and I reckon she'll be pretty busy making it nice so, honestly, Jenny, you won't have to see much of her.'

'But it'll be impossible to leave her out in the cold . . . Oh,' Jenny sighed, 'if you *knew* the trouble I've had with Lucy . . .'

'I'm sorry, Jenny. I've put my foot in it, haven't I?'

'Never mind, my dear – I'm not going to let it spoil the summer fun.'

Two days later the news got round the town. Mr Jamieson had found Mrs Corvill a small house in Scotts Place, and was looking for domestic staff at once. There was some discussion of reasons why Mrs Corvill shouldn't be staying at Gatesmuir, but the gossips explained it to their own satisfaction – Mrs Eynsham was staying with her little boy, and then you had to remember there were two other children, Max and Heather, and though of course there were rooms enough at the big house perhaps Mrs Corvill preferred a quiet place of her own, she being unused to children.

Then came the Braw Lads Gathering, and in the midst of the festivities the town forgot to worry about Mrs Corvill. The following week it was known she was in Peebles at the best hotel, and then she was seen walking up the path to the house where the servants had been busy for the last few days, and then what else but that her trunks arrived by special carrier's wagon from Peebles and the lady herself had moved in.

Goodheartedly, the local families sent invitations to Mrs Corvill for all the summer outings and parties. The Earl of Thornieburn, that unworldly man, told his wife he thought she should include Jenny's sister-in-law in her invitations to the Armstrongs. If it crossed his mind to wonder why the sister-in-law had put the Armstrongs to so much difficulty in buying her out last year, he put it down to her choice of Jamieson as her man of business. A foolish fellow, Jamieson, so people told him.

Lucy was very happy. Her little house was not as elegant as the one in Mayfair, but it had charm enough for a summer residence. It was pleasant to offer evening hospitality, and show the locals how such things were managed in London – little snacks of caviar or salmon mousse, white wine very well chilled, meat in pastry as light as air, crême bavaroise for dessert, a little music, candle-light, soft voices, muslin dresses and gleaming white shirt fronts . . . And garden parties – when Lucy arranged a garden party, it was a fête champêtre on a small scale, like a Watteau painting.

The younger members of Galashiels society were delighted with Mrs Corvill. Some even murmured that it would be very stylish to copy the idea of a black boy as page, but husbands and fathers were unsympathetic. In other respects, however, Mrs Corvill was approved of.

Her greatest admirer was young Heather Armstrong. Not only was it a source of pleasure to have an aunt so beautiful and so popular, but the popularity reflected off on Heather.

Heather had had few friends through her childhood. The silence that had come upon her when she was lost for a year, the shyness and timidity that had dogged her ever since, made it hard for her to be easy with other girls. At Thornieburn it was different – the two boys who shared lessons with her were like brothers by now. But when she went into the society of girls of the neighbourhood, she seemed to have nothing to say.

For their part, the other girls were wary of her. She had been 'odd', hadn't she? And then there was this strange business of having private lessons with Viscount Cairness and David Buchanan . . . Either she was to be envied because she was on intimate terms with the Thornieburns, or she was to be pitied because she couldn't attend normal school. Either way, there had been something strange.

But now, if you wanted to learn more about the fashionable Mrs Corvill, you could do so by asking Heather Armstrong. Heather spent a lot of time with her aunt. At weekends, when she came home from Thornieburn, she would go to the little house in Scotts Place after her morning ride, and sometimes she would spend all day there. So if you wanted to know what colour Mrs Corvill was going to wear to the Charity Ball, or whether she had ordered French or German wine for her next party, you asked Heather.

Surprisingly enough, Heather turned out not to be so odd after all once you got to know her. True, she still seemed to talk a lot less than anyone else. And her voice had a creaky sound to it, as if she didn't use it enough. But there was nothing wrong with her wits. She caught the point of a joke as fast as anyone else. She didn't have much fund of small talk, however. Clothes didn't seem to interest her, nor did flirtation. In fact, it was doubtful if she even knew why boys wanted to get the pretty girls called out in a game of Postman's Knock.

Heather enjoyed her relative popularity. She understood, of course, that people weren't really interested in her, but in her aunt. That was only to be expected because Aunt Lucy was so generous with her hospitality and her attention. Why, she even took the trouble to listen to Heather's problems.

'My dear, I don't think you should trouble yourself too much about feeling shy. Gentlemen don't like young ladies who are too forward, in any case.'

'Oh, it's not gentlemen,' Heather said. 'They hardly ever speak to me, except Allen and David – and they're only boys, really.'

'With whom do you feel shy and awkward then?'

'Well . . . Mrs Jamieson, for instance. And the minister's daughters.'

'The minister's daughters!' Lucy echoed, raising her eyes to heaven. 'Why should you worry about two such dowdy girls!'

'They're awfully clever. They can read Latin as if it were English.'

'Much good that will do them! They'll never get anywhere in the world until they learn to brush their hair more thoroughly and air their clothes to get rid of the smell of mothballs.'

Heather laughed, but stopped when she realised her aunt hadn't intended a joke. She went back to the matter in hand. 'I never know what to talk *about*,' she said. 'I told Mary Anderson about Mulberry's foal, and she was shocked.'

'Well now, that is a little puzzling. What's shocking about a foal?'

'I really don't know. I was telling her about how Lord Thornieburn chose a stallion for Mulberry so he'd likely get speed as well as stamina, and she clapped her hands over her ears.'

There was a little pause. Then Aunt Lucy said in a tone of gentle reproof, 'My dear, perhaps you should understand that horses are not tremendously interesting – '

'But they are,' protested Heather, even daring to interrupt her aunt in her eagerness. 'Allen and David love to talk about them.'

'Perhaps that is the problem. Perhaps, spending so much of your time each day with boys, you've come to think horses are important. But to a lady they are only, after all, a means of transport.'

Heather couldn't help finding that sad. To her, horses were one of the wonders of the world: so strong, so gentle, so willing to do whatever you asked of them. Beautiful to look at too – glossy coats, proud heads, and in action the very poetry of motion.

In every other respect Aunt Lucy was perfection. How strange that she couldn't seem to share Heather's view on this one point. Yet Aunt Lucy knew best. Perhaps it *was* boring of her to want to talk about horses.

'If I don't talk about horses,' she said humbly, 'what should I talk about?'

'Certainly it can never be wrong to speak of the weather, or of any coming event such as a party or a ball. Other than that, it would be best to let some other member of the party choose the subject. And decidedly, if you're with a gentleman, you should let him lead. Gentlemen always like to take the lead.'

'But gentlemen often talk about things I don't understand. Politics, and economics . . . things like that.'

'Why should that trouble you? You aren't expected to understand, my dear girl. All that's expected is agreement. But in any case, *young* gentlemen don't talk about such things to a young lady. They talk about poetry, or the opera, and so forth.'

'Not to me,' Heather muttered.

Her aunt surveyed the thin, unformed figure, the plain day dress, the honey-coloured hair in straight pigtails tied with black bows. 'Perhaps later,' she remarked. 'When your mother lets you put your hair up . . .'

Heather put a hand up to touch her hair. Why should that make any difference? Would her head suddenly become full of amusing chat just because her hair was done up in curls and combs?

In recent weeks it had become clear to her that some girls were attractive to boys, and some were not. She seemed to be in the latter category, except in the case of Allen and David – and that was different because their friendship had more to do with habit and shared time than with attraction.

Heather made a secret vow. From now on she would try to be like Aunt Lucy, who knew how to attract gentlemen to her side and, equally important, keep them there once they came.

In October Dinah Eynsham took Clive back to London to resume his schooling. Young Max, missing him, moped and whined and was disagreeable. To amuse himself, he took to pieces a vanity case which Lucy had given to Heather – an amusing trick box which would only open in certain ways.

Unfortunately Max, although very deft with his hands, couldn't put the box together again.

'Oh, you stupid, stupid child!' cried Heather when she saw the pieces lying on the nursery floor. 'How could you! Oh, Baird, why did you let him?!'

'Dearie, I never saw him at it until it was too late – '

'Oh, you always let him do just as he likes! It's too bad!'

Heather ran to her room, to indulge in a storm of tears. Whether these were brought on by the wreck of the vanity case or by some feeling of general malaise she couldn't have said.

When her mother got home from the mills and heard of the upset, she went to Heather's room to inquire. 'It's always the same!' cried Heather, her creaky voice made even more odd by the tears which clogged it. 'He spoils everything, and no one checks him!'

This was so palpably untrue that Jenny disregarded it. 'My love, we can buy you another box – '

'But not like that one! Aunt Lucy gave it to me, it was special – '

'Then we'll ask where she obtained it and order another – '

'And let her know I valued it so little I let my baby brother play with it?'

'Now, Heather, I'm very sorry Max broke the box, but there's no need to make a fetish of it just because Aunt Lucy gave it to you – '

'Oh, you always speak like that of her! I sometimes think you don't like her! It's shameful, Mama!'

Jenny felt a little cold shock. She did dislike Lucy, and her dislike had not lessened during the enforced 'family reconciliation' brought about by Dinah, yet she thought she'd concealed her feelings pretty well.

'I think you should lower your voice, my dear. There's no reason to make such an outcry. If you don't want Aunt Lucy to know the box got broken, I shan't mention it to her, of course. I'm sure she's forgotten she gave it to you by now.'

'No she hasn't! Aunt Lucy likes to give me things because she wants me to have the proper equipment for a good appearance. You don't know how kind she's been to me, explaining all about dress styles, what is becoming, what is not – '

'Heather dear, at fourteen years old you're far too young to be bothering your head – '

'That's just where you're wrong! I'm sure Aunt Lucy is right when she says wearing plain school dresses and dark colours is stultifying – '

'Stultifying!' This was an extraordinary word from one so young. In fact the spate of words was unusual in one so unsure of herself as a rule. 'My treasure, most young girls wear plain dresses and dark colours for school – '

'But they have pretty things for outings and parties.'

'But so do you, Heather! What are you talking about? You have poplins and cambrics for summer days and you know yourself you were pleased with the pale blue gauze for parties – '

'But they're so *babyish!* They have no line, no style – '

'I won't have this, Heather, that is quite enough! Your clothes are suitable for your age and your place in life – '

'My place in life! I wonder that you even think I have a place in life! What am I, really? I'm a plain, gawky, shy girl who spends most of her life boxed up with two boys who – '

'Boxed up? I thought you enjoyed your lessons with Allen and David?'

This interruption brought Heather up short. She did in fact enjoy lessons, and the company of Allen and David. How exactly they had come into this complaint she was making, she couldn't quite explain. Nor, indeed, what she was complaining of. She felt that she was somehow inadequate: not pretty enough, not amusing enough, not *feminine* enough. It must be *someone's* fault.

She changed tack. 'Aunt Lucy says London is the place where a young lady can learn what society really expects. She says that living in the country is all very well for a child, but that London society – '

'That is quite enough, Heather. Your welfare is in the hands of your father and mother, not in the hands of Aunt Lucy. You can leave it to us to do what is best for you.'

'Oh, really? Really? Papa is off somewhere else most of the time talking politics with dreary old men. And don't pretend that *you* are here, because you spend most of your time at the mills and we all know that.'

Jenny was genuinely hurt. She had poured out love and attention on this child, this daughter who had been lost to her and regained by her unstinted efforts. Although she had had to divide her time lately between her family and her business, she had tried not to let the family suffer.

But yet . . . could it be true? Since the beginning of the year, when Corvill's had come into the hands of the Armstrongs as owners, life had been hectic. There had been a hiatus in production caused by uncertainty about the future. Then there had been a necessary catching-up, and now she was in the process of re-organising the mills.

It was important to run Corvill's profitably, because out of the profits they had to repay the bank loan and make a good living. Ronald drew no salary as a Member of Parliament. His journeyings to and from London, the upkeep of the house in Eaton Square, his activities in various parts of the country as representative of the Scottish weaving industry – all of this had to be financed out of the money earned by William Corvill & Son.

Jenny laboured gladly to improve the business. Now, of course, she did it partly for the money, because the money was absolutely necessary. But she did it as she had always done – from pride in the cloth, from a desire to use her talents.

She found herself asking if she put these things before the needs of her family. Clearly she'd been inattentive, or else she would have sensed that Heather was going through some sort of crisis.

Yet what, exactly, was troubling the child? She had always been shy in company, a fact with which she herself and her family had come to terms. But now she seemed to think her shyness was a fatal defect. In addition she now seemed to think she wasn't attractive to look at.

Jenny studied her daughter as she faced her now. The girl was angry about the broken trinket, so her colour was higher than usual. She had a fine clear skin slightly tanned from the sun of the past months, and sprinkled with freckles. Her hazel eyes were fringed with lashes of a dark honey colour, her brows were well shaped. Her hair, extremely fine and silky, was tied back in plaits that looked like shiny, tawny ropes.

She wasn't pretty. Not yet. But one day she might be. She might be more than pretty, she might be a beauty.

Why the hurry? Why the anxiety? Such things ought not to be troubling her yet, for she was still in the schoolroom and could not be 'out' in society for at least another two years.

Jenny knew the answer. It was Lucy's influence.

Perhaps after all she had been too taken up with the business. She ought to have realised that Lucy was weaving her spell around her daughter.

'I'm sorry if you feel I've been neglecting you,' she said. 'You may be right.'

Heather gaped, and coloured up in a fierce blush. 'Oh, Mama!' she cried, rushing to Jenny to throw her arms around her. 'Oh, mama, I didn't mean it!'

With a lightening of the heart, Jenny hugged her daughter. The stranger who a moment ago had been berating her about fashions and London society was suddenly once again her own loving little girl. 'There, there,' she soothed, 'I know you didn't mean it. You were upset about the vanity case – '

'Oh, it doesn't matter about the vanity case. I didn't have anything to put in it, anyhow!'

'What was supposed to go into it, really?'

'Oh, hair ribbons, and little scent bottles – '

'Heather! You're far too young to be using scent!'

'Oh, Mama!' cried Heather, this time in amusement. 'Of course girls use scent – or at least, they cadge empty bottles from elder sisters and keep them with their hankies and hair ribbons. Jeanie Angus has two scent bottles – one has a few drops of attar of roses in it and it's heavenly.'

'Attar of roses?' Jenny said. 'I do hope you won't develop a preference for attar of roses. It's a very heavy perfume. I don't really think, Heather . . .'

'No, no, it's quite all right. I use perfumed lozenges instead; you know, the kind that are supposed to improve the breath.'

'Goodness gracious! I had no idea you were so perturbed about perfumes or things of that sort.'

'No, I suppose not, Mama. From what you say about your upbringing, you didn't have much fun of any kind. And then afterwards you've always been wrapped up in business affairs. Oh, it's quite all right, I do really see that you have to be,' she added hastily as she saw her mother's lips open in protest. 'But of course it does cut you off from little feminine things, doesn't it.'

'Oh,' said Jenny. She hesitated. 'Do you feel I am unfeminine, Heather?'

'Unfeminine?' Heather considered it. 'No, certainly not, in most ways you are very feminine – very well-dressed and well-turned out and good at being a hostess and all that. But . . .'

'But what?'

'Well . . . You do sometimes speak very crisply. And you have opinions.'

'I couldn't run a business unless I knew my own mind, Heather.'

'Yes, that's just what I mean. You've had to make yourself hard, I suppose, because business is a hard world.'

Hard . . . The word tolled like a bell in Jenny's mind. Was this how her daughter saw her? Hard, dictatorial?

'But of course, we've grown used to it,' Heather continued, hammering the nails into the coffin without being aware of it. 'When you give orders we know you do it because it's for our own good or for the good of Corvill's. So we try not to mind.'

The conversation stayed with Jenny all that day and all the next. She promised herself that she would take care how she spoke. If she heard herself sounding 'hard' she would check it. She wasn't going to allow herself to grow into a bossy old lady.

But as the year drew to its close, circumstances conspired to make it imperative that the Mistress of Waterside Mills should give orders – and in no uncertain terms.

In November Ronald had to be at the opening of a new Liberal Club in one of the Yorkshire towns, where the Party Leader, Lord Hartington, was to speak. Ronald thought it only good sense to extend his visit so as to see something of the Yorkshire textile industry.

From there he had to go to Greenock for the opening of a new museum and lecture hall in the Watt Institute. After that he went straight to London to catch up with his Parliamentary duties. He also had an invitation for a City banquet, at which Lord Beaconsfield spoke of what was being called 'the Eastern Question' –

should Britain intervene in the troubles between Turkey and Russia even if it might mean another war?

At about this time, the middle of November, tremendous gales began to lash the entire country. The Thames in London rose over its embankment, flooding houses on the south side of the river so that the inhabitants had to take shelter in the upper floors of schools and factories. Ships were driven on shore, lives and cargoes were lost, the main railway lines were damaged by falling trees. Ronald was unable to travel home when Parliament rose because committees were formed to begin urgent relief work.

December came in, with no abatement of the bad weather. Afterwards it was ascertained that six inches of rain had fallen in the month of December, the biggest rainfall in one month for over sixty years. The North of England was under water, so was Norfolk, to say nothing of low-lying fields in every county.

In Galashiels the meek little Gala Water overflowed its banks. The Mill Lead backed up and went surging through the woollen mills.

'Mistress, mistress!' shrieked Gaines, rushing into Jenny's office. 'The watter's coming!'

'Coming where?' Jenny cried, jumping up in alarm at his tone.

'Here, here, it's coming here, mistress! The river's coming into the mills!'

She rushed to the window. One glance was enough to show her that the loading bay with its railway line for freight cars was already under a few inches of water.

'Quick, close all doors. Send for the loading porters and the men from the dye-room.

They're to fetch all the bales of wool that they can manage and use them as a barricade against the water – inside all doors but particularly the doors that open onto the river side of the building.'

'But mistress – the wool!' wailed Gaines. 'It's going to be ruined!'

'Nonsense, we're in the business of cleaning and purifying wool. We'll sort it, after the water goes down. Quick, man, don't stand here wringing your hands!'

Her orders were carried out but not in time to prevent a low brown tide from coming into the ground floor on the northwest side, the one they reached last in their efforts to build a barricade.

The result was two inches of water in two of the carding-rooms. Jenny had all bales of made cloth carried up to the first floor, no matter what stage they had reached in the chain of production.

Little damage or loss ensued in Waterside Mills. But the town was under a foot of water and in the lower areas as much as two feet. Horses reared and shied when their drivers tried to get them to move through it. Men rolled up their trousers, women pinned up their skirts. Perforce they had to wade through the icy flood.

Though the rain continued, the flood level didn't rise by much – perhaps at most it reached thirty inches. But it hampered everything. Although production continued on the upper floors of most mills, goods couldn't be got away without tremendous efforts.

Jenny gave up going back and forth between home and mills after the first day, and had a truckle bed put up in her office. She sent a lad with messages to Gatesmuir when it seemed necessary, and in return had news from Baird: all was well, the house being on a slope remained untouched, a certain siege spirit was enlivening the household.

Christmas came and went almost unnoticed. At New Year, the usual celebrations were much subdued.

Lucy had made the mistake of remaining in Galashiels because until the bad weather came she was enjoying herself. Then, alas, she found herself marooned in her little house, with flood water creeping up the garden towards her front door. No possibility of going out on visits and to parties, unless one risked draggled skirts and hair styles losing their curl because of the damp.

At New Year, she let it be known she would hold open house for first-footers. No one came except her immediate neighbours. Yet to her chagrin she heard that many people struggled through the floods and the mire to first-foot at Gatesmuir.

Heather, riding to bring greetings on New Year's Day on her well-trained mare, found her aunt in a state of nervous irritation. 'Scarcely a soul has been near me since all this nonsense began!' Lucy cried, indicating with an angry gesture the watery exterior.

'I'm so sorry, Aunt Lucy, I'd have come but I was more or less marooned at Thornieburn until Allen's father set a team of plough horses to pull the carriage and bring me home for the New Year holiday. You haven't been in want of anything, have you?' she added anxiously.

'Oh, I haven't *starved*, if that's what you

338

mean, but it's been very unpleasant not having anyone to talk to except the servants. And it goes on and on – when shall we ever get out and about again?'

'Mama says the water is going down now that the rain has stopped.'

Lucy thought of the news this morning that there had been quite a gathering in Gatesmuir last night whereas she had been practically alone. Envy made her say: 'Your Mama is in her glory at a time like this, no doubt. I hear she's taken to sleeping at the mills? That shows where her priorities lie, does it not?'

This was a new thought to Heather. It was true that Mama had not been seen at home for more than a few minutes at a time, until last night. And though Papa had not been able to be there, Mama seemed hardly to mention him – she and the gentlemen had been talking almost exclusively about the damage to business.

Today being a holiday, Mama ought to have been at home. Where was she? At Waterside Mills, supervising a cleaning-up operation.

When she left Aunt Lucy, Heather rode on to the mills. A team of men were using brooms to push water across the yard towards the Mill Lead, which at the moment ran muddy and dark but would eventually clean itself as Gala Water received fresh forces from the hills.

'My dear, how nice to see you,' Jenny said. 'Have you come to admire our labours?'

'I came to ask if you would be home for lunch.'

'I think not, dear. It's hardly worth struggling home and struggling back.'

'But it's New Year's Day!'

'I haven't forgotten that, but it's a very unusual New Year's Day – '

'I don't see it's so very unusual. It's just another example of putting business first.'

'Heather!' Now for the first time she heard the reproach in her daughter's voice. 'Heather, I have to get the mills back into proper working – '

'That's what I just said, isn't it? I quite understand, you have to take the hardheaded view, even at a time like this.'

One of the foremen came up to ask if the volunteers should manhandle the bales of soiled wool to the scouring shed. While Jenny was dealing with that, her daughter hurried off to continue her ride and brood over her mother's un-motherly behaviour.

Whenever Jenny tried afterwards to touch on the subject, she found she was up against a settled attitude on the part of her daughter. Somehow she had been cast in the role of unfeeling, business-obsessed female. And the trouble was, all through the early part of 1877 she had to fulfil that role. Business had suffered a bad setback, just at a time when Corvill & Son could least afford it.

She was aware that she grew nervy and tense. Ronald was away often. This made matters worse, for she needed his comfort and support more than she ever had. Even when he was at home, their love-making seemed to have less power to heal her doubts: it seemed hurried, something that was only fitted in as world events allowed.

Not unnaturally, Jenny began to look rather pale and drawn. Archie Brunton, who watched her with the eye of unrequited love, noticed it.

'You're doing too much, Jenny. You ought to hand over some of the mill work to an office manager.'

'Archie, if I could find a man whom I could really trust to step into my shoes, I'd hand over to him this very minute.'

He was startled. It was so unlike Jenny to admit she was feeling the strain that he almost put an arm about her. But they were at a May charity bazaar in the grounds of his house, and they were surrounded by people.

'Take a holiday, at least,' he said.

'I can't spare the time.'

'A few days, my dear. Get away from it.'

'Well, I am getting away from it next week,' she said, smiling and making her tone lighter. 'I'm going to Paris.'

'Paris! My word, that could be a very enjoyable holiday – '

'No, it's business. You won't have noticed but all the new styles for women this year are based on silks and velvets and cashmeres. Corvill's agent in Paris is selling almost nothing to the big dressmakers. So he's arranged for me to meet one or two in an effort to get them to use Scottish tartans.'

Archie was called away to greet the Sheriff-Substitute who was honouring the event with his presence. But while he bowed and smiled for this dignitary, his mind was on what Jenny had said.

That was how it came about that when Jenny walked into the Hotel du Roi Soleil in Paris on Wednesday evening of the following week, Archie Brunton rose from a chair in the vestibule to greet her.

CHAPTER SEVENTEEN

Jenny went first white and then red.

'Good evening, Mrs Armstrong,' said Archie, beaming at her. 'Did you have a pleasant journey?'

'What are you *doing* here?' she cried, aghast.

'I've come to make sure that you enjoy a little break – '

'But I'm here on business, Archie! I shan't have time to enjoy – '

'Havers, that's just what's wrong with you these days! You never get a moment to relax and enjoy yourself. And since no one else will make you do it, I'm taking it on – '

'This is extremely improper, Archie. You have no right to be here.'

'I do have a right. I've loved and admired you for years, so I take it to heart when you begin to look haggard. Now, Jenny,' he said, taking her hand while the hotel porter moved her luggage towards the lift, 'don't get in a tither about it. There's nothing wrong in my being here. You can spend all day on business if you must, but I shall see you have a chance to enjoy something of Paris in the evenings. Paris is very beautiful in May when the gloaming comes on.'

'I shall certainly not be with you in the evenings! What would people say?'

He laughed. 'Jenny, this is Paris! People don't say anything about a quiet dinner for two and a stroll in the Bois. It's been going on for centuries – '

'Exactly! "Going on" – that's the phrase. I don't have room in my life for "goings-on".'

'That's your Huguenot upbringing speaking. Just because we share a meal or perhaps a visit to a concert, it doesn't mean anything.'

'It would mean something to our friends and neighbours if they heard of it! Suppose I had brought Baird with me?'

'But I knew you intended leaving her behind to look after the children. I found out all about it by talking to her about your French trip. And as to what people would say, that would depend on how it was put to them. And besides,' Archie said innocently, 'who is going to tell them?'

The receptionist was looking anxiously at Jenny, wondering if she was going to register or not. The porter stood holding open the elaborate gate of the lift.

'I really can't discuss this,' Jenny said, her tone very cold. 'I'm tired and I want to settle into my room.'

'Of course, of course. Shall we say eight-thirty?'

'Eight-thirty? For what?'

'Dinner. I've already discussed the menu with the restaurant chef. A light soup, *mousse de crevettes*, and then I thought perhaps some – '

'Archie, this is ridiculous!'

'Not in the least. You have to eat, so I've planned a meal.'

'I intended to have something light sent up to my room – '

'My dear girl, this is France! You can't shock the staff by eating little things brought up on trays! You must have French cooking, and French wine, and if possible a little French gaiety!'

'Now look here, Archie – '

'I shall knock on your door at eight-thirty. I hope you have something elegant to wear – but then you always look elegant.'

He bowed and moved away towards the hotel exit. Jenny, perforce, went to the desk to be told the number of her suite. Once there, she rang for a maid to unpack, took off her travelling gown, put on a negligée, and sat down to get her breath back.

When the maid appeared, she brought a box wrapped in green tissue paper. 'For you, madame,' she said. 'It comes from Grasse today. I expect it is very beautiful.'

Jenny took the box, unwrapped it, opened the lid. She found a perfect corsage of deep pink roses and fern. Their perfume drifted up to her. She saw the note nestling among the blooms.

'To welcome you to La Ville Lumière, from Archie.'

'*Eh bien*,' said the maid on a note of envy, 'I run the bath and while you bathe I unpack. Which gown do you wear this evening?'

'I shan't be dressing. I shall be staying in my suite – '

'*Mais non!*' cried the maid. 'With a so beautiful corsage to wear? Unthinkable! You must dine in the restaurant, madame – if you have a gown with pink, it will go very well with the flowers and the decor, which is *couleur d'huitre*.'

'I intend to stay here.'

'Madame, madame, what a pity not to let the rest of the world see those beautiful flowers – and they go so good with your dark hair. Do not deny to others the pleasure to see you wear them.'

Truth to tell, the charm of the flowers and the gesture of sending them had touched Jenny. Moreover, she had spent twenty-four hours almost entirely alone on her journey so far, so that the thought of eating in her room wasn't entirely attractive.

She took her bath, still supposing she had no intention of going down to the restaurant. But when she came out into the bedroom the wily chambermaid had laid out an evening gown of cream and blue taffeta, on which the deep pink roses would look delightful. Moreover, she stood ready with brushes and combs to do Jenny's hair.

When Archie tapped at the door at eight-thirty, the maid opened it. As Jenny went past into the light of the corridor chandelier, Archie drew in a breath of admiration.

And it was a fact that she looked well, despite being tired and perhaps a little thinner than usual. Her hair was done high on her head with combs of ivory and silver. She wore long earrings of ivory and filigree, to match a cameo round her throat. Her gown left her shoulders bare, emphasised her narrow waist, and by its long train gave her carriage a regal air. On her hands were wrist-length kid

345

gloves. She carried a fan of ivory. Archie's flowers were at her shoulder-frill.

For his part Archie was in an evening suit of dark blue lightweight cloth, with pearls in his shirt front and a dark blue tie at his gleaming starched collar. His shoes of the new patent leather sparkled as he walked. He offered his arm, Jenny took it. They entered the hotel restaurant expected and admired by the waiters.

Contrary to her expectation, there was no attempt at flirtation while they ate. Indeed, they talked of home – of Archie's fields and the new strain of oats he had sown this year, of Heather's mare and its new foal, of Mr Kennet's growing disablement and whether he should take to a bath chair as his wife suggested.

At eleven, pleading a weariness that was only too real, Jenny went to bed. She slept well, waking next morning feeling better than for many months.

The first business was with Corvill's agent, M Brissac. He called for her at eight-thirty, to take her to his office in the Boulevard Haussmann. There they spent two hours going over the order books.

'One cannot blame any particular factor,' he said, shaking his grey head in regret. 'It is simply that *le tissu tartan* has lost the charm for the moment. The dressmakers all say the same – the cloth is still beautiful, the quality excellent, but they do not want it.'

'Have you emphasised the plain cloth we now make? Have you shown them the sample books?'

'Of course, extremely! They agree, the colours are pretty – gentle, natural colours. But they don't want them. That is all, Mme Armstrong. They do not want what Corvill's make any more, or at least not to anything like the same extent.'

'We must get back the French market,' Jenny insisted. 'Paris is such a leader – it influences New York and Buenos Aires and Berlin . . .'

M Brissac looked pleased. He was a Parisian born and bred, so that any praise of his city made him glow.

He had made an appointment for Jenny to meet Madame Erlanger, one of the dressmakers now in the lead in the making of fashion. They went to a house in the Rue de Porthieu, where a footman in breeches and powdered wig ushered them into the presence.

Madame Erlanger had intended to be kind to the little provincial Scot who made the cloth. When this elegant woman in cinnamon poplin and lace was shown in, she rose rather hurriedly to her feet to greet her with more politeness than she'd intended.

'Madame, how delightful. Please be seated. *Henri, du thé au citron.* You will take refreshment, madame. The weather is warm, I think.'

They chatted amiably, the lemon tea was brought. M Brissac hovered. By and by large albums of designs were carried in by the footman, a vendeuse was summoned, there were discussions about fashions on sale already for the summer season and those being planned for the autumn show.

The room was airless, the windows tight shut. By the time noon came, Jenny was glad to make her escape. M Brissac took her to lunch with some fellow cloth agents who

worked for Italian and Swiss firms. In the afternoon she had another appointment, this time
with M Agarat, the ruling power in the matter
of day dresses.

M Agarat spoke no English. Jenny spoke
only broken French. M Brissac had to translate.

'My dear lady, I appreciate the honour of
your visit. I wish I could use your cloth. But it
is not in fashion here in Paris.'

'But you do still use it.'

'Not to the same extent as before. You see,
according to the styles now, we can use *tissu
tartan* for the *sous-jupe* or the *sur-jupe* – '

'That is the under-skirt or the over-skirt',
Brissac interjected anxiously.

'Quite so. In *la mode princesse* you observe
there are two skirts, sometimes more, one
partly showing, one wrapped over, and perhaps a third drawn back to form the *tournure*
where the train begins. Now, madame, *one* of
these skirts may be in tartan, but not more than
one. Or else the bodice can be in tartan, and
the skirts plain. But then there arises the problem of decoration. You observe, Mme Armstrong, that the decoration is much. We use
braid, and garlanded lace, and flounces of contrast colour, and embroidered flowers, and
ribbon, and fringe, and sometimes swansdown
or fur – that may be the rage next winter, fur as
a trimming.

'*Alors*, to put the decorations on tartan
would be bad. It would lack good taste. Tartan
is itself a beauty but it does not lend itself to
decoration.'

'Perhaps there could be less decoration – '

'Less decoration?' M Agarat was scandalised. 'How absurd! Decoration *is* fashion at the

moment: that, and the slender line in front leading to the gatherings at the back. The line is lean and slender, it was evolved so that it could be decorated with elaborate taste, with splendour of detail. Use less decoration? Madame, half the *ateliers* in Paris would go out of business. Where would they go, our embroideresses and braid-makers?'

He snapped his fingers. A personal assistant bounced in from the outer office. He was commanded to send the mannequins out to the show-room.

'Come, madame,' ordered Agarat, leading her out.

They sat on spindly chairs in the show-room. Young women with the figure demanded by fashion paraded in front of Jenny: of medium height, very slender in the waist, high-bosomed, with short arms and small hands and feet. Their clothes seemed moulded upon them from the shoulders to the hips, then the fabric swelled out in layers and flounces and wrapping to fall at the back into a train which rustled over the floor as they walked.

The colours were lighter than previous years, and these were summer clothes she was seeing. For the winter they would be darker, city streets being hard on pale clothes in bad weather. Every gown was of plain cloth decorated with a multiplicity of motifs and materials – much more elaborate than anything worn by most London women. But London usually followed Paris after a season or two.

At the end of the parade, M Agarat offered wine and tiny cakes. He spoke reassuringly: 'In a few years, Mme Armstrong, the fashion will

349

turn again. It is always so. Look towards 1880 or 1882.'

Jenny didn't tell him that by that time William Corvill & Son would have suffered a very great loss. She drank her wine, thanked the couturier for his kindness, and went away.

The third dressmaker was an old lady in the Rivoli. She too assured Jenny that decoration was the kingpin of Paris fashion at the moment and that plaid cloth did not take decoration well.

'But we make a plain cloth,' Jenny objected. 'M Brissac, show Madame the sample book.'

Brissac sprang forward with the book, opened at a suitable page. It showed fine tweed cloth in faint mixtures of brown and beige, brown and blue, blue and grey, grey and green.

'*Oui, oui, très charmant,*' Madame said, fingering the corners of the samples. 'But they are too heavy – consider, madame, if a woman wears two layers of skirt made of such cloth, she would be heavy laden.'

'But we can make it in finer grades – '

'I have no doubt, madame. But then, why should I buy fine plain cloth from Scotland? Do you not see, it has more cachet if I am using *cachemire d'Inde* or *velours de Bruxelles*?'

It was disheartening. It was also true. Jenny offered her thanks for the plain speaking, said her farewells, and let Brissac conduct her back to her hotel at about six o'clock.

Her head ached, she was discouraged. It was therefore a great pleasure to find on her dressing table another box wrapped in green tissue containing another corsage, this time of dark red carnations.

350

With it another note. 'Shall we dine in the open air this evening? I know a charming place by the Seine. At eight o'clock in the vestibule?'

The French maid said nothing as she helped Jenny dress later. She eyed the red carnations complacently, however, and smiled when the lady pinned them on with care at the shoulder of her pale beige summer gown so that they were not hidden by the folds of her soft lace shawl.

The restaurant was a short drive by carriage, on the left bank near the Quai de la Tournelle. Once again Archie had made arrangements in advance. They were shown at once to a table under a pergola of summer jasmine, lit with candles in a glass guard to protect them from the soft river breeze.

'What have you done with yourself all day?' Jenny asked as they sipped an aperitif.

He told her he'd looked up an old school friend, now working and settled in Paris. After that he'd gone to an exhibition of antique sporting guns, and bought some gloves. In return he asked about her day.

She gave him a resumé, acting the parts for comedy at first but falling into thoughtfulness as she tried to explain the trade situation. Then she pulled herself up short.

'I'm sorry. I must be boring you to death!'

'My dear Jenny, you could never be boring.'

'It's nice of you to say so, but I was told not too long ago that I had turned into the kind of person who thinks about business first, last and all the time.'

'Who on earth said such a thing to you?' Archie cried, ready to be angry on her behalf.

'Well, in fact, it was my own daughter.'

351

'Heather said that to you?'

'Oh yes, She thinks I've turned into a hard-bitten businesswoman.'

'Good gracious, I never thought the child could ever talk such blethers!'

'It surprised me too, I must say. But ever since, I've caught myself out using a certain tone, or going on and on about commerce – '

'Now don't be silly, Jenny! I've known you a long time and I haven't noticed anything hardbitten about you.'

'Are you sure?' she said, half-laughing and half in earnest. 'You don't find me intimidating?'

'Not the least. I find you fascinating, interesting, and at this moment extremely inviting.' He leaned across the little table to place a light kiss on her lips.

She drew back. 'Don't, Archie.'

'Very well. We'll go back to talking business, if you like. When do you think you'll have finished your conversations with these Parisians?'

'I thought of going home on Monday.'

'So soon? But Jenny – it would do you so much good to have a break! I mean, after the business discussions are over. Why don't you stay a little?'

'And do what?'

'Frivol. Play. Amuse yourself. And if you need any guidance, because I don't think you've done much of that, I'm here to help.'

'Oh, Archie, you are such a blessing in some ways . . . !'

Their food came. They ate in companionable silence. Jenny's headache began to abate. Occasionally a boat or a barge went by on the

Seine, lights beginning to glow in the gathering dusk. Within the restaurant music began, a guitar and piano accompaniment to a sentimental song: 'Last summer when I met my love, She said, "My heart is thine", But now a year's gone fleetly by, Where are you, sweetheart mine?'

Tears came foolishly into Jenny's eyes. Everything had its season, as the Bible said. Even love – it came, it grew strong and rich, and then it began to fade. Was that what she was coming to understand? That if her life seemed to be losing its warmth, it was because the love between herself and her husband had dwindled to a mere spark?

Archie took her hand. 'What are you thinking, my love?'

'Only that nothing lasts for ever.'

'And so we should seize happiness when we can – isn't that so?'

'I don't know, Archie. I'm . . . I'm too *tired* to think. I'm weary of being the head of the house, the head of the business. I'd like to wake one morning and not have to face decisions. I'd like – I know it's selfish – but I'd like to live for myself once in a while, instead of having responsibility for others.'

He pressed her fingers. 'I can't share all that with you. I've never been one to take on responsibilities, I've always been able to live for myself. But I can tell you this: I feel I've missed something. Most of all, I've missed you, Jenny my dear heart. I regret that more than anything else in my past – that I threw away the chance to be your husband.'

'It was so long ago, my dear.'

'Yes, but it still casts its shadow over me. I've

loved you for years, Jenny, you know that. When I see you uncertain and troubled like this, it hurts me. I long to comfort you.'

She sighed. He poured the last of the wine. They sipped it, and then he said, 'Shall we walk along the river bank?'

'I'd like that.'

He paid the bill, they strolled out onto the Quai de la Tournelle. Now the sweet-smelling twilight had come, the stars were coming out overhead. As they walked towards Notre Dame that huge shadow was black against the light May sky. Carriages went by on the roadway with a jingling of harness, a rush of wheels.

On a bench by the bridge, a young couple sat wrapped in each other's arms. Archie's arm pressed Jenny's hand to his side. They walked on a few yards. Then, in the light from the bridge lamps, he turned, swung her to him, looked into her upturned face, and kissed her with the force of passion long reined in.

When they broke free, they walked on again, unspeaking. They went up on the road. He hailed a chaise. When they reached the hotel they received their keys. He went up with her in the lift, escorted her to her room. There, he took the key from her and unlocked the door.

He swung it open. She walked in. She paused with her back to him in the dim light from the table lamp turned down low.

She said in a muffled voice, 'Don't go, Archie.'

Next moment the door had closed with a crash. He swept her up and carried her into the bedroom. With trembling fingers he undressed her, laid her among the pillows on the bed. In a moment he was beside her, and their bodies were searching for the release that physical need had built up between them.

Through that night, with her body alight once more from the old, sweet fire, she blanked out of her mind any thought of guilt or shame.

CHAPTER EIGHTEEN

Their love-making had been inevitable since the moment she saw him in the hotel lobby. If she had wanted to evade him, she should have left the hotel at once and registered somewhere else.

But she had chosen not to do. Deep within her, desire had taken hold. She had wanted the experience of being loved, of giving love in abundance. Some deep need had dictated her actions.

Her fortieth birthday was past. It had been an unconscious milestone. She had felt some important part of her life was over, the part that had to do with being sensuous, passionate, a true woman.

Heather had reinforced that verdict by telling her she had grown hard and domineering. It had hurt her more than she could admit to herself.

Archie had been her reassurance, her proof that she could still make a man want her. And she for her part had wanted him, the warmth of his arms about her, the strength of his longing for her. Like a warm tide he had bathed her body in pleasure, and washed away her fears.

In the morning when she woke, he had gone to his own room. She stretched out luxuriously, watching the sunlight filter in through the almost closed shutters.

By and by came the maid with her *café complet*. 'Bonjour, *madame*, you have slept well?'

'Very well, thank you.'

The Frenchwoman fetched a wrap from the wardrobe so that Jenny could slip it on before sitting up to receive the tray. She plumped up the pillows behind her. There was the merest hint of a conspiratorial smile on her lips. For a moment Jenny felt a blush of confusion, but then she recollected herself. This wasn't a little provincial hotel in Scotland, this was a room that had perhaps known many lovers.

A note was brought to her as she ate her croissants. 'I know you have appointments. Shall we meet at eight this evening in the vestibule?'

She nodded to the maid. 'The answer is yes.'

'*Très bien, madame.*' She went to the door, passed on the message. When she returned to lay out Jenny's day dress she murmured dreamily, '*Il est beau, l'anglais . . .*'

Yes, thought Jenny, he is handsome. And he loves me.

The day seemed tedious, the business talk seemed empty. She knew by now there was nothing she could do to improve exports to Paris, at least not for the present. By and by she'd put her mind to alternatives. In the meantime she would go through the motions of attending to affairs but in reality she was thinking only of the moment when she would see Archie again.

They dined in a restaurant near the Opera. Then they went back to the hotel and spent the night in each other's arms, this time with more awareness, with more enjoyment and appreciation of each other.

'I never ever thought you'd give in to me, my joy,' he murmured into her hair. 'I thought you'd always keep your guard up somehow.'

'I suppose I meant to. But when I opened that box the first evening and saw the roses . . .'

'I never thought your armour could be pierced by such a simple thrust. I've sent flowers to hundreds of girls, Jenny.'

'Don't tell me about your other conquests, you vain man! Although I know of course I'm by no means the first.'

'But you're the only one I've ever really loved, dearest. I mean it. I love you.'

'Ssh . . . That's too big a word to speak at this moment. We have each other and we're happy – that's enough.'

'More than I ever expected,' he said, his face buried in the curve of her shoulder.

He persuaded her not to keep the one business appointment for next morning, but to send an excuse. They spent the day walking and driving about Paris. He insisted on buying her a pair of absurd little jewelled evening slippers. She bought him a pearl cravat pin. They had lunch in a pavement café in Montmartre.

Next day, Sunday, Jenny didn't go to church. She was forty years old and the times she had missed morning service could be numbered on the fingers of one hand. But she felt she couldn't go to church and pretend to be holy. She had committed a sin, yet she felt no guilt, no regret.

In the afternoon there was racing at Longchamp. Jenny had never even been to a horse-race, and to go to one on a Sunday seemed the depth of depravity. But the French appeared to think that having given their thanks to God in the morning, they would not be condemned for enjoying themselves in the afternoon.

She picked a winner and two losers by sticking her bonnet pin in the race card. Seeing that she was losing interest, Archie took her to the river, hired a boat, and rowed her upstream under the branches of low-growing willows. There they lay alongside each other on the boat cushions and kissed to the lazy murmur of the river current.

That night, when they were in each other's arms, he said: 'Don't go home tomorrow, Jenny.'

'But I must. I've got my passage booked.'

'What does that matter? Let it go. Stay a few more days. No one is expecting you back particularly, are they?'

'Well, I told Baird I'd be back by Tuesday, and Gaines – '

'Oh, to the devil with Gaines. Send a telegram tomorrow. Stay on with me. We can go out of Paris to some quiet little spot, I know a little inn in a village called Barbazon, you'd love it there.'

'But I ought to go back, my dear. There are things I've got to see to – '

'Let someone else see to them. Jenny, we'll have few opportunities in the future to be together alone like this. Don't throw this chance away.'

She shook her head against her pillow. He wasn't aware of the movement. He said, 'You agree? That's my angel. We'll walk under the chestnut trees and watch the swallows skimming over the pond . . . They have big feather beds at the inn . . . We'll be lost in ours, lost in each other . . . Like this, my dearest love . . .'

When he rose in the dawn light to leave her, he leaned over to kiss her. 'When the maid has packed, have your luggage taken down to the lobby. I'll have a carriage brought round.'

She made an indistinct sound, for she was half-asleep. He put his mouth on hers then laid his cheek close to her cheek. 'Until later, darling.'

About an hour later she awoke fully. She went to the bathroom to splash cold water on her face.

What had she promised last night? Had she said she would go away with him to some village?

Echoes of his words came back to her. 'Few opportunities in the future to be together like this . . .'

What was he thinking of? What had she allowed him to think?

Here in Paris – in romantic, tolerant Paris, the city of light and of lovers, they could make love and enjoy each other without any restraint or guilt. But back in her real life – in workaday old Galashiels – they would never be lovers without endless deceit, endless subterfuge.

She had been all through that when she was a girl. She recalled only too bitterly the anguish and remorse that seemed to live with her then. The fear of discovery, the sense of unworthiness . . .

And now she was a married woman. She had a husband and two children. She couldn't do this to them. She couldn't put them in danger, put her marriage in danger. She would be mad to think of it.

When breakfast came with the maid, she was up and already partly dressed. She gave instructions for her trunk to be made ready and taken down for transportation to the station. 'I'm catching the boat train,' she said.

'*Oui, madame.*' The maid didn't ask, '*Et monsieur?*' She could tell only too well that they were parting. It was in the face of madame as she sat by the window sipping her coffee, in the droop of her shoulders as she glanced out at the street.

When her luggage was in the hall, Jenny went up to the next floor where Archie's room was. She knocked. A valet came to the door. 'Tell M Brunton that Mme Armstrong wishes to speak to him.'

'*Bien, madame.*' He went back into the room. Next moment he had ushered her in and taken his leave, one glance having told him he wasn't wanted.

'Jenny!' Archie's glance took in her travelling costume, the bonnet and gloves in her hand. 'Ready so soon? I thought we wouldn't leave until – '

'I'm going home, Archie.'

'No! Jenny!'

'I must go home.'

'But you promised!'

'Did I? I don't remember. If I did, I was wrong. I can't go away with you to your little French village. I have to go back to my husband and children.'

'But there's no need to go at once – '

'Oh yes. I realise now that I was quite wrong in ever letting this happen between us. When you spoke last night about opportunities to meet in the future, I knew it was impossible. I can't carry on a clandestine affair, my dear. It must end here and now.'

He sank down on a chair in front of the dressing stand. 'Jenny!'

'Hate me for it if you must, but I can't go through a hole and corner – '

'Then let's come out into the open about it! We love each other – come away with me, leave Ronald – '

'Leave Ronald?'

'Don't sound so astounded. Wives have left their husbands – '

'Lucy did that! Do you remember?'

'But that was different. She ran away to a man who didn't love her. But I love you, Jenny – '

'But I don't love *you*, Archie.'

'You do!' he exclaimed. 'You do, you've shown me you love me. You couldn't have given yourself to me so completely unless you really cared for me.'

Tears were brimming at her eyes. She didn't want to hurt him. He was so open, so simple – and she had let him throw himself over a cliff for her.

'This is complete honesty, Archie. You came upon me when I was feeling lonely and unwanted and vulnerable. You brought me reassurance and new confidence, and I took those. In return I gave you . . . physical passion, yes, that was real and deeply felt. And I'm very fond of you, Archie . . .'

'*Fond* of me?' His voice broke on the words.

'That's much too little, isn't it? I'm sorry. It's

the truth. I don't love you in the way I love Ronald.'

'But how can you love that man?' he burst out. 'He's only half-educated, a nobody by birth, and since he's got into Parliament he's got so conceited, never at home, always off being important with political bigwigs!'

Jenny sighed and shook her head. She smoothed the ribbons of her bonnet through her fingers. 'Archie,' she said, 'in a love affair there's always one who loves more and one who loves less. It just happens that in this case I'm the one who loves more. I'll never stop loving Ronald, though I know I don't fill as much of his life as he does of mine. And I'd certainly never take his children from him to go off to some foreign part with another man.'

'I can't believe you're saying this! You – Jenny Corvill who swept all before her when she first came to the Borders – you admit you're prepared to take second place in his life?'

'Once and for all, believe it, Archie. I can never love you as you want me to love you.'

He had been tying his cravat when she came. Now he put up his hands to it as if to continue, but instead his fingers wandered to cover his face as he bowed his head against the dressing stand.

Jenny didn't know what to do. She came timidly towards him, stretched out a hand, but to lay it on his shoulder in comfort seemed a useless gesture.

After a long moment he muttered: 'What am I to do? You were all my world. If you go, there's nothing left, nothing but emptiness, loneliness.'

'I can't answer that for you, my dear old friend. I wish I knew what to say . . .'

'I'm well past forty, Jenny. I know I'm not the man I used to be, life's passed me by . . . And for the past few years, as Armstrong's been more and more tied up with politicking, I've lived with the hope that I'd make you come to me somehow. I followed you here because . . . because I thought you and he were growing apart and that just one push . . .'

'No, you judged it a little bit wrong. Things weren't right for me, but they weren't so wrong that it could break up my marriage. I'm sorry, Archie. Find someone else to love.'

'Who, for God's sake! Who is your equal? There's no one else for me.'

'Archie, Archie.' Now she had the courage to come to him and touch him. She laid her hand on his shoulder, gave it a little shake. 'Come to terms with yourself, as I've tried to do. I know Ronald and I aren't the passionate pair I once thought, but I love him, he loves me, we're happy. Settle for that – love that meets the day-to-day needs. Find yourself a nice good-natured girl and marry her.'

'But it seems so . . . so puny, when I hoped it was going to be you and me . . .'

'That's got to be forgotten, Archie dear. From now on, it's you and someone yet to be found. You can be happy yet, lad. I hope and pray you will.'

She slipped out of the room while he was still sitting with bowed head, dreary and forlorn.

All through the journey home, she couldn't forget that sad figure. Archibald Brunton, the

most sought-after bachelor in the Borders . . .
And she had hurt him, wrecked his dreams
once and for all. She was filled with regret
and remorse, useless as they were. There was
nothing she could do now for Archie Brunton,
except wish him well.

At home she found Ronald had come back
from London for a long weekend, 'to get his
breath back,' he told her. Parliament had been
in a state of turmoil since the end of April,
when word reached them that Russia had at
last carried out her threats and declared war on
Turkey.

'It's a madhouse there, lassie,' he told her,
stretching out in the drawing room with his
long legs dangling over the sofa end. 'I had to
get away, to a calm place where folk speak
kindly to one another instead of shouting and
arguing.'

'Oh really?' Jenny said, smiling. 'This is a
haven of peace and quiet, is it?'

He reached out a hand as she passed, caught
her skirt. 'I wish I didn't have to be away so
much,' he mourned. 'The children are growing
up, and I hardly see them.'

'Max will be six next birthday. And Heather
– Heather's getting to be quite the young lady.'

'What's the matter with that girl?' he
demanded, sitting up suddenly. 'She moons
about when she's home – and though she's
polite to me, she never seems to be listening to
a word I say.'

'Now, now . . .' She sat down beside him on
the sofa. 'You've never been close to Heather.
Admit it.'

'Well . . .' He always looked half-ashamed
when he discussed any failing of Heather's. He

365

had lost contact with her when she was brought home after being lost. She had been greatly changed by her experience, so much so that for two or three weeks he even doubted she really was his child. Now there was a gap between them, so that when he compared their relationship with those of other doting fathers and daughters, he knew theirs lacked something important.

'Lady Thornieburn sent a message with her when she came home on Saturday, asking me to call when it's convenient. I wonder if there's any trouble there?'

'Trouble?'

'Oh, it can't be anything much. There's no urgency in Her Ladyship's note. Since you're home, shall we both go this afternoon?'

'Didn't you have work to do in the office?'

'Oh, let it wait,' she murmured, still under the influence of that Parisian interlude. 'Work will still be there when you and I are gone, my love.'

It was a fine afternoon in late May when they set off in the brougham. The hills were emerald green with new grass. Even the old stone walls separating the fields seemed to glow in the gentle sunlight, their lichen golden and creamy-grey, their stones sparkling with particles of silica. They splashed through the ford at Cadden, sending up a spray of little rainbows.

'This is so nice, Ronald,' Jenny said, leaning back against the leather cushions but letting her shoulder weigh on his. 'Why do we get so little chance to go out in the sunshine together?'

'If I thought you really needed it explained to you, I'd say you were sickening for water on the brain. But it is nice, you're right. So, then, apart from being told we couldna sell them anything, what did you learn in Paris? Did you spend money on flighty clothes? Did you go to the theatre?'

'Neither of those things, husband. But I did learn something in Paris, all the same.'

'And what was that?' he asked, turning to look at her in surprise, for her tone was serious.

'I learned to value what I have. Being away from Gatesmuir for a week, I was able to look at it from a new angle. I realised I was a very lucky woman, and should stop feeling sorry for myself.'

'Guid sakes! When were you feeling sorry for yourself, then?'

'Oh, for quite a long time – since New Year or thereabouts.'

'But what for, lassie?'

'It's too complicated to go into. Let it be enough to confess I'd begun to believe I was turning into a sour old woman – '

'You? Sour? My dear Jenny-wife, you're talking hay-haddins! Is this what happens when I'm away – you get yourself into a silly state over nothing?'

'I can be as silly as anybody else, Ronald, when I get depressed. But I've recovered now, and having you at home for a few days reinforces the improvement.'

'Na, na, dinna talk about improvements.' He was laughing. 'You only want me to say there's no room for improvement in you, and I never take the hook o' anybody fishing for a compliment!'

He put his arm about her shoulders, hugged

her, and in good humour with each other they finished the journey to Thornieburn.

Her Ladyship was delighted to see them. 'Mrs Armstrong! Now this is providential! I need some advice about bunting.'

'Bunting?'

'Yes, we're opening the grounds for athletic and archery competitions on Saturday – the local Church Boys and contestants from neighbouring villages. Now tell me, should bunting be – ' She broke off. 'But this won't interest your husband! Go round to the back, Mr Armstrong, you'll find the Earl conferring with the gardener about our new fountain. It won't play – such a disappointment.'

Jenny was led away to a section of lawn down by the stream, where workmen were putting up marquees. 'Such an upset, but one can't refuse to hold the games . . . Well now, you've come in response to my note.'

'Is something wrong, ma'am?'

'Wrong? What should be wrong? I'm sorry if I gave the impression – '

'Not at all, ma'am, but generally we write out our messages or they wait until we see each other. I wondered what – '

'Of course you did. It's this. Heather is fifteen next month, yes?'

'Quite so.'

'I wondered whether you had considered having her presented at court next year?'

Jenny stopped in her tracks. Her ladyship, unconscious, walked on, still talking. 'It's full early to talk about it but – Oh, Mrs Armstrong, why have you stopped?'

'I've stopped because I'm thunderstruck! Present Heather?'

'Yes, I wondered if you wished it?'

'But . . . but . . . she's not entitled . . .'

'Indeed she is. Wives and daughters of the aristocracy, wives and daughters of Members of Parliament, wives and daughters of merchants, bankers, or those engaged in commerce on a large scale . . . That's some of the categories, I've no memory, I can't remember quite how it goes. But you see, on two counts, Heather is qualified – she's the daughter of a Member of Parliament and of a man who is engaged in commerce in a large way.'

'Oh . . . would you say Corvill's was "in a large way" of business?'

'I would say so – but then I've no head for business, my dear, as you well know. However, if anyone asked me I should always say you are in the forefront of the clothmaking industry and as far as I can see that's true. Besides, that's only one of the supporting factors, there's the Parliamentary connection. So what do you say?'

'But doesn't one have to have a sponsor?'

'Certainly. I have the privilege of taking my own daughter, if I had one, and one other girl. If you'd like it, I'd be glad to send in Heather's name to the Chancellor at the end of the year, as a nominee for presentation next year.'

'What . . . what does it entail?'

'Well, I should have to go up to London with her, in, let's say March. She needs a certain amount of coaching – in how to curtsey in those confounded long skirts, and how to walk backwards out of the salon – that's even harder because your train's in the way. Then there are the clothes. Court dressmakers know what to suggest, but it takes a bit of discussion. I remember I hated it all; sitting about in my underwear while they tried various silks and brocades against me . . . And it's not just the presentation gown – you need dresses for the whole season. But in the end, of course, it was worth it for me because that was how I met Henry . . .'

'It sounds expensive,' Jenny said, trying to visualize it all.

'Yes, very. And that's why I thought I'd better put it to you now. Mention of her birthday made me think about it in the first place, and then I said to myself, "It's not cheap, and things have been a bit tight for them." ' Her Ladyship blushed. 'You don't mind my being so tactless about your affairs? But Henry has told me of the problems you had in finding the money to buy the business. And I thought, if you were going to go in for a London season next year, you'd better start planning the money side of it now.'

In strolling on while they talked, they had come to a pile of little flags at the side of the tented area. 'These are the bunting flags,' said the Countess. 'Do you know if they have to be strung up so that they all face the same way?'

'I think not, your ladyship,' said Jenny, divided between amusement and perplexity at this conversation. 'I think they flutter in the breeze and so they face whichever way the wind takes them. No one ever really looks at bunting, in any case.'

'I *know*, it's all such nonsense, isn't it, but people expect it. I told the Earl, if it was a point to point, I'd feel more at home with it, but foot races and Cumberland wrestling . . . Well, what do you think?'

'About the bunting?'

'No, no, about the presentation! Heather would have to be in London in the spring, but of course she could stay at your place in Eaton Square so she wouldn't feel strange. There would be the presentation dress, and all that goes with it, and I suppose you'd have to say eight or ten ball gowns for the season, and day and afternoon dresses enough so she wouldn't appear in the same clothes at parties and gatherings too often, because that *is* remarked upon, you'd be surprised how sharp some of the gossip is . . .'

'Heather is very shy,' Jenny said. 'I wonder if she would be able to stand up to it?'

'Well, as to that . . . I was shy too . . . You know what a hayseed I am, Mrs Armstrong, and woolly-witted too!'

Jenny made sounds of disagreement, but the Countess laughed and swept on. 'I think it would be good for her. Once a girl has been brought out, she's learned a lot, she's been launched into society, and afterwards she has a certain *je ne sais quoi* that stands her in good stead whoever she marries. And there's no knowing who Heather will get – she's turning into a very pretty girl.'

'Do you think so?' said Jenny, with a surge of pride.

'Oh yes, indeed, Henry was just saying the other day when he saw her go past on Princeling, he said to me, "Jemima, that child sits her horse like a little queen!" Oh, well, that was more about her horsemanship than her appearance but . . . indeed, he has said something to me about her looks and he's said other gentlemen have remarked on her.'

'That's very good to hear, ma'am. There was a time in her life, you know, when the poor little soul looked like a changeling.'

'Oh, children go through these phases,' Her Ladyship said with an aimless wave of her bony hand. 'Look at Allen. He was as thin as a riding-crop but with far less sting in him, yet look at him now . . . *I* think he's turning out quite goodlooking, though Henry says I need to put my glasses on . . . But he's a nice boy, and his bad chest is much better – though mind you, the doctors always did say it would improve as he approached maturity.'

'What are his plans? You're so kind as to think of Heather, but what do you intend for the Viscount?'

'Well, he'll probably go to university. I think he's fit enough for university. He ought not to go on with private tutors for ever. We think of sending him up in the autumn of next year. What's your opinion?'

'Mine? Well, my lady, I think it would be good for him to have the experience of being away from home. Will he take up any particular studies?'

'He says he'd like to read classics. Why not? It's not as if he's going to have to earn his living, and books are always a help when the weather's bad at Thornieburn . . . So what about Heather?' said the Countess, with one of her sudden turns of subject.

'I feel I must discuss it with my husband. He'll be as grateful as I am for this very generous thought, ma'am – '

'Oh, nonsense, nonsense, it's no trouble to me – except staying a season in London, which I must admit I hate, but then, now and again, it's just as well to be in Town, and as things are these days, with the Russkies being so horrid and so on, Henry feels he might go back into the Lords and say a word or two, so being in London wouldn't be a bad thing, although of course things may be different by then, but wars do tend to drag *on*, don't they? Where was I?'

'You were saying, I believe, that you would do the London season – ?'

'Yes, so I was, and you'd have to as well, wouldn't you. It would mean at least four months when you wouldn't be able to think about Corvill's, because either you or I would have to chaperone Heather.'

'I've had the thought recently that I ought to find and train a really reliable manager for the mills.'

'What a good idea! Well, what else is there to think of? There's the expense, of course, and there's the decision what to do about the offers she'll get – '

'Offers?'

'Certainly. Young men crowd around during the season looking for a good match. And Heather, with her pretty looks and her gentle manners and her probable inheritance . . . You see?'

'I think it's much too early to think of offers of marriage,' Jenny said, her breath suddenly seeming hard to catch. 'Why . . . she's still only a child!'

'You're protective towards her. I know there are special reasons for that. But one day, you know, she will choose a husband and we can only hope and pray she makes a wise choice.

That is, unless you prefer the old fashioned way of choosing a husband for her?'

'Of course not!'

'Then a London season will let her see a good number of young men – and some not so young – and she will learn from it. Yes. So we wouldn't encourage offers of marriage, and I suppose you wouldn't want her to go abroad at the end of the season to do a tour of the spas or anything like that.'

'Your ladyship, the more you talk about it the more I think the expense would be beyond us. At the moment we're going through a difficult period and though I hope that by next year things would be better, I still feel . . .'

'Then the following year!' said the Countess, with another of her flapping gestures. 'She'd be seventeen. That's a very nice age to be presented – I certainly don't approve of leaving it until eighteen, because that means a second season at nineteen makes the poor girl seem long in the tooth, but of course if she had a second season at eighteen – '

'No, no!' cried Jenny. 'If she is presented and does the London season at seventeen, that will be enough!'

'Talk to Mr Armstrong about it. I think that if we set our sights on the season after next, that is a good plan. It gives Heather a chance to get used to the idea, and if in the meantime you or I can take her to London so that she grows accustomed to the atmosphere . . . Don't you think so?'

Jenny didn't quite know what she was being asked to agree to but murmured she would speak to Ronald. They went back to the house, to find the men already in the shade of an awning over the terrace, awaiting afternoon tea.

'This man,' declared the Earl, 'is a genius! He took one look at the pumping mechanism for the fountain and declared he could see a blockage. My dear, you never saw the like! Old McDaniels stood there glowering like a thundercloud and declaring the thing was an invention of the devil, and Armstrong was there in his shirt sleeves wrestling with a coupling and swearing . . .'

A pair of footmen appeared bearing tea trays. The housekeeper followed, to supervise, and a moment later the children came running through the house from the hall.

'Mama, Papa!' cried Heather. 'They told me you'd come a-calling!'

She ran between them, putting out an arm each side to seize them and drag them round in a celebratory jig. The governess, bringing up the rear, smiled and murmured gently that she ought to be less boisterous.

The Viscount came up to make his bow and say he was glad to see them. At his elbow David Buchanan beamed amiably. They were a contrast, Allen Cairness tall and thin, David twice the girth and bidding fair to be plump in years to come. He added strength to this suspicion by looking for the plum cake with eagerness.

The Earl recounted again, with added flourishes, the tale of the fountain. David said through a mouthful of cake, 'It is a simple matter of hydraulic pressure, is it not?'

'Yes, though I wouldn't say I find it simple. However, I know a little about machinery –

I've been close to it most of my life,' Ronald said.

David began a dissertation on the idea, recently popular, of installing lifts in tall buildings which could be raised and lowered by hydraulic pressure.

'I shouldn't care to go in one,' said Lady Thornieburn. 'Suppose the water supply failed? In a drought, for example?'

'Oh, Maddie, you don't understand a word about it!' her son said.

'Well, neither do I,' cried Heather, always ready to spring to the defence of the easily confused Countess.

'Well, I wouldn't expect a *girl* to understand it,' Allen said with scorn. 'Girls don't understand *anything*.'

'My boy, that's a very sweeping statement.'

'It's true, though, Paddie. When you talk to a girl about anything important, they always give you a blank look. Cousin Amy couldn't understand a word I was telling her about the Argonauts the other day.'

'Cousin Amy is quite bright enough to beat you at croquet, though.'

'She cheated.'

'Allen!' cried the Countess. 'Even though it's true, you mustn't say so!'

Allen groaned and hid his face by taking a great swallow of tea. He then choked, and from a small cough began to gasp for breath.

'Here we go!' said Heather in a bored voice, and arose to thump her schoolmate on the back. 'Breathe in . . . breathe out . . . breathe in . . . There, is that better?'

'You needn't hit so hard,' Allen said, sitting back with a few coughs and hiccups. He reached up behind his ear, caught a dangling pigtail, and gave it a tweak.

'Beast!' cried Heather, jerking back.

'Double beast and spiders to you!'

'Yes, who screamed because a spider came into the schoolroom this morning?' David put in, advancing upon Heather with arms outspread and fingers dangling.

'Rotten beast to clype! Tell-tale-tit, your tongue shall be split!'

'Pigtail Peggy, Pull hard and steady,' chanted David, reaching for the pigtails.

Heather took off like the wind towards the shrubbery. The boys went racing after her.

'Children,' said Lady Thornieburn, shaking her head. 'What energy they have.'

And this is the girl, thought Jenny, of whom we were speaking as a debutante only a moment ago . . .

When she told Ronald about it on the way back, he was as astounded as she. And began at once to protest against it. 'Why, she's only a bairn! Look at the way they were behaving – she's not old enough to be put through the society mill.'

'It's not an immediate scheme. Lady Thornieburn thinks of it for when she's seventeen.' She went on to give all the details she could recall, though some of it eluded her because she'd been taken so much by surprise.

'Humph,' said Ronald.

She'd wondered if he might be totally against the idea, for he had strong views about equality. His favourite quotation from Robert Burns was the one about the guinea stamp: 'The rank is but the guinea stamp, The man's the gowd, for a' that.'

But that evening, after he had romped with Max in the garden and had a relaxing drink, he began: 'You know, Jenny, the idea of having the child presented is by no means a bad one.'

She looked at him with raised eyebrows. 'You were against it at first?'

'Yes, but I have to remember always to be particularly careful about Heather. I'm not the one who knows what's best for her. You proved yourself to be better at it than me. Do you think we should take it on?'

'First let me hear your own views.'

'Well, I'm against the society circus in general. But since I went into politics I've had dealings with all kinds of people, and one thing I've learned – it's a mistake to turn your back on an advantage.'

'You feel it would be an advantage to Heather?'

'Other men's daughters have had the privilege – I wouldn't say I know too much about what use they made of it, but it certainly does no harm in certain circles. Look here, Jenny, I think we both know that Heather isn't going to follow in your footsteps as a businesswoman. She shows no aptitude. Max is more interested in the mills than she is, even at his age. So I suppose we have to say that Heather's career is going to take her into matrimony. And a season as a debutante would presumably be a help.'

'I suppose that's so.'

'I must say it's extremely kind of Lady Thornieburn. I can't think why she should put herself out for us.'

'Well . . . That little scene at tea-time, you saw how Heather took it in her stride that she had to cope with what looked like an asthmatic attack. And how completely the three of them were involved with each other. I think in a way this offer is a sort of thank-you for the years of Heather's companionship.'

Ronald wandered to the decanter to pour himself another tot. 'Put like that . . . perhaps we ought to accept? Although really we owe the Thornieburns as much as they owe us.'

'It would cost a lot, Ronald.'

'We've got eighteen months to lay the money by.'

'But business is difficult, lad, you know that.'

'All the same, we're not at the stage where we're singing Poverty Knock.'

'No . . . And I do feel that if I follow up my idea of developing markets in Northern Europe and Scandinavia . . .'

'We'll do it somehow, Jenny.'

'All right. But I don't think we should mention it to Heather yet, in case we have to give up the idea on financial grounds.'

'Agreed.'

With renewed purpose Jenny went back to work. She had seen colours and shades in Paris that gave her new ideas for designs. She hired agents in Copenhagen, in Stockholm and Oslo, in Dresden, in Warsaw. She even began to develop markets in Canada, where the cities were growing fast as the wheat plains helped men to make fortunes.

When the London season ended, Lucy Corvill returned to Galashiels, having forgiven the town for the miseries of its winter. She was heralded by a wagon-load of new furniture for her rented house. Everyone was agog to be invited to her first party.

It was a select affair. The Armstrongs had received invitations but excused themselves on the grounds of a prior engagement. The young set of the district came, and took away ideas for redecoration and for new fashions. Hairstyles, they learned, were more elaborate in London these days, following the lead of a lady friend of the Prince of Wales. Curls were to be worn on the forehead and the hair swept up at the sides to expose the ears and – in the case of the aforesaid lady – valuable earrings given by the Prince.

Interesting gossip, good food, plentiful wine . . . What more was wanted from a hostess? In return Lucy was invited everywhere. And this was exactly what she wanted.

Yet another London season had taught her that she was not going to catch a titled husband. The competition was too keen. Every year, pretty girls were launched, with the advantage of youth and freshness and sometimes beauty. Often they had money too, and many of them were from aristocratic families.

Why should a man turn to a widow of no particular breeding, even if she were rich and pretty? This was the harsh question Lucy had had to face as August turned to its close and London emptied.

She had wept into her pillow when the answer presented itself in those hours of the morning when we face the cruel truth. She would not succeed, she was outshone by younger and more beautiful women. And she herself wasn't getting any younger. There were only two more years to go to her fortieth birthday – and at forty, she knew, hope would be gone.

So she had come to Galashiels, where the struggle was not so hard, where she was respected and courted because she was a member of the Corvill family. Titled men were not particularly plentiful here but men with money abounded. There were men of business who had been too busy to find a wife in their early years. There were widowers who might be glad of a sweet and sympathetic smile. There were bachelors, though not as many as she would have liked.

Among the men of the district, she hoped to find herself a husband. She had lowered her sights. He must be presentable, he must have money, he must be the kind of man she could manage – one like Ned, but without Ned's tiresome, half-hearted idealism.

She moved about the late summer gatherings of the Borders, casting about for a suitable man.

And her eye lighted on Archie Brunton.

CHAPTER NINETEEN

Archie took a long time to come home from Paris. He went by way of Monte Carlo, where he lost a lot of money at roulette but found a *petite amie*. A boating accident left him with an arm in splints and a slight case of concussion. The *petite amie* dropped him when he had to sit quietly recuperating in the hotel garden instead of spending money liberally at the gaming table.

When he had recovered, he felt the need of city life. He went to Marseilles, but Marseilles in July was hot. The mosquitoes were troublesome. He went to London, where he had friends. The season was ending, most of his friends headed out into the country for the shooting.

It took another two weeks before he could nerve himself to go back to his estate at Bowden. He argued with himself. After all, he would have to go home some time. He need not see Jenny Armstrong. In the past, if he were honest with himself, it was always he who had sought her out – Jenny had never made the slightest move towards him except in common courtesy. If he wished to steer clear of her, he could easily do so.

So at the end of September he went in

through his own front door. He had left telling his factor he would be away for a week or two. He had been gone four months.

There were estate problems to solve, decisions to take. The factor cornered him in his study where he kept him practically a prisoner for four days. Friends and neighbours came a-calling. Where had he been, what had he done? Ah, you rogue, you, the men seemed to be saying, imagining the fine time he'd had stravaging around Europe at his leisure. The women eyed him and thought he looked less robust than when he went away.

He was urged to take up the social round. His mantelpiece was crowded with invitations from every family of note in the Borders. He sat himself down to write a few acceptances.

His first encounter with Jenny came at a banquet in honour of two new baillies in the town of Kelso. The guests were lined up to be received by the Provost and his wife. Archie was escorting the maiden sister of one of his neighbours, with whom he had made up a party. Ahead of him in the queue he saw Jenny and Ronald Armstrong.

He couldn't take his eyes off her. She was even more beautiful than he had remembered in the lonely nights after his little French girl left him. Shining green silk, pearl drops at her ears, white hoya and fern in her rich dark hair . . . No wonder Armstrong looked pleased and proud as they moved forward to shake hands.

The diners were seated at three long tables placed in horse-shoe fashion. As luck would have it Archie found himself on the opposite side of the same table as Jenny and about three places down from her. As the waiter pushed in her chair, she nodded and smiled to fellow-guests. Her eye caught Archie's.

He saw her go pale. It was only momentary. She made her lips move in faint greeting, bowed to him.

It was over. They had met. From now on it would be something he need not dread. She had smiled and nodded. They were still friends, at least.

It was less of a pleasure to him to encounter Lucy Corvill. He knew she came and went in Galashiels, but he had not seen her since Cowes week almost two years ago. Now he saw her sitting across from him in a box at the Royalty Theatre in Peebles, with a party of friends.

In the second interval of the play, when visiting to other boxes was the rule, he went nowhere near her. He recalled that at Cowes she had been totally taken up with the grandees of the yachting world, and almost slighting because he preferred to play with Clive.

After the performance, when carriages were being awaited, he glimpsed Lucy's fair head in the midst of a little crowd. He skirted the group and was almost out under the street canopy when someone touched his arm.

'Brunton! Hold on! Come and say hello to Mrs Corvill.'

'Thanks, if you don't mind I'll get away. I want to walk to my hotel, clear my head – a dram too many in the bar, Kershaw.'

'Och, do come: just say hello. Mrs Corvill was just saying, she never sees you nowadays.'

'No, I'm busy on the farm – trying to take an

interest, you know. I stay at home more than I used to.'

'You're getting to be a dull dog, are you? That's a change. Well, if you won't come, you won't. Shall I give Mrs Corvill your respects?'

'Of course.'

He made off, glad to have escaped. But next day he wasn't so lucky, for they were both at the Assembly Ball in the town hall. Kershaw once more approached him, and this time excuses would have done no good. He was brought across to speak to Mrs Corvill, who looked angelically pretty in ivory taffeta.

'Mr Brunton!' she said with a friendly smile as he made his bow. 'I hear you went to the play last night.'

'Indeed. Kershaw told me you were there – I hope you enjoyed it?'

'Oh, these melodramas! One expects the worst, of course, from a play called *The Storm Fiend*. And touring companies can never measure up to a London cast.'

'Quite true.'

He was uncertain what line to take. He could see she wanted to be friends, and she was undoubtedly an extremely attractive woman, worthy to enter any assembly on his arm. In the past he had wanted her so much that he had pursued her and won her – but that had been merely the desire for conquest. Love had had nothing to do with it on his part.

Nor could he think she had really loved him, although there had been much romantic talk and vows of eternal devotion. He had thought her a silly woman, if the truth were told, beautiful but silly.

He knew that Jenny thought her more than

silly. Jenny distrusted and disliked her. There was the story about Lucy having had some part in the disappearance of young Heather – he couldn't now remember the details but he recalled the earnestness with which Jenny had spoken when she confided the facts to him.

So on the whole he would prefer not to be on close terms with Lucy. But on the other hand, truly beautiful women were few and far between, and she seemed quite willing to forget the embarrassing liaison of the past. If they could start off on a new footing – simply as people who moved in the same circles and shared the same interests – perhaps there was no harm in being at least amiable to her.

It was at this meeting that Lucy first thought of Archie Brunton as a husband. There he was: still a bachelor, still rich and handsome although without the fine flush of youth that had first won her heart. She remembered his house at Bowden – the Mains Farm, an old farmhouse much extended and improved in the past, with land stretching from it in all directions.

What couldn't she do with a house like that! A wide shrubbery and a copse to hide the farmland, a lake – easily managed, there was a burn that could be dammed – and a terrace like the one recently made at Gatesmuir. As to the furnishings, they would all have to go: as she remembered them, they all dated from about 1800.

She made sure she danced with Archie at the ball and then, having found out the name of his hotel, intended to happen upon him next day. But when she sauntered into the King James to take afternoon tea with a friend, she learned to her annoyance that Mr Brunton had left.

'I thought he'd be staying the Assembly Week?' she remarked to the informative waiter.

'No, ma'am, it was only the half-week. He was off to London at midday.'

To London. Should she follow him there? But London was so big – how could she find him without appearing to be on the hunt?

She decided not to be in a hurry. At the end of Assembly Week she herself went south as she had planned, to try her luck in the Brighton season, which had just opened with a Grand Charity Ball at the Pavilion. She was determined to avoid another cold wet winter in the north and the possible humiliation of an almost empty house at Hogmanay.

Brighton was pleasant, even though the salt air was bad for the complexion and the sea spray was even worse for silk decorations on bonnets. Yet there was no really reliable suitor except The Hon. Justus Territon, who would have gone down on one knee in a minute if she had given him the least encouragement. What was the use of that? He was a younger son with no money of his own and a very healthy married brother between him and the title.

From Brighton she went in late January to her house in Mayfair. She amused herself with a little shopping, looked up a few friends, attended a few parties, but found time was hanging heavy.

So she decided to pay a visit to her naive little friend Dinah Eynsham in her cottage in Bohemian Chelsea. And there, somewhat to her consternation, she found Archie Brunton.

If she was surprised, so was Archie. Mrs Eynsham spoke of Lucy from time to time, so he knew they kept up their acquaintance, but he hadn't thought they were on dropping-in terms.

Lucy saw that he was sitting with his hands resting on his gold-headed cane, in an attitude of waiting. After immediate greetings Dinah explained. 'Mr Brunton's going to take Clive to Wellington Barracks when he gets home from school. Clive is mad about soldiers.'

'How very kind,' said Lucy with an admiring smile. But mentally she was saying, He spent all his time with the brat when we were at Cowes. And now he's taking him to play soldiers . . . This is something I must deal with.

'I have a friend in quarters there,' Archie explained. 'He's promised to show the boy around – let him see how his batman polishes his accoutrement, all that kind of thing.'

Dinah remarked how wonderful it was to see leather really well polished, a conversation ensued about how to make a good mixture to bring a shine up on old leather, Lucy thought she would die of boredom.

All at once there was the sound of running footsteps on the garden path. The door burst open, and Clive came rushing in like a hurricane, his cheeks red from the cold breeze, his jacket buttoned awry, his schoolbooks swinging from a strap. 'Mr Brunton! I ran all the way! I didn't keep you waiting long, did I?'

'Not a bit. Besides, I've had pleasant company.'

Clive gazed from his mother to the visitor. He looked as if he greatly doubted that the company of two ladies could be pleasant. 'Say good afternoon to Mrs Corvill, Clive,' Dinah prompted, taking his books from him and making an attempt to unbutton his jacket.

'Hello, Mrs Corvill. I saw your page boy outside, he looks awful cold. Don't take off my coat, Ma, I'm going right out again – '

'Not in that state you're not. Upstairs with you, wash your hands and face, brush your hair, and put on your Sunday jacket.'

'Oh, Ma!'

'Do as you're told. Mr Brunton won't take you if you look like a street urchin.'

'That's right. Soldiers have to be smart, you know, Clive.'

'So they do. Right.' Clive straightened, saluted, about-turned, and went out with much stamping of the feet to obey orders.

'He's a real boy,' Dinah said fondly.

'Never a dull moment when he's around,' Archie agreed.

Lucy, her ear finely tuned, realised that to gain Archie's attention and approval at the moment it was necessary to be interested in the ill-mannered little boy who had just marched out.

'What a darling he is,' she said. 'Has he seen the Drury Lane pantomime this year?'

'Well, no. We don't as a rule – '

'I say, Mrs Eynsham, we ought to take him.'

'Oh, I don't know, the performance goes on so late – '

'But he *must* see it, the stage effects are stunning, Dinah,' urged Lucy.

'I really don't feel – '

'We'll make up a party!' she swept on, giving a little flourish of her engagement diary which she had produced from her reticule. 'Let me see now . . .'

They were still discussing it when Clive reappeared, soaped, scrubbed, brushed and in his best jacket. When he heard the proposal he made such an outcry in his enthusiasm that somehow it was agreed they would all go to a performance of *Robinson Crusoe* the following week. 'Now, Archie,' cried Lucy, 'I leave all the organising to you – men are so much better at understanding seating plans and things of that kind. But of course since it was my idea, I must pay.'

'Not at all, my dear, I wouldn't dream of it – '

And so on, a friendly wrangle over details, Dinah beaming and nodding, Clive clutching Archie's arm and urging that they would be *late* at the barracks, and in the end Lucy adroitly sweeping man and boy up with her. 'I ordered my hackney to wait,' she said, 'it will save you the trouble of ordering up another.'

Jubal hurried from his place in the hall to open the carriage door for them. 'Hello, Jubal,' said Clive. The boy gave him a half-smile but said nothing in reply until Lucy said sharply, 'Answer Master Clive, then!'

'Hello, Maz Clive.'

'He never seems to learn proper English,' Lucy said as they took their places. 'Sending him with a message is hopeless.'

'Speaks some sort of dialect, does he?'

'Yes, slave talk. My poor dear Ned spent so much time trying to get them to express themselves like human beings. Wasted effort. I don't really think they have the same intelligence as us, you know.'

'Maybe he's just numb with cold,' Archie said, half-laughing.

'Can't he ride inside with us?' Clive put in.

'Certainly not!' said Lucy, then, hearing the sharpness in her own voice, added more sweetly, 'You don't understand these things, Clive dear.'

She dropped them off at the barracks, bestowing a kiss on Clive's cheek before driving off for home.

On the whole, she was pleased with this unexpected encounter. Of course, at the moment, she was having to share Archie with this hoyden of a girl from Australia, but soon she and Archie would be in the Borders. Then it would be easy to happen upon him, to be in the same gathering, to invite him to her little parties. Oh yes. Things would go well from now on.

Spring came early that year. Lucy was pleased to find the trees already showing green buds when she got to Galashiels in March. Her first visitor at her house in Scotts Place was Heather, to whom she had written announcing her coming.

Lucy was almost startled at how much Heather had grown up since last she saw her in the autumn. She would be sixteen in three months' time, and though still thin and girlish there was a look about her that foreshadowed a slender beauty.

'You should wear this colour,' she remarked, holding up a fold of the gown that Heather was helping to unpack.

'Amethyst? I don't think Mama's ever thought of it. Nothing I've got would match it, at any rate.'

'Then you shall have a parasol and a bonnet to match if you can persuade Mama to let you have an amethyst dress.'

'I think it's too late. Mama and Baird have planned my spring wardrobe by now – '

'Surely you have some say?'

'Well, no, really. Mama has to see to such things when she has time. She's really busy now, showing the pattern book for the spring cloths – '

'But you must begin to take control of your appearance, Heather. You must develop a style of your own. Too many girls make the mistake of being mere copies of others, so naturally gentlemen never pay them any attention.'

Heather sighed and put the gown on the padded cane hanger, covering it with muslin to protect it from dust and fading. 'I don't really think that's important where I'm concerned,' she said. 'I told you before, I never know what to say or do. I shall just have to hope that someone will understand I'm not stupid or proud, just tongue-tied.'

'That's no way to catch a good husband,' Lucy cried, much put out. 'You can't rely on luck!'

'But what else can one do? There are only so many young men that I'm likely to know – '

'Good gracious, you can put yourself out a little to attract the best of them! That's obvious.'

'You mean . . . one should actually make a conscious effort?'

'My dear Heather,' Lucy said in a rather severe tone, 'it's a young woman's duty to make the best marriage that she can. That's a fact, is it not?'

'Well . . .'

'Come now, you know very well that your parents wouldn't let you marry someone beneath you. Naturally they want to see you better yourself in life when you choose your husband.'

'They've never said so – '

'They don't have to say so! It's taken for granted. And you must look about you when the time comes and think who would give you the best style of living, the best role in society – '

'But . . . one should be in love, surely?'

'Love comes with the married state, Heather. Simple liking or affection is enough as a basis. But it is essential that the man is able to offer something in exchange for the wifely graces with which you will surround him. Look around you – who among your acquaintances would be the most eligible, the most likely to give you standing and influence in society?'

'Well, who?' said Heather, perplexed.

'Viscount Cairness, of course.'

'Allen?'

'Yes, Allen, your classmate.'

'Allen?' cried Heather, laughing. 'Allen is never going to ask me to marry him!'

'Why not?'

'Well, because . . . because he doesn't think of me in that way.'

'What does that mean? He doesn't think of you as his equal in rank? He thinks you beneath him?'

'Oh, heavens, no, there's no swank or anything like that about Allen. No, he just doesn't think of me as a woman – he scarcely even thinks of me as a girl, I'm just someone who exercises the horses with him, and can't use a protractor when we're doing geometry, and goes off to deportment lessons when he's doing Virgil with Mr Barbour.'

The maid and Jubal came in, carrying another hamper of clothes between them. 'Whaur d'ye want this, ma'am?'

'Take it out again! There's no room in here.'

'Shall we leave it at the stairheid then, ma'am?'

'Take it to the box room for the moment. Really, Maisie, can't you think for yourself?'

'Sorry, ma'am.'

Lucy shook her head as they staggered out with the trunk. 'Servants are such a problem,' she said. 'I keep trying to find a good personal maid, but either they're so stupid they can't do new hair styles from a book or else if they're any good they only stay a few weeks . . .'

'Jubal's been with you a long time,' Heather pointed out.

'Yes, such an expense! He grows out of his uniforms. And he really doesn't *do* anything.' Lucy spread out the skirts of a day gown. 'I suppose this will have to go to the cleaners, since I haven't got a maid who would know how to get that stain out . . .'

'Well there, you see,' Heather said, laughing. 'Jubal is useful: he can carry things to the cleaners for you – '

'Oh yes, he can fetch and carry. And when I marry again the expense of his upkeep won't matter, really.'

'You're going to marry again?' Heather said, startled.

'Of course! Women weren't meant to live alone, my dear. The married state is our proper condition. And that is what I've just been saying,' she went on, wagging her finger at her niece. 'You must begin to think seriously about it. You shouldn't allow your advantages in being so much with Viscount Cairness to go to waste.'

'But I just explained – '

'You said he paid no attention to you. Well, you must make him pay attention.'

'But how, Aunt Lucy?'

'There's that other boy – the one who seems to eat up all the seed cake and shortbread at garden parties – '

'David Buchanan,' supplied Heather, chuckling at this all too accurate description.

'Yes, he's still sharing your lessons at Thornieburn?'

'Of course. We're to go on for another year at least – until Allen goes to university.'

'Allen is to go to university? I understood his health made such things impossible?'

'Oh, he's much better these days. His father thinks he could go to Edinburgh when he's eighteen.'

'It would be helpful if you could attach him before he goes, Heather. At university young men meet all sorts of people, fall into all kinds of involvements. You ought to act now.'

'But act in what way?'

'If you want to make Allen pay attention to you, *you* must pay attention to David.'

The girl looked as baffled as she felt. 'I don't follow that, Aunt Lucy.'

'It's perfectly simple. You must show that you like David very much indeed. You must rush to meet him when you first get to Thornieburn of a Monday morning, you must hang on his every word, laugh at his jokes, admire his cleverness . . .'

Heather, though bewildered, felt an impulse of amusement. 'He'll think I'm out of my mind.'

'Not at all. My dear Heather, men are all alike, even very young men. They all like to believe they are wonderful.'

'But you said I was to make a fuss of David, whereas it's Allen – '

'Certainly. Allen will soon notice that you make a fuss of David. You said you didn't know how to make him notice you, and I've explained how.'

'But what's the good of that? I mean, if the idea is to make Allen feel attracted to me?'

'It's in the nature of things that Allen will wonder why you prefer David. He'll begin to pay court to you simply because he doesn't want to take second place. There you are.'

Her niece stood staring thoughtfully at the dresses draped on the bed and the chairs. 'Isn't that rather deceitful?' she murmured.

'Deceitful? In what way? You do like David, don't you?'

'Of course.'

'Then how can it be deceitful to show that you do?'

'But I don't like him better than Allen, Aunt Lucy.'

'Who says you do? That is not the point. You can show you like Allen too – later, when he has wakened up to the fact that he wants to come first with you.'

'Is that really a correct thing to do?'

'I just explained to you, Heather. It is the duty of a girl to do well in marriage. If to achieve that end you have to find a way of fascinating a young man, that is perfectly permissable.'

'Is . . . is that how you and Uncle Ned came to get married?'

'Oh, my dear, I didn't have to make any great effort to fascinate your uncle! He was devoted to me from the outset. No, no, that was a different matter.'

'Of course, I see that. You were pretty and lively . . .'

Lucy gave a smile. 'I may say, without vanity, that I had no problems in being agreeable to gentlemen. I could have married *anyone* among a great following of young men . . .'

'But you chose Uncle Ned because you loved him.'

'Indeed, it was a love match.' Lucy always said this with such conviction that she almost believed it herself by now. 'But I must tell you, my dear child, that Ned was so unsure of himself that I had to give him quite a lot of encouragement. So I can tell you from my own experience that my plan of campaign will work.'

'I don't know if I could really do it. I should feel so odd, telling David I thought he was wonderful.'

'Dear child, you don't have to say it in so many words! Just look impressed, agree to his opinions, seem delighted when he smiles at you. It's very simple.'

'If . . . if I tried it . . . and it worked, and Allen began to be interested in me . . . You see, Aunt Lucy, I've never thought of him in that way. I don't know whether I should like it if things changed.'

'Then you go back to the way things were before,' Lucy said impatiently. 'Good heavens, Heather, the whole business is in your control! You can make men do almost anything you like if you put your mind to it. But, I must point out, it would be a great mistake not to further your chances with the Viscount. I don't believe you will find a better match anywhere in the Borders.'

This was obviously true. The words recurred to Heather all through the ensuing weekend. If, as Aunt Lucy said, it was her duty to make a good marriage, then Allen Cairness was the best she could make. And when she thought about it, she felt she probably might like to be married to Allen. Certainly he was the boy she felt on easiest terms with out of all those she'd met.

Aunt Lucy was so clever and had so much experience of the world. What she said was important. She ought to follow her advice. So on the following Monday, when she stepped out of the carriage, she put it into practice.

The two boys were waiting for her as usual in the courtyard, with three of the Countess's dogs for company. The dogs leapt and cavorted round Heather as she alighted, getting in the way of the footman taking down her portmanteau.

'Heel, Trounce! Heel!' shouted David at the largest of the dogs.

Trounce obeyed immediately, as he would

have obeyed anyone who called out the terms he had been trained to heed.

Heather gave David an admiring glance. 'What a way you have with animals,' she remarked.

Her attention was then needed in directing the footman. As she went indoors she glanced back. David Buchanan was looking after her with a smile.

Nothing unusual about that. He was an amiable boy.

All the same, she knew that she had caused that smile. It was a heady sensation.

CHAPTER TWENTY

Mindful of Lady Thornieburn's hint about giving Heather some experience of London, Jenny took her daughter with her on her March business trip. Between them she and Ronald would find time to take the girl about and if not, Dinah was always delighted to do so.

Baird would be left to supervise Max in the nursery. As she packed for Jenny she remarked, 'It's a' the crack that Herself has set her cap at Mr Brunton.'

'Lucy?'

'Aye. Have you no noticed she singles him out?'

'I've only seen them in the same room about twice, I think. But . . .' Yes, Lucy had seemed to give her smiles to Archie.

'And Mr Brunton likes it,' Baird went on. 'Mair fool he.'

'Baird, surely he has enough sense not to . . .'

'D'ye think so? For his sake, I hope it. She'll lead him a bonny jig if she gets control of his household.'

This conversation remained with Jenny. She was reminded of it when she took her daughter to Peter Robinson's in Oxford Street on a shopping expedition. Heather allowed

400

herself to be led through the department of ready-made clothes, but refused to like any of them.

'Well, let's go to the dress materials, then. Perhaps you'll see something there that you like and then we can have it made up.'

Heather looked about in the materials department. Nothing seemed quite right.

'Well, what are you looking for exactly, dear?' Jenny asked, glancing at her watch and thinking she would soon be running late for an appointment with her wool factor.

'I want a gown made of amethyst velvet.'

'Amethyst velvet? Don't you think that's a little too – '

'Aunt Lucy has a gown of amethyst velvet.'

'But Aunt Lucy is nearly – ' She broke off. She'd been about to say, Aunt Lucy is nearly forty, but realised in time that it would sound catty. 'Aunt Lucy leads a less active life than you, my pet,' she amended, 'and what is suitable for a lady like her isn't necessarily right for a girl who still likes to ramble about the countryside with her little brother.'

'Well . . .' Heather had to admit the justice of this. 'Aunt Lucy says I should wear amethyst. She says it would suit me.'

'So it would, I daresay. Very well, let's see if we can find some amethyst poplin or fine Swiss.'

Later, the cloth chosen and paid for, they made their way out to the hustle and bustle of the street. Wheels rattled, horses whinnied, whips cracked, wagons rumbled, newsboys shouted, dogs barked, whistles shrilled, pavement vendors shouted their wares, beggars whined for alms, the fire wagon went galloping by with its bell clanging.

'I suppose,' Heather said with a stifled sigh, 'that you get used to it. Aunt Lucy says London is very agreeable so I know it must be so.'

'One need not take everything Aunt Lucy says for gospel, my love.'

They waited for the sweeper to clear the crossing, then went on to the other side.

'You often sound rather critical of Aunt Lucy,' Heather remarked, 'but let me tell you, she knows what she's talking about.'

'In which particular department of information?'

'Well, if you want to know, she was talking to me about gentlemen the other day, and what she said was quite right.'

'What about gentlemen?'

'That if you want them to pay attention to you, all you have to do is let them think they're wonderful.'

Jenny laughed. 'I can't argue with that. But it's true of women as well as men. Anyone in the world – '

'When she first said it to me, I couldn't quite believe it, but it's quite easy, and then I happened to see her with Mr Brunton and could tell she'd quite captivated him because he was talking so delightedly to her. So you see what I mean when I say we ought to respect her opinions.'

A hackney came by, Jenny hailed it, and when they had settled themselves and she had given directions, Heather's attention was elsewhere.

Perhaps it was just as well. Jenny found no

pleasure in the idea that Archie was falling under Lucy's spell.

Through the ten days she spent in London she returned from time to time to the thought. She didn't love Archie Brunton, but she had a care for him.

Once back in Galashiels she nerved herself to speak to him. Interfering . . .? Yes, but Auld Acquaintance urged her to it.

She invited him to tea at the mills. Archie was mystified by the invitation – he had no business of any kind with cloth mills. Nevertheless he came.

When tea had been brought and the door closed, Jenny began. 'You must forgive me for what I'm about to say, Archie.'

He looked both nervous and curious.

'It's about Lucy.'

'Oh, I suppose you're wondering how I could . . . but then you see, Jenny, she seems to want me, and nobody else does.'

Jenny put her teacup down with a bang. 'Good God, man, have you no more initiative than that? Can't you go out and find a proper wife?'

Embarrassed, he pushed his little piece of madeira cake about his plate. 'It's this way, Jenny. I've wasted so much of my life already, I can't afford to waste any more. I can't waste time getting to know a perfect stranger and then finding I don't like her or she doesn't fancy me. I really don't have time to go out prospecting. And there is Lucy, clearly ready to get married again and not averse to marrying me, by the looks of it.'

'Archie, it would be a disaster! You know what she's like!'

He shrugged. 'That was years ago, after all. She's changed a lot.'

She was silent for a while. They both busied themselves with their teacups. Jenny asked if he would like more. He said yes. They were trapped in a very difficult conversation.

'I ought not to sit in judgement on Lucy, I suppose,' she said at length. 'Forgive me for seeming to do so, and for interfering in your affairs. But I should hate it if you were made unhappy, Archie. And it's my sincere belief Lucy would make you unhappy. Very unhappy.'

'Well, at least,' he said with a wavering smile, 'I shouldn't be unhappy alone. I'd have company.'

'But good heavens, man, there's better company than Lucy!'

'Who, for instance?'

Jenny decided to wager everything on one throw. 'There's Dinah Eynsham.'

'Dinah?' He was staggered. 'But she . . . she's got a ten-year-old son!'

'And what's wrong with that? You like him, don't you?'

Archie leapt to his feet and went marching about the cluttered office. 'Great heavens, Jenny, think what you're saying! It doesn't count that I like Clive. For that matter, I like Dinah too. But after all . . . she had an affair with Ronald before she got married.'

'And how many affairs have you had, Archie?'

'That's different.'

There it was, the old demarcation line. Men could have mistresses and father illegitimate children, and no one thought the worse of them. Woman could not have lovers nor could they have illegitimate children without being despised for it.

'Sit down, Archie.'

'Damned if I will. If I'd known what you had in mind, I'd never have come!'

'I didn't mean to mention Dinah until the moment I said her name. But if you think about it, Archie, she'd make you an ideal wife. She's beautiful and unspoilt and goodnatured. A bit hot-tempered, but she never holds a grudge. The lad is a lovely child – noisy and demanding, but intelligent.'

'And he's Ronald's son.'

'So you say. You can't prove it, though.'

'I don't have to prove it – '

'No, you don't, and you don't have to let it obsess you either. You have to take them both in the same way as the rest of the world – a handsome widow with a small income and a fine sturdy boy. All I can say is, if I were asked to choose who I'd rather spend the rest of my life with, those two or Lucy Corvill, I know which I'd pick!'

'No one asks you to choose, or to stick your nose in my affairs! Who the hell do you think you are?' roared Archie.

'I'm the woman you've followed about for more or less ten years. Archie my dear lad . . .' She went to him, took his hands though he tried to shrug her away, and tugged at him so that he was looking directly down at her. 'Archie, I don't want to see you make a terrible mistake. I know I was wrong to start talking about Dinah but at least promise me this – promise me you won't marry Lucy.'

'I won't promise a damned thing – '

The door opened, the chief clerk put his head in. 'Is anything wrong?' he inquired, then drew back in surprise at the tableau before him. Mrs Armstrong holding hands with Mr Brunton and the both of them white with passion! Dearie me!

'Everything is fine, McCraw, thank you. Mr Brunton had a coughing fit.'

Coughing fit! Havers! The chief clerk withdrew, much put out.

Archie's angry face melted into a sheepish smile. 'There,' he said. 'Your reputation's gone!'

'Not it. McCraw will never say a word to anyone.'

'A fine thing – we could go to bed together in Paris and nobody knew a word about it, but the minute I raise my voice above a whisper in Galashiels, the watch committee turns out.'

She blushed at the reminder of Paris. She turned away.

'More tea?' she said helplessly.

'I could do with something stronger!'

'There's Madeira . . .'

'That'll have to do. What I really need is a stiff whisky.'

She took the Madeira out of the wall cupboard, poured, and offered it to him. He gulped it down. Then he said, 'Sorry I roared at you.'

'It's all right.'

'I'm sorry I swore at you and told you to mind your own business.'

'I deserved it.'

'I . . . I promise not to marry Lucy.'

'Oh, Archie!'

'There, there. Don't cry. I suppose I knew I

was being a fool. But you see . . . I've grown so devilish lonely these last few months.'

'I know, my dear, I know. I understand.'

'I wish I could have married you, Jenny,' he broke out, with tears in his voice. 'You can't know how I regret the past . . . Oh, God, what a mess I've made of everything!'

'No no, you mustn't think like that. You've plenty of years ahead of you, man. You'll be happy yet, you will, I know it.'

He took out a handkerchief, blew his nose, blinked a few times, then made for the door. 'Since the business of the meeting is over, I think I'll take my leave.'

'Au revoir, Archie. Take care.'

'Aye, I'll try. Au revoir, my treasure.'

As he drove home in his gig he thought over the scene he had just played. He was in a state of confusion. Jenny's concern for him touched him deeply, only making him the more certain she was the only woman in the world for him.

Yet on the other hand the idea of Dinah began to take shape in his mind. Dinah was a very good, kind sort of woman – unpolished, without pretensions, perhaps not even a lady and perhaps not likely to be one.

She was almost the exact opposite of Lucy except that she too had beauty. But Dinah's beauty was of a different kind – a strong, warm loveliness. Temper – yes, he knew she had a temper, he'd witnessed little bouts of it. But as Jenny said, she was over it quickly and she never bore a grudge. Nor was she a clever woman, but then, thought Archie with honesty, he himself was no genius.

As for the boy . . . Ronald's son . . .

Could he really ever accept the idea of being stepfather to Ronald Armstrong's son?

Impossible.

Yet two days later he was on the train for London.

Easter was late that year. He made it the excuse for his visit, arriving with yet another addition to Clive's collection of lead soldiers.

'You spoil him,' Dinah protested.

'Not at all. Besides, these are the only toys he plays with. I think the boy is really interested in soldiering, Mrs Eynsham. Perhaps something could be – '

'Oh, dear me, his schoolfriends are all the same. One wants to be a train-driver, another wants to be a ship's captain. They'll all grow out of it before they're twelve.'

Archie was dashed. He'd intended to offer the help of his friend at the War Office in furthering Clive's career as a soldier. Clive could be heard upstairs in the playroom making trumpeting sounds as he led his leaden soldiers into battle.

'Do go up,' Dinah urged. 'I know you and he were fighting the Crimean Campaign the last time you were here.'

Next day, Sunday, he arranged to take Clive to Hyde Park to see the Easter turn-out of carriages and horses. Alas, Dinah had taken it for granted the invitation was for Clive only. When Archie got to the house in Chelsea, it was to find the boy waiting alone in his best clothes. His mother had gone to have tea with a friend.

Two days later Jenny Armstrong received a letter from Dinah, who tried faithfully to keep in touch but generally had almost nothing to write about. This time after the usual remarks about health and schoolwork, Dinah went on: 'Mr Brunton was here on Sattiday with yet another gift for Clive, and yestiday took him to the Park. I have a feeling he was vecksed about somthing, but don't know what because I made myself scairse both times knowing how he likes to have fun with the boy. I went to tea with Miss Kinsman, she sends her love.'

Poor Archie, thought Jenny. That's a gey hard row to hoe!

She sat down at once to write inviting Dinah to Gatesmuir. 'The weather is so good I thought you would enjoy some country life, and this time perhaps you could stay a while. Don't worry about Clive's schooling, he can go with Max to the dame school at Miss Gavin's, which is quite good. Please do come, I know Max would love to see Clive and I should love to see *you*.'

The response was an immediate acceptance. Jenny arranged a little dinner party for the day after Dinah's arrival, to which she invited a few close friends, among whom was Archie Brunton. She didn't even blush when she arranged the seating at dinner so that Dinah and Archie were sitting next to each other.

The result of that was an invitation to bring the children, Clive and Max, to the Home Farm next day to see the Jersey calves. Jenny excused herself – she had business, she said.

So it went. By and by Heather said to her mother, 'Does Mr Brunton particularly like Mrs Eynsham?'

'I believe he does,' Jenny replied with a smile.

'But I thought Mr Brunton particularly liked Aunt Lucy?'

The smile vanished from Jenny's face. 'I think not, Heather.'

'But . . . I feel sure Aunt Lucy thought . . . She once said to me she intended to marry again and I thought she meant . . .'

'Your aunt's intentions – ' She broke off. 'Your aunt may well marry again. But that's nothing for you to concern yourself over, my love.'

'But she'll be so disappointed!'

Lucy wasn't disappointed, she was enraged. For about a month Archie had more or less neglected her, and when it dawned upon her that this period co-incided almost exactly with Dinah Eynsham's presence, she understood at once what was happening.

She fought back with the weapons she had always used well – she took particular care with her appearance, she made sure she was always full of smiles and winsomeness whenever she encountered Archie in the social round. But she knew she was not only failing to regain his regard, she was losing ground. Mrs Eynsham, her unsophisticated friend from the outback, was winning Archie Brunton away from her without even trying.

Lucy kept up her association with Dinah, invited her to her house for card parties and tea al fresco on the little lawn. They had always talked about fashion. This continued to be their main interest, but Mr Brunton often seemed to come into it when Lucy discussed clothes. 'Mr Brunton does so love to see a woman in pink,' she would remark, knowing full well that Dinah could never look well in pink, or 'Mr

Brunton teased young Agnes Simpson about her freckles.'

'Oh, I always get freckles in the sun,' Dinah would mourn.

'Then you must take steps to clear them up. Although, dear Mrs Eynsham, if you've had them all your life it may be a hopeless task.'

'Reckon you're right.'

Nothing seemed to perturb Dinah. She hardly even seemed to be aware that Archie liked her.

In that, Lucy was wrong. It was slowly beginning to seep through to Dinah's consciousness, but she couldn't bring herself to believe it. In the first place, she had long ago decided that she was finished with 'all that sort of thing'. She was a widow, she had a little boy to bring up, she had no fortune – nobody was ever going to want her and she for her part wanted no one.

Then there was her humble view of herself. Mr Brunton couldn't *possibly* be paying court to her. He was one of the richest men in the Borders, he was goodlooking in his bluff, fair-skinned way. He could have anybody he liked. He couldn't really be interested in a nobody like Dinah Eynsham. It was all in her imagination.

'Nothing of the sort,' cried Jenny when she hinted at the subject to her. 'I'm sure Archie likes you very much. In fact, I shouldn't be surprised if he made you an offer any day now.'

'Mr Brunton? Make me an offer?'

'Yes, my dear. Why not?'

'Oh, Jenny,' Dinah said, blushing deeply, 'you know why not.'

They were sitting by the scarred old table in the old reading-room which Jenny used as an unofficial office. Jenny had been working on a new design. She laid aside her sketch pad, took one of Dinah's hands in both of hers, and looked serious.

'Dinah, I hope you're not going to say you're unworthy of Archie because you were indiscreet years ago and fell in love with a married man.'

'Well, it went a bit further than that, Jen. I had his baby.'

Jenny sighed. 'As far as the world knows, Clive is the son of Tim Eynsham, who died in a knife fight at Cootamundra years ago.'

'But . . . but . . . If Mr Brunton really did ask me to marry him, I'd . . . I'd feel bad about deceiving him.' She paused. 'D'you think I should tell him, Jen?'

'He knows.'

'Eh?' Dinah said inelegantly.

'He knows, Dinah.'

'You mean you *told* him?' Dinah cried. Although she'd been fighting for the courage to tell him herself, she felt hard done by that someone else should do so.

'I didn't have to tell him, dear. He guessed most of it.'

'But I don't see how . . . How could he guess, Jenny?'

Jenny got up and began restlessly tidying books and papers on the table. 'Dinah, Archie and I have known each other twenty years. There's not much about me he doesn't know, and one of the things he's aware of is that I went rushing to Sydney about a dozen years

412

ago to rescue my husband from some designing hussy – '

'Aw, come on, Jenny, I never was designing!'

'No, of course not. But from here, when I first heard of you, that's the way it looked. Archie guessed the minute you arrived on the scene in London that you were the woman who'd tempted Ronald away. He guessed that Clive is Ronald's son. He doesn't *know*, you understand – but he'd wager money on it. So you see, you don't need to confess to him.'

Dinah was struck dumb.

After a moment Jenny faced her and said almost sternly, 'Look at this sensibly, Dinah. Your little boy needs a man to handle him. At the moment his boisterousness is endearing, but if someone doesn't take him in hand he could end up a very rackety young man.'

'Oh, there's nothing bad in him, really – '

'Of course not, but it would be better if there was a man to control him. And Archie is very fond of the lad, and of you too, Dinah. And you need him. You don't want to go on for ever on your own, do you?'

'Well, I thought I'd have to. I was more or less resigned to it. I certainly never thought of marrying again.'

'You're not still in love with Ronald, Dinah?'

Dinah took a moment before replying. 'No,' she said with a sigh, 'I reckon not. Somewhere along the line I grew out of it. But then, you know – I'm not in love with Archie.'

'He knows that, my dear. But you do like him, don't you?'

'Sure. He's a very nice man. In a way he's more my type than Ron ever was – I think I could keep up with Archie, but I don't think I could ever have been a proper wife to Ron.'

'There you are then,' Jenny said.

'You think I should say yes, then, if he asks me?'

Jenny surveyed her handiwork and the tidy book table. Then she said, 'Dinah, one thing I've learned as I've gone along is that life keeps offering you chances to start again. The thing is to recognise the chance when it comes. You've got a chance now – but whether you take it or not must be your own decision.'

'Yair,' Dinah said. 'I reckon . . .'

June came, and with it Heather's birthday. The weather being perfect, there was a birthday tea on the lawn. Heather had invited Allen and David, and of course Max and Clive were of the party. Ronald was at home, for a wonder. Jenny had let Archie know he'd be welcome if he dropped by. Dinah and Baird helped to decorate the table in the shade of the chestnut trees. It was a grand occasion, not even marred by the little spiders who came down on fine threads from the branches overhead to see what was going on.

'More cake, Dinah?'

'Thanks, I won't. I'll have some tea, though. I'm so thirsty and dry . . .'

'You're flushed again. Is your throat still bothering you?'

'Ssh, Jenny, it's nothing – a summer fever.'

'You should have stayed indoors in the shade – '

'I didn't want to spoil the party. Honest, it's nothing.'

Jenny's attention was called away by the game of conundrums being played round the table. All the same, she cast an eye at Dinah now and again.

For the last four or five days Dinah had been plagued by a low fever. Her throat felt scratchy, her stomach seemed uneasy, she looked flushed and though she wouldn't allow her temperature to be taken it was probably a degree or so above normal. Yet nothing seemed to come of it. She didn't take to her bed with laryngitis or summer influenza. Each morning she seemed normal, each day the symptoms gradually came again, each evening she went to bed feeling poorly and then again in the morning she seemed better.

Jenny had suggested calling the doctor, Dinah insisted it was nothing. 'Back home there were all kinds of things that bit you and gave you a bit of a go,' she said, with a shrug and a smile. 'Your doctor prob'ly wouldn't know what to do with an ailment from down under!'

By and by the youngsters grew bored with sitting sedately at table. A game of hide and seek was proposed. Allen was 'it'. Just as he had found both Max and Clive, who were incapable of hiding in silence for two minutes, a visitor arrived.

'Good aftahnoon,' said Jubal, with his uncertain smile. 'Miz Corvill sent me with a present for Miss Heather and a packet for Miz Eynsham.'

'Oh, how lovely!' cried Heather, coming out of hiding at the sight of the prettily wrapped long box. She unwrapped it. Inside was a parasol in amethyst silk, an almost perfect match for her amethyst dress.

'What did you get, Ma?' Clive demanded.

'It's nothing,' Dinah said, colouring a little.

'Open it, open it!' demanded Max.

'Ssh, quiet, now, Max. It's for Mrs Eynsham, nothing to do with you.'

'Open it up, Ma!' Clive ordered. 'Come on, let's see what you got – it's a non-birthday present, mebbe.'

To quiet him, Dinah undid the stiff white paper round her packet, to reveal a pretty bottle decorated with painted flowers and closed with a glass stopper shaped like a little bird.

'Oh, isn't that nice!' cried Heather. 'It's just the kind of thing Aunt Lucy would send!'

'But what on earth is it?' said Ronald in perplexity. 'Perfume?'

'Well . . . as a matter of fact . . . it's a recipe that Mrs Corvill uses to clear her skin.' Dinah looked in embarrassment at Archie and away again. 'I have these awful freckles . . .'

'There's nothing wrong with freckles!' Ronald said, amused. 'What do you say, Archie?'

'Quite right. I think freckles are rather bonny.'

Dinah set the bottle down on the tea-table. Heather opened her parasol and proceeded to try it against first one shoulder then the other.

'Ho, my, my!' cried her brother. 'Aren't we important! Must have a parasol to keep the sun off our precious head, mustn't we?'

'I think it looks jolly nice,' said David Buchanan, going pink.

'Oh, you're always saying you think Heather looks jolly nice,' Allen groaned. 'You're a mutual admiration society, you two!'

'Well, it does look nice – '

'Dinna be daft!' Max broke in. 'How can she look nice when she's got far bigger freckles than Mrs Eynsham, and squinty eyes, and teeth that stick out – '

'And frizzy hair,' put in Clive, tempted into evil by Max. 'And a squeaky voice – '

'And scared of spiders,' added Allen, 'and puts saddles on back to front – '

'And is getting terribly *old*,' suggested Max, 'and pretending to be grown-up – '

'Beast!' cried Heather, abandoning the parasol and throwing herself on her brother. 'Beast, little beast – can't spell or write well, put the duffer down the well!'

A mêlée ensued, from which Jubal extricated Max by the simple expedient of dragging him by one arm. 'You shoh say nasty things,' he remarked, 'an' hit yoh sister's birthday.'

'But she *is* always on about her dress and her hair and things like that. Let go, Jubal – ' He pulled himself free so as to make a face at Heather. 'If you're so keen to be pretty, you should take a swig at Mrs Eynsham's freckle mixture. Go on, I dare you.'

'Dare, dare, double dare!' chanted Clive. 'Go on, have some of Ma's beauty potion.'

'Heather doesn't need things like that,' David Buchanan said with indignation.

'If she lets Magnet run away so that she loses her hat again, she'll need something against sunburn,' Allen said, laughing and yet annoyed and wanting to hurt a little.

'All right then,' Heather said. 'I'll take a double dose and then Magnet can run away with me two days running.'

She snatched up the bottle, took out the stopper.

'No, no, Miss Heather – you don' take that – it for Miz Eynsham – '

'Don't be silly, Jubal,' cried Heather. 'Mrs Eynsham doesn't mind – do you, Aunt Dinah?'

'No, don't, Miz Heather!' The page launched himself at her.

Too late. Heather had drunk off half the contents of the bottle.

Jubal threw himself towards the tea table. 'Miz Armstrong, Miz Armstrong! Please – come quick – '

'What's the matter, Jubal?' Jenny said, starting from a daydream. There was no doubting the dread in the boy's voice.

'Oh, Miz Armstrong – she done drink it – I couldn't stop her. I tried but she won't listen – Miz Armstrong, you got to do sumpin!'

'What, Jubal? What? What's wrong?'

'She drunk de potion! She gwine be sick. Quick, Miz Armstrong – you got to help her!'

Jenny felt herself go cold and then hot. Realisation swept in upon her. Heather had drunk something harmful.

Allen Cairness had come hurrying after the black boy. 'What's got into him?' he demanded.

'Quick, Allen, run round to the vegetable garden. There are some boys working there – send one of them at once for Dr Allerdyce.'

'Send for – ?'

'Tell him to say he's to come at once – Heather has swallowed something.'

'I'll go,' Allen said. 'It's quicker than explaining. Which house?'

'The house by the bridge. It has a green door and a brass plaque – oh, quick, Allen.'

He was off running, to grab his horse from

the stables, throw himself on it, and ride off bareback at the gallop.

Meanwhile Jenny and Ronald got their frightened daughter into the house. 'I feel all right,' she kept saying, 'I don't know what the fuss is about, I'm all right!'

Baird mixed salt and water in the kitchen. She ran with it to the morning room, into which Heather had been taken. 'Drink it,' she said. And when, after one mouthful, Heather began to protest, she said grimly, 'Drink it or I'll hold your nose and pour it down you!'

Together she and Jenny got Heather up to her room. There she began to be sick. 'What is it?' she wept. 'Why are you doing this to me?'

'Oh, darling,' Jenny cried, holding her in her arms. 'Oh, my darling, my darling! Please – it's for the best!'

It broke her heart to have to be cruel to Heather – to Heather, whom she had brought back from the land of the lost and vowed to keep from harm for the rest of her life.

The doctor came, heard the story. 'Where's the black boy?' he demanded.

Jubal emerged from a corner of the landing where he had been hovering.

'Now, my lad, what's this all about?' said Dr Allerdyce, frowning sternly.

'That bottle got a potion in it. My mammy showed Miz Corvill how to make it. My mammy knowed how to do things with leaves and plants, you make good things and bad things but this is a bad thing, I dunno what's in it but Miz Eynsham, she be takin' dis potion, s'pose to make de skin white but I think it make her sick, I don' think Miz Corvill would give a good thing to Miz Eynsham.'

The doctor heard him with utter amazement. 'Look here, child,' he stuttered, 'you be careful what you're saying. You can't really mean – '

'He does,' Jenny intervened, 'he does.'

She knew it with certainty. Heather had swallowed poison.

CHAPTER TWENTY-ONE

Dr Allerdyce was inclined to discount the whole affair. He looked at the narrow little bottle which Baird had brought in from the tea-table, tipped a drop of the liquid on his finger, tasted it, and shrugged.

'It's some kind of herb tea,' he said. 'It's a little bit bitter but nothing out of the ordinary.'

'But Jubal said – '

'My goodness, Mrs Armstrong, yon wee creature can scarcely speak the Queen's English. You got the wrong end of the stick.'

'But Heather was sick – '

'Of course she was sick! You gave her an emetic.' Clearly he thought she had behaved in a panicky, foolish fashion.

They were outside the door of Heather's room. He put his head round to give her another glance, then came back to Jenny. 'Her pulse is a bit rapid but she's had a fright.' And whose fault is that, he said by the tilt of his head and the turn-down at the corners of his mouth.

'You don't think she's in danger?'

'Not at all, not at all.' He took his leave, clearly annoyed at having been dragged from his house by a nervy boy when he was just about to sit down to his tea.

Jenny went back to look at her daughter. Heather was lying propped up against pillows, her hair in a tangle. 'A fine birthday party,' she muttered.

'How do you feel, darling?'

'Quite all right. Can I get up again?'

'No, Dr Allerdyce said better keep you in bed.'

'What was supposed to be wrong with me?'

'That preparation you drank – Jubal said it was harmful.'

'Idiot,' sighed Heather, closing her eyes and looking drowsy.

Jenny went down to the morning room where Heather had first been taken. Ronald was speaking in a reassuring fashion to Allen and David. Baird had already taken the two younger boys to the day nursery out of the way. Jubal was sitting on the ground outside the windows that gave access to the terrace.

'How is she?' Allen asked in slightly gasping voice.

'Quite all right. The doctor says it was a fuss about nothing.'

'But Jubal said – '

'Doctor says he didn't know what he was talking about.'

David Buchanan smoothed down his hair and hitched his jacket. 'We ought to get back to Thornieburn, Allen. Are you all right to leave?'

'I'm perfectly all right,' Allen said with resentment, wheezing.

'You're not going to have an attack?'

'No, I'm not, stop fussing!' He went to Jenny, took her hand and shook it formally. 'Thank you for having us, Mrs Armstrong.'

'I'm so sorry I spoiled everything, Allen.'

'Not at all. Come on, David.'

Both boys bowed and went out.

Dinah and Archie were sitting together on the sofa. Dinah looked very shaken. 'I hope she won't take any harm,' she said. 'I should have stopped her.'

'Don't blame yourself, Dinah,' Ronald said. 'She took us all by surprise.'

Jenny gave a half smile and a shrug, then went out to the page boy. 'Jubal?'

'I hear you say, she gwine be all right.'

'Did you really think it was something harmful?'

'Sure did.'

'But . . . I don't understand. You were bringing a lotion to Mrs Eynsham that you thought would harm her?'

He nodded, his head hanging.

'You didn't mind?'

'I don' care 'bout Mrs Eynsham. She nevah look at me as if I was there. But when Miss Heather – ' He broke off. She could see tears glinting on cheekbones. 'You been real nice to me, Miz Armstrong. I din want to see yoh little girl harmed.'

She bent down, patted him on the back. 'Thank you, Jubal, you meant well. You'd better get back, Mrs Corvill will be wondering what happened to you.'

'You don' tell Miz Corvill what I done?'

'Of course not, Jubal. Off you go.'

He got to his feet, hunched his shoulders as if preparing to bear a burden, and trudged off. Jenny went back into the morning room.

'Lucy gave you that mixture or lotion for your skin, Dinah?' she asked.

'Yeh, to get rid of my freckles.'

'Silly girl,' Archie said, not quite patting her hand.

'What did you do with it – put it on your skin?'

'No, no, I had to take two teaspoons with my morning tea every morning.'

Ronald gave a snort. 'Damn nonsense,' he grunted.

'That was a second lot, the little bottle that came today?'

'Yeh, I told her I was running out. They're tiny little bottles.'

'When did you first start taking it?'

'She gave me the first little bottle . . . let me see . . . it would be about a week ago.'

'And you've taken it every morning since?'

'That's right.'

'And you've had that temperature every day now for four days.'

Archie stood up. 'What are you saying?' he gasped.

'I don't know, Archie. Perhaps I'm being silly.'

About eight o'clock Heather began to run a temperature. Her eyes took on a slightly glazed look. She complained that her throat hurt, that she felt sick.

Ronald himself went to fetch the doctor. Dr Allerdyce took his time over examining her, then came out on to the landing looking perturbed. 'I don't want to raise a false alarm,' he said, 'but it would be a good idea if you kept the other children away from her. I think she's got the first stages of scarlet fever.'

'What?' cried Jenny.

'It may be nothing. But the throat, the temperature – and she has the beginnings of a rash.'

'Surely it's to do with that stuff she swallowed –'

'Now, now, Mrs Armstrong, that's a pure co-incidence. And in any case, it may not be anything much, she may have some form of prickly heat, we've had an unusually warm June. Don't alarm yourself. I'll send you an alkaline mixture for you to bathe the rash and if you just keep her on fluids we'll see how she goes on.'

'Look here, Allerdyce,' Ronald said in a hard tone, 'you're taking this very calmly. But from my point of view my daughter has suddenly gone from being a healthy, lively girl to –'

'It's probably nothing. Don't upset yourself, Mr Armstrong. If Heather can get a good night's sleep she'll probably be much better in the morning.'

That proved to be the case. Jenny, Dinah and Baird took turns sitting up with her through the night and it happened that Jenny was there when, in the early morning light, Heather opened her eyes.

'Mama!' she said, in a perfectly clear voice though full of surprise. 'What are you doing there?'

'Just keeping you company, sweetheart. How do you feel?'

Heather paused as if testing the matter. 'All right,' she said. 'A bit fuzzy in the head, but all right. What time is it?'

'About five.'

'It won't be breakfast for a long time, then.'

Laughing in relief, Jenny went to order tea and thin porridge for her daughter.

The routine of the house was totally upset. Jenny should have gone to the mills by eight to attend to various matters, but Ronald went in her place. She herself, feeling a reaction, went out into the garden after breakfast and stretched out on one of the cane chairs by the roses. She drifted off into a light sleep, to be wakened by a shadow falling over her.

She sat up. Lucy was standing a few feet away with her parasol up to protect her complexion from the sun.

'Good morning, sorry to disturb you,' she said in her gentle voice. 'Thirley told me you were out in the garden so I walked round.'

'Oh . . . Lucy . . .'

'I came to inquire after dear Mrs Eynsham.'

The haze of sleep left Jenny's mind. 'Why should you inquire after Mrs Eynsham?'

Lucy looked surprised. 'But . . . I heard the doctor had been called here yesterday.'

'So he was. But why should you think he was called to Mrs Eynsham?'

The other woman stiffened. The parasol tilted as if she had momentarily lost her grip on it. She turned her head to look up at it, took control of it, and then said casually, 'I think someone said so. Who needed the doctor, then?'

Jenny was watching her narrowly. 'It was Heather,' she said. 'I got in a panic because she was taken suddenly ill.'

'Heather!'

'Yes, but it was all a mistake,' Jenny went on. 'Dr Allerdyce thought it might be the onset of scarlet fever but she's much better this morning.'

'Heather?' Lucy repeated.

426

'Yes, at first I thought she'd taken something that disagreed with her but it was this summer fever – Dr Allerdyce is quite cross with me about it.'

'She's all right?'

'Much better. She was very sick, but after all we were having a birthday party – I daresay she ate too much.'

'Yes, I suppose so . . . I hope . . . I hope she's all right. Give her my love.'

'Yes,' Jenny said, 'I will. Now if you'll excuse me, Lucy, I mustn't lie around here like a lady of leisure. I have work to do.'

Lucy knew she was being told to go. She said a graceful goodbye and walked away round the side of the house to the drive.

Jenny went indoors. To Thirley she said, 'Never let Mrs Corvill into this house again.'

'Mistress?' Thirley gasped, astounded.

'Never give her access to any of the family. Do you understand?'

'Yes, mistress.'

'Now send a boy to ask Mr Armstrong to come home at once.'

'Yes, mistress.'

Ronald came home in a hackney although it was only fifteen minutes' walk from the mills. 'Is Heather worse?' he cried as he rushed in.

'Oh – husband – I'm sorry, I didn't think of that! No, she's all right, she's had more tea and some toast. No, that's not why I sent for you. Come upstairs.'

Sitting on the landing table was the little bottle which Jubal had brought the previous afternoon. It was almost empty. Heather had taken a large gulp and some of the remainder had been spilt when Jubal tried to snatch the bottle from her. But the stopper had been put back and the quarter-inch that remained had been kept safe.

'Ronald, when you used to go to listen to lectures about the properties of aniline dyes at the Royal Institute, you made friends among the scientists, didn't you?'

'Aye, I did.'

'Are there any within reach of us here?'

'Well, there's Walter Davison . . . He's a lecturer at Surgeon's Hall in Edinburgh.'

'Take you this phial, Ronald. Go there and ask him if he or a colleague can tell us what the contents are.'

He took the bottle from her. He held it up to the light. The liquid tilted innocently behind the painted glass. 'Why do you want it analysed?'

'Lucy was here. She expected *Dinah* to be ill.'

He turned, frowned at her, his mind racing. 'Dinah?'

'Jubal said it was harmful. Dinah had been unwell for four days. When Lucy heard we'd called a doctor she thought it was for Dinah.'

'But that's weird, Jenny. Why should Lucy want to harm Dinah?'

'Because Archie is thinking of asking her to marry him.'

Ronald gasped. 'You're joking!'

'I am not.'

'He wants to marry Dinah?'

'Aye, he does.'

'But . . . why should Lucy –'

'Lucy wants him. Ask any of the servants. They'll tell you it's all the gossip in the servants' halls. Yet in the last few months Archie has been showing quite clearly he has no intention of falling into her trap. Instead he's turned to Dinah. So Lucy wants Dinah out of the way.'

Ronald walked along the landing and back. 'Wife, you're saying that Lucy was attempting to commit a murder.'

'That's what I'm saying.'

'On very slight evidence!'

'It's evidence enough for me. Lucy supplied Dinah with some concoction that was supposed to clear away the freckles. Instead of putting it on the skin, as you'd expect, she had to take it internally. For four days she's been ill with very much the same symptoms that Heather has had –'

'But wait – Heather took a big dose. If it's harmful . . . if it's poison . . . Heather should have been very ill indeed.'

'No,' said Jenny, 'because we made her vomit it all up, or most of it. She's had a mild attack of poisoning, with the same effect as Dinah's had.'

'No,' Ronald said, 'it's impossible. No one would do such a thing.'

Jenny's mind had been hunting and searching ever since Lucy's inquiry gave her away. Now something came to her, unbidden.

'Ronald,' she said, 'how did Ned die?'

He stared at her. In the light coming in from the window at the end of the landing, his face took on the look of candle wax.

'No, Jenny . . . You're wrong.'

'My brother died of a fever.'

'Yes, but he was under a doctor's care.'

'He was under *Lucy's* care. Wait,' Jenny muttered, 'I have the letter still – it's in the book room.' She hurried along the landing, went into the book room, opened a wall cabinet, and took out a box in which she kept personal papers. A moment's search put the lawyer's letter into her hands. She unfolded it, searched through it.

'Here it is: ". . . A medical certificate . . . denotes scarlet fever inducing nervous excitement and toxaemia . . ." Wait, there's a bit about Lucy . . . Here it is: "His widow nursed him with great devotion during his illness." Do you remember how we disbelieved that at the time? Lucy never nursed anyone with devotion, and certainly not Ned. She never cared a jot for Ned.'

Ronald had come and put his arm about her shoulder, reading as she did. She felt him shake his head. 'It can't be, Jenny. Even Lucy wouldn't do a thing like that.'

She folded the letter into its envelope, put it back in the box. 'Go to Surgeon's Hall. Get that tincture analysed.'

'I'll catch the noon train.'

While he was away Lady Thornieburn sent to inquire after Heather. The messenger was David Buchanan, whose plump face was full of anxiety. 'She's really all right?' he insisted.

'As far as we can tell.'

'May I see her?'

'I think not, David.'

'I specially want to see her, Mrs Armstrong. The thing is, I've been offered a post in Calcutta.'

Jenny was startled. 'India?'

'I've been offered a place in a shipping agency. I wanted to ask . . . I wanted to ask . . . Heather and I . . .'

Jenny frowned at him. 'I beg your pardon?'

'I wanted to ask her if she would wait for me.'

'In what sense?'

'To be engaged when I could afford it.'

Oh dear. From all she had ever heard her daughter say about David, she thought him a rather dull fellow.

'Heather is much too young to bind herself in any way, David,' she said with great firmness. 'I shouldn't allow it even if she wanted to.'

'Oh, she'd want to –'

'No, she would not. Heather has no notions about being unofficially engaged to you or to anybody else.'

He looked so dashed that she put a hand on his shoulder. 'No, really, David. It's quite out of the question. She's never spoken of you as if she cared for you in that way.'

'You don't know anything about it!' he cried.

'Now, now. I know you think I'm an interfering mother, but I want to prevent any misunderstanding. I'll let Heather write to you. When do you leave for India?'

'The first week in July.'

'Very well. I'll have a talk with her, and then she shall write to you. But I must tell you not to expect anything that would raise your hopes.'

Flushed with anger which he knew he must repress, David rode off. Jenny went to her daughter's room. 'David just came to bring good wishes from Thornieburn, and more or less to ask for your hand in marriage,' she said lightly.

Heather gave a little cry, and went bright red.

'Darling!' exclaimed her mother. 'You don't *care* about him, surely?'

'Oh, of course not! He's such a nuisance!'

She sat down by the bed. 'What is this all about, Heather?'

'He's . . . he's got rather fond of me. It was all a mistake. He probably thinks I'm fond of him, and of course I am, in a way, but . . . I never thought he'd take it so seriously!'

'Have you been trifling with that young man's affections?' Jenny said with mock sternness.

Heather's eyes filled with tears. 'I wish I'd never started it!'

'Started what?'

'Nothing, nothing! It's just that . . . I must have done it wrong . . . I only wanted to . . . Oh, what a stupid mess!'

The last thing Jenny wanted was to upset the child. She patted her head and said, 'There, there. His heart isn't really broken, and if it was it'd mend soon. He's going out to Calcutta where there will be far too much to do to remember how you let him kiss you behind the library door.'

Heather knuckled her tears away. 'It's not funny,' she said, in a trembly voice, but half-giggling.

'No, and you won't enjoy it when you write to him and tell him you don't want to be unofficially engaged. But there you are, if you play these little games, you must expect to pay for them.'

Despite this little flurry of emotion, Heather continued to improve. She was allowed up next day. Her father came home that evening, ran up to her room where she was reading with cushions behind her and her feet on a footstool, and kissed her with an almost ferocious fondness.

'Papa! What a bear hug! Have you just got back?'

'Yes, and you've never been out of my thoughts all the time I was away!'

Heather laughed, thinking it a fatherly foolishness. But he meant it, every word.

'Davison took me to a friend of his in the laboratory,' he told Jenny, when he went to her boudoir to talk in private. 'Collins did a variety of tests. He gave me the results this morning. The liquid is a steeped tincture of datura stramonium.'

'What on earth is that?'

'It's a poisonous plant that grows in warm climates. It's well-known in India as a secret poison used by criminals.'

There was a long silence.

'Jenny?'

At last she managed to get breath enough to speak. 'She could have been killed,' she quavered. 'Our daughter could have been killed!'

'Yes, you were right and I was wrong. The so-called skin tonic is an easily obtainable poison in hot climates.'

'But how would Lucy get hold of it?'

'Didn't Jubal say something about his mother?'

'I don't remember. It's all a hazy mix-up now. Ronald, we have to know the whole truth.'

'But how can we find it out? If Lucy really did something bad to your brother, that was three years ago and a whole ocean away.'

'I'll never rest until I know.'

He nodded, holding her close. For a moment they were utterly together in the face of this terrible knowledge. No thought about his Parliamentary career or her duties at the mills intervened. They were finding comfort in each other after a frightening escape.

Next day Jenny had come to a decision. 'I'm going to London to speak to Mr Baxter,' she said. 'You remember Mr Baxter, Ronald? The agent we asked to help us when that man was pestering Dinah at her house.'

'I remember.'

'If anyone can find out what really happened to Ned, he can.'

'My dear, are you sure you want to do this?'

'I have to know for sure, husband.'

He agreed with her, but he wondered what they would do if they got evidence their sister-in-law had committed murder.

Mr Baxter listened to Jenny's exposition of the case with a concerned expression. 'There seems no doubt there was intent to harm Mrs Eynsham,' he said. 'Why don't you inform the justices?'

'Because Mrs Corvill will say Dinah misunderstood her, that she wasn't supposed to take it by mouth but use it as a lotion. And Dinah's so unsure of herself she'd probably agree she made a mistake.'

'But this substance – stramonium – is it used for cosmetic purposes?'

'I've no idea. Many strange things are, Mr Baxter. I believe actresses use white lead to increase the whiteness of their arms and throat for the stage. I simply don't know anything about this plant. But what I should like to know is how Lucy came to have it, and whether she's used it before.'

'It'll cost a penny, you know.'

'That's understood. I have a cheque here for the initial outlay on your passage and so forth, and a letter to our New York agent for any further funds you may need. Will you take on the inquiry?'

Henry Baxter was no longer young, but he liked Mrs Armstrong and the case piqued his curiosity. So on a sweltering hot day in July he found himself walking across Bowling Green near New York's quays, in search of Leopold Derrington, agent for William Corvill & Son.

The weather being so warm, the immediate suggestion was that they should go to a neighbourhood bar and quench their thirst with rye whiskey. They were soon on first name terms.

'Making inquiries in Richmond?' said Derrington with a grimace. 'Have you any idea, Hank, how difficult that could be? A Limey wanting to find out something about the doings of the Richmond nobs?'

'I'd appreciate any ideas you can put forward, Leo.'

'What you want,' said Derrington, 'is a Pinkerton man.'

CHAPTER TWENTY-TWO

Even with the help of the soft-spoken Southerner supplied by the Pinkerton Agency, Mr Lawford, it wasn't easy to find out much about Mrs Edward Corvill.

The cover story was that Baxter was a friend from England who at Mrs Corvill's suggestion was looking up her old acquaintance in Richmond. Few wished to discuss her. One man's face lit up when she was mentioned: 'Such a charmer,' he said. Another turned away with, 'Don't mention her name to me.'

The women were more willing to talk, almost universally against her. The most talkative was Mrs Corvill's former dressmaker, Madame Laflore.

'I oughtn't to cry her down,' she said over her third bourbon and water, 'for Lordy, I made so much money offa her! Hard to please, but if you told her the Governor's wife was wearing that style, she was wild to have it.'

She was a woman of about sixty with a weakness for bourbon. But she was shrewd.

'Mr Corvill? A softie! He didn't have a notion how to handle her. But I don't know many men that could have . . .'

'She speaks very fondly of her husband,' Henry Baxter prompted.

'Does she now? It's true, they had the look of a real loving couple when you saw them together.'

'But you thought otherwise.'

Madame Laflore took a sip of bourbon and gave him a broad wink. 'You're getting me drunk so I'll be indiscreet, is that it? Well, what the heck, I don't care. If you want to know what I thought, I saw her as a self-centred little hussy. I'd take a bet she broke up Bub Calder's marriage, and there was another feller she was mixed up with just around the time her husband took and died.'

'What happened then?'

'What d'ya mean, what happened then? Ned Corvill got the fever and passed on. Louis Mattiron came to his senses and cleared out.'

'That was the man friend?'

'Yeah, I think poor Mr Corvill found out about him. She told me her husband was insisting they move to New York. I think it was to get her away from Louis. Then, when after all Fate made everything easy for her, Louis had changed his mind.'

'Why was that, do you think?'

'God knows, mister, but I think he made the right decision. She was very strange around then – her temper was as touchy as a cat in a thunderstorm. And then Louis was the kind that didn't want to be tied down. Sure, he liked to romance and make a big thing of it, but marriage. . . No, I don't think he wanted to be married.'

Baxter and Lawford withdrew from her parlour, Baxter leaving a token of his gratitude on the drum table. Lawford said, with a shake of the head, 'She sounds a difficult lady, this Mrs

Corvill. What's your interest in her, Mr Baxter?'

'That's confidential between me and my client.'

'Of course,' Lawford agreed.

Thereafter they seemed to strike barren ground. Two days went by, nothing except the merest small-talk emerged.

On the evening of a hot and humid Monday, having nothing better to do, Baxter went to look at Edward Corvill's grave in the churchyard of St Thomas's. A handsome grey marble headstone had been erected. 'Sacred to the Memory of Edward Corvill of Scotland and of this Parish. "Rich in Good Works". Erected by the grateful citizens of Richmond Virginia.'

A voice spoke at his elbow. Baxter leapt several inches into the air from alarm.

'You the whitey that's askin' about Miz Corvill?'

He recovered his dignity. 'Yes, I am.'

'You know her?'

'I've met her, shall we say.'

'How's my boy doin' among the white folk?'

'Jubal? He's well, I believe.'

'She beat him a lot? I hope she don' beat him.'

'I don't know about that. The lady who sent me here has been a friend to Jubal. Is he your son?'

'Yessir. I'm Selina.'

'Mrs Corvill's maid?'

'Yessir.'

'My employer, Mrs Armstrong, had a warm coat made for Jubal last winter. He was going around in a suit of cotton sateen.'

'Jubal feels the cold. I sure hope it ain't snowy and icy there.'

'Sometimes it is. But Mrs Armstrong does her best to look after him when she can.'

'He learnin' to read and write?'

Baxter floundered. He knew very little about Jubal, but he was almost certain that Mrs Corvill had made no effort towards the boy's education. 'I don't think so,' he confessed.

'She promise!'

The woman's eyes widened with anger and distress. She had a broad, bony face, very black. She was dressed in a loose grey and red cotton dress with her head tied up in a red bandana. She stood with a slight stoop, as if she had worked hard all her life and was now permanently weary.

'Tell me what Mrs Corvill promised.'

'Why you want to know? Why you askin'?'

'Mrs Armstrong hired me to find out about Mrs Corvill. If you were her maid you must know a lot – '

'I ain't sayin' nuthin'!'

'Please, Selina, we think Mrs Corvill has done something bad.'

'Huh! What's that to me!'

'But your boy is in her hands.'

She frowned.

'Why did you give him to Mrs Corvill to take to England?'

She made as if to speak, then shivered and drew back. 'I cain't talk here. *He* might be listenin'.'

'He? Who? Oh . . .' He saw her glance flash to the tombstone and away. 'Come to my hotel, then,' he said. 'Come, and talk to me. I'll tell you all I can remember about Jubal.'

439

She hesitated. 'I cain't come till after's dark.'

'All right. Let's say ten o'clock. My hotel is the – '

'I know where you's at, white man. I knowed all about you from the minute you walked into Richmond.'

He went back to the hotel in triumph. When Lawford heard the news he smiled. 'You'll be lucky if you get any sense out of her. Black people are very chary of saying anything about white people.'

But when a tap came on Baxter's door soon after ten, he felt in his heart that he was going to learn something important.

She stole into the room, sat gingerly on the edge of the chair he offered. 'You got to promise to look out for my boy when you get back. I sent him with her to get a' education and a good start in life where they ain't so down on us. You promise?'

'I do, Selina.'

She nodded once or twice. 'Well, I worked for Miz Corvill almost from the first when she arrive here in Richmond. She promise me she get her husband to pay for my Jubal to get a education, but the time's a-goin' on and nuthin' come of it.'

'Go on.'

'See, my mammy come from Africa. She knew 'bout herbs and medicines from the old country. She teach me. Miz Corvill knew I got the Wisdom from her. 'Long about midsummer, three years ago, she asked me to make her a mix o' Jimson weed. You know Jimson weed?'

He shook his head.

'Hit a tall plant, grow round here, plenty of

440

it. Burn the leaves, hit good for the asthma. Drink the brew, hit good for the cough. But too strong, hit bring on closed-up throat and sickness and loose-the-mind. Six or seven days, a man dies.'

'Selina,' muttered Baxter, appalled.

'My mammy used it, if that what you wonderin'. She tole me, they had a bad overseer, liked to hit the slaves, she put Jimson weed brew in his coffee every mornin' for eight days, two weeks later they laid him in the ground.'

'Why did Mrs Corvill want you to make her the mixture?'

'She don' say, but Mr Corvill fall sick. Ev'body say he die of the scarlet fever, and I'm just a stupid darkie that don' know nuthin' about nuthin'. So I don' say nuthin'. But Mrs Corvill she know I know, so she tole me to keep my mouth shut, and I say I ain't goin' to say a word to anybody so long's she does what she promise – give my Jubal a' education.'

'But you let her take Jubal away.'

'Yeah, she had to go to Scotland to get her legals, she tole me – the money her husband leaves, hit in Scotland. She was gwine come back, cos they was this big lover she wanted, but he took off and kept goin', so she decided to go to Scotland and start all over. So I tole her, you take Jubal, or I ain't gwine be so quiet any more.'

Baxter had been listening intently to catch the meaning in the unfamiliar accent. Now he asked, 'Was there any of this poison left after Mr Corvill's death?'

'Oh, sure – plenty. Li'l packet just like tea, you take a good pinch and pour boilin' water on, boil it a while till the liquid go strong.'

'Selina, will you write this down so I can take it to Mrs Armstrong?'

'Man, I cain't write.'

'Well, then, will you repeat the story in front of a shorthand writer and sign it?'

'You think I'm crazy? They'd arrest me and dangle me at a rope's end.'

'But I wouldn't tell anyone in Richmond.'

'Where you gwine get this writer, then? From the Man in the Moon? No, mister, I don' sign nuthin'.'

He attempted a new tack. 'Mr Corvill wasn't unkind to you, was he? He tried to help your people?'

'Reckon so.'

'Didn't you feel sorry to see him harmed?'

'You think I care what white folks do to each other? All I care about is stayin' alive and seein' my Jubal grow up well.'

Baxter wrote it all down and sent it express mail to New York, where Leo Derrington put it aboard the first ship to Liverpool.

'You understand,' Baxter wrote, 'that this testimony is not admissible in any court of law. Selina herself will not testify and from me it is mere hearsay. Besides, the case would have to be brought in Virginia.'

Jenny Armstrong read it, then took it with her to London. Ronald was already there for the beginning of the Parliamentary session of 1879. Heather was also there, staying at Eaton Square but spending most of her time with Lady Thornieburn being 'groomed' for the London season.

When Ronald had read the letter, he laid it by. ' "Not admissible",' he sighed. 'And of course Lucy explained away the accident with the bottle.'

Lucy's story had been perfectly logical. Of course the skin-clearing tonic contained some disagreeable substances. Of course they had had a bad effect on Heather. Heather was really still a child – an adult would only have felt nausea. This explanation, given to Dinah, had brought forth Dinah's agreement.

'It's right,' she said to Jenny. 'That's all I felt – just nausea. It wasn't really intended to do any harm, Jenny.'

All the same, Dinah had taken the advice of Archie and Ronald, and given up the attempt to get rid of her freckles.

The Armstrongs discussed Baxter's report endlessly. When Baxter himself got back and fleshed out the details, they could see it was hopeless.

'The woman Selina is frightened – rightly so, she was an accessory to murder. Moreover, she don't care a jot about justice. All she cares about is her son. Can't say I blame her, Mrs Armstrong.'

'What can we do, then?' Ronald asked, since his wife remained silent.

'Nothing, I'm afraid.'

'Dammit, the last time that little gypster hurt Heather she got away with it! I'm not letting her slip out from under it this time.'

'There's no case you can bring against her in this country. I'm sorry, sir, but there it is.'

In the middle of the night Ronald Armstrong awoke. He had been roused by muffled sounds. As his mind cleared he realised it was the sound of his wife sobbing.

'Jenny?'

443

She tried to burrow further into her pillows.

He sat up, leaned over her. 'What's the matter, my dove?'

'Nothing. I'm sorry I woke you.' Her voice was thick and slurred with grief.

'Tell me what's wrong, Jenny.'

She turned towards him, leaned against his shoulder. 'My poor brother,' she wept. 'Poor, poor Ned! She never loved him. I disliked her for that but I never thought . . . I never thought she felt so little for him that she could just *extinguish* him like a guttering candle.'

'She's a bad woman.'

'And he loved her, you see. It's so unfair – so cruelly unfair! If he'd had the right wife he might have made something of himself, really been someone of value. Because he had a good heart, you know. He genuinely wanted to do something worthwhile. If he'd had someone to help him, who knows . . . ? But he fell in love with Lucy. Oh God, it's so unjust!'

'My little wife, my jewel . . . Don't cry. So far as we know, he never stopped loving her. Even when she ran off to another man, Jenny, he convinced himself she wasn't to blame. So in his way, he was happy – '

'Happy in his illusions! What an epitaph! It seems so hard. I was lying here remembering him – he was such a *nice* boy, Ronald. And suddenly I felt how wrong I'd been to cut myself off from him for so many years. I left him in her clutches.'

'But you couldn't foresee – no one could have foreseen what she'd do. Even I – and God knows I hate and despise the woman – I never thought she'd do such a thing. You mustn't blame yourself, my joy.'

'I can't help it. . . !' She abandoned herself to her tears, helpless in his arms, grieving at last for a man whose life had been wasted.

Ronald held her and soothed her, calling her by all the pet names that are the wealth of a happy marriage. By and by she quietened, letting him comfort her with kisses and caresses. Until at last in the early hours of the morning they made love, in passion that was like the resurgence of their first coming together. In the past few years there had been some barriers between them – worldly matters had dragged them away from each other, they hadn't been quite in harmony.

But that was forgotten in those moments in the quiet dawn. They were lovers again – young again, richly fulfilled.

Not far away on the far side of Green Park, Lucy Corvill was also awake, but alone. She slept badly these days.

She had had a very bad scare over the skin-clearing mixture for Dinah. That one encounter with Jenny in the garden at Gatesmuir had told her that she was under suspicion. She'd gone scuttling home to pack up and leave for London. There she had remained in fear and trembling until Dinah returned to Cheyne Terrace in Chelsea – a fact known at once to Lucy because she had tipped the odd-jobs boy generously to let her know.

Dinah, artless and open, answered all Lucy's questions without suspicion. Yes, Heather had made a complete recovery. Yes, Jenny had seemed to think there was something seriously wrong with the herbal mixture. Yes, she understood what Lucy said about the strength of the brew being too much for a child. No, she herself felt no illwill towards Lucy; she was too happy in her new relationship with Archie.

Lucy Corvill understood that she had to accept the fact – Archie Brunton was going to marry Dinah. There was no way she could now prevent it without bringing down catastrophe upon herself.

But she had something new to hope for. Heather wrote to her saying she was coming to London with Lady Thornieburn to prepare for presentation at Court. Lady Thornieburn had the entrée. If she could make friends with her, Lady Thornieburn might agree to present Lucy.

It was possible, though not usual, for a married lady to be presented. If she could achieve that, new prospects would open up for her. And it was important to have something to hope for, because her life seemed to be going nowhere.

She had come back to her homeland with all kinds of ambitions. None of them had been fulfilled. The opposite, in fact. She was losing ground – growing older, facing loneliness, failing to make the important and rewarding friendships she'd expected.

Sometimes she had the feeling she was in a train that was not going to the destination she intended. A sensation of powerlessness, of being at a loss, would come over her. Where was she headed? Had she made a mistake somewhere? Who was in control?

But everything could still be different. She still hadn't reached that awful watershed, the age of forty. She still had her looks, although in a good light some mornings she could see the crow's feet in her fine skin. But no one else could see them because no one else cared to peer so intently at her. If there were occasional silver threads in her hair, they didn't show in the still glowing gold of her curls.

Still young-looking, still attractive, still with a fortune at her disposal. And if she were presented at court, that would be the seal of respectability.

She began to cultivate the Countess, who knew her a little but liked her much less. However, Lady Thornieburn was too polite to let it show, particularly as the creature was aunt to dear young Heather. Lucy therefore began to dwell in a dream-world, where she would be ushered into the Throne Room in white satin and ostrich feathers, make her curtsey, and retire with all eyes fastened upon her in admiration.

She wouldn't let herself remember that the Princess of Wales would probably be taking the presentations this year since Her Majesty preferred to stay at Windsor. It was well-known that the Princess of Wales had very strict views on propriety. She caused inquiries to be made about debutantes by the Lord Chamberlain. When it became known to him that Mrs Corvill had once run away from her husband and been dragged back in hysterical disarray after her lover abandoned her, she would be struck off the list.

Not that Lady Thornieburn had the least intention of putting her name forward in the first place.

Lucy Corvill clung to her ambitions, determined not to allow difficulties to dishearten her. In the long hours of the night when she couldn't sleep, she looked forward to a future when everything would be different, when the world would accord her the respect and affection that were her due.

Fretful and unrefreshed, she rang for her maid to bring her early morning tea. As usual, there was a long delay – they seemed to take positive pleasure in making her wait, she thought angrily. Why couldn't she find decent servants? She paid enough, perhaps more than some of her acquaintance, yet they came and went, seeming always pert or sullen. Only Jubal had stayed with her through the years since she came home, but of course he had nowhere else to go. And she was beginning to feel bored with Jubal and his black face and his reproachful presence.

She dragged herself out of bed, throwing a soft woollen dressing-gown about her shoulders. She went to the window to see what the weather was like, so that she could spend the next half-hour planning what to wear for the morning's outing.

Her window looked out over a small paved garden to an alley along one side of her little house. As she looked out, a man moved in the drizzle of the March morning. She gave a gasp of alarm and drew back. She had seen him before, in almost the same spot. He was watching her house!

Alarmed, she grabbed the bell-pull. But there was still a delay in answering. At length Daisy came in with her tea-tray.

'There's a man loitering in the alley! Send Arthur out to tell him to clear off!'

'Really, ma'am?' said Daisy, going to the window to look out. She turned with a shrug. 'Nobody there.'

'I tell you I saw someone – '

'You sure? It's misty and drizzly, mebbe you saw a stray dog – '

'Don't be impertinent! I know what I saw! Send Arthur out!'

But the report came back as she was dressing. Arthur had seen no one.

'Prob'ly someone just using the alley as a shortcut, mum,' the footman said.

'I saw him there two days ago, I tell you.'

'Well, prob'ly he uses the shortcut reg'lar, mum.'

Of course. She hadn't thought of that. She mustn't start getting nervy and silly just because things weren't going well in her life at present.

'You may go,' she said to Arthur, who went, muttering under his breath that if she was going to send him rushing about in the mornings she wasn't going to get her shoes cleaned, now was she?

She felt a need to cheer herself up after that little scare. She ordered a hackney from the livery stables, telling Arthur to make sure they sent a smart carriage with a civil driver, as she wished to hire it for the entire day.

When Jubal presented himself as usual to clamber aboard with the driver, she waved him away. 'Not today.' So tiresome – she was bored with him.

She had an engagement to lunch with a friend, after which they went to Marlborough Street Police Court to hear the case against Madame Rachel, a lady trading on the name of the famous actress, charged with obtaining jewellery by fraud from poor dear Mrs Pearce.

This was so thrilling that afterwards she and

the friend comforted themselves with tea and cakes at The Belgian Patisserie in the Strand. Her companion then left her, having an evening engagement.

Unwilling to go home, Lucy had herself driven to the shops of Holborn. She tried on gloves, bought a fan, looked through a copy of *Joshua Haggard's Daughter* by Miss Braddon but decided it looked too gloomy. To fill in the time before she must go home to a solitary dinner, she sat in the dress materials department of Meeking and Company in Hatton Garden, and had lengths of cloth brought to her for inspection.

'Is madam looking for something in particular?'

No, if the truth be told. Only something to while away the early part of a dismal evening. 'Materials for a court dress,' she said, imagining the dressmaker exclaiming in delight at her elegance as she tried on the half-finished gown.

White or ivory, of course. She would wear her diamonds to go with it, and the head-dress should be of the best French paste, with the feathers attached in front. The Countess of Thornieburn would be at her elbow so that she could take a last minute decision on whether to carry a fan or a nosegay.

'. . . Milanese silk,' the salesman was saying, 'very fine so that it would need to be mounted on muslin.'

'No. It's insipid.'

'Then perhaps madam would prefer this?'

Soft French velvet, Chinese shantung, Indian silk muslin, georgette, Japanese zephyr, guipure lace, *peau d'ange*, taffeta, brocade . . .

At last he unrolled a length of silk damask, snowy white with a pattern of ferns, crystal clear and smooth. Not for her – too cool, too tame. But for Heather it would be ideal.

Lady Thornieburn had mentioned a few days ago that so far they had seen nothing to inspire Heather's court dress. Here it was, the perfect cloth – made up with plain ribbon ruching and worn with white carnations wired in fern – yes, perfection.

'I want two yards as a sample,' she said. 'Put the rest of the bolt away; the Countess of Thornieburn will probably be sending for it in a day or two.'

'Yes, madam,' said the salesman, triumphant after more than an hour of what he'd thought of as wasted time.

It was eight o'clock. She would take the sample now to Eaton Square, show it to Heather and her mother. Heather would adore it, Lucy knew. And then of course Jenny would more or less have to invite her to stay to dinner en famille unless she'd happened on an evening when they had a party.

She got into the hired carriage. 'Eaton Square,' she said.

'Yes, mum,' said the bored driver. What a day – in and out of the shopping streets, long waits outside shops, and now back West again to Eaton Square when everybody was coming the opposite way for the theatres and music halls . . .

Jenny and Ronald had already had dinner. Heather had gone up to her room to read and rest after a long day practising court deportment.

It had not occurred to Jenny to tell her servants at Eaton Square that Mrs Corvill was not to be admitted. She gasped when Graves came into the drawing room, announced 'Mrs Corvill,' and showed her in.

'My dear Jenny,' Lucy began almost with gaiety, 'you'll think me mad to come dropping in like a skylark but I happened on this material in Meekings and I knew at once it was *just* what Heather's been looking for to wear at her presentation, so I came *at once* – '

'What the hell are you doing here?' Ronald said, leaping to his feet.

Lucy stopped. Her hands, holding out the package wrapped in tissue paper, were drawn back convulsively.

'Get out of here!' he snarled. 'Out!'

'Ronald – you – '

'Out!' he said, advancing on her.

She shrank away. No one had ever spoken to her in that tone of voice before. Her frightened glance turned to her sister-in-law. 'Jenny! What's the matter with him?'

Jenny too had risen. She put a hand on her husband's sleeve. 'Don't, Ronald.'

'She's not staying a moment more in my house!'

'I agree. But we'll just ring for Graves to show her out – '

'We won't give him the trouble. I'll throw her out myself – '

'How can you speak to me like this?' Lucy quavered. 'You must be mad!'

'You're the one that's mad! Do you imagine we want you here? After what you've done?'

'What have I done?' Lucy cried, genuinely bewildered. In her dream world, she had done nothing wrong. 'What do you mean?'

452

'You nearly killed Heather – '

'I? I harmed Heather? You're insane! I *love* Heather!'

'Oh, you do? Perhaps that's true. In your own strange way you're fond of Heather. But you're not to see her or speak to her or write to her, ever again. And don't ever come to this house, or the door will be slammed in your face. Don't come here, don't come to Gates-muir – do you understand?'

'No, I *don't* understand. Heather loves me. She'll tell you – all I ever want is what's best for her.'

'True perhaps. The poison was meant for Dinah, wasn't it?'

'Dinah?' Lucy echoed. 'Dinah?' She shook her head. 'Dinah and I are the best of friends. She'll tell you so herself – '

'Only because she's got no idea what you were up to last June – '

'You're talking nonsense! Last June? I was in Galashiels last June, in my own house – '

'And you sent Jubal with a little bottle of poison – '

'That's nonsense! I explained all that. Ask Dinah, she knows it wasn't meant to harm anyone.'

'No? It wasn't meant to harm Ned either? But he died of it!'

Lucy felt a thrill of terror go through her. The packet of cloth slid through her fingers to fall on the floor at her feet. She put a trembling hand up to her mouth.

'Ned?' she whispered.

'She's going to faint,' Jenny said. She set a chair behind their visitor. Lucy sank on to it. 'Are you all right?'

'Who the hell cares if she's all right?' Ronald shouted. 'Damn it, Jenny, don't be kind to her! Let's just throw her out and be done with it!'

'Wait – calm down – she's coming round.'

Ronald stooped to look into Lucy's white face. 'Never thought you'd ever have that dragged up, did you?' he said, his voice grim and hard. 'Thought it was all safely behind you. But we found out all about it. Jimson weed. Ever heard of it?'

Lucy made a fluttering gesture. 'Don't . . .'

'You dry the plant and make a sort of brew of it. Then you feed it to the victim – a big dose polishes him off in a few hours, one or two wee doses give him symptoms like a fever and then it takes a week or two for him to die. And of course you nursed him devotedly, didn't you? Poor Ned, poor hapless gomeril.'

'I don't know what you mean!'

'Jimson weed. It grows wild in Virginia. Your maid knew how to use it. Her mother had taught her in the old days before the plantation was broken up in the War. A sure poison, not easy to detect. Just what you needed.'

'I didn't need . . . You don't know what you're saying . . . I didn't . . .'

'You poisoned your husband, Lucy.'

'I didn't! The doctor will tell you – it was on the death certificate – '

'Scarlet fever. Yes, we were sent a copy. But the symptoms of poisoning by Jimson weed are just like the onset of scarlet fever.'

'No. It's not true. How dare you? How dare you say things like that? I loved Ned. Anyone will tell you – '

'Your maid Selina told us. We know all about it.'

'Selina?'

Jenny took it up. 'Your maid. Jubal's mother. Remember her, Lucy? She confessed it all. We know all about it.'

'All about what?' Lucy cried wildly. 'What did she say? If she says I harmed my darling husband, she's lying. She's lying!'

'No, Lucy. She has no reason to lie.'

She shook her head from side to side. 'You don't know her! You don't know what they're like! They make up any story they want to, they can't be trusted, and in any case' – a sudden thought – 'why would she give her little boy to me to look after if she thought I'd done something wicked?'

'She *made* you take Jubal. That's one of the things that's so convincing. You had to bring him with you. But you don't even like him – anyone can see that just by watching the way you treat him. So you must have had a reason to bring him from Richmond, and that's the reason, Lucy, that's the reason – it was her payment for helping you to kill your husband.'

Lucy had watched and listened while Jenny made this accusation. Her mind began to function. She said, more calmly, 'It's just a made-up story. There's not a word of truth in it, a wild story from an ex-slavewoman. I can't imagine how you heard such nonsense. Someone from Richmond – some silly spiteful person you've come across, talking utter nonsense!'

'No, Lucy.'

'I tell you it is! Utter nonsense. Whoever told you this tale is out of his mind.' She broke off. 'It was Mrs Calder, wasn't it? She never liked me! As if I'd ever look twice at that stupid husband of hers! Oh, if it's something Susanna Calder told you – '

'We obtained this information from a very reliable man,' Ronald said, weighting his words. 'We sent him out to Richmond on purpose to find out – '

'Sent him? But . . . But why? I don't understand!'

'I believe you really don't.' He shook his head at her self-delusion. 'You didn't think we'd be worried after you nearly killed Heather – '

'I never harmed Heather! Stop saying that!'

'Only because her mother took immediate action – otherwise our little girl would have died, Lucy. And you would have been a murderess twice over.'

The dreadful word made her shudder. She hunched her shoulders to ward it off. 'I'm not! It's untrue, all of it! I don't care what you've been told! This man you sent – he must be mad to believe such a lie. Who is he? He must be a fool!'

'You want to know who he is? You want to meet your accuser?'

'Yes,' she said, rising to her feet. She knew she could triumph – she knew she could face any man and make him admit she was wrongly accused. Believe a black woman, a former slave, against the word of Lucy Corvill? He would see in a minute how absurd it was.

'Very well,' said Ronald. 'Come with me and I'll introduce you to Henry Baxter, who spoke personally to your maid Selina.'

Her hired carriage still stood outside. She let Ronald conduct her out to it. They both got in.

456

'Meach Street, Marylebone,' Ronald said to the driver.

The route led through one of the less salubrious quarters of London. By now it was about nine o'clock on a dark March evening. The two passengers in the carriage sat in silence, watching the shuttered shop fronts and the houses where light gleamed from between closed curtains.

In a quiet lane the carriage drew to a standstill. Ronald let down the window. 'Why have you stopped – ?'

The door was pulled open under his hand. He heard the door on the other side jar open. He turned in surprise.

He saw a dark-clad figure leaning in. Lucy was dragged to one side.

'Hi!' Ronald shouted. They were being robbed! He struck out at the hands hauling at Lucy. From behind came a swishing sound.

A thousand stars exploded in his head. Darkness came down.

Darkness and oblivion.

CHAPTER TWENTY-THREE

The universe was a great bell which tolled in unison with the throbbing pain in his head. Beyond the pain a voice spoke indistinctly.

He opened his eyes. The light hurt him. He caught a glimpse of a triangle of white – a face. He let his lids slide shut.

'Ronald! Ronald, can you hear me?'

With tremendous effort – a labour of Hercules – he managed to get his eyes open again.

'Ronald. Do you know me?'

How absurd. 'Dinna be sae daft,' he said, 'you're my wife Jenny.'

'Thank God!'

It seemed aeons later that he opened his eyes again. A man was looking down at him – frock coat, satin cravat. 'How many fingers am I holding up?'

Idiot. 'Two.'

'What is the capital of France?'

'Paris. Is this a game of forfeits?'

'You'll do,' said the man.

'Oh, God,' groaned Ronald, 'My head . . .'

'Sir, can you answer some questions?'

Dark blue uniform with upstanding collar, bluff face, dundreary whiskers.

'You're a policeman.'

'Right you are. What can you remember of the occurrence, Mr Armstrong?'

'Uh . . . We were in a hansom . . . no, a fourwheeler. We stopped in an alley. I . . . let down the window to ask why . . . Oh, my head hurts . . .'

'Did you see anyone?'

'It was dark. The only lights were the carriage lights.'

'How many men do you think there were, sir?'

'I suppose . . . one opened the door on my side, one hit me . . . from behind . . .' Something was nagging at his consciousness. He tried to sit up. 'Where is Mrs Corvill? Is she all right?'

The police sergeant pressed him back. 'Did they speak?'

'No.'

'What did you have on you, sir? In the way of valuables?'

He frowned, trying to recall. The pounding in his head grew worse. 'A pocketbook with two banknotes and some letters. A sovereign case with three sovereigns. Some loose cash – say five or six shillings.'

'Watch?'

'Yes, a gold half-hunter and chain. A gold cravat pin shaped like a weaver's shuttle.' He brought his hand up to look for his wedding ring. Still there. But it was more important to find out . . . 'Is Mrs Corvill all right?'

'Could we just stick to –'

'Damn you, answer my question! Jenny? Is Lucy all right?'

There was a whispered colloquy. Then Jenny

said in a low voice, 'Perhaps she tried to run away or cry out. They hit her too hard.'

'Oh, God . . . You mean, she's dead?' He closed his eyes and lay back.

A time went by. At last the police sergeant said, 'Is there anything else you can tell us? Did you hear their voices, did they speak to one another?'

'No.' He thought a moment. 'What about the driver? Can't he tell you anything?'

There was a hesitation. 'That's the curious thing, sir. We found the driver half-conscious, bound and gagged in the mews behind your house. It was a confederate who drove the carriage to that alley where you were waylaid, presumably.'

Ronald said no more. He felt terribly ill and confused. His head throbbed unbearably. Jenny sat beside him holding his hand. By and by the police surgeon brought him a draught. The pain in his head subsided a little.

'Can I go home?' he asked.

'When you feel like it.'

'What time is it?'

'Just after two in the morning. You were found about midnight – a porter going off duty from one of the hotels found you.'

About an hour later, still groggy but able to manage on his own two feet, he was helped out to a carriage and taken home from Marylebone Police Station. He went to bed, fell instantly asleep, and woke about eight in the morning feeling as if he might live.

Jenny sat with him as he drank tea and nibbled dry toast. 'How do you feel?' she asked.

'Gey dreich . . .'

'No wonder.'

'Was Lucy robbed?'

'Yes, her reticule is gone, her rings, a pearl hat-pin. I didn't pay attention to what she was wearing but I think I remember an amethyst brooch. The police are going to ask her maid this morning.'

About midday, feeling more himself, Ronald got up. A reporter came, asked a few questions about a robbery only noteworthy in that a Member of Parliament had been the victim, and left.

Heather came home at mid-afternoon from her session with the dancing instructor at Lady Thornieburn's. She had to be told what had happened – if they left it any longer, someone else might tell her.

'Heather, we have something very sad to say to you.'

'Yes?' Heather said, looking at them with anxious eyes.

'Your Aunt Lucy is dead.'

'*What?*'

'She was killed last night – '

'Killed?'

'In a robbery. Her carriage was waylaid – '

'No!'

'My darling,' Jenny said, putting her arms round her daughter, 'it's terrible, I know. Try to be brave about it.'

'Killed? How was she killed?'

Ronald had to leave it to Jenny to explain. He himself had no idea how it had happened. 'Her skull was fractured. The police surgeon says it was done with something called a blackjack.'

Heather broke into a storm of weeping.

'My precious, my treasure, don't,' soothed

461

Jenny. 'Don't cry. She knew nothing, she didn't suffer –'

'Oh, poor Aunt Lucy! Poor, poor Aunt Lucy! Have they caught the man who did it?'

'No, dear, there seems to be no clue –'

'It doesn't matter – nothing will bring her back.'

'Ssh, ssh, my pet,' Jenny murmured. 'She wouldn't want you to weep –'

'What do you know about it?' Heather flashed at her, wrenching herself from her mother's embrace and turning on her with anger in her tear-drenched eyes. 'You never liked her, you never understood her – you don't care what happened to her! I hate you!'

She flew to the door, dragged it open, and raced upstairs to her room.

Ronald made as if to follow.

'Where are you going?' Jenny said, catching his sleeve.

'I'm going up to tell her she can't speak like that to you!'

'Leave her alone, husband. Let her have her cry.'

'But she ought to be told –'

'No, Ronald, no. Let it be.'

Late that afternoon they went to Lucy's house in Mayfair. Her personal maid had already absconded, taking with her as much in the way of perks as she could pack easily – a few gowns, an ivory fan, some hair combs, some underwear. The cook, the parlour maid and the footman received their wages and a sum in lieu of notice.

There remained Jubal. 'What are we going to do about him?' Jenny said to her husband.

462

'Damned if I know. We'd best take him home to Eaton Square with us.'

They locked up the house and took the unresisting Jubal with them. He was handed over to the care of Graves, who looked puzzled at the trust but accepted it.

Henry Baxter had been summoned to the house to see if he could explain the how and the why of the robbery. 'It's unusual for hold-up men to knock out the coachman and put their own man on the box. In fact, I've never heard of it before,' he said. 'There's no need – they just lie in wait in some good spot – Hounslow Heath, for instance, or the edge of the Rookery. And then they stop the coach and drag the driver and passengers out.'

'But they hit the man on the head and tied him up while he was waiting outside our house,' Jenny said.

'Odd. It may be some new dodge.'

Heather came in, looking pale and subdued. Her grief over her aunt's death had subsided but she was clearly very shaken.

'Have the police found the men?' she asked.

'No, dear.'

'Will they find them?'

'It ain't likely, miss,' Baxter said.

'The carriage was waiting outside our house. Why did they pick on it?' Ronald mused.

'No idea. It was just an ordinary hired carriage, wasn't it?'

'Yes. It didn't even have the black page-boy on the box – that might have attracted them, made them think it was someone rich who was using the carriage.'

'What are we going to do about Jubal?' Jenny wondered.

'We could have him here,' Heather suggested.

'My dear child, I have no use for a black page!'

'Well, perhaps we could get him a post with someone else. It's quite a fashionable thing.'

'Do you think we have the right to dispose of Jubal like this?' Ronald put in, his voice rising in anger. 'What about what *Jubal* wants to do?'

There was a shamed silence. 'Let's ask him,' said Jenny. She rang for Graves and asked him to send Jubal in.

The boy came in looking scared and subdued.

'Jubal,' said Ronald, 'you know Mrs Corvill is dead.'

'Yessir, I heard you sayin' that to the others.'

'What would you like to do now?'

'Me?'

'Yes. Would you like us to find you a post with some other family?'

Jubal looked down at his shoes and said nothing.

'How old are you, Jubal?' Ronald asked.

He shrugged. ''Bout twelve, I reckon.'

'Don't you know?'

'Nossir.'

'Can you read and write?'

'Nossir.'

'Not at all?'

'I kin read "Stables" and "Hotel" – things like that.'

'Jubal,' said Jenny suddenly, 'have you any money?'

'No, mam.'

'Wages? You got wages?'

'No, mam.'

464

'Mrs Corvill didn't pay you any wages?'

'No, mam.'

'Did you ask for any?'

Jubal looked at her and then looked down. It was clear the idea of asking for wages was to him ludicrous.

'Well, you have wages owing to you,' Ronald stated. 'If you've never had any, they must be back-dated to the day you first took service with Mrs Corvill.'

The boy said nothing.

'Jubal,' Ronald said, 'why did you stay with Mrs Corvill?'

'Where I gwine to go, Mistah Armstrong? I don't know nobody heah.'

'That's true,' Ronald said, 'that's only too damned true.'

'Ronald,' Jenny reproved, 'mind your language!'

'Language! My God, the boy's been kept like a slave! And slavery has been abolished, as I'm sure you must have heard!'

There was a silence. Mr Baxter cleared his throat. 'Seems to me,' he said, 'if the boy's a free agent, he ought to be asked where he'd like to go.'

'Oh yes!' cried Heather. 'Jubal, what would you like to do? Where would you like to go?'

Jubal fixed his great dark eyes upon her. 'Oh, Miss Heathah,' he breathed, 'I shore would enjoy to see my mammy again.'

'Go home, you mean? To Richmond?'

He drew in a careful breath. 'It a long ways to go,' he said. 'There's an ocean, and a piece on a railway. But if I got wages comin', I kin pay. I shore would enjoy to go home to Richmond.'

465

It was agreed. Jubal would go back to his mother. Baxter undertook to find a minister of religion or some other reliable person to accompany the boy and deliver him to his mother. As to using his wages to pay for his passage, that was ruled out. He must go home with what he had earned during his painful years of exile.

The family went to bed very late that night. Jenny noticed that Heather was thoughtful and silent. Perhaps she had learned something about her adored aunt in the conversation about Jubal's future.

Lucy's funeral was arranged with the expected pomp and ceremony. Almost no one attended except the Armstrongs, and of that family only Heather really grieved.

The question now was, should Heather go on with the plans for her presentation? Lady Thornieburn urged it. 'I know some debutantes withdraw on the death of a member of the family, but I think since Mrs Corvill spent almost all of Heather's life abroad, and Heather only got to know her recently, it would be carrying things too far to expect her to mourn as if for a close relative. I've spoken to the Chamberlain – he says there is no objection if Heather goes on with her presentation.'

So a month went by, six weeks. Jenny had to go home to Galashiels but returned to London in May. Heather's presentation gown was being made, most of the wardrobe for her season had been finished. Now she needed matching gloves and stockings, she needed fans and combs and trinkets.

After an afternoon's busy shopping, Jenny took her daughter to have tea at Bainbridges in the Strand. Heather, although only a few weeks from her seventeenth birthday, took a childish delight in ordering strawberry ice. Jenny contented herself with tea and scones.

She was pouring her second cup when her ear caught a voice she recognised. She looked up. Across the tea-room, Maud Massiter was talking with friends.

Their eyes met. Mrs Massiter gave a triumphant smile, a slight toss of her head. Puzzled, Jenny watched her. But the other woman had gone back to her friends, her feathered bonnet nodding as she talked emphatically.

'What are you looking at, Mama?' Heather asked, half-turning.

'Nothing, dear. Just an acquaintance I haven't seen for a long time.'

Maud Massiter, wife of the man who had run away with Lucy all those years ago. Maud Massiter, who had hired a man to haunt Dinah's house in hopes of learning something harmful to the family of Lucy Corvill. Maud Massiter, who had had a frightening scene with Lucy outside the Haymarket shop.

Jenny made herself concentrate on what her daughter was saying about kid gloves. She was therefore surprised when she felt a presence at her elbow. Mrs Massiter was standing by their table, her back to Heather, her formidable attention focused on Jenny.

'I must offer my condolences on the death of your sister-in-law,' she said in a hard tone. 'Very sad.'

'Thank you,' Jenny said, taken aback.

The other woman bent a fierce glance on her. Her face was suffused with a dark flush, a flush of triumph. 'The streets of London are so

467

dangerous, are they not?' she remarked. 'Even *innocent* people come to grief.'

'Yes,' said Jenny, feeling a little thrill of alarm.

'And people who are not so innocent get their just deserts, perhaps.'

'Mrs Massiter!'

'Good afternoon, Mrs Armstrong.'

With a stiff bow, she made her portly way out of the restaurant.

Jenny understood what she had been told. Maud Massiter had had a hand in the death of Lucy. She got to her feet. Heather looked at her in astonishment.

'Stay here, daughter!' she ordered, and hurried out.

Mrs Massiter was waiting on the kerb for her carriage. Her friends had made their way along to their own conveyances. She was alone.

'One moment, Mrs Massiter!' Jenny exclaimed, catching her by the back of her cape.

The other woman turned to her, stout and formidable. 'My dear woman,' she said, 'please don't pull at my clothes!'

'Mrs Massiter – I must speak to you!'

'I have nothing to say to you.'

'Wait! This is important! Lucy is dead – '

'So I was told,' said Maud Massiter with a fierce grin of satisfaction.

'Please! I need to know! I have a family to think of. Are any others likely to have . . . accidents?'

The carriage trundled up. The coachman leapt down and opened the door. Mrs Massiter got in, waited for the door to be closed on her. Then she leaned forward.

Her face was suddenly altered – suffused with dark colour, sombre, full of grief.

'He died in Athens,' she said in a stifled voice. 'A gentleman has to pay his gambling debts but, you see, the money I sent arrived too late. So he blew his brains out, my poor, poor Harvil.'

'He is dead?' Jenny said, startled. She recollected herself. 'I'm so sorry, Mrs Massiter –'

'No, you're not sorry! You blame him for what happened to your brat. It wasn't his fault! It was that witch, it was her fault. *She* took him away from me, *she* led him astray, *she* parted us, parted us for ever. My beloved, my darling husband . . . He died. And she had to pay for it. She had to pay – you understand that?'

Jenny stood on the kerb, gazing up at the woman looking down from the oldfashioned carriage. She tried to read what was in her face. She was frightened, bewildered.

'Mrs Massiter . . . I have a family to protect . . . Are there likely to be any more . . . unexpected tragedies?'

'Tragedies? You call her death a tragedy? It was justice! Justice! No one else could mete it out, so I had to undertake it.'

'Mrs Massiter – !'

'Oh, don't worry about your family. I care nothing for you or your breed! Live, if you must, all of you! What does it matter to me?'

She leaned back into the carriage, signalling to the driver to move off.

Jenny stood outside the restaurant watching it trundle away and become lost in the traffic of the Strand.

So, it was over. Maud Massiter had had vengeance for the loss of her husband by taking

Lucy's life. Jenny felt she meant what she said, that with that final act she had lost interest in the rest of the family, that she felt they were unimportant.

She was filled with strange feelings: relief and thanksgiving, dismay and distress, wonder at so much grief for an utterly worthless man, at so much cunning expended on taking revenge. The hiring of thugs, the planning of a murder . . .

Should she tell anyone in authority what she'd just learned? Should some action be taken to bring Mrs Massiter to justice?

But there was no proof, only the woman's own words. And of course she would deny them if Jenny tried to bring them before a judge.

Maud Massiter had caused murder to be done. She had planned it, had hired men to execute the plan. Perhaps they had been following Lucy for days, waiting for an opportunity. And then one evening Lucy calls in Eaton Square, her driver is knocked unconscious and tied up, a conspirator takes the driver's place and takes the carriage to a suitable spot for the murder.

Ronald's presence had perhaps been unexpected. They had thought Lucy would come out of the house and drive off alone. Certainly Ronald had been dealt with comparatively lightly. Only a slight concussion, and for that Jenny was profoundly thankful.

But for Lucy it had been death. The police surgeon had told Jenny: 'Three severe blows to the cranium – I wonder at it for they must have known one blow was enough to render her unconscious.'

The motive for the hold-up had not been robbery. Ronald's money and watch, Lucy's jewellery and reticule – those had been taken as a blind. The plan from the outset had been to kill Lucy Corvill in revenge for the death of a worthless man who had taken his own life over gambling debts.

The perpetrators would probably never be found. They were lost now in the rookeries of London, hard men who had been paid for their work, paid well. Jenny had no doubt Maud Massiter had poured out money on them unstintingly, glad to find hands ready to carry out her plan.

Maud Massiter. Only a few minutes ago Jenny had seen her sitting in the tea-room, chatting with friends – an English country lady, plump, rich, badly dressed. Who would ever have guessed the passion that had forced her into action against her hated rival? Who would ever have imagined this frumpish figure held a heart that was broken because a bad and selfish man had taken his own life?

After a few moments Jenny took a deep breath then went back into the restaurant to sit down with her daughter among the elegant tea-drinkers, and play the part of a debutante's mother.

CHAPTER TWENTY-FOUR

Since the beginning of the year, the newspapers had been in a hubbub. A few were against war with the Russian Empire but most argued vehemently in favour of it. The song of the moment in the music halls was:

> We don't want to fight, but by Jingo if we
>   do,
> We've got the ships, we've got the men,
>   we've got the money too
> We've fought the Bear before and while
>   Britons shall be true
> The Russians shall not have Constanti-
>   nople!

Ronald was against war. He had read accounts of the Crimean Campaign and knew that if British troops were sent to that area more were likely to die of dysentery than ever might die of wounds.

The Navy was sent to the Dardanelles. Lord Derby resigned in protest. The Fleet was recalled. Derby withdrew his resignation.

In Parliament, Members snarled at each other. Fights broke out. Within the parties, men who held the same basic principles were at odds.

Lord Hartington, the Whig leader, called Ronald in for a confidential chat. 'As things are going,' he remarked, 'what with the Tories changing their mind every few days, it may well be that an election will be called.'

Ronald shook his head. 'Dizzy will tell them to calm down,' he said.

'But if there *is* an election, and we win it, I shall need to know whom to call upon.' He studied the Member for West Tweed. 'Would you be willing to take junior ministerial office?'

'Me?' cried Ronald in astonishment.

'Why not you? You keep your head, you steer clear of parliamentary quarrels, and you're quite an effective speaker.'

'Well, I . . . I'm greatly honoured.'

'It would only be a junior post, you understand,' Hartington said, stroking his moustaches. 'I thought perhaps you would like to serve in the Board of Trade, or in some department to do with industrial development. You have the background for it.'

'Yes, perhaps that is true.'

'Shall I add your name to my list, then?'

'If you think I could be useful, sir.'

'Well, it's in the future – we still have to win the next election. But I have my hopes, Armstrong, I have my hopes.'

When he related this interview to his wife, Jenny was elated. 'A ministerial post! Oh, Ronald!'

'Now, now, remember about chickens being hatched. It may all come to nothing. Besides, Mrs Massiter's flunkey may put a spoke in it somehow.'

'Unsworth? What could he do?'

'We-ell . . . not much, I suppose. He's been

lying doggo for a long time now. But that woman is so unhinged . . .'

Jenny shook her head. 'I told you, Ronald. She's lost interest in us.'

'That's what she said outside Bainbridge's. Who knows if she meant it?'

'She meant it, husband. Now that she's taken her revenge on Lucy – '

'I still think we ought to tell the authorities. That woman hired a gang of *murderers!*'

'Ronald, it's over.' Jenny clasped her hands and held them out towards him in supplication. 'Don't stir it up again. The Massiters have done enough to us, one way and another. Besides we agreed, didn't we – what's the evidence? Only hearsay – wild things said to me by a hysterical woman. She'd deny every word.'

'It's not right,' he muttered, pulling at his sandy hair as he did when perplexed. 'An MP should uphold the law.'

'Didn't someone once say that politics is the art of the possible? It's just not possible to do anything about Mrs Massiter. Besides, if you're thinking about punishment – I assure you, she's in her own kind of hell, poor mad creature.'

'You're not sorry for her?' he countered in bewilderment.

'No. No, of course not.' Yet she was. Absurd and illogical though it might be, she was sorry for Maud Massiter, who had lost everything – including perhaps her sanity. For a moment or two she saw again that plain, raddled face, its grimace of grief and pain . . .

'Did Hartington feel that an election is imminent?' she asked, forcing herself to return to the question in hand.

'No, so you see it's all castles in the air – '

'But even to be thought of! It's an honour. Does Lord Thornieburn know?'

'No, I'll write him a line.'

'I'll call in while I'm at home,' she promised. 'He'd probably like to have a chat. He must be missing Her Ladyship by now, stuck at home on his own.'

Jenny was going home to look after various matters of business. Heather was to stay on at Eaton Square, though still under tutelage at Lady Thornieburn's London home. Her father, busy in the House, came home each night and formed a stable centre for her home life.

Jenny was taking Dinah and Clive with her to Galashiels. Dinah had been upset by Lucy's death – upset by the fact itself and the manner of it. 'It makes you feel you aren't safe going out of your own door,' she said in a shaky voice to Jenny when they first discussed it.

This feeling of apprehension had not lessened. Jenny thought it would do Dinah a world of good to get away from London for a few weeks and by now the idea of Clive taking his lessons at Miss Gavin's school was well accepted.

They arrived in Galashiels on a May afternoon that was surprisingly cool. The carriage was waiting for them with young Max sitting up on the box with the coachman. 'Hello, hello!' he shouted, jumping about and waving. 'I say, Clive, what do you think, our cat has four kittens!'

Waiting for Jenny was a businesslike letter from Mr Jamieson the solicitor, saying that as

he had heard she was returning to Gatesmuir
he had decided not to write at great length but
instead to ask her to come and see him. 'It
refers,' he said, 'to the estate of the late Mrs
Edward Corvill.'

Intrigued, Jenny went the following day,
leaving Dinah and the two boys to go visiting
at Archie Brunton's estate.

'Thank you for coming, Mrs Armstrong,'
Jamieson said, colouring a little. He had not
forgotten what a fool he had made of himself
last time they met. 'May I offer you refreshments?'

'Nothing, thank you.'

'Very well. Let us get straight to business.
Your sister-in-law, Mrs Corvill, died intestate.'

'Really?' Jenny replied. 'I would have
thought you would have insisted she draw up
a will?'

'I tried, dear lady, I tried. But she kept putting it off. People do, you know. And of course
she was still a young woman. There was no
reason to think it was urgent.'

'Quite,' Jenny said, and said no more. She
was waiting to see why she had been called in.

'The law in this country allows a holograph
will. That is to say, a will written in ordinary
handwriting by the legator. In the absence of a
will, a rational statement of preference is
allowed to stand as a legal document.'

'Yes?'

'Although Mrs Corvill never could be persuaded to make a will, she wrote to me on
several occasions. In one letter, when I had
been urging upon her the necessity to make
provision for the bestowal of her property, she
said with some annoyance that she had no

476

intention of wishing her life away but that if
she ever made a will in favour of anyone, it
would be in favour of her niece Heather.'

'What?'

'She had no living relatives on her side of the
family, at least none that I can discover. Her
mother died while she was in Virginia. Her
father died while she was still a child. Her only
relations were from her husband's side of the
family. And if you will look at this letter, which
she wrote to me over a year ago in reply to one
of mine, you will see the remark I mentioned.'

Unwillingly Jenny took the letter. She had
no wish to read anything in Lucy's handwriting, but clearly it was necessary.

It was written on pink-tinted notepaper, in
Lucy's scrawling hand. A passage had been
outlined in red ink and initialled by Jamieson.

Why you go on about it I can't think and I
ashure you I have no intention of making
a Will because it means thinking about
Death wich is very unpleasant. If I ever
did make a Will I'd leave my belongings to
Heather who altho' not clever is a nice
enough child and the only one with a kind
word for me. You might draw up something along those lines but I don't know
when I shall want to think about it seeri-
ous enough to sign it.

Jenny handed it back.

'You see, it is quite clear in intent. I therefore
intend to put it forward for probate and I
assure you, Mrs Armstrong, it is highly likely
to be approved. The property, which is very
substantial – ' he hesitated, coloured, and

added, 'Well, it is the purchase price of Corvill's invested very profitably.'

'I remember.'

'Yes, indeed . . . Miss Armstrong, being a minor, will inherit under the care of yourself and your husband as her legal guardians.'

'I see.'

'I preferred to explain this to you in person. But I shall of course write to you formally, and the probate will be going forward.'

'Yes. Thank you.'

'So your daughter is quite an heiress, you see.'

'Yes.' She was divided between the wish to say she wanted her family to gain nothing from Lucy's death, and a sense of vast relief that the great expense of Heather's London season could be met from this inheritance.

She wrote to Ronald as soon as she got away from Jamieson and into her office at Waterside Mills. 'I wanted at first to say "keep the money", but of course he can't keep it,' she wrote. 'And since it has to go somewhere, it may as well come back to the family who made it in the first place!'

She sent the letter to the post at once, attended to a few problems that had awaited her arrival, and set about walking to Gatesmuir. As she went, the carriage caught up with her. Dinah and the two children were in it heading for home after a visit to Bowden.

'I'll get down and walk with you,' Dinah said.

'No, don't bother –'

'I'd like to. I've something to tell you.'

The children were perfectly happy to drive on with the coachman. Dinah in her pretty dress of fine green wool walked alongside Jenny, her head bent slightly away. But the bonnet, set far back on her head, could not hide the faint blush when she began to speak.

'Archie asked me to marry him.'

'He did!' Jenny cried, catching her hand. 'About time!'

'I thought you might be pleased.'

'You said yes, of course.'

'Yes, I did. I reckon we might have a very happy marriage.'

'I quite agree with you.'

'Do you, Jenny. Do you really?'

'Of course. I've been hoping for it for months. I don't know why it's taken the pair of you so long to get to the point!'

'Well, it was me. I wasn't sure it was right. But he's real fond of Clive, and Clive really likes him and will be ready to have him as a father. So I said yes and we're going to be married next month.'

'A June wedding! How lovely!'

'Oh, it'll only be quiet. No ta-ra, Jenny. It would hardly be fitting, all things considered.'

'I don't know why you say that! You have every right to –'

'No, Jen. Archie's going to Glasgow to get a licence and we'll be married as soon as the three weeks' qualification is up. I hope you don't mind – we aren't even going to invite *you*.'

Jenny pressed her hand. They walked on in companionable silence. Lucy would have hated this, Jenny thought to herself. But Lucy is part of the past. It's time to think about the future now.

Archie left Bowden the following day,

dropping in at Gatesmuir en route to Galashiels station. 'I thought I'd ask for your blessing,' he said to Jenny.

'You don't need any blessing from me,' she told him. 'You're getting two – Dinah and her boy.'

'I'm going to London to see Ronald,' he told her.

'To London? I thought you were going to Glasgow?'

'I'm going to London first. I can't be easy until I've spoken to Ronald. After all,' he said, looking very straight at Jenny, 'the boy is Ronald's son.'

Jenny said neither yea nor nay to that. 'It should be a very interesting conversation,' she said drily.

It was, indeed, interesting. It took place in a room at the House of Commons, where Archie had sought out the Member for West Tweed in the early evening of the day he arrived.

'What's this about?' Ronald said with some perplexity. 'I'm not your MP.'

'Of course not, it's nothing to do with Parliamentary business. It's something private,' Archie said in a vexed tone. He was nervous and in some alarm at what he was going to say.

'Private? You want to talk to me on a private matter?'

'Yes. It's about Dinah.'

Ronald stiffened. 'What about Dinah?'

'She and I are getting married next month.'

Ronald drew in his breath. 'Married?'

'Yes. You don't seem too surprised?'

'Well . . . no . . . it's been somewhat in the air for a while. But to tell the truth I thought you'd shy off in the end.'

'Shy off? Why the hell should I?'

'Well, because . . . I don't know. I felt you just wouldn't ever have the strength of purpose . . .'

'Look here,' Archie said in a tight voice, 'you and I have never liked each other, Armstrong. I never thought you were good enough for Jenny and you probably thought I was an empty-headed idiot for letting her slip through my hands in the first place.'

'Nicely put.'

'Well, even if we don't like one another, we can respect each other. I know – at least I have good reasons to suspect – the truth about Clive. No, wait – ' as Ronald began to speak. 'Let me finish. I'm going to be frank. For a long time that put me right off the idea of marrying Dinah.'

'Did it, by God. Who are you to be so holier-than-thou?'

'Quite. I agree with you. I began to see I was being a fool. I like Dinah a lot – she and I understand each other pretty well. And as for the boy, I think he's an absolute winner. So finally I told myself to stop being a fool and I popped the question and the result is, Dinah and I are all set for the matrimonial stakes.'

'And why are you telling me all this?' Ronald wanted to know, frowning.

'I wanted to tell you that I'm determined to be a good father to the boy. You know how awful that word is – "stepfather" – it's in all the old legends about cruel plots and so on. Well, I'm going to do my best to be a good father and if in the course of time Dinah and I have children of our own, I want you to know that

481

Clive will never suffer by any neglect or comparison with them.'

'Mmm . . .' Ronald leaned back on the wooden chair until it was tilted on its back legs. He surveyed the decorated plaster of the ceiling. 'I must say, that sounds gey honourable, Brunton.'

'Coming from you, that's a great compliment.'

'Aye, it is. As you say, we've never liked each other, but I can appreciate an honest man and so I wish you well, Brunton, I wish you well in your marriage.'

'Thank you,' Archie said, offering his hand formally.

Ronald stood up and shook hands. 'Ach, man,' he said, 'come on, let's you and me go to the Members' Bar and have a wee dram to celebrate.'

As Jenny had promised, she went to see Lord Thornieburn to tell him of the conversation between her husband and the Party Leader.

'Really?' said the Earl. 'Hartington said that, eh? Good, good. I hope he gets a chance soon to put it into practice.' He hesitated. 'I have something to tell you that may surprise you.'

'A good surprise or a bad surprise?'

'I think it's a good one.'

'Go on then, please. I'm all attention.'

'Allen has been talking to me. He wants to ask for Heather's hand in marriage.'

'What?' It was a gasp of amazement.

'Well may you be surprised. I nearly died on the spot. They're a pair of babies! But it seems he's in earnest.'

'But . . . but . . .'

'Do you think your husband will agree?'

'Good God, she's only a child!'

'No, Mrs Armstrong, she's seventeen next month and about to undergo her first London season. It's quite the thing, you know, to get engaged in your first London season.'

'It may be so, God knows,' gasped Jenny. 'Look here . . . excuse me, my lord, but – have you got this right?'

'Oh, you think I'm so impractical I didn't understand him,' he said, grinning. 'No, no, Allen came to see me in my gunroom and asked for my permission to seek Heather's hand in marriage.' He beamed at her in delight.

'And you gave your permission?'

'Yes.'

'But she's too young to marry!'

'Oh, they're not thinking of getting married tomorrow. He's going to university, you know. I think that'll be about three years. He'll be twenty-one by the time he's completed his studies and then he wants to come back here and breed good sheep and cattle and horses. And, as he tells it, Heather thinks that would be a very suitable kind of life.'

'You mean Heather has already discussed this with him?'

'Oh, dear Mrs Armstrong, of course! You know what these modern girls are like! Well, no,' he amended, giving a little wriggle of embarrassment, 'in fact Heather is much more shy and reticent than most modern girls. But they *have* discussed it. Allen was very upset for a time. He thought she'd decided on David. But David set off for India and Heather didn't seem to be breaking her heart about it, so the boy took his courage in both hands and asked her. Seems she's pleased with the notion. So what do you think?' He waited, fixing an anxious gaze upon her.

'Well, in fact, I should think they would suit each other very well,' she agreed. 'Heather doesn't take after me – she's got no interest in business. But she's mad about horses. She never seems happier than in the country. Perhaps it is the ideal life for her.'

'Well, that's very encouraging. Allen is going to London in a day or two to ask your husband's consent to the marriage. Perhaps you wouldn't mind writing him a note to prepare him for it? Because, to tell the truth, the boy's damned nervous and when he's nervous he gets these wheezing fits.'

'What does Lady Thornieburn think?' Jenny asked, pricked by anxiety. The Countess was so wrapped up in Allen. Would she think Heather a good enough match?

'Oh, Jemima'll be delighted! Meantersay, Mrs Armstrong, why d'you think she took the child up and offered to present her? I think she had it at the back of her mind all the time. Bring the girl out, launch her, throw the pair of them together in the London season, and bob's your uncle.'

'Really?' murmured Jenny. How could it be true? Heather was still a young girl who ordered strawberry ice in a restaurant. And yet . . . and yet . . . At Heather's age, Jenny herself had fallen passionately in love.

But with quite the wrong man. There was the difference. Heather was in love with Allen – who could be better? As Jenny thought about it, she realised how right it all seemed. Heather was so shy, so bad at making new friends. Lady Thornieburn might talk about the London season giving her self-assurance, but Jenny felt in her heart the assurance would only be a facade. Within herself, Heather would still be timid and uncertain. The events of her childhood ensured it.

So if she had given her heart to Allen, that was perfect. She knew him, was at her ease with him, teased and trusted him, turned to him for his opinion, shared her chief interests with him.

And Lady Thornieburn had seen this. Lady Thornieburn, constantly at home in her household as Jenny was not, seeing the youngsters together every day – Lady Thornieburn had perhaps said to herself, 'Here is the perfect wife for my poor son, someone who understands his ailment and isn't alarmed by it, someone he has always been fond of.'

Hence the idea of giving Heather a London season. It would be the right preparation for a girl who was to marry into the Thornieburns.

Was Her Ladyship managing the two youngsters? Had she manoeuvred them into it?

Well, what if she had, Jenny thought to herself. They would make a happy pair. Arranged marriages were often very successful.

As she prepared to leave, Allen himself came in. The May weather somehow never seemed to suit him, it always seemed to bring on his wheezes. He said apologetically, 'Forgive the streaming eyes. How are you, Mrs Armstrong?'

'I'm well, and all the better for hearing the news your father has just given me.'

'You told her, Paddie?'

'It seemed the ideal opportunity, my boy.'

'And . . . and what do you think, Mrs Armstrong?'

'I think it's a wonderful thing,' she said, with a good deal of conviction. She wouldn't be entirely at ease with the idea until she'd spoken to Heather.

Allen and his father came to the courtyard to see her into her carriage. Allen opened its door for her and stood leaning on it, to detain her a moment.

'I want to tell you, Mrs Armstrong,' he said, his young face very earnest, 'that I'll try to make Heather happy.'

She studied him. His hay fever made his eyes bright, his thin face had a slight flush. He wasn't exactly handsome but he had a good bone structure, a fine carriage of the head. He waited now for her response, anxious but quiet.

'Do you love her, Allen?' she asked, surprising herself. 'You aren't taking her because she happens to be someone you know?'

He flushed. 'How can you say such a thing!' he exclaimed. 'Of course I love her. I suppose I always have, but I didn't really know it until I thought I'd lost her to David Buchanan.'

'That was never anything important,' she said, dismissing poor David with a little wave of her hand. 'When he came to ask if he could offer for her, she was . . . I think you could say she was embarrassed, and quite relieved when I said she could write her refusal to him.'

Allen shook his head. 'I suppose I got the wrong end of the stick. I really did think the pair of them were . . . well . . . There you are, you see. It's easy to make mistakes. So after she'd gone to London to get ready for the season, I thought about it, and then when I went to Town to see Maddie I thought, well, why not tell her how I felt, to make sure how things stood. And she said . . . it was wonderful . . . I couldn't believe it.'

'I'm finding it hard to believe myself, Allen,' Jenny sighed. 'But as long as you're both happy, that's what matters.'

The horses moved restlessly, the coachman fidgeted with the brake handle.

'Come on, you two, stop wasting time on clash,' scolded the Earl. 'Your horses are telling you it's time to go home, Mrs Armstrong.'

Allen moved as if to stand back. Impulsively Jenny leaned forward to kiss him on the cheek. 'Goodbye for the present, Allen.'

In a few days he would be her daughter's fiancé. In a year or two he would be her son-in-law. Extraordinary.

When the subject was broached with Heather there was none of the hesitation, the embarrassed silence, that Jenny had expected.

'Allen asked me to be unofficially engaged a few weeks ago. I was delighted to accept.'

'Delighted to accept?' echoed her mother, surprised by the phrase.

'Of course. You're pleased, aren't you, Mama?'

'Certainly! Allen is . . .' She let the words die away. She'd been about to say, Allen is the only young man I could entrust you to.

They were in Heather's room. Heather, her head bent over a row of plants she was tending, didn't look up. 'Allen is a dear,' she said.

'Yes, one of the nicest lads I know.'

'We've so much in common.'

487

'That's true.'

'We both love horses and country life.'

'So you do.'

'And he doesn't mind that I'm shy, and I don't mind that he wheezes.'

But do you love him? That was the cry that wanted to burst from Jenny's smiling lips.

Something prevented her from asking. Perhaps physical passion was not to be expected in her daughter's marriage. There were women like that – Jenny had met them. Fondness, friendship – many a good match had been founded on those.

She thought of the damage that had been inflicted on Heather by the abduction, the long months of childhood separation, the struggle to come back into normal family life. Ronald scoffed at her fears, but Jenny felt in her heart that there were wounds to the soul as well as to the body.

Perhaps the ability to fall deeply in love had been destroyed in Heather by those childhood experiences. But perhaps it was simply that, as always, words were difficult for her. She didn't know how to express what she felt. Better not to make her unhappy by asking questions for which she could find no answers.

'All I want,' Jenny said, and to her dismay her voice faltered, 'is for you to be happy, my treasure.'

Heather picked up a dead leaf from her ivy plant. 'Happy?' she repeated. 'Well, of course, any girl would be happy to be engaged to someone like Allen.'

To which Jenny's response was a loving hug and fervent good wishes.

She didn't confide her news to Dinah. In the

first place it wasn't for public discussion yet. In the second Dinah was too busy with preparations for her marriage. She was in a flurry over new dresses urgently being made by Baird and a professional dressmaker, and writing to the staff at her Chelsea house to say she would be closing it and they should look for other posts.

'I dunno if I'm going to be able to handle Archie's household,' she mourned. 'I'm getting in a tizz over just these few things!'

'You'll grow into it,' Jenny soothed. 'And anyhow, you'll have a housekeeper. Don't worry about it.'

'No. I'm not really worried. And I told Clive he's to have Archie for his father, and he was really pleased. So . . . I don't know what I'm getting in such a state about!'

'It's called bridal nerves, I believe.'

In due course Jenny saw her off on the train to Glasgow. Young Clive remained for the time being at Gatesmuir keeping Max company. At ten, Clive Eynsham was the ring-leader, the organiser of games. He had Max marching up and down the garden carrying a stick for a rifle, drilled him, gave him orders to 'Charge!' or take sentry duty.

Yet Max could hold his own. He would make his friend accompany him to the mills with his mother, and drag him into the works to watch new carding machines being bedded in to replace an old set.

'How long are we going to stand here watching old spindles bobbing about?' Clive shouted in his ear.

'But it's interesting.'

'What's interesting about making rotten old thread?'

'It isn't thread, it's yarn, you stupid.'

'Well, rotten old yarn –'

'If you didn't have yarn you couldn't have cloth. And if you didn't have cloth you wouldn't get uniforms for your soldiers, so there.'

Jenny, who was keeping an eye on them while watching the new machine's trials, smiled to herself.

'Come on, let's go and watch the shunter.'

That was more to Clive's liking. A small locomotive brought goods trucks into the yard, where orders were loaded ready to be added to the train at the station. Jenny led them up on to the loading bay where the gantry picked up large packages to swing them over into the truck.

'Messrs Gradov, Merchants, Minsky Prospekt, St Petersburg,' Clive spelled out from the large label in waterproof ink. 'St Petersburg, that's Russia – Mr Brunton says we'll be at war with them any day now.'

'I hope not, Clive,' Jenny said.

'Course we will. If there wasn't wars, there'd be nothing for soldiers to do.'

'You know, Mama,' Max said, watching Tam Muir work the controls of the gantry, 'that's awful slow.'

'What is, my love?'

'Getting that arm over to the truck. I bet you could make it go faster. Couldn't you, Tam?'

'Not wi' these levers, laddie.'

'What you have to have,' Max said, 'is extra little wheels. I saw them in a thing when you took me to see how the scenery went up and down in the Theatre Royal, Mama.'

'Come on,' Clive said, 'let's go and buy some ice-cream. Mr Brunton gave me sixpence last week, I've still got it.'

One soldier and one mechanical engineer, Jenny thought fondly as they raced out of the yard. And luckily, the mechanical engineer was in the Armstrong family. By and by, it might well be that Max would interest himself in the running of the mechanical side of the mills.

Perhaps he would never be as much in love with the patterns they wove as his mother. Perhaps he would never have the same instinct for blending colour that had made his father a byword in the cloth industry.

But everyone contributes in his own way, thought Jenny. I gave what I could, Ronald has played the part that was just right for him. In some strange way, there's a pattern to life just as there's a pattern in the cloth we make. Her daughter's pattern would lead her away to a different life – to marriage and quiet country pursuits. Her son's pattern might bring him into the world of technical invention for the weaving trade. Time would tell, for time was part of the pattern.

When Dinah came home from Glasgow with her husband, Jenny took Clive to the Home Farm to welcome them. Clive's first question was, 'Did you see the parade for the Queen's Birthday? What regiment was it?'

Any stress or embarrassment was immediately done away with. Soon Jenny took her leave. She shook hands with Archie, kissed Dinah on the cheek. 'I know you'll both be very happy,' she murmured as Archie helped her into the carriage. 'But mind, I'll be keeping my eye on you!'

He was laughing as she drove off.

Now Jenny set off for London, taking her little boy with her. It was rare for Max to go, but this was a special trip. His sister was to be presented. She wanted him to see Heather in her presentation gown, to wave her off as the carriage took her to the Palace. It was an occasion for the whole family to share.

Baird was of the party, in control of a mountain of luggage. 'Whit's this?' she asked in annoyance as Jenny insisted she should carry a special parcel.

'It's a piece of fine tweed for Miss Ellen Terry.'

'And who's Miss Ellen Terry when she's at hame?'

'Oh, Baird! She's the beautiful young actress who's just joined Mr Irving's company at the Lyceum Theatre.'

'What! cried the old servant, scandalised. 'Ye're no presenting lengths of cloths to *actresses*? You that's had the patronage of crowned heads!'

'Baird, it's good publicity. Times are changing. It's fine to have the patronage of the Queen and the Princess of Wales, but Miss Terry's name is on everyone's lips – if she'll wear my cloth, it could have a very good result on sales.'

The cloth was a new design she had had made up specially for Miss Terry – a soft umber colour flecked with grey. With the actress's beautiful dark colouring it should look lovely. A walking dress made from it would be a pleasant addition to any woman's wardrobe but if Miss Terry would just mention the maker's name – or allow Jenny to give the name to a gossip columnist – there would be profit as well as pleasure in the transaction.

Ronald met them at King's Cross. 'Good God, have you brought the contents of the house?' he demanded when he saw the luggage.

'My dear man, if we're to go through a London season, we must have clothes to suit the occasion.'

'Jenny, the whole thing is driving me mad. I'll be glad when it's over.'

Though he might complain, he summoned up porters and had the whole thing organised in ten minutes. Max rushed indoors at their London home to find his sister. He somehow thought that in the long absence in London she would have been totally altered in some way.

And she had been. It was strange, but seeing her through Max's eyes, Jenny realised that her daughter was different. Perhaps the lessons with the teacher of deportment, the sessions with the dressmakers and the *chapelières* had had some effect – the *desired* effect.

For Heather was no longer a gawky girl. She was a young lady – tallish, slender, light-stepping, her toffee-coloured hair up now in a high chignon at the back and loose curls on her brow, a ribbon about her white throat, her waist no bigger than the span of a man's hands.

'You do look funny,' remarked her little brother. 'I bet you can't run up and down stairs in those silly little boots.'

'Race you up them,' Heather said, and

convinced him she was still the sister he remembered by proceeding to do so at once.

The presentation was a week ahead. When Jenny called on Lady Thornieburn in Wilton Crescent, she was told that all was going well. 'Her gown is to be delivered next Monday. I hope you'll approve of it, Mrs Armstrong – it cost an awful lot but it's special taffeta from Hungary, ice-taffeta it's called, it has a hint of blue in it and it just brings out Heather's colouring to perfection.'

'I'm not worried about the cost any more,' Jenny said, and proceeded to tell her Ladyship about Heather's inheritance.

'My word! That is rather fine,' murmured the Countess. 'I mean, Harry and I wouldn't have started talking about dowries and so forth for quite a while, and I know you'd have done as well as you could for her, but we knew – forgive me – after that business about buying out your sister-in-law . . . We knew you might be a bit pushed.'

'We'll still do our best for her,' Jenny said. 'But certainly it's changed things to know she will have money of her own.'

'Splendid! I'm so pleased about it, my dear! I must admit I always half-hoped . . . You'll think I'm silly, but I was always worried about whether Allen would find a girl who understood him. He's got this complaint, you see, and in some ways it's a handicap, but he's not a *weakling*, you know, he's not an *invalid* . . .'

'I understand perfectly. And so does Heather.'

'That's it. That's just it. She understands all about it. *Such* a comfort,' said the Countess.

Everything seemed perfect. And yet something was wrong. While doing her hair for her two nights later, Baird said to Jenny, 'Mistress, what ails yon lassie?'

'Ah? You've noticed it too?'

'She's aye the look of being on the verge of tears. I askit her yesterday to tell me what was wrang, but she walked away fra me.'

'Perhaps it's just presentation nerves,' said Jenny.

'Perhaps it is. She's aye been shy and easily frichted. But I dinna quite believe it.'

'Do you think I should speak to her about it?'

'Weel . . . If she doesna perk up afore the week's oot, I think ye should.'

But there was no necessity. On the following Sunday morning, when Jenny and Ronald came home from church, Jenny found Heather waiting for her upstairs in her boudoir.

'Mama, I've something to tell you.'

'I thought you had,' she replied. 'Come and sit down, my treasure.'

Heather shook her head. 'I'd rather stand,' she said, and stood – like a prisoner in the dock.

'Mama, I've broken off my engagement to Allen.'

'What?'

'I felt it was only right.'

'But . . . but when did this happen?'

'I went to see him in Wilton Crescent while you were at church.'

'Heather! What's the meaning of this?'

Tears glinted in her daughter's hazel eyes. 'Mama, I'm so ashamed. I *tricked* Allen into asking me to marry him.'

Jenny stared at her. 'Explain yourself,' she said faintly.

'It began a long time ago, last year. Aunt Lucy –'

'Aunt Lucy,' echoed Jenny with a groan.

'She explained to me it was my duty to make Allen propose, because he was the best match in the neighbourhood. And he is, isn't he?'

'I dare say.'

'Aunt Lucy . . . At the time it seemed true . . . She always seemed . . . I don't know how to explain it but she was so beautiful and elegant and gentle . . . I felt she must know best. So I asked how you made someone propose and she told me you had to "fascinate" a man, and it was quite easy, especially if you made him jealous of someone else.'

'Oh,' sighed Jenny, 'David Buchanan.'

'Yes, David Buchanan.' Heather went fiery red. 'Poor fellow! I was absolutely beastly about that, Mama. I let him believe I thought he was wonderful.'

'But you didn't.'

'No, of course not. I like David but in some ways he's awfully dull. The only interesting thing about him is that he got a job in Calcutta.'

Despite herself Jenny gave a little laugh.

'All the same, it worked,' Heather went on in her husky little voice. 'After he'd gone and Allen realised the coast was clear for him, he . . . well, he showed me he liked me a lot.'

'He loves you,' Jenny said softly. 'I saw it in his face when he spoke to me about you.'

'That's what so awful! I couldn't do it! I couldn't cheat him! It suddenly seemed so terribly dishonest! I found myself thinking, Aunt Lucy may have said this was all right, but it *isn't* and so I . . . I . . .'

Now, at last, she sat down droopingly on a

silk-covered chair, all her lessons in deportment forgotten.

Jenny tried to think what to say. Her mind was on her dead sister-in-law. 'Your Aunt Lucy was a strange woman,' she said. 'You once told me I often spoke sternly about her. That was because I disagreed with most of her ideas.'

'And this one in particular, I imagine,' Heather murmured.

'Heather, it was so *unnecessary!* Allen has been fond of you for years and would have come to realise he loved you without – '

'I know,' Heather said, and burst into tears. 'And I've spoiled everything! By pretending and play-acting I've made a fool of him! I hate myself for it, I absolutely hate myself!'

'No! No, my darling,' said Jenny, flying to her and putting her arms about her heaving shoulders. 'It's not your fault. It's that damned woman!'

'Mama!' cried her daughter, sitting up and staring at her through her tears. 'Mama! You've just used a profanity!'

'And if I could get my hands on your aunt I might do something worse. But she's dead, and we mustn't speak ill of the dead. Heather, she misled you. But you mustn't blame yourself because she misled a lot of people cleverer than you, cleverer and older.'

'I've been thinking, Mama. I wonder if I ought to accept this inheritance from Aunt Lucy? I'm beginning to wonder if I liked her as much as I thought I did.'

'Dear girl, the money you're inheriting has almost nothing to do with your aunt. It was money *we* earned – your father and I. It came

497

from William Corvill & Son. It just happened to fall into Aunt Lucy's hands for a little while because in a way that was part of the pattern of life at that time. But that part of the pattern is finished, and the money is yours. It's money that came from Corvill's, and that's your family.'

'Are you really sure? You don't think it's tainted?'

'Good heavens! You've really had second thoughts about your aunt!'

'Well, I've been thinking about her a lot. I believe she was wrong about catching a husband. I think it's . . . well, I feel uncomfortable about it. And then there was the way she treated Jubal. It shocked me, you know, when I found out she'd never paid Jubal any wages. I should have thought more about Jubal when she was still with us.'

'Don't blame yourself. She cast a sort of spell. Other people felt it too. The sad thing is, you're the one that's suffering.'

'Oh, I deserve to suffer,' sobbed Heather. 'To treat Allen like that! I must have been mad. And you see, I had to tell him, because we were going to go out and ch-choose the ring t-tomorrow!'

'How did he take it?' Jenny asked with a sigh.

'Oh, he was so wonderful, Mama! He said,' wept Heather, putting a sodden handkerchief to her wet cheeks, 'that he of course accepted my wishes and only marvelled that I had ever thought him good enough. Good enough! Mama, he's twice as good as me, and I never did deserve him, and though he was calm and controlled while we were speaking, I *know* he got an attack of his wheezes afterwards and I hate myself, I *hate* myself!'

Her mother went to her and drew the tawny head against her breast. 'My dearest, my pet, don't distress yourself like this. If you don't love him, then it's best to find out now and not later. No matter what it's cost you, and how much pain you feel – and Allen too – honesty is best.'

'I haven't been quite honest,' Heather confessed. 'I begged him not to tell his mother until after the presentation ball. Lady Thornieburn's been so kind to me and worked so hard to get me ready – I didn't want it all spoiled for her.'

Spoiled for her, thought Jenny. The poor soul had only undertaken the task of presenting Heather at court so as to make her a fit wife for the darling son. Months in the noisy, smelly city of London, which she hated, to groom this pretty girl for a great event that would make her a society debutante – and all for nothing. Worse, all for a great unhappiness for Allen.

A merely practical point caught her attention. 'Heather, I don't see how you can hide the breaking of the engagement. I thought it was to be announced at the ball?'

'Yes, but Allen is going to tell her we couldn't find a ring we liked, and ask her to postpone it for a few days. Then the morning after the presentation ball he's g-going to t-tell her,' Heather stammered. 'She'll hate me when she hears, of course. And serves me right.'

'Heather, you're not the first girl who's

changed her mind about her engagement. Don't be so hard on yourself.'

'Mama, I ought to be hung, drawn and quartered.'

'No, that's too much. But bread and water for a year, perhaps.'

Heather gave a trembling laugh.

'Do you want me to tell your father?'

'Oh, not yet! Not until after the presentation! He can say what he likes about it's being a lot of nonsense but he's as pleased as punch about it. Don't spoil it.'

'Very well,' sighed Jenny. 'We'll keep it between ourselves for a week. And in the meantime, now that you've made a clean breast of it to Allen and me, try to look less miserable.'

'Have I been looking miserable?'

'Like a wet Sunday developing into a wet Monday. Baird remarked on it too. Cheer up, my little dove. It's not the end of the world, though it may seem like it.'

Briskness of manner seemed the only recourse. She was disappointed, and surprised at the depth of her disappointment. Only now did she realise how happy she'd been at the thought of confiding Heather – nervy, quiet Heather, her darling, her long-protected treasure – to the loving care of Allen Cairness.

The secret weighed heavy with her. She was sorry for Heather, and equally sorry for Allen, in whose face she had seen the glow of a deep attachment when he spoke of her daughter.

But under her concern and disappointment there was another emotion – a muted anger. Lucy . . . Even from the grave she had the power to harm.

Jenny had business engagements which took her mind off the affair to some extent. But the only pleasing thing in the next few days was a note from the actress Miss Terry saying she was delighted with the cloth Mrs Armstrong had sent on behalf of William Corvill & Son.

So much so that I am having it used for a stage costume in the next play at the Lyceum, which will be the comedy *Olivia* with Mr Irving as Dr Primrose. I think Mr Irving would disapprove of my having the clothmakers given any particular mention in the programme notes, but I shall see your name is used in any discussion of my costumes during the publicity for the play . . .

Jenny smiled as she sent the note north to be framed and hung on the wall of her office at Waterside Mills. When she had buyers in each new season, it was always helpful to have tributes of this kind for them to read as they sipped their Madeira.

Heather's court gown was delivered. Jenny saw it tried on. Baird and the modiste clucked round her daughter, smoothing out a fold here, pinching up a tuck there. The headdress was carefully placed – at the moment artificial gardenias but on the day they would be real. Three white ostrich feathers would go behind the bandeau, mounted on a deep comb which would be hidden in the chignon of light brown hair.

'Perfect,' sighed the dressmaker's representative. 'Don't you think so, madame?'

'Yes, I like it.' Which was just as well, as it was costing a fortune.

The great day came. A day of high summer, the London trees in full green leaf, roses out in the gardens, brilliant displays in the flower beds of the parks.

Heather was allowed to sleep late and was made to take breakfast in bed. Then a short walk for fresh air and exercise, then the toilette in the afternoon. She bathed and put on the specially made underwear of crepe de chine and lace. She wrapped herself in a soft cotton robe, tied it with a silk sash.

The hairdresser came. For an hour she brushed and curled and pinned.

The headdress of flowers was delivered. Baird took it upstairs as if it were a gold crown. 'Is it a *wreath*?' Max whispered as he noted her respectful tread.

Evening came. A light meal was served. Heather, still in the cotton wrapper, came to table. Her little brother was scandalised. 'Is she allowed to come to dinner in her dressing-gown?' he demanded with indignation.

'Ssh, Max, your sister's allowed to do anything she likes today,' his father told him. 'She's being presented at court.'

'Will it hurt?' asked Max.

'No,' said Heather, 'but it'll take me weeks to recuperate.'

Ronald glanced at her. It was the first thing by way of a joke that he'd heard from her in about two weeks. But when he had asked his wife what was wrong the answer was always the same: presentation nerves.

At mid-evening the carriage came. It was still too early, but there would be a long queue of vehicles waiting to pass through the Palace gates. The Mall would be blocked with them. And it was necessary to be in the right place in the queue so that the Chamberlain would find your name on his list.

At eight-thirty Heather came downstairs. The ice-white gown gleamed in the lights of the hall. The gardenias looked like ivory against her hair. The white feathers rose above her head in a little cloud.

Long white kid gloves covered her arms. Her shoulders rose from the ruched neckline and merged into the creamy throat, slender as a swan's. Around it she wore the gift of her parents, a treble row of small pearls fastened in front with an ivory cameo.

She carried a fan of plain white silk. Jenny saw it tremble between her fingers.

'My darling girl,' she said, kissing her gently, 'you look lovely.'

'Thank you.'

As she drew her head away, she saw the glint of tears on her daughter's lashes. 'Heather,' she said, 'what's the matter?'

The girl gave a little shiver. 'Can I speak to you alone, Mama?'

'What, now?'

'It's important.'

Jenny cast an anguished glance at Ronald, who was hovering in the background with Max's hand in his.

Mother and daughter went into the drawing room. Heather walked to the empty fireplace, then turned and walked back.

'Mama, you know what I told you on Sunday?'

'About Allen?'

'Yes. Mama, what am I going to do?'

'But . . . you've done it. You released Allen from the engagement.'

'But Mama, I love him.'

Slowly Jenny sank down on to the nearest chair.

'Oh dear.'

'What am I going to do? I've lost him!'

'When did you find this out, Heather?'

'I don't know. I've always known it. I just seemed to get in a muddle. It was because of deceiving him, I thought perhaps I'd been deceiving myself. But I wasn't. I love him, Mama. And I'll have to face him at the ball this evening – and I don't think I can!'

'What exactly did you say to him when you broke it off?'

'I don't remember.'

'Did you tell him you didn't love him?'

'I think I did.'

'You're sure of your feelings now? You really love him?'

'Oh, Mama, of course! He's been my best friend for years and years! There's no one else in the world I care about the way I care for Allen!'

Jenny climbed to her feet again. Though her knees were shaking, she had regained control of herself.

'My dear,' she said, 'don't worry about it. It'll be all right.'

'How can it be all right? After what I've done? After I've admitted I cheated, after I told him I couldn't wear his ring?'

Jenny threw out her hands in a gesture of encouragement. 'You only have to look at him the way you look now,' she said. 'You only have to tell him it was all a mistake. He'll know, Heather. He'll understand.'

'Oh, no, he'll despise me – '

'No he won't. I promise you, it will be all right.'

'But how can it be? I've hurt him, I've shown myself to be silly, selfish . . . How can you think Allen would just "understand"?'

'There are two reasons, my little daughter. The first is that he's known you for years – you yourself said it, he's been your best friend ever since you first met him. He can't have been best friends for years without knowing you well. So he'll understand that you got in a muddle, that Aunt Lucy put you into a misapprehension which you felt you had to explain to him – '

'But – that's just relying on his kindness – '

'Wait. Let me go on to the second reason, my dove. Allen loves you.'

The beautiful girl in white put her gloved hands up to her rosy cheeks. 'Truly, Mama? I mean – in *that* way?'

'In that way. I've seen love in the eyes of men, Heather, and when Allen looks at you I see it there. His life will be empty without you. And if you look at him with love in your eyes, as I see it now – he'll know.'

Heather turned to look at her reflection in the great mirror over the fireplace. She saw a face alight with a fearful joy, a half-hope that might turn into a miraculous certainty.

'You really think so?'

'I do. Now dry your eyes and go out to the carriage. You can't keep the Princess of Wales waiting.'

A faint smile turned up the corners of her

daughter's mouth. She dabbed at her eyes with a lace handkerchief. Jenny picked up her fan and gave it to her. She led the way to the drawing room door, opened it, and ushered Heather through.

Ronald looked with anxiety at his wife. She smiled and nodded. Max stood holding his father's hand, over-awed. The servants had lined up in the hall to watch the young mistress leave for the Palace. They made sounds of approval as, looking like some fine porcelain figurine lit from within, she walked by with her head held high.

Jenny watched her. And the thought, the wonderful thought, came to her: She isn't afraid. My little timid girl, facing one of the greatest ordeals of her life – she's full of confidence.

But of course, she added thankfully and without irony, love can work miracles.

Graves went to the front door and opened it. Heather walked through and down the steps to the kerb. The hired carriage glowed under the evening sky, fresh glossy varnish, polished leather, the horses with their manes braided, the coachman in his best livery.

'Good luck,' Jenny whispered in Heather's ear. 'And remember, when you get to Wilton Crescent for the ball, smile at Allen as you go in. Just smile at him, and when he comes to you tell him you love him. And everything will be all right.'

'Oh, Mama,' Heather whispered back, 'what would I do without you?'

She got into the coach. With a wave of the whip the driver called up the horses. The carriage moved off.

Jenny went back into the hall.

'Are you sure she'll be all right?' Ronald asked. 'She looked as if she were burning up like a church candle.'

'Nerves, husband, presentation nerves.'

'Can we go in a coach like that some time?' Max demanded. 'I don't see why Heather should get a special coach and not me.'

'It's time you were in bed, young man.'

'Oh, *Mama!*'

Baird took him upstairs. The servants had dispersed.

'Well, I suppose we'd better go up and put on the glad rags,' Ronald said. 'When does this ball start?'

'Eleven o'clock.'

'Eleven o'clock! What an hour to start dancing and exchanging toasts! Is it right, by the way, the engagement will be announced tonight?'

'It might be and it might not. They couldn't find a ring they liked,' lied Jenny. 'If you can stay awake, you'll find out.'

'Sensible folk ought to be going to bed at eleven o'clock.'

'Nobody in this household is being sensible at the moment.'

'Jenny lass, you're right.' He put his arm about her waist so that they went upstairs together, their heads almost touching. 'I feel strange,' he confessed. 'A daughter about to curtsey at court, her engagement about to be announced, a son growing up so fast I can't keep pace with him. It ought to make me feel old, but somehow it doesn't.'

'It's part of the pattern,' Jenny murmured.

'What?'

'Never mind.'

He went into his dressing room. Presently she heard him singing to himself as he took off his frock coat, untied his cravat, took the studs out of the front of his shirt. It was the old Borders song that went with the summer festival.

> Braw lads, braw lads, tramping o'er the
>   heather,
> Gie's your hand, my ain true love, we'll
>   follow them thegither.

She was suddenly happy. Not for this moment only but with a happiness she knew would remain with her through any troubles that might yet come.

Her daughter would also be happy – two young people who loved each other would soon clear up any misunderstandings.

Her husband and her son – the men in her life – they would be her chief concern from now on.

She would guard the inheritance that would be handed on to Max, she would further its good name with her designs and her care for fine quality.

She would help Ronald in his career and if in the course of time he obtained a Cabinet post, she would turn herself into a political hostess for his sake.

But above all she would be happy. Because happiness was part of the pattern too.